Praise for other books by Kim Iverson Headlee

Dawnflight:
"Compelling." ~*The Dallas Morning News*
"Intense." ~*USA Today*

Morning's Journey:
"Magnificent."
~Kathleen Foley, author of the Faith in Uniform series

Liberty:
"A true masterpiece."
~Jill M. Roberts, *To Be Honest*
"Epic."
~Heidi Ryan, *Drue's Random Chatter*

King Arthur's Sister in Washington's Court:
"Entertaining." ~*Publishers Weekly*

Snow in July

KIM IVERSON HEADLEE

PENDRAGON COVE PRESS

Published by
Pendragon Cove Press

Snow in July by Kim Iverson Headlee

http://kimheadlee.com
https://twitter.com/KimHeadlee
http://www.facebook.com/KimIversonHeadlee

Interior art copyright ©2014 by Jessica Headlee
Cover design copyright ©2014 by Natasha Brown
All fonts are in the public domain.
Imprint name: Neverwinter
Title and chapter headings: Iglesia
Author name and page headers: Lightfoot Narrow
Body text: Cambria

FOR
*My family, as always, and for
Patricia Duffy Novak, at long last.*

Contents

Chapter 1

FIFTEEN THOUSAND MEN and horses writhed across
the valley below, appearing as toys in a children's
game.

Many might consider war a game, but Sir Robert Alain de
Bellencombre, knight of Normandy bound to the service of
Duke William and commander of a unit in the cavalry reserves,
did not number among their ranks.

Edward the Confessor, King of England via his Saxon father
but Norman by his mother, was dead. This battle, raging near
the coastal hamlet called Hastings, would decide the right
of one man to wear the English crown: William the Norman,
acknowledged by Pope Alexander to be Edward's lawful successor; or Harold the Saxon, brother of Edward's wife, the man
alleged to be Edward's deathbed choice.

Stroking his war horse's glossy charcoal neck to calm her,
Alain pondered Harold's claim. It had to be true. This many

men would not sacrifice their lives for a lie. Yet the vast majority of Harold's supporters were Saxons harboring no wish to bear the Norman yoke. Perhaps such men might be desperate enough to fight for a lie that promised to restore Saxon rule.

A trumpet blared. He signaled his men forward, couched his lance, and spurred Chou to send her careening into the melee.

Harold's shield wall, which had seemed impregnable, began to crumble under the onslaught of Alain's unit, hastened by the desertion of men who no doubt decided they weren't quite so willing to die. Their lord stood exposed just long enough for a Norman archer to sight his mark. Harold fell, screaming and clutching an arrow that protruded from one eye.

Harold's supporters closed ranks around him, blocking Alain's view and giving him more than enough to do as the Saxons redoubled their efforts to guard their lord's body.

A familiar whirl of colors caught Alain's attention. The saffron leopard prowling on a green field—Étienne! A Saxon knight, with a blue arm and fist blazing defiance across his gray shield, bore down upon Étienne with leveled lance. Étienne tumbled from his horse. He scrambled to his feet and retrieved his sword, putting it to good use on the Saxons surrounding him, although the knight who'd unhorsed him had already ridden in search of other targets.

Lance long since discarded and sword now rising and falling with fatal precision, Alain surged to reach his brother's side. Protection of her youngest son had been their dying mother's wish, and he had sworn on his own life to keep Étienne safe.

Before he could close the distance, another Saxon knight fought past Étienne's guard to thrust a war-knife into his throat. Through the visor the knight's eyes gleamed with startling, fathomless malice. Alain could only watch in stunned disbelief as he laid his hand upon Étienne's chest for a few moments. Uttering a soul-freezing howl, the Saxon yanked out his seax and disappeared into the press with Étienne's shield, denying Alain vengeance.

Shame and grief rent his heart asunder.

He had failed the two he loved most; failed them so utterly that he could never beg their forgiveness in this lifetime.

Pain slammed into his shoulder, toppling him from the saddle. Étienne's body broke his fall. He tried to roll clear, but a spear through his chest pinned him to Étienne. His gut convulsed, and bile burned his throat. Blinding agony killed his struggle to free himself. Death's stench invaded his nostrils.

He closed his eyes and waited for his final journey to begin.

THE MOUNTED band crept through the forest, constrained to the pace of the wagon. The new moon helped to conceal their progress but also concealed obstacles in their path. With each jolt, the wagon's passenger moaned.

Thane Ulfric spurred his horse even with the knight driving the wagon. "Have a care, Eosa. He must survive, else all is lost."

Eosa's thick blond braid whipped across his shoulders as he turned and spat over the wagon's side. He raised the reins in one fist, teeth bared in a snarl. His misshapen bottom lip gave him a draconic appearance. "Take them if you think you can fare better. My lord."

With an angry jerk on his own reins, Ulfric pulled his horse back to join Del, guarding the wagon's rear.

Secrecy had forced them to hide by day and travel at night. It had been nothing short of miraculous that they'd even survived the disaster at Hastings, to say nothing of being able to spirit away the battle's most exalted casualty—or keep him alive this long. They'd been obliged to field dress each other's wounds, and their lord lay in dire need of better care than the three of them knew how to render.

The wagon lurched. The plunder bumped into the passenger, who groaned a feeble protest. Eosa halted the wagon, and he, Ulfric, and Del dismounted to secure the cargo.

"This journey would be easier," Ulfric grumbled to Del, "if you would change your mind."

Privately, Del conceded his cousin's point. Their present speed would put them at the gates of Edgarburh, Del's home, by daybreak. Del had every confidence in Kendra's healing skills.

But the action could carry deadly consequences for her and their father, Thane Waldron, and everyone else Del held dear.

"Nay. I cannot put my family and our people at risk of being executed for treason."

"If we succeed," Ulfric said as he gave the rope a savage tug, "we shall be hailed as saviors."

"If." Del grasped Ulfric's arm as the thane of Thornhill prepared to mount. "Your feelings for Kendra should prevent you from involving her in this perilous venture."

Ulfric shrugged him off and swung onto his horse. "My feelings for your sister pale in comparison to the magnitude of what I—we must accomplish."

Their supine companion thrashed his limbs, his moans sounding louder and more delirious.

Del waved an arm toward the wagon. "Look at him, Ulfric. Even if he survives this journey, he shall be fortunate to ever ride again, never mind his ability to rule."

"If he survives, I can handle the rest," Ulfric insisted.

"How? With sorcery? A divine miracle?" Del snorted. "Be reasonable. The loss at Hastings has sounded the death knell for our way of life. England is changing—has changed already," he amended sadly, recalling the number of Normans King Edward had appointed to key positions at court and in the largest churches. "A wise man will accept this fact and adapt to it."

Del mounted, the wagon creaked forward, and they rode in taut silence.

"Do you fancy yourself a wise man, Delwin Waldronson?" Ulfric asked at length.

An image of the Edgarburh shield pattern came to mind, the dark blue upward bend on a gray field. The variant Del had carried into battle featured an arm, bent at the elbow and terminating in a fist, a dangerous design for a Saxon to brandish in an England ruled by a Norman king.

Del resolved to adapt his shield to his father's pattern at the earliest opportunity.

"I fancy myself a realist, Ulfric."

"A real fool," Ulfric muttered.

Del refused to dignify the insult. He spurred his horse into a trot. "I shall ride point for a while," he told Eosa as he passed the wagon.

Although Del could hear no human sounds, the wagon's noise assured him that Eosa was following as best he could, with Ulfric presumably guarding the rear.

Lost in his churning thoughts, he had no idea how far he'd ridden when he realized he hadn't heard the wagon in quite some time. Mayhap his companions had stopped to answer nature's summons. Whatever the reason, he deemed it best for them to stay closer together. He wheeled his horse around and galloped it back up the trail.

He burst into a widening of the cart path to find Eosa, still seated on the wagon's bench, confronting a mounted warrior wielding a sword and carrying a kite-shaped Norman shield. As Del watched, the foe's dim silhouette seemed to waver and grow to impossibly huge proportions, prompting Del to scrub his eyes.

The Norman's intent, as he advanced upon the wagon with leveled sword, was horrifyingly clear.

Del thought he heard crunching in the bracken, as though Ulfric was returning to the wagon, but he only had time enough to shout for Ulfric to hurry.

Sword drawn, Del urged his horse between Eosa and the Norman and landed several furious blows in the hope of turning the attack upon himself.

His tactic worked too well.

The Norman cocked his sword arm and smashed the flat of the blade against Del's helmet, sweeping him out of the saddle. He hit the ground with a heavy thump and tried to roll clear of the hammering hooves. Weakness engulfed him, and his traitorous body refused to obey.

As if bound by a dream, he watched the Norman dismount, stride closer, raise his sword, and thrust it downward. Searing pain ripped through his gut.

His final thought centered not upon the liege lord he had failed to protect but upon his dear sister and their father, both of whom would be devastated by his death.

"My God—Alain!"

He heard a strangled noise, offspring of a groan and a gasp. Pain resumed its vigil, and he realized the sound had come from him.

He'd lost count of how often he'd conjured the battle in his dreams, reliving his failure to keep his vow to protect Étienne, and now the failure to die, to prevent himself from failing anyone else. He groaned again.

"Alain, for the love of the Blessed Mother, wake up!"

Even through pain's fog he recognized the voice. Sir Ruaud d'Auvay had removed the spear embedded in his shoulder, dressed his wound with strips of Étienne's surcoat, hustled him from the battlefield, and secured for him the best of care through several weeks of fevered semiconsciousness, first in the Hastings field hospital and later at Ruaud's chambers in London. Of any living soul, Ruaud knew Alain best, but he had no inkling of the depth of Alain's anguish, nor would he ever find out.

No one had any business invading his purgatory.

Alain opened his eyes to find Ruaud peering at him, his candle's glow warming Alain's face. Alain attempted a shooing gesture. As he glanced away, ashamed by how weak he felt, he noticed the frost that had etched the windowpanes. Two months' convalescence had done little to improve the condition of his body or spirit. His hand dropped to the coverlet. "A bit of air, if you please." He regarded Ruaud with a limp grin.

"God be praised." After straightening and setting the candleholder on a table, Ruaud ran his fingers through his thick, dark blond hair, his usually jovial face tense with concern. "You looked so pale and still, I almost summoned a priest."

"I am glad there was no need for my services, Sir Ruaud," boomed a man from the threshold.

The speaker strutted into the room, his sumptuously embroidered, wine-colored velvet robes rustling across the floor rushes, a bulky gold crucifix hanging from his neck: Bishop Odo de Bayeux, Duke William's half brother and one of the duke's most trusted advisers. A stoop-shouldered cleric shuffled behind the bishop, clutching a leather folio to his chest.

As Ruaud hastily vacated his bedside seat and bowed to kiss their visitor's ring, Alain tried to push himself up. Pain bolted through his chest and down his arm in pulsing waves. Nausea clawed at his stomach. He fell back against the pillows, gasping.

"Be at ease, Sir Robert," said the bishop. "No need for formalities on my account." He balled a fist, raised it to his lips, and cleared his throat. "I am here to pay you honor at King William's behest. His Majesty conveys his regrets that he is unable to visit in person, but with the coronation less than a fortnight away, those details consume his every waking moment."

Not to mention William's recuperation from his battle wounds, Alain thought wryly. Rebellion could erupt at the slightest display of weakness. "I understand, my lord bishop."

Bishop Odo nodded at the cleric, who extracted a parchment leaf from the folio. "William, Duke of Normandy and King of England," began the cleric in a nasal voice, "to Robert Alain de Bellencombre, Knight of Normandy, greetings. In deepest appreciation for your assistance in securing for us the Throne of England, we grant you deed to the estate of Edgarburh in Somerset, Wessex, the title for which property shall be conferred to you upon the occasion of your wedding to Kendra Waldronsdotter, the daughter of the estate's present lord—"

"Your pardon," Alain said, throat constricting, "but may I see that?" Bishop Odo arched an eyebrow but granted his consent. The parchment rattled as the cleric passed it to Alain, who perused it and met the bishop's inquisitive gaze. "Duke William wishes me to marry the thane's daughter? Does she know yet?" He hadn't intended to sound so querulous and felt his cheeks heat.

"*King* William wishes to quell any remaining spirit of rebellion in the most expedient and bloodless way possible," Bishop Odo replied. "Couriers were dispatched with his decrees at first light. Marrying his bachelor knights to English noblewomen, especially those living nearest to London, is a sound and merciful policy."

Merciful for whom?

"Please forgive Sir Robert, my lord bishop." Ruaud shot Alain a warning glance. "His fever and wounds have left him addlepated. I am certain he appreciates the king's generous boon."

Alain nodded and swallowed, heart plummeting. Marriage meant making more vows . . . vows to love and honor and protect.

Vows too easily broken.

THE PEWTER goblet hit the trencher with an ungodly clatter. Bloodred wine seeped across the white table linens, reminding Kendra of what Del's blood must have done the night he was ambushed.

As a servant rushed to right her goblet and blot the stain, she leaned against her carved, tall-backed chair on the dais of Edgarburh's feast hall, certain she had imagined the voice that had startled her.

She wished Del's condition could be righted as easily.

Her seat gave her the best view of the Cristes-mæsse festivities, which at present consisted of a muzzled, scruffy bear being goaded through its awkward paces by an equally scruffy man to the raucous amusement of the crowd.

Kendra couldn't share in the laughter.

With the tip of her dagger, she chased slices of stewed apples around her trencher, racking her brains for something—anything—she hadn't yet tried to help her brother, either to heal his wound or cure the fever and cough invading his lungs.

Invasion. She gave a soft snort. Not three months earlier, Del had risked his life in the service of King Harold against the invading William of Normandy. Del had been one of the lucky few to survive the battle, only to be cut down on their father's lands by one of William the Bastard's knights. The enormity of the outrage still blazed within her heart.

Even greater kindled her wrath over the decree accompanying the coronation announcement: she must wed one of these ruthless Norman warriors.

This very day, her father was paying court upon the new king, offering his—though not his daughter's—acquiescence to the betrothal in hopes of currying favor enough to present his complaint about Del's attacker. He possessed the knight's shield, though the coward had eluded capture. Waldron kept the shield locked in his quarters, for he couldn't risk losing his one tangible link to the Norman swine.

Kendra's heart had screamed the truth, although her father had refused to hear it: Sir Delwin Waldronson had fought for King Harold, his attacker was one of William the Bastard's retainers, and justice would be denied.

Unable to avenge Del, she'd channeled her energy into helping him as best she could.

She gripped her dagger's haft in white-knuckled frustration. There must be some herb or simple she hadn't tried . . .

To heal the pain, you must endure the thorn.

Kendra jerked her head up. The dagger slipped from her fingers and dropped onto the table. Sheepishly she looked around, but the others seemed enthralled by the bear's antics.

Petals from the Glastonbury thorn, the thousand-year-old tree purported to have sprouted from Joseph of Arimathea's staff when he established the first Christian church on the ancient sacred site, were reputed to work every manner of medicinal miracle in the hands of the pure in heart. But when she had tried to use some of the herb to heal her mother, the petals had ignited in her hands, leaving naught but ash.

Her unworthiness provided the only possible explanation.

Ashamed of her failure, she had concocted a story about falling into a bed of nettles to explain the lurid rash on her palms.

She turned her hands to catch the fickle torchlight. Though the discoloration had faded, and the pain had long since subsided, the effects remained visible after nearly a decade.

Endure the thorn.

Her mother's dying request wrenched Kendra's heart with renewed shame and guilt and fear.

Mayhap, now that she had gained more experience in the healing arts, she could avoid suffering the same consequences. She doubted whether she had grown any more pure of heart, but she had to try this remedy for Del's sake. She turned her thoughts toward how many petals she'd need and how much her request would cost.

"Lady Kendra?" She glanced up at the worried face of her maidservant, Rowena. "My lady, he asks for you."

No need to ask which "he" Rowena meant. Kendra rose. So did the rest of the company, but she forced a smile and bade them to be seated and enjoy the entertainment. The bear and its handler yielded to a troupe of brightly clad jugglers whose feats and ribald jokes soon had the people laughing again.

Just as well, Kendra thought. The time for tears would arrive swiftly enough.

She donned her cloak trimmed in rabbit fur and left the hall, stopping first at the kitchens. While Rowena prepared a hot onion poultice, Kendra brewed a tisane of lungwort and lady's mantle. Not that, after all these weeks, she had much faith left in either remedy, but she had nothing else to offer.

Cradling the lidded terra-cotta mug against her chest to preserve the warmth of its contents, she scurried along the roofed walkway toward the manor house. After navigating the building's slick exterior staircase, she ducked inside the upper story's door and hastened down the rush-lit hallway toward Del's quarters. Only by the extra set of footfalls echoing off the walls did she know Rowena was keeping pace.

Inside the chamber, Kendra almost dropped the tisane.

To say that Del's condition had declined since tierce, when she'd torn herself from his bedside to oversee the final preparations of the Cristes-mæsse feast, was an understatement. His face, already pale, had developed a waxy sheen. Sweat-darkened blond hair framed his sunken cheeks and pain-furrowed forehead in a damp halo. His eyes were closed and his lips parted, his chest moving erratically.

She shut her eyes against the sting of unshed tears. Inhaling to compose herself, she blinked and rounded on her maidservant, fighting to keep exasperation and fear from dominating her tone. "Rowena, why did you not fetch me sooner?"

"Not her fault." The voice sounded hoarse and frail, not like her brother at all. "My wish."

Upon setting the mug on the tray beside the onion poultice and shedding her cloak, Kendra strode to Del's side. She directed the maidservant to clear a place amid the clutter of bandage rolls and half-empty potion vials and salve pots on the nearby table. The candles' flames wavered in time with the women's hasty movements, throwing restive shadows against the wall. Rowena shifted the tisane to the table and piled the discarded items onto the tray. After reviving the fire by turning the logs and heaving on another, she picked up the tray, dipped a curtsey in response to Kendra's murmured thanks, and left the room.

Hefting the poultice in one hand, Kendra loosened the ties of Del's tunic with the other.

His hand gripped hers with unexpected strength. "Don't bother." When she began to protest, his face cracked into the lopsided grin she loved so well and would miss so much. "Please. I'd like to leave this world not reeking of the kitchens. If it's all the same to you."

To combat her alarm, she adopted an aura of mock haughtiness. "It most certainly is not the same to me, Delwin Waldronson. The poultice will help you breathe." She hoped.

His bark of laughter sparked a cough that made him release her hand. She abandoned the poultice on the table so she could help him sit up, rubbing his back and feeling otherwise useless, until the fit subsided. When it finally did, he lay back against the pillows, wheezing. Blood spattered the coverlet. Her stomach twisted. Their mother had died so, though not because her body had been weakened by a festering sword wound.

Refusing to surrender, she snatched the mug, removed the lid, and lifted it to his lips. He took a swallow, though whether just to humor her or not she couldn't tell. Kendra told herself his wheezing had eased, but of that too she could not be certain. She felt certain of nothing.

She left the mug on the table and perched on the stool beside his bed. He caressed her hair, her cheek, her lips. His fingers felt too cold. She grasped his hand and kissed it, wishing yet again for the gift their mother was rumored to have possessed, the ability to heal with but a touch.

Gently she laid Del's hand down but did not let go. His smile seemed laden with as much sorrow as affection.

"Promise me something, dear sister."

She squeezed his hand. "Anything, Del! You know I would give you . . ." As she cast about for an absurd example, she glanced out the slotted window and noticed the weather's bleak turn. "If it were within my power, I would give you snow in July." If only he would live that long, she prayed. Long enough for her to obtain some of the Glastonbury thorn's petals and overcome her fear of using them.

He smiled. "You'd find some way to do it, Kendra. I know." The smile vanished. "Promise me you'll strive to find happiness."

She withdrew her hand to cross her arms, irritation over their old argument rising despite her worry. "And how am I to do that, pray tell me, if I am fated to marry a man of the accursed race responsible for doing this"—she waved her arm over his body—"to you? I would rather die! And Father knows it. But he cares for naught save his own status, that he retains some vestige of control over our lands."

"Do not speak so. Father loves you and is doing what he can to ensure that you will be provided for. You and all the folk who look to Edgarburh for protection."

Stung by the truth of his rebuke, she bowed her head. "I know, Del. It's just that . . ." She clenched her jaw. "I shall never marry the retainer of a king who lets his knights attack men returning home under the banner of truce."

Del's lips twitched in an unreadable grin before his piercing blue eyes adopted a frank look. "Even if such a vow would deny you your heart's contentment?"

She was on the verge of repeating her vow when he gasped, beset by another bloody coughing fit. After helping him get through it, grieving at how light his once-robust body felt, she dipped a cloth in the water to swab the sweat from his brow and blood from his lips.

"Please, Kendra. I need to know . . ." The wheeze returned, along with an ominous rattle. "Seek happiness. Promise me that."

"Oh, Del." Her voice caught, and she swallowed. She dropped the cloth into the basin and grasped his hand in both of her smaller ones, thankful that the ravages of injury and illness had spared this much of the powerful knight he had been. "If there is any way to fulfill both vows . . ." Doubts laid siege to her tongue.

"You will, dearest Kendra." He closed his eyes, nodding slightly. "I know you will."

Surrendering to the trembling of her chin, she fell to her knees and laid her head beside him. His hand came to rest upon her hair. He drew a long, shuddering breath. The rattle stilled. Her heart hammering, she raised her head. His hand slid away. His eyes were open, staring; his chest, unmoving.

She collapsed over his body, keening and hugging him to her as if sheer force of will could bring him back. Knowing she craved the impossible, she railed at God for taking the person who loved her best, at Del for letting himself be taken, at his demon-spawned Norman murderer, at her mother for failing to bequeath Kendra her rare healing gift, at her father for condoning her barter to a Norman knight. And at the architect of her misery, whose crown, bought by Saxon blood, was being set upon his head this Cristes-mæsse day: the Bastard of Normandy.

Kendra rose, dried her face, and set her jaw. Tenderly she closed Del's eyes and folded his arms across his chest. Bending to kiss his brow, she affirmed her promise to find happiness wherever she might.

But it would never be in the arms of a man whose race was responsible for her brother's death.

Chapter 2

IR Robert Alain de Bellencombre despised being noticed.

Being noticed wrought problems in myriad forms: a matron's lewd grin, a priest's glare, a Saxon's spear, a king's unwanted boon.

For a scout, being noticed wrought death.

Grimacing, he leaned his good shoulder against the church's rough stone wall, the stench of urine and offal from the nearby tanneries so heavy in the air he could taste it.

A king's boon. Most men would kill for estates as rich as Edgarburh was reputed to be.

A knot of worshippers left the church, casting surreptitious glances his way, doubtless wondering why a Norman knight had chosen this dingy backstreet church rather than offering his petitions at the Minster with Winchester's affluent residents.

Alain wondered the same thing.

He'd attended vespers mass to pray for a way out of the predicament King William had thrust upon him. Since a woman lay at the heart of the problem, he had chosen St. Mary's Church in hopes of placing his petition before the Blessed Mother. But the worship service had been a nightmare of poor Latin, worse singing, restless parishioners, the tanneries' stench, and sundry other distractions.

Alain wished he'd yielded to Ruaud's insistence that he accompany him to the tavern instead.

Cutting his reverie short with a rueful shake of the head, he set off toward the prearranged meeting place. Mindful of the planking that crossed the brook bubbling down the center of the road, he strode south along bustling Tanner Street. At High Street, he turned right, continued for a block to the Sign of the Rose, and descended the stairway to the underground tavern while a plan coalesced in his mind.

The darkness, relieved by a few rushlights, provided stark contrast to the evening sky's summer brightness. He squinted into the gloom.

"*Ici, Alain.*" The deep Norman voice pierced the background hum of English. "*À gauche.*"

As directed, Alain turned to his left, took a few steps, and stumbled into Ruaud. Ale splashed onto Alain's tunic. He bore his frothy baptism stoically. Ruaud's laugh shook his paunch, and more ale threatened to fly forth as he pounded Alain on the back, near the wound he'd taken at Hastings nine months before.

Alain massaged his shoulder, wondering when its pain would cease. He had long since resigned himself to the fact that the pain of failure never would abate.

Several years Alain's senior, Sir Ruaud d'Auvay had become Alain's mentor and friend at Duke William's court at a time when Alain had stood in sore need of guidance. Comte Philippe FitzHugh, Alain's elder half brother, had looked upon Alain with suspicious dislike, always fearing Alain coveted their father's title, never believing Alain's fervent and sincere denials.

Philippe had undercut Alain at every opportunity, the most recent blow being Alain's intended bride, whom Philippe had lured into his own bed.

No. Marie had gone willingly, lusting after Philippe's wealth and title. They deserved each other. Ruaud had helped Alain recognize that. Afterward he had implemented Ruaud's suggestion to transfer from the scouting corps to the cavalry, following William to England to let battle cauterize the wound of Marie's betrayal.

If not for Ruaud's agreeing to accompany Alain on this personal mission to Edgarburh, he doubted he'd have undertaken the journey.

The more he pondered it, in fact, the more attractive the idea of turning back became.

"Did the Blessed Virgin look with favor upon your request?" Ruaud's breath exuded ale, and Alain detected a slur to his words. "Do you think the Holy Mother will grant you a wife worthy of such a fine and pious young knight?"

Alain's eyes had adjusted sufficiently to note that only two other Normans numbered among the tavern's patrons, the crimson cross emblazoned across the front of their white tunics marking them as men employed by Bishop Odo, who had been appointed coregent and charged with governing the affairs of southern England while the king held court in Normandy. King William's other close friend and adviser, William

FitzOsbern, had been ordered to establish his headquarters in York to serve as the bishop's counterpart for governing northern England.

Odo's men greeted Alain with friendly nods and continued sitting near the back, drinking ale with a passing fair Saxon woman. If they had heard Ruaud's remark, they didn't respond to it. The Saxon patrons most likely would not understand a word. Alain knew many Englishmen in London who spoke fluent French, but in Winchester he had met few men with command of the language.

In answer to Ruaud, he shrugged. "I could not concentrate."

"What, Sir Robert the Pious having trouble at his prayers? Did a pretty pair of eyes distract you?" Ruaud laughed again—a bit too loudly, Alain thought. He wondered how many flagons his friend had consumed. Despite his bulk, Ruaud's ability to hold his alcohol remained tenuous.

"Sit." Alain took Ruaud by the arm and steered him toward an out-of-the-way bench. "I must discuss something with you."

As they seated themselves, a short, ill-featured serving woman appeared with a flagon, which she thrust into Alain's hand. "From your companions, my lord," she said, nodding toward Odo's men. Returning her attention to Alain, she offered him a provocative smile.

He understood all too well the implications of such a smile, and even if the woman had been a peerless beauty, he had no wish to accept her unspoken invitation.

Mercifully, she retreated to attend other men clamoring for service. Alain saluted the Normans with the flagon and took a long pull.

The brew's bitter taste compounded the bitterness frothing in his heart. Months of resentment roiled to a head. He lowered the flagon and met his friend's bleary gaze. "I have a plan. I need your help."

"Plan? We do not need a plan," Ruaud scoffed. "All we need is a guide across the plains of Somerset. Our friends"—he tossed a nod at the bishop's knights, who sat too engrossed in their conversation to notice—"have said the road to Sarum is easy. We would be wasting our coins to hire a guide here, when cheaper and more reliable service is available in Sarum."

"I am not going to Edgarburh."

"What?" Ruaud roared the word, attracting the attention of a pair of burly Saxons seated a few tables away. "You drag me from London to this armpit of a city for no purpose? You ignore King William's command? Do you yet suffer battle fever? Or have the vapors of this accursed dung heap robbed you of your wits?"

The Saxon men were frowning. Alain gave Ruaud a warning stare. "I am sorry," he said. "But I refuse to be William's pawn in his chess game with the English."

Ruaud rolled his eyes. "You have a choice?"

Alain curled one hand around his flagon and the other into a fist. "I will travel to Anjou, hire out my scouting services and my sword, and outwait William's wrath. I need you to buy me time. Go to Edgarburh, introduce yourself as my spokesman, and make excuses for my absence as long as you can." He drained his flagon and set it down with a solid thump.

His decision didn't make him feel a fraction as satisfied as he'd hoped.

Puffing his cheeks, Ruaud blew out a sigh. "Merciful Mother of God. Your brains would make the flowers grow. What am I to tell the thane or his daughter? That your wound still troubles you? This long after the battle, do you think they will believe it?"

Alain gave a stiff shrug. "It does, sometimes."

Ruaud snorted. "You have brooded about this wedding for half a year. William rewards you well. Forget this Anjou lunacy. Take the rich estate and the woman, and be done."

"Easy advice for you to dispense." The echo mocked Alain from the bottom of his empty flagon. "You did not have to marry into your English estate." He held the mug aloft to signal the serving maid, which she acknowledged with a gap-toothed smile, took his penny, and hurried off. After downing half of the replacement brew, he eyed Ruaud over the rim.

"I am already married." Ruaud grinned. "Or have you forgotten?"

"I have not. But by the way you consort with the London women, it seems you have."

Ruaud let out a hearty laugh. "And that is the best part of being a knight, lad. Marry the wench, get some sons on her, and do as you please with other women."

"Trouble visits a married man who dallies." And their children, Alain mused, recalling William's rocky rise to power because Duke Robert had never married William's baseborn mother.

The absolute last thing Alain wanted was an army of bastards scattered about the world.

Ruaud ran a hand through his hair and canted across the table, his gaze as earnest as his state of inebriation would permit. "Dalliance has never caused me any trouble. And it need not cause you any, if you are careful. Marry the Saxon and leave her in Wessex to bear your sons. Then hie yourself to France or Normandy or Jerusalem—or hell itself, for all I care." Ruaud finished his ale and brandished the empty flagon. "Ale of more!" he yelled in his atrocious English.

"Some friend you are."

Ruaud remained silent as the serving maid approached. Mumbling something Alain couldn't hear, she extracted the flagon from Ruaud's hand and vanished with it into the shadows at the back of the tavern.

"You do have another option." Ruaud gave Alain a long stare as though taking his measure for the first time. Alain felt his brow furrow. "You could go to Edgarburh in disguise."

Alain recoiled as if he'd been struck. "Why should I?"

"You are the scout. You tell me."

"To see the woman and her land for myself?"

Ruaud tapped a finger on his nose. "If she is not to your liking, you have lost nothing."

"Nothing except the easiest way to sidestep this matter." Alain took another pull. "And how would you propose I explain the deception if I choose to reveal myself?"

"A jest, a harmless ruse. Some portion of the truth. All of it, even." Ruaud scrunched a shoulder. "You are clever enough to think of something suitable."

Alain had no desire to think of a suitable reason, no desire to come within five leagues of Edgarburh. "I leave for France tonight, with or without your help."

"You are serious." Ruaud sucked in a long, contemplative breath. "Very well. I will no doubt regret this, but I will do as you ask." The woman returned with a full flagon, which Ruaud took and raised to Alain. "And I hope the bitch of Edgarburh will be easier on the eyes," he bellowed, "than this mongrel of a serving wench."

The two Saxons Alain had noticed earlier exchanged a glance, rose from their table with a clatter of toppling benches, and stomped toward Ruaud. Well muscled, they moved with the wary grace of seasoned warriors. Alain's senses sharpened to danger.

"What did you say, you Norman pig?" said one of the men in flawless French. "It is bad enough that you loot our land, but I will not listen to you insult our women."

Ruaud's face flushed dark red as he stood, swaying, to meet the challenger. He and the Saxon were of a size and build that promised an equal match. The second Saxon hung back, perhaps waiting for Alain's move. Odo's men rose, fists on hips.

The regent would not be pleased to hear of a tavern brawl. William had urged his knights not to drink in public places and had charged the coregents with enforcing the fragile peace. Alain studied the faces, measuring the fury glittering in each pair of eyes.

"My good sirs," he said in lightly accented English as he stood. "This little jest is not worth a fight. My friend will apologize to the woman, if that is agreeable to you."

The second Saxon gaped at Alain. "Who are you? You dress like a Norman and associate with one, and yet you speak our language as if you were born to it."

Alain inclined his head. "I am Norman by my father, Hugh FitzWalter. My mother was English. After my father's death, she took me to the London court of good King Edward." He summoned his courtliest smile. "It would not be seemly to profane the king's blessed memory by brawling in the town where his widow yet lives, agreed?"

Ruaud turned to Alain, eyebrows puckered. "What say you? You speak the English too fast."

"I told them you will apologize to the serving woman," he whispered rapidly in French. "Which you will do, and then we will leave. There is much to be done ere I depart for Anjou."

Ruaud hesitated, his gaze shifting from Alain to the Saxons, Odo's knights, and back to Alain. He shrugged. "As you wish." He signaled to the serving woman, who answered his summons with alacrity. Ruaud swept her a bow. "My apologies, good woman," he said in French, "if my jest insulted you."

The woman shook her head, clearly mystified.

"My friend apologizes for any bad behavior," Alain explained to her. He withdrew a farthing from the pouch at his belt and pressed it into her callused palm. "We would not want the fine people of Winchester to think Norman knights are ill-mannered."

"Thank'e, my lord. You're a fair-speaking man, you are." Her grin did nothing to alleviate her homeliness. She pocketed the coin, curtseyed, and continued about her business.

The two Saxons nodded grudging approval. Alain and Ruaud bade farewell to the regent's men and strode toward the steps.

"I left half a flagon of ale," Ruaud complained.

"Better to waste ale than blood." An image of his brother's lifeless body tortured his mind. He tried to banish the scene, and the guilt it evoked, without success.

He could almost feel the hot stares of the Saxon warriors burning into his back. He ascended the stairs into the soft evening light and began a brisk westward hike toward the far gate of the ancient walled city and Regent Odo's half-built hall, where Alain and Ruaud would spend their only night in Winchester. Ruaud lumbered along beside him.

"I still think this plan of yours is a bad idea," Ruaud said, "but I suppose I owe you something for averting that trouble in the tavern."

"My thanks for your help. This will work out for the best, you will see."

Ruaud grunted.

The street wasn't busy, probably owing to the fact that most residents had retired to their evening meal, if the beefy aromas wafting on the breeze gave any clue. Alain's stomach rumbled. He and Ruaud hadn't walked far when a mounted courier rounded a corner and sped toward them. The courier reined his mount to a sliding stop.

"Sir Robert Alain de Bellencombre?" When Alain nodded once, the courier said, "Well met, Sir Robert. Regent Odo commands your presence in his private audience chamber."

"Now? What about?" The courier shrugged. Alain's spine tingled a warning. He plucked at his damp tunic that reeked of the tavern, no thanks to Ruaud, and curbed a sigh. "Then I would appreciate the loan of your horse to make better time." He spared a wan grin for his friend, who looked none too steady on his feet. "And your assistance to accompany Sir Ruaud back to our quarters in Regent Odo's hall."

"Understood, my lord." The courier dismounted and held the bridle for Alain.

"I do not need a nursemaid," Ruaud muttered as Alain mounted.

"Tell me that again if you are still awake after I return." He turned the gelding about, dug heels into the horse's flanks, and clattered off.

Two hours later, Ruaud not only was very much awake— and sober—but demanding every detail.

"Thieves. Hellish beasts. Grisly deaths. Rumors of curses and practitioners of the black arts." Alain ground the words between his teeth as if that could somehow solve his problem. Ruaud's cocked eyebrow bade him to explain. "The regent has received dozens of reports from the monks and merchants in the Glastonbury district, two days' ride west of Edgarburh. God alone knows how much of it has been exaggerated. Regent Odo has ordered me to investigate and enforce the king's laws there."

Clasping his hands behind his head and tipping his chair backward on two legs, Ruaud stretched his unshod feet toward the fire. "I thought that was the local thane's task."

"Apparently that thane is not preserving the peace." Bitterness overpowered Alain's tone.

The chair's front legs came down with a sharp thud. "The father of the woman you are commanded to marry?"

"Ulfric of Thornhill. The regent wants me to learn why he has not stopped the mayhem."

Alain spat onto the slate floor. That, for plans. Evading an unwanted wedding was one thing. No power under heaven could make him shirk duty to king and country when people's lives stood at risk.

Restoring order to Glastonbury might begin to atone for his failure to protect Étienne.

He stared into the snapping gold flames, questing for answers and finding only more questions. Nothing could ever atone for his broken vows.

Ruaud's chair grated on the slate as he turned, grinning. "You will go to Edgarburh posing as my squire."

Alain wrenched himself from his depressing thoughts to regard Ruaud. "You're joking!" Ruaud's grin widened. "Dear God above, you're not joking."

"You are too old, of course, but that comely face of yours makes you seem youthful enough if no one looks closely." Alain snorted in denial. "Well," Ruaud pressed, "have you a better solution to scout the land, the lady, Thane Ulfric, the outlaws, and heaven knows what else is plaguing the people? I have seen many a man quake dumbstruck in front of a knight and moments later reveal all to a lowly squire."

"True enough. It may work." Alain fingered his chin. "If I can keep myself from drawing undue attention."

Ruaud chuckled. "That could pose a problem. The ladies always notice you."

"The ladies notice this." Alain looped a finger through the lone symbol of knighthood he wore when not armed, a thick gold chain draped over the finely tooled leather jerkin he'd donned for his audience with the regent.

"You are wrong, my friend. Your face has been collecting hearts all over London for weeks. You have been brooding too much to notice. So, what will you call yourself, squire?"

"Alain," he snapped, irritated at Ruaud's blithe attitude. In the next breath, he recognized the reaction's unworthiness and gave Ruaud an apologetic smile. "I do appreciate your help." Thankful that his preferred name was common enough to avoid suspicion, he pursed his lips, trying to construct an innocuous surname. This evening's tavern flashed to mind, Sign of the Rose. It reminded him of his shield's device: a white rose nestled in a graceful tangle of greenery, symbolic of the Norman town of his birth, Bellencombre, "pretty entanglement." His lips parted into a smile that felt more genuine. "Call me Alain Bellefleur."

Outlaws, hellish beasts, and mysterious deaths. Sorcery. An English estate. And a woman he must claim as his bride before claiming her land.

Alain felt more like a thief than the men he'd been commanded to bring to justice. His smile vanished.

He stood, crossed to the slotted window, braced his hands on the cold stone ledge, and gazed at the partially constructed towers rising above the castle's far wall. The carpenters, stonemasons, and other workmen had long since returned home for the night. The scaffolding, barely visible in the twilight's final moments, made the structures look as delicate as a child's pebble-and-twig fantasy.

Given time, many other Norman castles would defend the English countryside. He hoped it wasn't a childish fantasy to believe that someday, God willing, one of those castles would be his, with or without Lady Kendra Waldronsdotter of Edgarburh at his side.

Preferably, for her sake as much as his, without.

STROKING THE black velvet cord at her neck, Kendra inspected the rosebushes, engrossed in her evening ritual of selecting the best bloom with which to adorn Del's sarcophagus at vespers. This was the one blessed moment of her day not devoted to either the burh's mundane concerns or preparations for her impending marriage . . . or to meaningless oblations to a God who'd turned a blind eye to the Norman sword that had cut her brother down.

Although the gardens perfuming the expanse between Edgarburh's church and manor house were not private, by tacit agreement no one disturbed her, for which she felt abundantly grateful. Here amidst the sanctity of the roses, gifts from Del the spring following their mother's death, she could reflect upon the whirlwind her life had become since her father had returned from King William's coronation.

Waldron's news had been just as bad for Kendra as Del's death had been for their father. He'd been unable to secure from the king a firm promise to investigate Del's attack. And, worse yet, Waldron had been "strongly encouraged"—forced, in her opinion—to establish a date for the arrival of Sir Robert de Bellencombre, her Norman bridegroom.

Because of the severity of Sir Robert's battle wounds, Waldron had selected mid-June, giving her more of a reprieve than she'd expected, but her vows lay in grave danger of being compromised.

Even with the delay, she'd had no choice but to spend her every free moment preparing her wedding garments, dreading with each stitch the dawning of the day when Sir Robert would ride up to claim her like a sack of plunder. Today was the eve of that hateful day.

For pride's sake, she'd made each stitch perfect and each seam straight and sturdy, applying the same exacting standards to her maidservants' work. To Hedda and Rowena she assigned the tasks of crafting her soft linen undertunic and bedgown, while Kendra embroidered the midnight-blue overtunic and scalloped the paler veil's hem. She could not bear the thought of her own hands making the clothes she would be wearing when this Norman would force himself upon her in their bridal chamber. His coarse, violent fingers and rancid breath, his sweaty body crushing hers beneath him, his bony hips grinding against hers to make their union legal in the eyes of Church and King, mayhap making an heir in the process . . . the imagery made her flesh crawl.

Chafing her arms, she returned to the decision at hand, which she had narrowed to two candidates: a red and a white, growing on adjacent bushes, their stems slanting toward each other as if striving to entwine. Both were flawless blossoms, full and fragrant. But she always laid a single rose on Del's tomb, over the place on his effigy where his heart would have been. By this time on the morrow, whichever of the two flowers she did not select would be opened past its prime, its petals beginning to curl and die.

Which rose should I choose?

Red for Del's heart or white for his soul? Red for the blood spattered with his final breath? Or white for the snow swirling outside that night, the snow embodying her fervent wish for his recovery?

The vespers bell startled her. She whipped her head around to see the laborers lay down their tools and head toward the church.

She glanced at the bushes swaying in the breeze. Her two favorites had blown closer, petals brushing.

Which one?

Red for her vow not to marry the countryman of her brother's murderer, or white for her promise to seek happiness?

The bell tolled again, sounding more insistent.

Her ivory-hilted dagger flashed in the shortening sunlight. Both roses fell into her basket.

She sheathed the dagger and hurried toward the church as fast as decorum allowed, making sure her necklace did not slip free of her tunic. She harbored no secret that she wore at her bosom a slim silver case containing a lock of Del's hair, cut from his head the night of his death by the dagger he'd given her and taught her to wield. Those who didn't understand might consider her practice idolatrous, however, so she kept it hidden.

Inside the main doors, she genuflected before the altar and moved to her customary place near Del's sarcophagus, where his remains guarded the church's entrance and their mother's tomb. His sarcophagus's newly completed marble panel depicted Del, limned in gold, standing within the ranks of King Harold's doomed shield wall. Upon their father's orders, Del's shield bore the family's bent blue bar rather than the cocked arm-and-fist variant Del had carried into that fateful battle.

If ignorant generations later presumed that Sir Delwin Waldronson of Edgarburh had lost his life at Hastings, so much the better. The truth was hard enough to bear without sharing it with the rest of the world.

While Father Æthelward mumbled through the service to the choir's less than tuneful responses, she took advantage of her position, screened by the other worshippers, to finish adorning Del's tomb. She picked up the previous day's offering, a yellow rose that reminded her of their friendship. The rose's head hung as if in mourning, its petals already falling. Heedless of the thorns, she pressed it to her chest before stooping to lay it in her basket, along with the loose petals she swept from the lid. She would save these with the others in the tall earthen jar in her quarters, to be strewn on her wedding day, providing she could find a way to keep both vows.

No boorish Norman would trample these sacred flowers underfoot.

She hoped her brother's memory would never wilt, but as the weeks had stretched into months, she found it harder to preserve his features in her mind's eye, and it goaded her grief.

Running her fingers over his cool granite effigy helped. The image faithfully portrayed Del as fair of face and broad of shoulder and brawny of limb, facing death as he had life: head-on and arrayed for battle, his hands folded in eternal prayer. The only missing detail was his smile.

Her heart ached. That Godforsaken Norman sword may as well have pierced her too.

She blinked and retrieved the red and white roses. Avoiding the thorns, she twisted the stems together. The white's stem was much longer than the red's, casting the illusion that it overshadowed the other. She separated them and adjusted the stems to make the blossoms even. Pleased with the effect, she kissed both and laid them on the effigy in time to ease to her knees with the rest of the congregation.

After the priest's prayers ended and people began shuffling past her, she kept her eyes closed and head bowed, adding her silent petition for the redemption of Del's soul and for the means to fulfill her vows.

"Daughter. Walk with me."

Her father was looming over her, his arms crossed and face stern. She swallowed hard. Such a look brooked no disobedience.

Gazing at Del's tomb, he sighed, expression softening. "Come." He offered his hand to help her rise, which she accepted with resignation. Tensions had flared between them since his return from London, and she braced herself for another bout.

She genuflected again, grasped her basket's handle, and turned to accompany Waldron from the church. Not across the yard to the feast hall, as she'd expected, since that was where most Edgarburh business—including private matters—transpired, but past the garden toward the manor house. In silence they ascended the outer wooden staircase, entered the building, and trod the corridor containing the bedchambers. Specifically, she realized with a start when their course became apparent, Waldron's.

Several paces from their destination, curiosity compelled her to blurt, "What's wrong?"

Pulling up short, he gave her an odd look. "Wrong? Let me see." He snorted, ticking the points on his fingers. "Taxes are due ere long, and the tenants have barely recovered from the war to scrape together their payments. A Norman is on his way to take possession of my daughter and the estate." Waldron's gray eyes gazed at her levelly. "My son is dead, and my daughter acts like a widow rather than a bride." He inclined his head at the black woolen veil she wore even as these final spring days warmed toward summer.

This time it wasn't the sun that made her face heat. "My choices honor Del's memory." She gripped the basket with both fists, raising it before her like a shield. "Do yours?"

"My choices, Kendra," he grated between clenched teeth, "are made for the good of all. Including yourself, though you're too stubborn to acknowledge it." Despite the limp that was the legacy of an old war wound, he strode the remaining distance so briskly that she felt obliged to break into a trot.

Waldron yanked open the door, ushered her inside, and pulled it to with a timber-rattling thud. She tilted her head to meet his glare.

"The good of all, Father? What possible good is it to surrender me—and, by extension, Edgarburh lands—to this barbaric Norman?" When Waldron didn't answer, she pressed on, "What good can come of forcing me to break my vows to Del?" After setting down the basket to fold her arms, she lowered her gaze to the floor rushes, lowering her voice to match. "If I had accepted Ulfric's suit, this matter never would have come to pass."

The irony forced a laugh from her lips. Ulfric, a relative of her mother, had petitioned for Kendra's hand five summers after Edwina's death. Fifteen years Kendra's senior, he had given the then eighteen-year-old Kendra the impression that he possessed a dual nature. Nothing she could explain beyond vague suspicions, but Waldron had honored her decision to reject the suit.

She looked up, emboldened by the memory. "You promised me that I need never marry save for love. Have you forgotten in just three years?"

He dropped into the chair beside his worktable, propping his elbow on the dark, smoothly planed oak surface and bracing his forehead against his fist, his thatch of white hair falling over the scarred, gnarled fingers. Never could she recall him looking so old and weary. "I remember." His care-lined face adopted a plaintive look. "And nothing would delight me more than to honor that promise. But this is a royal command you would have me break."

"Made by the royal bastard—"

He glared at her. "Spare me your opinion of our new king. I cannot control your thoughts, but his lineage has no relevance to this or any other conversation you might have. In a thrice William will execute any Saxon lord he perceives as a threat, and treasonous speech is as valid an excuse as any other." His eyebrows knotted into a thick white line. "And do not dare to presume these Normans will not understand you. Many of them know our tongue as well as we do. Do I make myself clear?"

She nodded, chastened, realizing there was no wisdom in inciting this Sir Robert to wrath by insulting his king—their king, she amended. "I understand, Father," she whispered, gazing at the floor.

She felt his leathery fingers slip beneath her chin, and she lifted her head. "Be of good cheer. By all reports, Sir Robert is pious, courtly"—he winked—"and handsome."

Shrugging free, she rolled her eyes. "By Norman reports, you mean. That hardly qualifies as an honest assessment."

"So you would call King William a liar too?" Her father's tone rumbled as ominously as a summer storm.

"Nay! I—I had presumed—" She clamped her mouth shut. After a few moments, she said, "Please forgive me, Father."

Waldron nodded and crossed to the wall where the chests containing his clothing and other personal effects stood. The longest and newest chest—and one of the few secured with an iron lock, the key to which lay in Waldron's possession alone—contained the shield of Del's murderer. To her surprise, he stopped before the first in the line, bent over, and swiped its age-darkened, leather-hinged lid with his tunic sleeve to clear the dust. He pushed it open and started sorting through its contents. She shifted from foot to foot to peer inside the chest, to no avail.

He extracted a length of finely spun linen, gave it a gentle shake, and turned to hold it up before him. She gasped. It was a lady's veil, edged in an elaborate pattern of silver thread and dyed a delicate shade of slate blue, the precise color of her eyes, and her mother's.

Waldron's smile was tinted with a mixture of affection, pride, and sadness. "Your dear mother made this and wore it the day we wed. I couldn't bring myself to bury her in it. I had hoped—" He drew a swift breath and thrust the veil toward her. "I know you have been hard at work making your wedding garments, and I commend you for that. But it would please me if you would wear this veil to greet Sir Robert."

Though she'd always known that her father loved her, never had he shown it so tenderly. She drew near to caress the fabric. It smelled faintly of must, but that could be remedied with fresh lavender and a good airing. The silver threads glittered in the candlelight. Waldron laid it across her outstretched palms. It weighed next to nothing, far lighter than her mourning veil, which at times felt as if it had slid off her head to bind her heart.

"Father . . ." A quiver threatened to block her throat, and she swallowed. "I will be honored." Edwina's veil clutched in one hand, she stood on tiptoe to throw her other arm about her father's neck. Tears burned her cheeks. Waldron completed the embrace with fiercely protective strength.

She would never surrender the lock of Del's hair she had taken such pains to preserve, but she had to admit it would feel good to shed her black veil for a while. And she would savor giving her would-be bridegroom a glimpse of what he would never possess.

Chapter 3

ALAIN LAY ON his back beside the raucously snoring Ruaud, right hand beneath his head, staring at the ceiling's dark oak timbers. The guide they'd hired in Sarum, a man named Ecgfrith, hadn't returned from his evening's entertainment—likely in a woman's arms. Ecgfrith had recommended keeping to the Winchester road until it intersected the road to Ilchester in front of this decaying excuse for an inn.

He scratched absently at his chest. While he distrusted Ecgfrith's furtive manner, the man's advice had proven sound, for their choices had been limited to braving the creatures inhabiting this lumpy mattress or the ones creeping into their bedrolls atop some windswept hillock. As an unwelcome Norman traveling across unfamiliar English territory, he preferred the sensible solidity of walls any day.

Or night.

Hoofbeats thrummed outside. It seemed a strange hour for someone to be arriving unless it was a courier, but the irregular drumming sounded like several horses. Alain honed his senses but couldn't discern anything else above the snores. He rose, padded to the shuttered window, and stooped to peer through a knothole.

Light from the half-moon illuminated the scene well enough to wrench a soft curse from his throat.

In the courtyard below, five men had dismounted and were throwing their reins over the rail. The horses' bridles and harnesses had been wrapped with rags. The men eased out their swords, speaking in tones too low for Alain to catch. Outlaws, he guessed. A sixth man joined them from the inn. Though the gloom prevented him from being certain, the chill prickling his spine told him the sixth was Ecgfrith.

One by one, they crept inside.

Alain withdrew from the window. Reaching for his sword, he breathed a prayer of thanks that he'd remained in his squire's garb of plain jerkin and trousers. Ruaud had scoffed at Alain's caution. If they survived, he doubted that Ruaud would ever scoff again. He drew his sword and battled the shiver wrought by the *if*.

"To arms, Ruaud!" he rasped, giving his friend's shoulder a shove.

Years of battle propelled Ruaud awake, and his brow furrowed. Finger to lips, Alain pointed with his sword toward the door, where footfalls shuffled in the corridor beyond. While Ruaud dressed, Alain scooped a shovelful of embers from the brazier, blew to redden them, and stationed himself near the door.

No match for the combined weight of a half dozen men, the door yielded with a crash. Alain launched his surprise, shovel included, catching some men in the face and others on the arms and hands. Howls of rage and pain split the night, followed by curses and stomps and the clatter of steel on steel as Alain drove the intruders back into the corridor.

Two men nursing burn wounds fled. As Alain fought with the apparent leader, he felt Ruaud pressing at his back, surging like a leashed hound scenting the quarry. Alain dodged aside, and Ruaud joined the fray, spouting a cheerful stream of French insults.

Alain found nothing entertaining about this fight. His adversary, though dressed in poorly tanned and patched leather such as an outlaw might wear and wielding his sword with both hands when one should have sufficed, landed his blows with the might and precision of one well trained in the military arts. Alain couldn't see his face, but a memory nagged that he'd fought this man before. He squelched it, redoubling his efforts. His shoulder began aching, and he prayed the old wound wouldn't betray him.

Saxon screams and thuds behind Alain told him Ruaud had finished the last of his attackers. Faced with two Norman swords, the man fighting Alain disengaged and ran off. No one else of the erstwhile band was in any shape to accompany him.

Of Ecgfrith there was no sign.

As Alain's opponent fled down the corridor, his silhouette seemed to blur. Thinking it a trick of the quivering torchlight, Alain blinked but couldn't shake the sensation. After a few moments, the sound of boots pounding timber ceased, replaced by a mad scrabbling, as if an animal had been loosed.

Puzzled, Alain took a step or two after his foe, but fatigue and the aching of his shoulder halted him.

Silence reigned save for ragged gasping as both knights struggled to regain their breath.

Ruaud clenched his sword, glaring. He didn't appear to have suffered more than a few scratches, for which Alain was thankful. "Aren't we going after the bastard?"

"To what end?" Massaging his shoulder, Alain didn't bother to leach the disgust from his tone. "So he can lead us into another trap like Ecgfrith did?"

"Is that what you think happened?"

"Absolutely."

"But why?"

Good question.

Most likely they'd fallen afoul of Sarum outlaws. If these attacks occurred with regularity, Alain wondered why Bishop Odo hadn't acted to combat them. Even if all the other victims had been murdered, surely such reports would have reached the regent's ears by now.

The men could be part of the Glastonbury band; a remote possibility, given the distances involved, but worth considering. Such a connection would imply that these outlaws were far better organized and informed—and dangerous—than Alain had presumed.

Rather than answer Ruaud's question aloud, he shouldered past his friend into the chamber that almost had become their tomb and tossed his sword onto the bed. After cross-gartering his trousers, he grabbed his boots and braced against the bed to tug them on. The outlaws had attacked too quickly for him to don footgear, and he thanked God it hadn't hindered him. He retrieved his sword belt, girt it about his waist, and sheathed his sword.

He snatched his cloak from the back of a chair and settled it across his shoulders. In the corridor, he joined Ruaud, who was attempting to converse in his halting English with the innkeeper.

Alain wondered whether the man's concern was an act. "How many other travelers have suffered a similar fate?"

The innkeeper blanched. "None, good squire! I-I beg you not to be angry with your humble servant." He bowed double as though baring his neck to a headsman's ax.

The odds of a Glastonbury connection jumped several notches.

The innkeeper looked so pathetic, Alain decided to take pity on him. "Be at ease. Sir Ruaud and I have taken no permanent injury." Ruaud was regarding Alain with puzzlement, and he switched to French to ask, "Have you searched the bodies?"

Ruaud shook his head, and Alain squatted to take a closer look. None of the three men was wearing or carrying anything to suggest he was anything other than what he seemed.

He stood and told Ruaud, "I am going to check on our horses."

"You think they have been stolen?" Alain shrugged, and Ruaud toed the closest corpse. "If so, then these poor sods will not need theirs. But wait." He laid a hand on Alain's arm, his grip radiating concern and urgency. "I will go with you."

As Ruaud returned to the room for his outer gear, the innkeeper sidled up to Alain. "You won't be—" Wringing his hands, he stared at the dead men and the open doorway to his Norman guests' room before returning his gaze to Alain. He swallowed and grimaced. "You and your master won't noise this abroad, will you?" he whispered.

"No worry there, friend." Alain laughed mirthlessly. "But don't take offense if you never see us again."

That coaxed a wavering smile to the man's lips. After bobbing another bow, he trudged off, presumably in search of someone to help him remove the corpses and mop up the blood before other guests stumbled upon the scene. Alain was a bit surprised that no one else had come out to investigate the fight; cowering in their beds, perhaps, or else too drunk to notice.

Ruaud joined him, and they headed for the stables. The outlaws' horses were gone, even the animals the dead men had ridden, leaving a morass of the imprints of boots and hooves in the dew-dampened dirt. Alain studied the swath of tracks leading toward the crossroads and released a sigh.

"Any idea where they might have gone?" Ruaud asked.

"I cannot be certain. On the road's hard-packed surface, they can ride anywhere without fear of being followed. But I do have a reasonable guess." Ruaud cocked his head as if inviting Alain to continue. "West. Back to Glastonbury."

Staring westward, Ruaud let out a low whistle. "For once, I hope you are wrong. I would not like the implications if you are proven right."

The implications that someone in Sarum knew who they were and the nature of their mission, perhaps having been warned by a traitor in the regent's employ . . . Alain couldn't agree more.

As he turned, an odd print caught his attention. He stooped to trace it.

"Did you find something?" Ruaud asked.

"The innkeeper must have a dog." An extremely large dog, he surmised, though he couldn't recall having seen such an animal on the premises. A howl pierced the gloom from afar. Alain stood and gazed in the direction of the eerie sound. "Or perhaps a wolf passed through."

"And the mere sight of us convinced it to keep going, eh?" Ruaud's grin looked wan in the moonlight.

Hellish beasts . . . Alain shrugged.

They warily resumed their course toward the stables and discovered one of the outlaws inside, lying facedown in a puddle of blood. Alain kicked him in the side. The man didn't move. With his foot he righted the body.

Ecgfrith. Eyes bulging, his throat bore wide, jagged slashes as if he'd been cut with a dull blade.

Or a predator's teeth.

Alain lifted an eyebrow at Ruaud. "Did you give him those wounds?" Extracting information from the guide would have been useful—and satisfying.

Ruaud shook his head. "Never saw him during the fight."

Very odd.

Could the rumors contain a spark of truth?

Shoving aside the mystery of the man's demise with a shake of his head, he noticed a small pouch that had spilled some of its contents into the straw. He drew his dagger, squatted to cut it from Ecgfrith's belt, and straightened. Inside he found the coins Ruaud had given the guide and a few muslin-wrapped packets of dried herbs. Most of them Alain recognized as medicines any scout would carry: valerian, willow bark, chamomile, feverwort, elder. One, however, eluded him. He nudged the tiny, whitish petals with a fingertip.

Wild rose? Alain's mother often had given him a tisane brewed from rose hips to ward off distempers of the nose and lungs, but he had never heard of any use for the petals other than garnishing delicacies at the king's table.

Shrugging, he handed the coins to Ruaud, who accepted them with a short laugh. Alain added the medicines to his supply.

A familiar whinny disrupted the silence. He hastened past the other stalls, relieved to find Chou and Azure unhurt, if wild-eyed and jittery. Not that he could blame the animals; the air reeked of death. Alain stroked Chou's velvety black muzzle, and the mare nosed his palm, questing for treats. He regretted not having anything to offer and scratched her jaw.

"You do not carry your saddle packs," said Ruaud behind him, "but I wager that will not stop you from returning to London."

"I shall forget you said that," Alain growled, staring at the whorls of hair on Chou's cheek. "But only because you are my closest friend."

Ruaud chuckled, stepping closer to drop a hand onto his shoulder. "Between last night's near-brawl and tonight's mishap, the omens do not bode well."

"Omens are for fools." He shrugged Ruaud's hand away. Omens had portended an easy victory for William at Hastings. On the eve of battle, Étienne cheerfully had equated "easy" with "bloodless." And, foolishly, Alain had believed him.

Now worms were feasting upon Étienne's bones even as worms of guilt feasted upon Alain's soul.

Ruaud's nod exuded sympathy. "Come, lad. You sleep while I stand watch." He poked Alain in the ribs, chortling loud enough to make the horses stamp and toss their heads. "At this rate, I shall have to play the squire to even our score."

Though Alain shared the laugh, he sensed that sleep would be a futile prospect. His mind's eye was already reviewing the incident, stroke by harrowing stroke. But he appreciated Ruaud's offer more profoundly than his friend could ever know.

KENDRA WOKE to the scraping of her bedcurtains' wooden rings upon the dowel. Light assaulted her closed eyelids, and she winced. Squinting, she pushed herself into a sitting position to see Rowena bustling about the chamber, twittering like a love-smitten sparrow.

Today was the day.

She retreated to the pillows with an inward groan. But returning to her dreams wasn't an option if it meant more arguing with Del about keeping her vows. He had looked so alive and was so insistent that she must seek happiness above all else. With her Norman bridegroom nearing her doorstep, she didn't believe she could ever attain true happiness. She squeezed her eyes shut against the threat of tears.

"Please, my lady, 'tis time to dress."

Touched by the concern in Rowena's voice, she opened her eyes. Her new slate-blue gown had been laid across the foot of her bed, and Rowena was shaking out Edwina's veil. "Now? Why?"

"Riders have been sighted and should arrive within the hour."

"Already?" Kendra threw aside the bedclothes and stood.

Not Sir Robert! Please, not Sir Robert!

Resigned to her fate, she held out her arms for Rowena to assist her in donning her overdress.

God chose to answer her prayer, though in an unexpected manner. The riders proved to be Ulfric and a few members of his fyrd. She couldn't decide whether to be thankful for the reprieve or annoyed that God had granted this trivial request but not her impassioned petitions for Del's life.

On the manor's stone steps, Ulfric dismissed his men-at-arms to the task of stabling their mounts.

"What brings you to Edgarburh?" Waldron asked. "Are you not busy dealing with the problems in your district?"

"My men and I were tracking one of the beasts," Ulfric said. "It led us on to your lands, but we lost the trail near the granite quarry. Have any of your people seen anything unusual?"

"Not to my knowledge." For a moment, Waldron looked dubious. "But I thank you for the warning. I shall alert my patrols."

Ulfric grasped both Kendra's hands and kissed her cheek. "My dearest cousin, you look more radiant each time I see you. The angels must weep for joy to behold your beauty."

She felt her face flush and resorted to her usual rebuttal tactic. His rugged good looks and charm were forever turning maidens' heads, but never hers. "And you, Ulfric, grow ever more silvery of tongue. Have you been practicing at court?"

His grin widened wolfishly. "I would love to show you what I've been practicing."

I'm certain you would, cousin. She pulled her hands from his. Her cheeks felt like fire. To ward off her embarrassment, she let ire surface. "I don't believe my bridegroom will be too happy with that proposition."

"Bridegroom?" Ulfric faced Waldron. Kendra could have sworn he'd feigned surprise. "Am I too late to renew my suit, my lord?"

"Aye," Waldron replied, giving Ulfric's broad shoulder a sympathetic clap. "By King William's decree, no less."

"Indeed?" Ulfric glanced around. "Where is this bridegroom? I should like to meet him." Those ice-blue eyes came to rest upon Kendra rather covetously, she thought. When he blinked, the look gentled. "To make sure he is worthy of you, dear cousin."

When he reached for her hand, she noticed a bandage swathing his wrist, bearing signs that the wound was oozing. "That needs changing. What happened? Can I help?"

Ulfric yanked back his hand, seemed to think better of his action, and smiled. Flexing the fingers, he studied his wrist as if for the first time. "'Tis nothing. A nip from that demon-spawned stallion of mine. I can change the bandage myself." He knotted the hand into a fist and thrust it behind his back, making her wonder why he seemed anxious to hide it. "So, tell me where this lucky bridegroom of yours is."

"Sir Robert de Bellencombre is not expected until after nones," her father answered. "You and your men are welcome to stay, of course, for as long as you wish." Waldron turned to instruct a waiting servant to prepare the hall to receive the visitors. The man saluted and left.

"You are ever gracious, cousin." Ulfric bowed. "But I'll not impose upon your hospitality past the morrow." He winked at her. "Unless my lady Kendra wishes otherwise."

His sly, faintly predatory smile awakened her old suspicions that not everything about Ulfric, whose name meant "wolf-king," was as it seemed.

What she wished was to be left alone, with no thoughts of Normans or marriage or vows or regrets to trouble her. Having yet to devise a way to escape the tyranny of her mind, she would settle for the solitude.

With Ulfric in attendance, however, even that wish seemed doomed to be denied.

Surrounded by Thane Waldron's men, Alain rode behind Ruaud, absorbing the details of the Edgarburh estate. The reports of its wealth were supported by vast stretches of cropland, some fields ripening with summer wheat and others being harvested for hay. Sheep dotted grassy knolls too steep to cultivate. Cattle gazed at the warriors from the shade cast by ancient willows at the river's edge, some preferring to chew cud while standing belly-deep in the placid waters. Most of the farmhouses looked tidy, well provisioned, and prosperous. Nor did the farmhands seem overly concerned to see Normans, although Alain attributed their apparent sense of security to the presence of the thane's men.

It was a fine estate Alain could become accustomed to governing if only it weren't encumbered with an emotional price.

Edgarburh's central compound had been built atop a hill with a commanding view of the plains. He nodded to himself with satisfaction. Of all the likely sites they'd passed, he'd have chosen this one too. Around its base sprawled a town that boasted a huge market, complete with livestock pens and all their attendant sights and sounds and smells. In size, the church was comparable to St. Mary's in Winchester, though Edgarburh's appeared to be in far better repair. The many merchants' shops, selling everything from apothecary's wares to wine, implied a more affluent patronage than those who frequented the church ministering to Winchester's tannery district.

Edgarburh's town reminded him of Bellencombre in Normandy, and the association sparked pangs of longing and regret.

He sighed. *Holy Mother, please let this lady of Edgarburh be a cost I can bear.*

As they plodded up the manor's road behind an oxcart laden with ale kegs and crated supplies, he tried to banish his concerns about his promised bride and imagined instead how the timber palisade would look replaced by stone walls.

The manor's compound was laid out with more precision than the town. Near the main gatehouse stood the stables and barracks, across from a training ground where more of Waldron's men drilled both mounted and on foot. As the gate sentries had done, the soldiers exchanged waves with the incoming patrol before returning to their drills. The smithy was situated next to the barracks, where a warrior stood waiting while his horse was being shod. Beyond the training ground, women and older children toiled among the long rows of a vegetable garden. A few of the women greeted the patrol with giggles that did not go unnoticed by the men. The kitchens stood between the hall and the manor house, connected by timber-roofed walkways. A chapel flanked the manor house on the right. Between chapel and house bloomed an exquisite rose garden.

The whitewashed, timber-ribbed manor house looked unassuming by Norman standards, though Saxons probably considered it opulent. Diamond-paned glass windows glittered across its double-storied face. Chimney pots bristled atop its timber roof in pairs, most disgorging gray tendrils of smoke in spite of the warmness of the waning June afternoon. A stout wooden staircase serviced the upper floor.

From each building fluttered a gray banner bearing a dark blue *V*. A memory nudged Alain, but he couldn't place where he'd seen the device.

The escort halted at the base of the wide granite steps leading to the house's main entrance. Ruaud dismounted, as did Alain, who moved to take Azure's reins in one fist while holding Chou's reins and the packhorse's tether in the other.

The massive oaken doors swung outward. Two men stepped forth. The elder, a white-haired man of at least three-score years, stood elegantly attired from head to foot in dark blue velvet. The tunic displayed a repeating *V* pattern wrought of silver thread. A matching cape draped from shoulders to waist. His cap sported a peacock plume. The other man, perhaps five and twenty years younger, which would make him a decade older than Alain, was similarly dressed. This one carried himself with a warrior's haughty air. A clean bandage showed from underneath the sleeve on his left wrist.

As Alain matched the younger Saxon's stare, he got the distinct feeling he'd seen this man before.

At court, perhaps? Or in battle?

Hastings, most likely. It would explain why the Saxon's face had folded into an expression of contempt. But who was he? Thane Waldron's son? For there could be no doubting the identity of the older man as he approached Ruaud with an extended hand and a welcoming smile.

No welcome resided in the younger warrior's expression.

And where was Waldron's fabled daughter? Alain felt his brow crease as he gazed past the Saxons into the shadows of the open manor house behind them.

"I am Thane Waldron. You are well come to Edgarburh. Please forgive the delay," Waldron said to Ruaud. "Lady Kendra is putting the finishing touches on her attire. By the time your retainer sees to the needs of your horses and returns, she should be ready, and we can complete the formal introductions."

Ruaud leaned toward Alain. "I hope you understood him," he whispered in French.

Alain pursed his lips to suppress a grin. "His daughter is not ready. Our host wants me to put up our horses and return."

"Go," Ruaud commanded loudly. "*Vite!*"

Hurry, indeed. Dawdling couldn't have been further from Alain's mind.

KENDRA CUSHIONED her head with the back of her hand on the window's frame, careful to remain hidden from the group that had gathered on the manor's steps, two stories below her window.

Sir Robert appeared every inch the brute she had imagined.

Even worse, it seemed as if he could barely speak English. Although the glazed panes prevented her from hearing the conversation, she could tell by the way he kept looking toward his manservant, who seemed to be responding as if in explanation.

If she'd not been born into nobility, she might have found Sir Robert's servant intriguing, Norman or no. While being deferential, he interacted with his master and Waldron with respect yet confidence. Distance prevented her from discerning details, but his body seemed far more fit than Sir Robert's.

What she found more surprising than her own attitude toward the squire was that Ulfric appeared to eye him with a measure of grudging respect.

Sighing for more reasons than she could count, she turned from the window and strode toward her destiny.

ALAIN LEFT the packhorse's tether with a member of the patrol, explaining that he would unload the animal upon his return. He led Chou and Azure to the stables, found a groom, and conveyed his wishes for their care. Anticipation mounting, he all but ran back to the manor.

A young woman was standing on the staircase's top landing as he approached. No, he amended, feeling his eyes widen and his blood heat, a goddess. The suggestive clinging of her grayish-blue gown made him forget his blasphemous lapse.

He shifted from foot to foot to mask his reaction. Her ash-blonde curls, creamy complexion, and alluring curves conquered his fear of failure. As his heart thrummed its praises of her beauty, he vowed to protect this lady unto the ends of the earth.

But he tempered his lauds with a petition for wisdom, for he needed to ascertain her heart. Experience had taught him the folly of loving a beautiful but title-hungry woman like Marie.

Yet sorrow enveloped this lady like a shroud. The slope of her delicately boned shoulders, the tilt of her petite chin, the hooded reserve of her slate-blue eyes, the slight pout of her full lips all sang the same dirge.

Blessed Virgin, could I be the cause of her misery? Please, let it not be so!

He wanted nothing more than to gather her into his arms and kiss those lips until their song transformed from sorrow to joy.

Their gazes met. Her look, a cross between appreciation and reprimand, made him remember his "station," and he looked down.

"This is Thane Ulfric, kin to Lady Edwina, my deceased wife," Waldron said.

Recognition made Alain glance up. The name had to be a coincidence. This Ulfric seemed fit to rule an entire province, to say nothing of a few thousand acres. If he were suffering problems from outlaws and murderous beasts, Alain would gladly feast upon Chou's fouled bedding for a week.

Ulfric's glowering softened as Waldron's daughter joined them. A suitor, then? Alain's jealousy fought with his need to maintain composure.

"And this, as you gentlemen may have guessed," Waldron continued, beaming at his daughter, "is the Lady Kendra." He placed her hand into Ruaud's. "Kendra, I am honored to present Sir Robert de Bellencombre."

Ruaud made no attempt to correct Waldron's error. Alain coughed into his fist. Ruaud shook his head and released her hand as if he'd been burned. *"Pardonnez-moi, mon seigneur et ma demoiselle, mais je m'appelle—"*

"En Anglais," Alain whispered, irritated and yet amused that the lady had befuddled his friend.

"Ah, *oui.* Apologies, my lord and my lady." Ruaud grinned, spreading his hands. "I call myself Ruaud d'Auvay. Sir Robert's—how say you? Man of speaking?"

Alain coughed again to hide his chuckle. Kendra looked downright relieved. Ulfric's expression grew pensive.

"Messenger?" asked Waldron, eyebrows lowered and fists on hips. "Why? Where is he? What's his message?"

While Ruaud struggled to answer the barrage of questions, Kendra repeatedly mouthed the phrase "man of speaking" until clarity lit her eyes. "Spokesman?" Her voice had a pleasing lilt.

Ruaud nodded. "Spokesman, *oui, ma demoiselle.* Yes, my lady. And friend. He is ill. Could not ride."

"Ill?" Ulfric asked with a level of interest Alain mistrusted. "Not injured?"

"Ill. Fever of more." Ruaud tossed a grin at Alain. "Sir Robert did not leave Winchester."

Ulfric frowned but said nothing.

"Perhaps we should go to him, daughter." That suggestion won Waldron a pleading look from Kendra. "With your knowledge of healing lore—"

"No!" Gentler, Ruaud repeated, "No, my lord. Sir Robert comes here soon. Sends *un cadeau*—a gift." He glared at Alain and switched to French. "Your turn, Squire Bellefleur."

He understood the sarcastic emphasis on the word "squire" and didn't like the implications. Ruaud had agreed to do the talking unless absolutely necessary.

And "absolutely necessary" had arrived far sooner than Alain had anticipated.

As SIR Ruaud babbled in his semicoherent English about Sir Robert, Kendra fought a jumble of emotions regarding Ruaud's squire. Not only was his station beneath her rank, his being Norman placed him beneath her contempt. And yet she couldn't tear her gaze from him.

Several inches taller than Sir Ruaud, the squire was trim where Ruaud sported a paunch, and he radiated quiet dignity to counter Ruaud's comic disposition. Both men wore their blond hair cropped close, but Ruaud's darker locks didn't curl about his ears and forehead in whimsical wisps begging to be touched. Ruaud's nose bore the lumpish evidence of having been broken at least once, but no scars marred the squire's face. And those eyes—merciful heaven, if the squire regarded her once more with those probing, sea-green eyes, she would faint from the delectable agony.

Relief washed over her when he broke eye contact and strode to the packhorse. Broad shoulders and sinewy arms rippled as he wrestled something from a saddle pack. For one wanton moment, she imagined being encircled by those arms, protected, cherished. Loved . . . happy . . .

She shook her head. One of his countrymen had murdered her brother. She must despise this man.

And yet that task was proving to be a major chore.

The squire turned and approached, bearing a small gilt box across both upturned palms. His smile, slow in dawning, nearly stopped her heart. He knelt upon one knee at her feet.

"My lady Kendra," he said in a rich, refined voice, "Sir Robert regrets the circumstances preventing him from being with you this day. I pray you will not be vexed by his absence. It shall be short, I assure you." His French-accented English was as flawless as his face. He rendered another heart-stopping smile, holding the box aloft. "Please accept this gift, bearing the de Bellencombre arms, as but the smallest token of Sir Robert's esteem."

He flipped back the lid. A gold brooch nestled in black velvet, its face enameled with a flower encircled by interlacing greenery, a white rose.

White for Del's soul, or white for my promise to seek happiness?

Her hand trembled as she reached for the brooch. Embarrassed, she snatched it back.

White for the snow that shrouded the ground as he lay dying in my arms? Her vision blurred with tears as the scene returned in all its agonizing detail: the biting cold, the onion poultice's stench, the blood bubbling from Del's lips, the death rattle, the profound powerlessness and loss . . .

"Nay!"

She gasped, hand to mouth. Everyone gaped at her, except the squire. Disappointment and sorrow dominated his face as he averted his gaze. She hadn't meant for the exclamation to slip out, and certainly not to be misconstrued as a refusal of the gift rather than a plea for deliverance from those dreadful memories, but she couldn't explain without ripping open the wounds of her soul.

"P-please forgive me," she forced past her quivering lips. She was unsure to whom she directed the plea: God, her father, Sir Ruaud, the absent Sir Robert, who would hear of her ill-mannered behavior and be wroth with her . . . or the last person on earth who deserved such treatment, the squire. The pain clouding his eyes wrenched her heart.

She spun, gathered her skirts in both fists, and fled for the stairs, sobs wracking her body for Del, for herself, and for the Norman stranger she had never intended to hurt.

Chapter 4

ALAIN FLIPPED THE lid closed with a sharp click, struggling for composure. This brooch had been a gift from his father to his mother on their wedding day. Comtesse Margaret had bequeathed it to Alain, and upon earning his spurs, he'd adopted its design for his arms to honor her memory.

A memory Lady Kendra had tarnished.

He rose, watching her retreat up the stairs and disappear through the door leading to the upper rooms.

Forgive her? Despite his staunch Christian upbringing, he wasn't sure he knew how.

Thane Waldron laid a hand on his shoulder. "Please excuse my daughter, squire. I'm sure she meant no offense. She—" He glanced in the direction she had gone, withdrew his hand, and sighed. "Kendra has much on her mind."

"She has no wish to marry Sir Robert," Ulfric said with a smirk.

Alain had guessed as much. What he didn't anticipate was the disappointment lancing his heart.

"She has no choice. She will not bring the king's wrath upon us." Waldron glared at the Saxon warrior. "Neither will you."

Ulfric bowed stiffly. "If you will excuse me." He jerked a nod toward Ruaud and Alain. "My men and I have a long ride on the morrow." He stalked toward the manor house's lower entrance.

"A long ride—to where, if I may ask, my lord?" Alain said to Waldron after he was certain Ulfric was beyond earshot.

"Thane Ulfric owns a holding a tenth the size of Edgarburh abutting Church lands near Glastonbury, a two-day ride west." Waldron glanced at the setting sun, a move for which Alain felt thankful else the thane would have seen his eyebrows shoot up. "Good Sir Ruaud, I believe there is ample time to unload your gear before vespers. Of course, you and your squire are welcome to join me in the chapel. Do you require assistance?"

After Alain translated, Ruaud shook his head. "My thanks, Thane Waldron, *mais non*. Alain and me, we carry—" He windmilled with both arms. "We carry all things."

Close enough, Alain thought with a private grin, resolving to help Ruaud improve his English. Much more of this, and he'd be forced to reveal himself just to save everyone the torture—although if Ulfric suffered, Alain wouldn't mind.

He rebuked himself. Ulfric might be arrogant to a fault, but he had not proven himself an enemy.

Yet.

As Alain stowed the brooch and began removing bundles from the packhorse, his thoughts strayed from Thane Ulfric to Lady Kendra. The forced marriage might explain much, but her actions and her father's words implied more. He hefted his rolled-up hauberk to his shoulder, looped the saddle pack over the other arm, grabbed his shield by its straps, and turned to face a quizzical Waldron.

"Two sets of arms, Sir Ruaud?" the thane asked.

Alain noticed his friend was similarly laden and said, "Sir Robert sent his gear with us so he can travel more quickly." He brandished the shield, emblazoned with the de Bellencombre rose.

The lie burned his tongue, but it seemed to satisfy Waldron. He beckoned them to follow him up the stairs to the upper rooms. The first door on the left stood open, where a pretty, auburn-haired maidservant was emerging with an armload of linens. She uttered a squeak of greeting, dipped an awkward curtsey, and tottered down the corridor. Ruaud watched her, a wistful smile tugging at the corner of his mouth.

Waldron took a few steps into the room, stopped, and shrugged. "Again I must apologize for my daughter." He gestured around the chamber. "Everything seems to be in order, but she would better know how to see to your needs, Sir Ruaud. Please do not hesitate to request her assistance." He gazed toward the narrow bed, scratching his chin. "Shall I have a pallet sent up for your squire, or will he be sleeping in the feast hall?"

Alain relayed the question in French for Ruaud's benefit, as well as his preference. "You snore worse than any ten men," he concluded with a grin. Ruaud chortled. Alain executed his courtliest bow to the thane and reverted to English. "The feast hall, if it pleases my lord Waldron." Having Ulfric's men for company might also afford the opportunity to learn something about the outlaws.

Waldron nodded and left, pulling the door shut behind him.

Stretching on his back across the bed, dirt-caked boots and all, Ruaud clasped his hands behind his head and uttered a low whistle. "Lady Kendra is one fine filly."

"Indeed." Alain paused in the task of unrolling his hauberk to give Ruaud a pointed look. "Do not think of riding her."

Ruaud let out a throaty laugh, slapping his midsection. "I've no wish to sheathe your sword in my gut." His expression sobered, and he sat up. "So, when does Sir Robert arrive?"

Excellent question.

Alain worked a pole through one armhole and out the other, and hoisted it onto a tall rack. Should he confess all and be done with this stupid ruse? Go riding out as a squire and return a knight? His limited dealings with Ulfric convinced him this would be the best way to confront the thane regarding the problems occurring in his jurisdiction.

What would Lady Kendra think? How would she react? Would she reject his mother's brooch again? Reject him?

Did he even care?

Yes!

The admission's vehemence surprised him.

However, he suspected that her apparent reluctance to marry Sir Robert de Bellencombre was but one of her secrets. A flash of insight showed him how to conquer those secrets, not as a knight of the Conqueror, but as himself.

He balanced his kite-shaped shield in a corner and faced Ruaud. "Sir Robert arrives to claim Lady Kendra's hand after Squire Alain has claimed her heart."

KENDRA SPENT a fitful night and woke with the disturbing realization that the tall Norman squire had dominated her dreams. Why, she had no idea, but she couldn't stop thinking about his courtly grace and perfect English, his muscular body and handsome face, his expressive eyes and smile . . . and the pain she had caused, which, in spite of her hatred of Normans, prompted a twinge of guilt. She sat up and pressed the heels of her hands to her eyes. The images intensified.

Weary of thrashing beneath the coverlet, she parted the bedcurtains, stood, and approached the window. Beyond the chapel's roof, the pearly gray of dawn was staining the dark blue sky. The chapel reminded her of a task she'd left undone because her emotions had been rendered undone first by Sir Robert's gift, then its giver. She had forgotten to change the roses on Del's sarcophagus.

An appraisal of the light convinced her there would be enough time to select a rose before prime if she hurried. Del would have to forgive her for being late this once. She'd have remembered had she attended vespers, but she had remained in her chamber, imprisoned by her tumultuous emotions. The tide had receded with the dawn, though an undercurrent of grief and regret remained. She doubted those feelings would ever ebb.

She strode to the chest containing her clothes, opened it, and pulled out a plain dress and veil. Not a black veil, however. She had no desire to explain mourning attire to strangers, though the squire might understand.

Where had that thought come from? She doubted he'd wish to speak to her in the wake of her unintentional rudeness.

As she settled the veil over her forehead and trapped it with the silver circlet, she tried to tell herself that she shouldn't care one iota for what he might think about her behavior.

She propped a foot against her bed to tie her shoe. She had no business swooning over one face when she was promised to another—one that might not be half as handsome but wielded fourfold power. She had no business swooning over a Norman, period. She gave the knot a final tug before repeating the process with the opposite foot.

Then there was her other vow, she mused as she fastened her cloak, the vow to find happiness. Sighing, she rubbed her temple.

An image of the squire surfaced, kneeling, offering a gift. The gift hadn't drawn her attention first. His expression had: expectant, kind, hopeful.

Hopeful? Hopeful of what?

She grabbed her dagger from the table near her bed, fastened the sheath to her belt, and strode for the door.

Hopeful that Sir Robert's gift would please her? She had to admit that it had, for it reminded her of Del. Even though the brooch had evoked painful memories, she was grateful for them.

She left her quarters, pulled the door shut, and crept past Sir Ruaud's chamber toward the stairway door. Anything else his squire might have been hopeful of she didn't dare contemplate.

ALAIN STOOD at a window in the hall, hands clasped behind his back, listening to the ragged chorus of snores emanating from Ulfric's men and watching the sky lighten around Edgarburh's chapel. Waldron's retainers had long since left for their duties. Between the Saxons' veiled hostility, Alain's wariness, the hall's chill, and the straw pallet's thinness, what little sleep he'd snatched had been fraught with dreams of this place and of its elusive lady, of wooing her and of her reaction to the truth.

One was a good dream, the other a nightmare.

He laid a hand to his shoulder to massage the stiffness, hoping, no, praying to bring the former to pass and avert the latter, God willing.

Movement in the rose garden caught his eye. He felt his lips stretch into a smile as he recognized the lithe figure. Time to start working on the good dream.

"Up, sluggards! Time to go," urged a rough voice. Ulfric's, Alain realized with a start.

Shadows still swathed the hall, but he slipped away from the window lest it betray his silhouette. He had no fear of a handful of Saxons, but neither had he the wish to provoke a confrontation. He'd endured a bellyful of that, without their leader, last night.

With curses, groans, coughs, and cruder noises, Ulfric's men rose and prepared to leave. Ulfric ordered them to stop by the kitchens for provisions before meeting him in the stables, and then strode from the hall. Alain waited until the last Saxon had departed before returning to the pallet for his cloak, which he draped about his shoulders and pinned with a plain iron brooch. As he passed through the doorway and crossed in front of the manor house, he prayed he'd find Kendra in the rose garden.

She was there. So was Ulfric. The mere sight of them standing together was enough to make Alain's blood pound. He darted behind a massive bush and parted the leafy canes to improve his view.

"I cannot, Ulfric." Frowning, she turned her back on the warrior, arms folded. "But I do appreciate your offer."

Offer? Of marriage? Alain glared at Ulfric. Hadn't Thane Waldron made the situation plain enough to him? If not, then Alain—no, *Sir Robert Alain de Bellencombre* would.

"It shall always stand, Kendra." Ulfric turned her to face him and cupped her chin. She didn't resist. Ulfric closed his eyes as if savoring the touch of her skin. "Remember that."

Ulfric lowered his hand, and Kendra nodded once. Alain relaxed fists he hadn't realized he had clenched. Ulfric bowed and took his leave, angling toward the stables, never once glancing in Alain's direction.

Too bad.

Eyes closed, he took several slow breaths. Woo the lady, he reminded himself; don't lock horns with the competition. He suspected that she would not be won with courtly manners, a disarming smile, and flattering words, although until he could learn more about her, those paltry tools would have to suffice.

The breeze freshened, bearing the scent of roses. Alain opened his eyes. In the strengthening light, he noticed the closest blossoms were red. Dewdrops glistened upon the bloom he selected, like tears on her cheek.

Kendra had moved to a bench toward the back of the garden and was sitting hunched over, forearms resting on her thighs, her hair a golden curtain obscuring her face, her hands stretched before her as though cradling something. Whether she was weeping or praying, the distance made it impossible to ascertain. He approached her slowly, as if she were a skittish mare, concealing the rose behind his back.

When he had come within a few paces, she raised her head, straightened, and slipped a silver pendant into the neck of her gown. Her eyes were dry, but their secrets had returned.

He bowed. "My humblest apologies for disturbing you, my lady."

"Not at all." The brief smile illuminating her face encouraged him to draw closer. Clasping her hands, she averted her gaze. "It is I who should apologize to you, Squire—" She looked at him, brow furrowed, and spread her hands. "Please forgive me. Sir Ruaud mentioned your name, but I've forgotten it."

Her innocent, winsome expression made it easy to forgive everything she'd done . . . or ever would do. He grinned. "Alain Bellefleur. My friends call me Alain." He shortened the vowels and stressed the second syllable in the Norman manner, "Ah-*len*."

"Alain." She repeated it several times as though sampling a new delicacy, making him yearn to sample her delicate lips. "A fine name." She captured his gaze with hers and sighed. "I apologize for my rudeness, Squire Alain. The outburst was an accident. Sir Robert's brooch reminded me of . . . something. I meant no offense to him." Her eyes darkened with the intensity of some emotion he couldn't fathom. "Or to you."

More secrets. So be it. As a scout he was accustomed to ferreting out secrets. "None taken, my lady. And to prove it"—he withdrew the rose from behind his back—"here is my gift to you."

She stared at the rose so long he feared she wasn't going to accept it. Finally, she did. Their fingers briefly touched. Blushing, she smiled shyly, inhaling the blossom's scent. "Thank you, Squire Alain. It's perfect."

Before he could respond, the chapel's bell tolled prime. Just as well. It delivered him from the temptation of resorting to insipid flattery. This woman didn't need his words; she needed action. He offered his arm. "May I have the honor of escorting my lady Kendra to church?"

She stood, sorrow again invading her gaze. "You are very kind, but—" Her chin began to quiver. She turned to retrieve something from the granite bench. "I'm very sorry, but I cannot."

Her head bowed, she slipped past him and hastened toward the church. He was too startled to follow her. In her fist, beside the blossom he had given her, she clutched a white rose.

A gift from Ulfric, or had she picked it herself? If so, why?

More to the point, why had she rejected his harmless offer of escort as though he'd suggested something improper?

And why, he hurled at the brightening heavens, gritting his teeth and knotting his fists, did it hurt so damned much?

As THE chapel's reassuring walls closed about her, Kendra felt the thundering of her heart subside. Even if the squire did choose to follow her into this house of God, she would be safe under the watchful eyes of those who had loved and protected her for as long as she could remember.

But no place on earth could offer her sanctuary from the raging confusion of her thoughts.

Needles of pain prompted her to look down. One by one, she unfolded the fingers clenching the roses' stems. Blood dotted her palm, blood the same hue as the rose Squire Alain had given her. Recollection of his captivating smile warmed her cheeks.

No doubt he believed she had rejected him again. She tried to make herself believe it too.

Sighing, she approached Del's sarcophagus. When she picked up the older flowers, their blossoms burst apart, releasing their perfume and scattering red and white petals across the tomb's lid and onto the floor with a soft rustling.

Too emotionally drained to do otherwise, she left the mingled petals where they lay.

With the priest's prayers but an echo in the back of her mind, she gazed at the white rose she had chosen this morning. Guilt had dictated the color: for failing to save Del's life, for blaming her mother for her failure and her father for her marital predicament, for her ineffectual prayers, for her reaction to the brooch's de Bellencombre device, and for how her reaction had affected the man who had presented the gift to her.

She twined the stems together, feeling a fresh surge of guilt for—nay. The squire was a Norman. She could not permit herself to become attracted to him.

The more she tried to shove him from her mind, the more persistently he invaded it.

Perhaps Ulfric had been correct in suggesting that she accompany him back to Thornhill to enjoy a respite from the pressures of awaiting her Norman bridegroom. As Ulfric had noted, it would be a fitting turnabout for Sir Robert to be obliged to wait for her.

The suggestion had appealed to her for that very reason, but instinct had warned her against acting upon it. To sort through her emotional turmoil, she needed to spend time away from all the men in her life: her father, her cousin, her bridegroom . . .

She kissed both blooms and laid them on Del's effigy.

Above all, she needed to distance herself from the two men exerting the most influence upon her, Del and Squire Alain.

Kendra practiced the routine of worship while pondering her goal. She couldn't stay away too long or folks would start to worry, especially her father. Perhaps even—nay! She must forget the squire, but a short excursion would have to suffice. But to where? For what purpose? Disappearing for too long a period without adequate reason would raise questions she had no wish to address.

Stymied, she returned her attention to Father Æthelward, who was preaching on charity. Charity . . . alms, of course, presented the perfect solution. The outlying farms would benefit from the receipt of medicines, and the people always appreciated a visit from their thane's daughter. She owned a full array of treatments for wounds and burns, sprains and breaks, fevers and chills, disorders of the stomach and bowels, and many other ailments. Anything she didn't possess she could procure from the Edgarburh apothecary, and if she ran short, she'd make arrangements to return with more.

For the first time in almost a year, her smile felt deep and genuine. A few days spent solving others' problems promised the best way to make her forget her own.

She could scarcely wait to get started.

Her sole regret, she grumbled to herself much later, while stopped for a meal in the shade of a birch copse after leaving the third farm, was her decision to bring Rowena. The woman's assistance had proven valuable for brewing tisanes and binding wounds, but Kendra wished she had selected a companion less prone to babble about every man within a fortnight's ride of Edgarburh.

Concentrating on her light meal of dried beef, bread, and ale, given by a grateful mother who claimed her son had been cured of a fever by the touch of Kendra's hand, helped her ignore Rowena's prattle. The mother's claims had disturbed Kendra more profoundly than she had first realized. For if she had healed the boy, either by touch or by the herbs' natural powers, then why couldn't she have healed her own mother or brother?

Not to mention the fact that the Church discouraged such claims with the threat of excommunication—or worse, which explained why Edwina had never spoken to Kendra of her gift.

Kendra had refused to leave the farmhouse before exacting a vow from the boy's mother to keep her opinions about Kendra's miraculous healing powers to herself.

"And that gorgeous Norman squire . . ." Spewing crumbs, Rowena uttered a noise halfway between a sigh and a moan. She brushed her mouth with the back of her hand and grinned at Kendra. "What do you think of him, my lady?"

Kendra looked away, seeking the men her father had sent with her. The fyrd veteran, Cæwlin, had taken the much younger Oswy to the far side of the hillock to spar with their swords, leaving no hope of a diversion from that quarter.

She stared crossly at their horses as they cropped grass a few paces away. Because she was trying not to think of the squire, her nerves felt bowstring taut. She leveled her glare at Rowena. "I am duty-bound to wed another. What am I supposed to think of him?"

A wounded look rippled across Rowena's features. "Your pardon, my lady. I meant no harm, truly." Glancing down, Rowena chewed her bottom lip. Her eyes widened, and the chewing stilled. "My lady, do you think—" She slid a shy, apologetic look toward Kendra. "Could there be a chance he might notice me?"

According to the servants' gossip, which Kendra tried to ignore but wasn't always successful, Rowena's long auburn hair and pleasantly shaped figure attracted the gaze of every man she met, providing Kendra wasn't in the immediate vicinity. Studying the woman now, she could well believe the rumors.

However, she suspected that Squire Alain was not just "any man." His poise, manners, and language skills bespoke service to kings, not the boorish knight whom he had followed to Edgarburh.

Who was this man?

Mayhap the squire had done something to displease King William, who had ordered him into Sir Ruaud's service as punishment. She suppressed a snort and downed a mouthful of ale. As entertaining as that idea might be, it didn't fit what she'd observed of the Normans' easy camaraderie. Nor did it make sense that he owed Sir Ruaud a debt. They behaved more like friends than master and servant. Kinsmen, then?

A thought jarred her. She hid her reactions behind another swig of ale.

Squire Alain probably was already involved with another woman; if not married, then surely betrothed. Kendra wasn't prepared for the rush of jealousy, and the ale soured in her mouth. She swallowed hard. But if he had another woman, why was he making such blatant attempts to flirt with Kendra?

Was he a rogue who used his charm and physical appeal to conquer women?

An even more disturbing idea struck her like a slap in the face. Had Sir Robert sent Squire Alain to test her steadfastness?

She resolved to be doubly mindful of her words and deeds around him.

'Twas a precaution she didn't wish to take.

Kendra engrossed herself in removing a pebble from her shoe, wishing Squire Alain could be as easily dislodged from her mind. Realizing Rowena was silent for the first time all day, she glanced at the woman, whose eager expression reminded her that she owed the maidservant an answer.

Would the squire notice Rowena and be attracted to her? Kendra suspected not, but she replied, "I hope so."

After replacing her shoe, she finished her ale and sent Rowena to fill the skin with water from the nearby stream. Humming, the maidservant glided off, hips swaying as though she were practicing her wiles for her next meeting with the Norman squire. With a smile and brief shake of her head, Kendra reached for her saddle pack to assess its contents. She still possessed a reasonable supply of dried elder, comfrey, chamomile, linden, willow bark, and lady's mantle, though the ground valerian root was almost gone. Salves also had been in high demand, especially those for fighting wound fevers. She gazed sunward. Time aplenty to visit at least two more farms on this, the eve of the longest day of the year, before finding a place to retire for the night.

The vibrating ground alerted her to the presence of riders. The copse crowned a hillock yielding a fair view of the stream and surrounding pastures, and she located the riders. They were headed straight for her position. Cæwlin and Oswy stopped sparring, weapons still drawn, to watch the horsemen approach. Kendra squinted into the distance but couldn't recognize them. There seemed to be five or six. Men from the fyrd, she presumed. Or mayhap her father was showing Sir Ruaud the estate, although why they were approaching from the west, when Edgarburh lay miles to the east, puzzled her.

If it was indeed her father and Sir Ruaud, she tried not to imagine who else might be riding with them.

Shrugging, she rose and caught Hilde before the mare got the notion to join the procession without her. Rowena had led her mount down the bank to the stream, which seemed like a fine idea. Kendra secured the saddle pack, checked the girth, tugged on Hilde's reins, and walked down the gentle slope, choosing a spot a few paces from Rowena and her gelding. Hilde slurped the calmly flowing water.

The whine of an arrow and a startled outcry made Kendra turn. Cæwlin had slumped to his knees and was struggling to remove the shaft embedded in his shoulder.

"Away, my lady!" Oswy yelled as he ran for his horse.

Shouting for Rowena, Kendra grabbed the reins, scrambled atop Hilde, set heels to flanks, and galloped across the stream. She despised having to leave Cæwlin and uttered a prayer for his life, and her entire party's. Crouched low over the mare's neck, she had no idea whether the hoofbeats pursuing her belonged to the mounts of friend or foe.

Screams and the clash of arms erupted behind her, and she slowed her mare to look back. And wished she hadn't. Oswy, engaged with two of the intruders, was struck in the head. He fell with a sickening thud and did not move. Rowena stood shivering in the grasp of a third man. The other two, still mounted, were bearing down upon Kendra with frightening speed.

With Hilde already laboring for breath, Kendra had no hope of outrunning them. Heart pounding, she halted her mare.

"Fortune smiles upon us," boomed one man. "She's given us gold treasure ripe for the plundering." Both laughed coarsely.

Cheeks aflame, she turned her mare to regard the men, who bore the ugliest faces she'd ever seen, their expressions rank with greed and lust. Their hair and beards were scraggly, their teeth broken, black, or missing. Scars crossed every inch of exposed flesh. The men's leather tunics and breeches were badly tanned, rancid, and patched in several places, and their boots had fared little better. Incongruously, their horses seemed sleek and well fed, if winded.

The men probably had stolen them.

Swallowing her fears, she squared her shoulders, thrust out her chin, and declared, "I have no gold." Her deliberate misinterpretation of the jest prompted another round of guffaws. She had to raise her voice to continue. "You are welcome to my medicines and food if you will leave me and my servants in peace." She'd need salve and bandages to tend Cæwlin and Oswy if either man was still alive, but the sick pit in her stomach cautioned her not to harbor such thoughts.

"We care naught for your supplies, Lady Kendra of Edgarburh," said a mountain of a man whose face featured a pale red scar on the left side from eye ridge to lip.

She gasped at his knowledge of her rank and name.

Grinning, he raised a hand. The others rode up to circle her, leaving Oswy where he lay. Kendra's mare shifted nervously. She knew exactly how Hilde felt.

The leader dismounted and sauntered toward Kendra at the speed of a cat toying with a cornered mouse. When he had drawn close enough, he latched on to her wrist and yanked her from her horse, catching her roughly. He turned her to face him and grasped her chin. Inwardly, she screamed at the forced pucker of her lips beneath his grip.

"What you carry does not interest us." His face loomed closer, and the reek of onions and ale on his breath made her stomach churn. "But you do."

Her heart began pitching wildly as he released her chin, drew a seax, and raised it to her neck. With its point he pulled her locket from its place of concealment beneath her undertunic. How he knew it was there she had no idea. "Please, nay, that has no value!"

"Oh, aye, Lady Kendra, it does." His laugh was a nasty rasp. "'Twill show Thane Waldron how serious we are."

With a flick of his wrist, he cut the cord. The pendant fell into his other hand. Her hopes fell with it.

Chapter 5

ENDRA FELT NUMB.

Numb from shock, from hunger, from fatigue, numb from the cramping and chafing inflicted by hours spent in the saddle, numb from the drenching rain and subsequent cold that stung her cheeks and hands and sliced through the folds of her cloak to attack other vulnerable places. Numb from worry about the fates of Rowena, Cæwlin, and Oswy, numb from fear that her captors would decide to have their sport with her.

Her greatest numbness, however, stemmed from despair.

'Twas no small miracle that she'd stayed astride.

Her fears sharpened when the outlaws drew rein, dismounted, and pulled her down. But she was too numb to struggle. They'd been traveling westward through a long, secluded valley that she recalled from her journeys, years ago, to visit Ulfric and other members of her mother's family. She also recalled that, because this valley's stream was seasonal, no crofter or farmer lived here.

Nothing about this Godforsaken valley had changed. The downpour had turned the streambed into a ribbon of mud, not much use to either man or beast.

As Kendra stood with a hand on Hilde's withers to steady herself, eyeing her captors and yearning for salve and bandages to soothe her raw thighs, the outlaw with the livid facial scar pulled his wineskin from around his neck and offered it to her. The unexpected kindness took her aback, and she hesitated, wondering where her wineskin had gone.

"Take it or not, 'tis your choice," he said, not unkindly. "Ever ridden on your belly?"

From the seriousness of his expression, she decided he was referring to a mode of horseback travel rather than making a vulgar sexual allusion. She shook her head.

"Nor would you want to." The man chortled, slapping his companion on the back. "Rat can vouch for that." The outlaw called Rat looked irritated by the comment. "By the by, you can call me Snake." He twitched his cheek, making his scar seem like a living presence upon his face.

"Pleased to make your acquaintance." She groped the saddle horn for her wineskin's strap without taking her eyes from the rat and the snake.

Snake elbowed Rat. "She may be nigh unto dead on her feet, but she still has spirit." Again, Snake thrust his wineskin toward her. "Take it. Methinks you lost yours"—he jerked his chin eastward—"back yonder. We still have a fair way to go before we camp. If you don't keep up your strength, you'll be riding facedown ere long."

She drank. Rather than the bitter brew she'd expected, the outlaw had given her a sweet wine that bore a hint of apples.

She hadn't realized how parched she was until that moment and took several more gulps.

Laughing, Snake pulled the wineskin from her grasp, and she groaned her disappointment. "That's plenty for now, my lady, unless you do have a wish to ride on your belly."

Her face flushed, only partially from the wine. She asked, "What of our horses? They must have water soon, and this stream is useless."

Snake regarded her with approval. "Not far from here is shelter and a well, though we'll have to lead our mounts up the last stretch to reach it. Think you can manage a bit of a climb, my lady?"

She nodded. "If I can tend to some personal needs first."

Rat grinned, baring pointed teeth suggestive of his name's origin. "Be pleased to help ye, m'lady."

"Imbecile!" Snake rounded on the man, drew back a meaty fist, and punched him in the gut. Rat doubled over, moaning and swearing. "The next blow will be lower. If her ladyship is harmed in any way, Dragon will feast upon our ballocks." Snake faced Kendra with a wink and a grin, hitching his trews in a suggestive manner. "Can't speak for Rat, but mine are of much more use to me where they are." His eyes narrowed. "You wouldn't be thinking of running, would you, my lady?"

The thought had occurred, but she had dismissed it. "I very much doubt I'd make it as far as yon hawthorn patch." She pointed at some thick, thorny bushes growing near the streamed a score of paces away, the sparse remains of their May blooms looking as bedraggled as she felt.

Snake nodded and cast another warning glance at Rat, who'd recovered enough to glower back at him. "Go do what you must, then, and don't worry none about us."

She didn't feel very reassured by Snake's implied pledge, but as she removed the saddle pack from Hilde's back and retreated from the men and mounts, her legs' stinging convinced her she had little choice.

Shielded by the hawthorn thicket, she hunted through the pack for a pair of bandage rolls and what was left of her elderberry salve, hiked her skirts, and set to work. The salve and bandages wrought a miracle on the abrasions caused by folds of her dress that had gotten caught wrong when she'd mounted. She wrapped each leg from thigh to knee while she pondered the outlaws' words and deeds.

That they intended to hold her for ransom she had no doubt. She did doubt that "Snake" and "Rat" were these men's birth names, not to mention the mysterious "Dragon" Snake had alluded to with a strand of fear threading his tone. Their final destination presented another mystery to which she doubted she'd get a forthright answer.

Then there was the matter of her father's reaction to her abduction. Would he pay their demands or send the fyrd after her? She guessed the former, though she couldn't be certain. Since the small terra-cotta salve pot was empty, she inverted it atop a low, flat rock beside the bush. She drew her dagger from its place of concealment beneath her overdress, cut off a lock of hair, and tucked it under the pot, hoping that if the fyrd happened by, one of the men would notice the odd arrangement and connect it with her.

She couldn't keep from imagining a certain Norman who might insist upon riding with them. In the next breath, she denounced it as a vain fantasy. She had done nothing but run from him each time they met, giving him no reason to risk his neck for her.

The discouraging thought didn't prevent her from harboring the fragile hope that Squire Alain might help rescue her. It remained the sole tether on her fears.

BACK AT the same window where he'd begun his day, gazing toward the chapel and rose garden, Alain wrestled with his concern for Kendra, whom he had not seen since their disastrous dawn meeting. Since he'd acted far too boldly for a squire, he doubted she would wish to speak with him again.

Around him drifted the soft chorus of sounds as Waldron's retainers settled in for the evening. A sleek deerhound wandered over to investigate the intruder into its domain. Alain gently but firmly discouraged the questing nose and stooped to inspect the magnificent animal. By the white patches interrupting the brindle pattern on forehead and chest, he recognized the dog as one of the bitches that had accompanied Waldron's hunting party.

Alain enjoyed a hunt as much as the next man did, but today his heart hadn't been in it. He suspected his heart could be found wherever Kendra had gone.

The dog butted his hand. He obliged by fondling the spot at the base of her ears that all dogs seemed to enjoy. Emitting canine groans, she cocked her head and leaned into his caress.

He hoped this animal's mistress would one day respond as ecstatically to his touch.

Instead, Kendra had left, ostensibly to dispense medicine and cheer to outlying farms, but the twisting of his heart proclaimed the truth. She was trying to escape him. Again.

And, again, he considered whether to reveal his identity and accept the consequences. Switching hands to stroke the dog's other ear, he envisioned the most probable scenarios.

None were pleasant.

He gave the hound a final pat and stood. The dog regarded him, tail wagging. When that failed to produce the desired result, she sighed, turned thrice in a tight circle, and sank onto the rush-strewn flagstones at his feet. Folding his arms, Alain glared at the darkening rose garden as if by force of will he could make Kendra appear. She didn't, of course; most likely, she and her escorts were sheltering with a farmer's family. By the fading sunset, he judged that Edgarburh's gates were already shut fast, and only in unusual circumstances would they be opened before dawn.

Movement across the central yard drew his notice. A rider spurred his mount to the manor house, halted, and slid from the saddle. The man didn't bother to tether his horse, who wandered, nose down, into the longer grass while its rider took the manor's stairs two at a time and disappeared through the door leading to the upper rooms.

One of Waldron's men, Alain mused, probably a gate sentry. But why the urgency? If Kendra had returned, there would be no need to alert her father. Someone else had to be at the gate, someone unknown to the sentries and demanding the thane's permission to enter. Someone desperate enough—or powerful enough—to refuse the sentries' injunction to camp outside until morning.

Foreboding gripped Alain's gut.

The rider appeared a few minutes later, raced down the staircase, caught his horse, mounted and spurred it toward the main gate. Alain followed their progress until the angle of the hall blocked his view. He glanced at the manor house in time to see a disheveled but determined Waldron emerge, descend the stairs, and stride toward the hall as briskly as his limp allowed.

The moment the thane shoved open the doors and crossed the threshold, he began bellowing to rouse his men and order the torches lit. The hall erupted into frenzied activity as the men started awake and rose to don armor and retrieve swords and shields from recesses around the hall. Even the hounds, including Alain's erstwhile companion, scrambled about, adding their canine voices to the din.

Alain remained beside the window, out of the way and yet feeling very much like the center of a whirlpool. He couldn't suppress the notion that, if this whirlpool had anything to do with Kendra, he would get sucked into it too.

As torchlight flooded the hall, Waldron stepped onto the dais, straightening his cap and tugging at his tunic. Rather than seating himself at his tall-backed chair behind the table, however, he remained in front of it, stroking his chin and pacing. One of the retainers approached Waldron and asked a question Alain couldn't hear. Emphatically, the thane shook his silvered head and spoke something else. The retainer saluted with his sword and turned to order the men into two ranks, forming an aisle from the doors to the dais. Waldron's lined face adopted a look of grim satisfaction as he leaned against the table to await his visitor.

Visitors, Alain amended as he watched three burly men swagger into the hall, escorted at spearpoint by more of Waldron's warriors. The spears appeared to be no threat to these men, who seemed capable of using the weapons to pick their teeth. At a nod from Waldron, the rest of the thane's men drew their swords, but even that gesture went ignored by the outlaws. For, by their shabby dress, vulgar speech, and arrogant demeanor, Alain realized these men could be nothing else.

Had the Glastonbury band extended their range to Edgarburh?

A diminutive, hooded figure was being held by one of the outlaws, head bowed and crying softly.

Please, Holy Mother, not Kendra!

Fists and jaw clenched, he strode toward her but halted behind Waldron's men. As a foreign visitor and, more to the point, a supposedly low-ranking one, he had no right to disrupt these proceedings.

Despising his helplessness, and hers, he maneuvered for a better view while her captor planted a hairy hand in the middle of her back and shoved her. She fell to her hands and knees with a scream. When she raised her head, the hood fell back, revealing a tangled cascade of auburn hair. Alain recognized her as the maidservant who had prepared Ruaud's chamber. His thanksgiving dissolved into dread when she turned to reveal blood, bruises, and terror disfiguring her face.

"What is the meaning of this? Where is my daughter and the rest of her escort?" Waldron thundered.

Getting no answer save insolent grins, he beckoned to the maidservant. She jerked a worried glance over her shoulder and scuttled forward to huddle, sobbing, at her lord's feet. Waldron bent down to speak with her in tones impossible to overhear, rubbing her back. She responded with a tremulous nod and more whimpers. Waldron told her something else, and she rose and fled through the rear door leading to the kitchens.

The thane stood to watch her departure for a few moments before folding his arms and sharpening his glare. "You men," he addressed the outlaws in a low, hard voice, "had better explain yourselves now, or I will have my men spit you where you stand, cut off your rotting members, and feed them to you."

Alain raised an eyebrow.

The outlaws guffawed. The biggest of the three, whose dark red hair hung in greasy strings and whose mustache looked even darker and greasier, spread his hands in a gesture of mock surrender. "'Twould be your choice, indeed, Thane Waldron." He cast a measuring glance at Waldron's warriors. "I've nae doubt ye can defeat us." The outlaw's grin turned feral in the shifting torchlight. "But then ye'd never learn the fate of your precious daughter."

"What?" Waldron roared, echoing Alain's sentiment. "Lady Kendra—"

"Is safe enough, my lord." The man exchanged a swift look with his companions. "Or was, last time we saw her. I canna say the same for her men. Likely they've fattened a flock of ravens."

No! Kendra can't be gone!

Yes, Alain's rational self argued. Evidence abounded, not just in the outlaws' words and the maidservant's wounds, but in the thane's ashen countenance. Even the men-at-arms seemed less sure of themselves, more dejected, as if their lady's abduction had robbed them of their self-esteem.

Alain wasn't immune either. Like Persephone, Kendra had been ripped from his world, and his springlike joy had vanished.

A stirring woke within him akin to the battle rage that had earned him Norman accolades and a Saxon spear. He, Robert Alain de Bellencombre, had grown weary of the outlaws' cat-and-mouse game.

Waldron's face grew stern. "How am I to believe you have her, that this isn't some idiotic ruse?" Alain flinched at his future *beau-père's* choice of words.

The spokesman executed a sloppy bow. "Thought ye'd ne'er ask, my lord." His fingers dipped into a fur pouch at his belt and withdrew a length of black velvet cord. As the silver pendant swung free to gleam in the torchlight, Waldron blanched. "Ah, ye know this wee bauble. Very fortunate for you—and for her."

Alain thought he had seen Kendra wearing something similar but couldn't be certain. He whispered a query to one of Waldron's guardsmen.

"'Tis her ladyship's and no mistake," the soldier whispered back. "Not one like it in all the world. Holds a lock of my lord Delwin's hair, it does."

Alain's head snapped up. Delwin? Another suitor? One so dear that she cradled a lock of his hair at her bosom?

Before Alain could question the guard further, Waldron extended his hand in an unspoken demand to examine the pendant. When the outlaw refused, the thane said, "I must be certain that it's not a forgery. Push on the top loop to release the catch, and show me what's inside."

The outlaw complied. After a few moments' fumbling, the locket sprang open in his palm. He inverted the piece, and a pale wisp fluttered to the slate. With a pained expression, Waldron scooped the hairs off the floor and closed them into his fist. The outlaw shut the case and stashed it and its cord in his pouch.

"Ready for our price, Thane Waldron?" asked the spokesman. The thane nodded once. "Fifty gold marks—"

"No!" Alain shouldered between two startled guards to face the godless rabble who had the audacity to threaten his wife-to-be and her father. Whether they belonged to the Glastonbury band or not, if this abduction had been planned, and these men had known about Kendra's Norman bridegroom, then the ambush at the inn made abrupt and terrible sense. Either way, Alain would learn the truth or else die trying. "Take me instead."

"You, Norman?" The outlaw spokesman eyed him skeptically, similar looks crossing the others' faces. "For what purpose?"

"Ransom. The king will pay thrice that for one of his"—he swallowed a groan—"one of his men." He hoped it didn't sound as lame to them as it did to his own ears.

"A hundred and fifty? For a squire?" Waldron challenged.

Alain felt heat rise in his cheeks, and not just from anger. Ignoring it, he glared at the outlaws to weigh his chances, pondering whether to reveal himself as a knight. Armed with wits and luck as well as armor and weapons, he could prevail alone against the three. As their captive, he'd have just wits and luck to rely upon—if that much.

He bowed to the thane. "Your pardon, my lord. In my earnestness to help the Lady Kendra, I forgot my station." Alain turned to address the outlaws. "I am certain I can convince my master, Sir Ruaud d'Auvay, to offer his life in exchange for Lady Kendra's. The king will make it well worth your while to return both of us, I assure you."

While the outlaws drew aside to debate the issue, watched by the thane's men, Waldron laid a hand on Alain's shoulder. "You may not own the trappings of a knight, lad, but you do possess the heart of one."

Alain acknowledged the praise with a brief smile. "If they accept this proposal, my lord," he whispered, "Sir Ruaud and I shall not go meekly."

Waldron glanced at the outlaws, who were still murmuring and gesturing among themselves. He regarded Alain for a long moment, expression wistful. "'Tis a pity Kendra is promised to Sir Robert. I suspect she could come to like you."

"I would be most honored to earn her favor." *And her love.* Alain chewed the inside of his lip to keep his smile from broadening. "But it is my fondest wish that my lady Kendra find happiness and love with Sir Robert de Bellencombre."

"Fairly spoken, squire." Waldron gave Alain's shoulder a squeeze. "I pray you can speak as fairly to Sir Ruaud."

Alain understood the implied command, bowed, and departed the hall. The outlaws, too deep in their deliberations, paid him no heed, but he detected an air of cautious respect emanating from some of Waldron's men as he strode past them.

Outside, he broke into a dead run.

He burst into Ruaud's chamber, panting from his dash across the yard and up the manor house's stairs. Ruaud was sitting on a stool near the hearth, his back braced against the wall and his hauberk draped across his knees. A pot of sand stood within easy reach.

"Well come, squire." Ruaud grinned, brandishing a fistful of sand. "You have been remiss in your duties of late."

Alain slammed the door. "Lady Kendra has been captured by outlaws. They have demanded fifty in gold. There is a chance they will agree to take both of us in exchange for her life." He advanced into the room and lowered his voice. "There is also a chance they belong to the band I have been commanded to investigate."

"What?" Ruaud threw the sand down. Most of it missed the pot and hit the floor rushes with an angry hiss. Without bothering to dust his hands, he heaved the mail aside, stood, and stalked up to Alain. "Bleeding wounds of God! Are you mad or just stupid?"

Arms crossed, Alain parried Ruaud's glare with his own. "Neither." He hoped. "There are only three—"

"Three." Ruaud snorted. "Plus the bastards guarding Lady Kendra at Glastonbury or wherever the hell they have taken her, and their sentries, and God knows how many more."

"We can take them all, I know it." Alain's conviction had never burned hotter.

"Take them? With what? Our bare hands?" Ruaud plucked at his tunic. "We would be lucky to be left with the clothes on our backs."

He refused to let Ruaud's skepticism quench his resolve. "Our bare hands if we must. Our heads most assuredly. We will have to stay alert to the slightest opportunity and follow the other's lead without warning. I doubt they will let us do much talking."

Ruaud thrust his head to within a finger's length of Alain's face, squinting and sniffing speculatively. "You do not seem drunk, but that is the only reason I can fathom for this lunacy." Giving a dismissive wave, he withdrew to his hauberk's mound of woven steel rings. "Come back after you have slept it off."

"I am not drunk." Fists clenched, Alain took two paces and stopped. Any closer and he might succumb to the temptation of throttling his friend. "I shall not stand idle while my"—lest someone overhear, he reined in his voice—"while Lady Kendra remains in peril. Since you are not with me in this, I shall go after her myself."

He spun and headed for the door, mind reeling. Ruaud's refusal meant having to track the outlaws instead. Burdened with Waldron's gold, they would return to their lair. Then he would need to devise a way to get past these three, plus the lair's sentries, Kendra's guards and, as Ruaud had speculated, God alone knew how many others. Minuscule odds, at best.

So be it. He grasped the door's handle.

"Alain, wait." Not a command but a plea. Upon releasing the handle, Alain turned to find Ruaud studying him, an odd pairing of resignation and pride fighting for domination on his ruddy face. "You think she is worth the risk?"

"Without question."

"Bloody fool, I knew you would say that. But I believe you." Ruaud stooped to lift his mail. "Come and lend me a hand." His tone sounded unusually subdued.

"You will surrender, then?"

"Against my better judgment, yes." Holding up the mail, Ruaud nodded toward the pole leaning on the wall, and Alain retrieved it. Together they worked it through the armholes and set the pole and mail on the rack beside Alain's. Ruaud gazed at their armor and weapons. "Someone must guard your back."

Alain's elation was brief. Ruaud's help increased his chances of success a hundredfold, but a hundred times minuscule was still minuscule. "You do not have to do this."

Laughing, he slapped his belly. "I have grown lazy with William's peace. Soft. A little exercise will do me good." He elbowed Alain's ribs. "You too. Being taken captive will enliven the sport."

Hastings had taught Alain never to view killing men as sport, but he understood that his friend meant to cheer him. He gripped Ruaud's shoulders. "We may regret our decisions ere this is over."

"Hah. At least you have not taken complete leave of your senses." Ruaud rolled his eyes. "First the squire ruse, now this.

What next? Shall we shave our pates and pose as bishops to visit the Pope?"

Alain had to laugh at the ludicrous image. "I doubt you would pass muster in a tonsure. But I do appreciate your help." Visions of Kendra, alone and terrified, battered his brain. The mental assault fortified his resolve. "So will she."

WITH SNAKE in the lead and Rat holding Hilde's reins, the party plodded south across the valley toward the tallest point on the ridgeline. As the darkness advanced and the ascent grew steeper and rockier, Hilde began to stumble more often. Finally, Kendra dismounted to complete the trek on foot.

What Snake had called shelter revealed itself as the ruins of a temple. Many of the columns had fallen from what she guessed to be generations of neglect. Why the stone hadn't been carted away for building materials she attributed to the temple's remoteness. Faded, chipped mosaics of bare-breasted women being chased by prancing, horned, goat-footed men-creatures with unconcealed genitalia proclaimed the temple's pagan origins. What rites had been performed atop such bawdy floor decorations she had no desire to ponder.

Snake sent Rat to draw water for the horses, an order the other man grumblingly obeyed. Apparently unconcerned by the vulgar mosaics, Snake drew tinder and flint from his saddlebag and knelt below one of the larger holes in the roof to start a fire. The small stones ringing a patch of blackened tiles proved this wasn't an original idea.

She studied the roof, trying to determine where she would be best protected from the weather overnight. Some of the curved red tiles, each as long as a forearm, had fallen through gaping holes, and fragments littered the floor. Though careful to avoid the large shards, she felt scores of smaller ones grind to ochre powder underfoot. She selected a spot at the base of the waist-high altar and hunkered inside her cloak while Snake collected twigs to feed his infant flame. Since she couldn't trust Snake as far as she could heave him, and Rat half that far, she appreciated the solidity of stone at her back.

Rat came stomping in only to be sent out to fetch deadfall for the fire. Each time he returned with an armload, he dropped the wood with a horrific clatter and shot a pointed glance first at the lewd mosaic and then at Kendra.

She did her best to ignore Rat, focusing instead on the growing flames as they devoured the wood.

Snake disappeared into the shadows between a pair of upright columns. A series of sounds emerged: the scrape of stone on stone, the clang of metal, Snake's sharp oath. He returned a few minutes later with a kettle in one hand and several iron rods tucked in the opposite armpit. While Rat departed for water, Snake set the kettle down and proceeded to fit the rods into a three-legged structure straddling the fire. A fourth, shorter rod ending in a hook dangled from the apex. Upon Rat's return, Snake ordered him to fill the kettle and hoist it onto the hook.

Again Snake rose and went to the kettle's hiding place, this time returning with a battered tin ladle, three tin mugs, and a small packet wrapped in muslin. When he offered to brew Kendra a posset, she politely declined, asking instead for a mug of hot water. He grunted and settled beside Rat to wait for the flames to complete their work.

Kendra grabbed her saddle pack and hunted for the ground willow bark, which she hoped would take the edge off her aches. She debated whether to add valerian but decided to conserve her dwindling supply. Her stomach noisily reminded her that she hadn't eaten since her capture, and she made short work of her remaining bread and cheese.

When Snake brought the mug to her, padded with a scrap of leather, she asked, "Is this where you live?" It would be a comfort to know she'd be held no more than a day's ride from home.

"This?" He surveyed the crumbling ceiling. "This be naught but a way station. Serves all who know of it." He grinned, though it seemed forced. "We enter Dragon's den on the morrow."

A chill crept up her spine that the mug's warmth was powerless to dispel.

Chuckling, Snake straightened and withdrew to the other side of the fire, where Rat had already bedded down, wrapped in his cloak with his saddle pack for a pillow.

She dropped in a pinch of powdered willow bark but didn't wait long for it to steep before taking a sip. Thinking better of it, she set the mug beside her and stared into the flames. For a moment, she fancied Del's face wavering there. Her fingers crept toward her neck, where the locket's cord should have been, and found naught but skin. With a start, she recalled that Snake had cut it off and given it to one of his men to take back to her father as proof of her abduction. She shuddered, imagining how easily he could have sliced her throat. Her dagger wouldn't be much of a deterrent against his seax.

Even after Del's death, she had never felt more helpless, afraid, or so utterly alone.

Stripped of her last tangible link to her dear brother, her mind grasped on to the memory of another man, one who'd given her a single red rose. She drew her knees to her chin, hugged her shins, and squeezed her eyes shut against the welling tears.

As THE Normans approached Edgarburh's hall, a burst of shouts emanated from within. The outlaws, Alain guessed, were still wrangling over his proposal. He and Ruaud stopped on the last step, and Ruaud shot him a glance as if to ask whether Alain intended to proceed. Alain pounded on the door. Beneath the noise, he heard Ruaud's sigh.

Two guards opened the doors, and a hush conquered the crowd. One would have thought the king himself had appeared. Alain gave Ruaud a subtle nod and he strode forward, with Alain trailing a discreet half pace behind.

Without even so much as a meat knife, Alain felt naked as they passed the outlaws, who gave them measuring stares. Since they concentrated most of their scrutiny upon Ruaud, Alain suspected "naked" couldn't begin to describe how his friend must feel. Yet Ruaud's stride did not falter as they traveled the aisle to approach Waldron upon the dais.

"Sir Ruaud d'Auvay," intoned Waldron, "what is your decision?"

Alain began to translate, but Ruaud held up a hand, expression grave. "I help daughter of you. I and my squire, if they"—he jerked a contemptuous nod over his shoulder—"agree."

"We donna give a bloody damn about your squire." The outlaws' spokesman looked as if he wanted to surge forward, but Waldron's men kept him at bay.

"Both or no deal!" Grinning, Ruaud added, "No gold of King William."

This prompted more arguing among the outlaws, though it seemed to Alain the sole dissenter would soon lose. As he watched in morbid fascination, he felt a hand touch his shoulder. He turned to find Ruaud also had turned, and Waldron was regarding them.

"Whatever happens, I cannot thank you enough. Both of you," the thane said. "Please know you go with my prayers, and the prayers of all Edgarburh. May God grant you mercy, strength, and courage."

Waldron extended his hand to Ruaud, and they gripped forearms with a depth of sentiment that needed no translation. Moments before Alain's turn, he noticed a flash of white in Waldron's palm. They too gripped forearms, but rather than letting go, Waldron slid his hand back. Since the outlaws had reached an agreement and were striding forward, Alain stashed the packet, unopened, in his pouch.

"For Kendra," whispered Waldron. "May it help you too."

Alain had no time to wonder about the gift as the outlaws produced lengths of leather cord for binding his and Ruaud's wrists. After they had finished, Alain gave several experimental tugs, feeling the cords scrape his flesh. The knots held fast.

The outlaws shoved Ruaud and Alain forward, and their march into captivity began.

The looks they earned from Waldron's men contained more pity than anything else, as though they didn't hold much hope for the Normans' success. Alain couldn't disagree, but neither could he fall prey to doubts, his or anyone else's.

Kendra's life—no, all of their lives, he realized as they passed from the torchlit hall's safety into the gaping maw of night—depended upon it.

Chapter 6

A BLOW TO THE ribs roused Alain from a fitful sleep. Rolling away earned him a kick on the other side. He rolled again, ending on his stomach.

"Hey, Pit, Pretty Boy wants a good buggering. You going to oblige him or should I?"

Despite being stiff and sore from sleeping on rocky ground, he couldn't sit up fast enough. He glared at the two men looming over him, trying to discern which one was "Pit." Both outlaws were of roughly equal height, though where one was florid and endowed with bulging muscles, the other had angular features, long black hair, a deep tan, and dark, darting eyes.

The outlaw with the flaming red hair, beard, and mustache, who'd acted as spokesman and whose bare arms were smothered with dark blue spirals from wrist to shoulder, grabbed Alain by the hair and yanked him to his feet. "We havena time for such sport." By the northern accent, which Alain recognized from a childhood visit to his mother's relatives, he surmised this was the man called Pit. Tightening his grip, Pit planted a hard kiss full on Alain's mouth. "Think that'll do ye for now, lassie?"

He itched to spit in Pit's face but decided that would buy him more trouble than he could afford. Pit shoved him to his hands and knees in the dirt, adding another kick. He spat out Pit's vile taste and dragged an arm across his face to erase the prickle of Pit's whiskers.

It didn't help.

Chortling, the two men stomped away, presumably to inflict their crude jests upon Ruaud, who'd been guarded across the camp. Alain rose to his knees, eyes shut and hands folded, trying to remember the morning prayer, but the only words to obey his summons were:

Do you think she is worth the risk?

Last night, he had felt certain. Now, he was anything but.

The dull thuds of flesh striking flesh, accompanied by chortles and oaths and groans, drew his attention. Pit and his companion obscured the view. Whatever Ruaud had done, they were making him pay. Alain's stomach twisted.

Is she worth the risk?

The hell of it was that now wasn't the time to make a move on their guards. They were heading westward, toward Glastonbury, but their course proved nothing. He had no guarantee that Kendra would be waiting at the place these men were taking Waldron's gold. The outlaws had insisted on Waldron providing half of their original demand to offset the cost of feeding extra mouths, though Alain expected to sup on no better fare than stale bread, moldy cheese, and sour ale.

Is she worth it?

He closed his eyes and bowed his head to pray for strength, wisdom, patience, guidance, opportunities—for anything useful that God might see fit to grant. An image hove to mind of the raped and beaten maidservant, sobbing in a wretched heap at Waldron's feet. This time, when she lifted her head to regard Alain, her face looked agonized, beseeching, accusing... and it was Kendra's.

Is she?

It galvanized him, and he redoubled the urgency of his prayer.

Forgive me, Ruaud...

A whack between the shoulder blades pitched him forward. He caught himself before hitting the ground, and regretted it as fresh pain lanced his left arm. Fighting to keep his expression neutral, he pushed to his feet.

The third guard said, "Prayer time's over, Saint Pretty Boy." He deposited the chest of gold into Alain's hands. "Go help your fonging mate load up." The man tossed a nod toward his companions, who'd seated themselves around the fire to break fast. "Hurry, or there'll be nothing left."

Alain watched in amazement as the man left him and Ruaud unbound and unguarded with the gold and horses as if knowing escape was not Alain's intent.

Faced with such a tempting opportunity, he considered bolting back to Edgarburh to enlist Waldron's men as reinforcements but discarded the idea. For one thing, these outlaws knew the land. Though it had been full dark when they'd departed, Alain had a fairly clear sense of the way back, but he suspected that obstacles he hadn't noticed before could slow their escape. Even if by some miracle he and Ruaud eluded pursuit, they would remain ignorant of Kendra's whereabouts. The passage of time and the confusion of trails would make tracking her nigh impossible, and her captors, alerted to the possibility of a frontal assault, would fortify their defenses.

In such a scenario, Kendra would be the loser.

With a glance at the outlaws, who were sharing a jest and not paying him any mind, he walked to the picket line. Face to face over the back of Waldron's packhorse was the closest the outlaws had permitted him and Ruaud to come. Ruaud's condition stabbed Alain with guilt. His face was bruised, his lip was split and bloody, and the darkening flesh around one eye was beginning to swell it shut. The other glared at Alain.

"I am sorry." Alain's words sounded pitifully inadequate.

Ruaud snorted and bent to secure the pack's frame. Straightening, he nodded toward their captors. "We should leave while we have the chance." Urgency dominated his tone.

Alain concentrated on securing the chest to the frame. With luck, he'd be able to recover Waldron's gold as well as his daughter. Not making eye contact with Ruaud, he said, "This is my only means of locating Kendra. You go, if you must. I will not give up now."

Ruaud squatted to check the horse's chest harness. "I expected you to spout some damned foolishness like that." Standing, he rubbed his jaw and winced when he touched a bruise.

"Why did they—"

"The one called Raven made a suggestion I did not like." Alain guessed he was referring to Pit's partner, the dark, angular man. Ruaud looked at Alain with a hint of his usual humor. "I will live."

"Get over here and make water on the fire," called Raven from his fireside perch. Alain cocked an eyebrow. "Move your shite-covered Norman arses, or we'll move them for you!"

A deep laugh rang out. "Think ye King William will pay us double for opening them up a wee bit for him?" Pit, again.

His back to the Saxons, Alain whispered, "She is worth it."

The look Ruaud shot back as they returned to the outlaws and prepared to carry out their command conveyed the thought that she had damned well better be.

THE DAY dawned cloudless, bright, and hot. Kendra and her captors broke camp early, taking time just to relieve themselves, eat cold travel rations, douse the fire's remains, and stow the cooking implements. Across ridges, high rolling plains, and valleys, they rode away from the rising sun. Sometimes they rode at a canter or trot, and sometimes they dismounted to lead their animals, the terrain dictating the pace. She couldn't decide which was worse: the aching muscles, the itchy trickles of sweat on her face and back and legs, the sharp smell of the men and horses, or the bone-deep fatigue.

Or the festering worry that she would never see anyone she loved again.

With the sun past its zenith, Snake raised his fist, and the party drew rein. For the past hour, they'd been riding the spine of a natural causeway across a marsh. As the causeway narrowed, the swarms of gnats and biting flies intensified. She pitied the horses, whose ears and tails constantly twitched the pests away, to little effect.

At the causeway's end, the marshy ground yielded to vast swampland. Cattails, horsetails, iris fronds, marsh grass, and other tall, water-loving plants waved in the languid breeze. Willows dotted the swamp, their branches sweeping across the water's surface as if testing the temperature. Wild geese and ducks abounded, their calls filling the air with noisy abandon, and a heron regally stalked fish in the green-hued shallows.

In the hazy distance stood what looked like an island, though Kendra knew from her mother's tales that it wasn't one. The conical hill was called the Tor. Its slopes were cloaked with the ruins of a maze, its summit crowned with a tower. In its bowels, according to local legend, slept the greatest enemy the Saxons had ever known, Arthur of the Britons. Some visitors claimed to have heard the faint but unmistakable sounds of battle. Others swore they'd seen King Arthur in the light of a full moon, spurring a fiery-eyed white stallion and wielding a fearsome broadsword, a fierce black war hound lunging at his side.

She closed her eyes, suppressing a shudder.

But even the thought of being rescued by her people's ancient enemy—however impossible—seemed more appealing than the wretched reality of her situation.

She heard the creaks and jingling of harnesses as Snake and Rat dismounted and tethered their horses. Not knowing what else to do, she opened her eyes and followed their example, looping Hilde's reins over a low branch.

Snake stumped over to a massive oak and thrust his arm into a hole in the trunk, to the shoulder. His face contorted in concentration. Finally, his expression transformed into triumph, and he withdrew his hand, clutching a hunting horn that looked to be in far better condition than its lodging suggested. He sucked in a breath, lifted the horn to his lips, and blew a deafening blast.

"What happens now?" she asked him after the ringing in her ears subsided.

Snake replaced the horn, returned to his mount, retrieved food and his wineskin, which had been refilled that morning from a cask stored in the temple, and motioned Kendra to join him in the oak's shade. She was glad that Rat had chosen to remain with the horses.

"Now, my lady"—Snake passed her hunks of bread and cheese, his grin shifting into a feral cast—"we wait."

She followed the line of his gaze toward the Tor, mesmerized by the ripples gouged by the relentless wind.

What they were waiting for, she dared not ask.

AN INSISTENT hand shook Waldron's shoulder. He started awake, trying to ignore the flush of embarrassment that he'd overslept in his chair on the feast hall's dais with a legion of attendant aches. He pressed a hand to his pounding forehead and winced at the worst ale-head he'd ever experienced. His hand thudded onto the armrest as he remembered why.

His daughter was missing, and his Norman guests had let themselves be captured in a foolish attempt to rescue her, leaving Waldron naught else to do but drink himself into oblivion.

His guard captain came into focus. "Thorgil, what news?" Waldron didn't voice the vain hope that Thorgil bore tidings of Kendra.

"The patrol found Cæwlin and Oswy, my lord." The big blond warrior's face remained impassive, but Waldron read tension in the set of his jaw.

"Dead." Resignation weighted Waldron's tone. He closed his eyes and tipped his head back against his chair.

"Oswy is, my lord, though he must have fought bravely," Thorgil replied. "Cæwlin is still senseless but alive. He suffered an arrow wound. Bassa is tending him."

Waldron's eyes snapped open, and he rose. Too quickly; the throbbing intensified, and his senses reeled. Thorgil thrust out his hands to steady him, but Waldron shrugged him off. A welcome sense of purpose displaced the helplessness. "See to it Oswy is buried with the fyrd's full honors. And have Lofwin report to me at the infirmary with a dozen of his best warriors and scouts."

"Thane Waldron, is that wise? The outlaws said—"

"I know what the outlaws said." Not repeating their threats helped to control the brutal imagery of Kendra's fate, but not by much. "This is why I expect Lofwin to select the best." Waldron was about to dismiss the warrior when another idea occurred. "And have our fastest courier report to me."

"Aye, my lord." Thorgil thumped fist to breast and bowed his head, stepping aside to let Waldron pass.

The warriors lay on adjacent cots in the infirmary. Father Æthelward was administering Oswy's last rites. Stopping on the threshold, Waldron bowed his head until the priest had finished. Waldron made the sign of the cross against his chest and resumed his course.

No matter how many times he had seen death, on or off the battlefield, he knew he'd never get accustomed to it. Oswy's strengthening stench, unmoving chest, pale skin, sunken face, and bloodstained tunic and jerkin were bad enough, but Bassa had wrapped his head with a bandage. Even so, it didn't hide the massive dent in the poor lad's skull. Waldron's gut twisted, and he crossed himself again.

"I don't believe he suffered, my lord," murmured Bassa behind him. The peaceful cast to Oswy's features lent substance to the physician's pronouncement.

"Thank God for small mercies." He gripped the lad's sword hand in farewell. To the sound of Æthelward's soft "Amen," Waldron faced the cot containing Bassa's living charge. "And how is Cæwlin? When will he wake?"

Bassa stroked his closely cropped beard. "Difficult to say, my lord. The arrow missed his heart, but the wound is infected. A day, perhaps two—"

"Damn it, man, I need answers now!"

"Which you won't get, my lord," said the physician, "if you kill my patient."

Mentally, Waldron began rehearsing his list of oaths but didn't get far before recognizing the truth of Bassa's claim. "Very well. Send me word the moment he wakes." He turned and started for the door.

"No need, my lord," said a raspy voice.

Waldron returned to Cæwlin's side. Bassa pressed a cup to the warrior's lips. Some of it dribbled out, and Cæwlin sputtered a cough. Waldron felt like quipping, *Now who's killing the patient?* Instead he asked, "Who attacked you, Cæwlin?"

"Outlaws." The veteran's brow creased and his gaze grew distant. "Five. From the west." He shrugged and winced. "More than that, my lord, I don't know. What of Lady Kendra?" The fragile hope in his tone shattered Waldron's heart.

"Being held for ransom." Shaking his head, Waldron grunted his frustration. "West" could mean anything. Ulfric lived to the west, and so did Cynewulf, Oesc, Wihtred, Thorgud, Edgert, and dozens of other thanes. Waldron didn't stand on amiable terms with many of them, especially after paying court to King William, but he couldn't imagine a thane in the lot who would resort to abducting his daughter in retribution. "Think, man. Are you sure you don't remember anything else? Distinctive clothing, adornments, mannerisms, speech?"

Cæwlin's fist weakly thumped the cot. "Don't you think I'd have told you?" His face colored, and he jerked his head aside. "Forgive me, my lord." Tears sprang from the corners of his eyes.

Waldron laid a hand on Cæwlin's uninjured shoulder. "I know you did your best, old friend." He glanced at the adjacent cot. *You and poor Oswy.* Waldron sighed.

The sound of brisk voices caught his attention, and he turned toward it. "Ah, Lofwin, well come." Waldron made a beckoning gesture. Lofwin ordered his men to wait outside while he entered the infirmary, stepping with catlike grace between men, cots, and implement-laden tables to reach Waldron's side. "I want you to track the outlaws who left with our Norman guests last night"—he lifted a peremptory finger—"and don't bother to lecture me about the risks. I've heard that one already. I trust you to be quick and quiet."

Lofwin cracked a grin and bowed. "My lord, not even the deer will mark our passage."

"God's speed to you, then," Waldron said. *You shall need it.* "Send word when you can."

Lofwin saluted and left with his men.

Cæwlin struggled to rise. Bassa tried to stop him, but the lean physician had trouble keeping his grip on the determined warrior. "Unhand me, you fool-headed physician! I must go with them."

"The only way you'll go anywhere is in a box if you don't heal," Bassa retorted.

Waldron nodded. "Don't make me order restraints for you, Cæwlin." He clapped Cæwlin's good shoulder. "Heal yourself, and take your vengeance another day."

The fyrd veteran let out a mirthless laugh. "I hope Lady Kendra will have another day." Doubt clouded his tone.

Waldron refused to share Cæwlin's doubts. He drew Bassa aside for assistance in composing a message that would, God willing, add a measure of insurance to his plan.

ALAIN'S HUNGER and thirst, compounded by the brutal pace and even more brutal sun, couldn't begin to compare with the abominable ache in his shoulders, especially the one that had taken a spear at Hastings. With their wrists bound together and attached to leather leads, he and Ruaud lumbered behind the mounted outlaws, sometimes being forced to break into a trot. Either that or be dragged.

Is she worth it?

Alain was beginning to revise his initial opinion.

He glanced past his shoulder but saw nothing more than the chalky downs rising to either side of the narrow valley, sporting a thatch of grass too sparse even for sheep. A rabbit venturing from its warren couldn't find cover on the ridgeline.

Still, he couldn't dispel the sense of being watched.

Their captors were watching them, of course, after a fashion. In their present condition, the knights had no means of escape, so the outlaws didn't deem it necessary to keep them under constant scrutiny.

No, this feeling ran deeper, more dangerous. The air crackled with deadly expectation.

He raised his hands to wipe his brow as best he could, chiding himself. While his instincts had served him well on many a scouting mission, in this instance he was most likely sensing the presence of sentries guarding the outlaw band's perimeter.

To the young man leading him, whom the others called Wart, he gave voice to his curiosity. Of the three, the strapping but spotty-faced Wart seemed the most approachable, perhaps owing to his apparent newness to their band. Or perhaps because, in some remote way, this youth reminded Alain of Étienne.

He ground his teeth against the familiar tide of guilt and tried to banish the uncomfortable association.

"Naw, we'll be lucky to make it by sundown." Wart eyed him suspiciously. "Why would you be thinking that?"

Pit guffawed. "Why, indeed? Saint Pretty Boy is eager to try the rest of the lads. Seems we're not good enough for the likes of him." He winked at Alain.

The suggestion leapt beyond ludicrous to genuinely amusing. Alain thinned his lips and averted his gaze to kill his smile.

And abruptly wished he wasn't bound. He stared at an inverted salve pot. As the distance lessened, he saw a golden lock of hair lying pinned beneath it.

His pulse quickened.

That they were following Kendra's trail comforted him only to a degree.

He feigned a stumble and fell, causing Wart's horse to rear and whinny and its rider to loose a barrage of epithets. Ruaud tried to rush to Alain's aid but was yanked back by an irritated Raven. Alain rolled toward the salve pot, snatched the hair, and stuffed it in his pouch.

Spouting a string of vulgar remarks, Pit stopped and dismounted. He stalked to Alain, hauled him to his feet, kicked the salve pot under the nearby hawthorn bush, cocked a fist, and gave him an uppercut to the jaw. Alain's head snapped back, exploding in needles of pain. He tried to focus on his attacker to steel himself for another blow but couldn't concentrate.

Is she worth it?

Numbness enveloped him as his vision went black.

Chapter 7

SAXONS DID NOT share the Welsh belief in a fey-peo-pled Otherworld, but Kendra could see how the fantasy could come to pass when lulled by the rhythmic rasp of fronds and splash of water on the barge's hull. Nothing else broke the journey's silence. Even the outlaws, after exchanging watchwords with the bargeman, seemed to prefer the company of their private thoughts.

She huddled against Hilde's comforting, horsy warmth, closed her eyes, and pictured herself drifting into the Otherworld, beyond the outlaws' reach.

The drawback, if such a wish could be granted, was that it would leave her trapped beyond Alain's reach as well.

She shook her head to dispel the traitorous notion. Of course it didn't work.

Sighing, she opened her eyes to watch the Tor slowly rise before her. Although the air didn't feel cold, she couldn't suppress a shiver. She drew her cloak more tightly about her chest, as if it could shield her from her uncertain future.

At the base of the hill, the bargeman poled the craft to the dock while sentries emerged from their posts behind a ruined rock wall. More of these chest-high walls encircled the terraced slopes all the way up to the summit: the remains of the ancient maze Kendra's mother had spoken of, she surmised. Huts clustered near the dock, displaying evidence that the builders had pilfered blocks from the maze. The stone tower seemed to survey the swamp and valley like an implacable lord.

"Dragon be awaiting you up there." Snake's tone sounded awed.

A plaintive howl drifted down from the summit, causing the horses to snort and stamp.

Rat led the horses into a nearby pen, and Snake escorted Kendra into the maze.

The journey had been a garden stroll compared with the arduous task of navigating the switchbacks and overgrown cut-throughs of the Tor's maze. As they ascended, the wind turned cold and tangled with the frequent howls to make them seem by turns dreamily distant and dangerously close.

By the time they reached the top, she felt so disoriented, chilled, weary, and out of breath that she doubted she could find her way down even if her soul's salvation depended upon it. She spent several minutes bent double, turned away from the biting wind, hands to knees, panting and trying to coax her heart back to its normal pace.

The prospect of having to meet this Dragon, whom even the dauntless Snake seemed to fear, didn't help.

"Come, my lady," he said as another outlaw opened the tower's door from the inside and ordered them to enter. "We've one more climb afore us."

Kendra straightened and groaned at the tower's spiral staircase, visible behind the guard's bulk. Steeling her resolve, and praying the eerie howling wouldn't start again, she marched onward, trying her best to ignore the guard's lewd stare as she was forced to brush past him.

The tower's lower chamber appeared to be a storeroom of sorts, with a straw pallet tossed against one wall. The chamber reeked of must, offal, urine, and sweat. Oddly, wooden planks comprised the floor, rather than dirt or flagstones. She thought she heard a faint growl as she crossed the room, but she had no time to wonder about any of these things, for Snake hurried her toward the staircase. This ascent, coming so close upon the heels of the other, left her legs wobbly and burning. She clung to the cool stone wall for support.

After a few moments, Snake took her elbow and ushered her to the door. He pounded thrice and gave the countersign in response to a muffled query from within.

The door swung open to reveal opulence beyond anything Kendra had ever imagined.

Jewel-hued tapestries and plush carpets hid almost every hint of stone. Plump pillows embroidered with gold thread lay scattered among ornate chests, tables, chairs, and benches. A hearth along one wall contained a fire that cast shifting shadows throughout the room. Thin slotted windows, their wooden shutters no match for the wind, punctuated the stone at regular intervals. Reedy music reverberated off the walls, accompanied by the shutters' rattling.

She pressed a hand to her throbbing temple and averted her gaze.

In spite of the ample hearth and the overabundance of fabric, she got the distinct impression that the cold outside was awaiting the best time to strike.

She tried to dispel the sensation with a toss of her head.

The piping stopped, and a rustling drew her attention. A man appeared, as if he'd stepped out of one of the tapestry scenes, and he approached her with haughty grace. His robes looked elegant enough to adorn any courtier's frame, although Kendra imagined that few courtiers could boast of having a frame as well muscled and proportioned as his. He wore his long, dark blond hair in a thick braid. His face she might have called handsome if not for his twisted lower lip, perhaps the legacy of an old battle wound, which gave his expression a perpetual snarl.

"I've brought the Lady Kendra, as ordered, my lord Dragon."

Dragon's eyes never left her as he accepted the statement with a curt nod, reached out, and began running his hands over her body. When he pinched her nipples, panic flared in her gut. She flinched.

Dragon yanked her closer, baring his teeth in an unpleasant grin. "Just making sure the merchandise is not damaged, my lady. For my king." His hands slid downward across her hips. "A sound business practice, would you not agree?"

"Your king? William?" she gasped.

His grin widened. "Not every man bows to the Bastard of Normandy."

She had no chance to retort as he encountered the bandages swathing her legs and straightened. Glaring, he rounded on Snake. The older man stood his ground, but Kendra saw sweat bead upon his brow.

"What did you do to her, you filthy excuse for a whore's son?"

"Nothing." Gratitude for Snake's kindness strengthened her tongue. "Snake did not cause this. My clothing chafed me, so I bound my legs to ease the pain."

Although Snake looked relieved, Dragon regarded her suspiciously. "Show me."

Guessing that any attempt to preserve her modesty would prove futile, she hitched her skirts over her knees and unwound the bandages. Dragon lost no time in stroking her thighs, probing farther than he had any decent right to do. She gritted her teeth against his assault.

After what seemed like an eternity, he withdrew his hand and let her skirts down. She nearly collapsed with relief.

"She tells the truth," Dragon growled to Snake. "Fortunately for you." He turned to a gilt chest sitting atop a nearby table, opened it to withdraw a small linen sack, and tossed it at Snake. It jingled as he plucked it from the air. "Now leave us."

She gazed beseechingly at Snake, who answered with a one-shouldered shrug and made for the door. As he reached for the handle, the timbers shuddered under the force of someone else's knock. Snake opened the door to reveal the man who had admitted them into the tower, grasping a sealed piece of parchment in his fist. Eyebrows knotted, Dragon strode forward and snatched it from the guard.

His reaction, after breaking the seal and studying the contents, was immediate and vehement. He flung the parchment into the fireplace.

"A summons, my lord?" Snake ventured.

Dragon did not answer but stripped off his robe to reveal a fine ebony leather jerkin and breeches. He stalked up to the guard. "Bring her food and wine. She does not leave this chamber until I return, and no one but me is to enter it. Understood?"

The guard nodded. Dragon ordered Snake to attend him and crossed the threshold without a backward glance. Snake gave her a short bow and followed his master. The door thumped shut with deadly finality.

Kendra hurried to the hearth, found a poker, and rescued the smoldering parchment. She moistened her fingers to quench the heat, but the embers had already obliterated much of the message. The only phrases she could make out with any certainty were "at once," "explain," and in a bold flourish at the bottom, "URTH." In the retreating sunlight, she squinted at the message and turned it at different angles, trying to discern more clues, to no avail.

In dejected misery, she sank onto the nearest mound of pillows. Even if she could divine the outlaws' plans, she had no prayer of escaping their lair, and no one who might help her knew where she was being held. She wadded the parchment and threw it into the fire. As it blackened, her hopes of rescue crumbled to ash within her heart.

Face in hands, she succumbed to sobs.

TOLERATING THE insults and the occasional yanks on his bonds, Alain trudged behind his captors, wrapped in a fog of fatigue and pain.

She *is* worth it!

Every stride he reminded himself: She *is*. Worth it.

When doubts threatened to overcome his resolve, he had only to recall the maidservant's battered form and terrified face. The idea that Kendra might be suffering thus sent a jolt of anger through him.

Although he despised its source, he welcomed the anger as the one thing keeping him alive.

Since late afternoon, the group had been traversing a causeway across a swamp. Gnats and biting flies provided merciless escort, and the creatures seemed to take perverse delight in inflicting their torture upon the captives, whose bonds made it impossible to brush them off.

Evening brought cooling temperatures and relief from the insects, but a quickening fog complicated efforts to find a suitable camp site.

"I say we press on," said Raven.

"Are ye daft, man? In this gloom, the lads'll be at our throats afore they ken it's us." Pit crossed his woad-painted arms and glared at his companions. "Or mayhap they'll recognize us and slit our throats anyway, for the gold." He leered at Alain. "Or for a go at Saint Pretty Boy here."

"Who else would know the signal besides us?" Wart put in.

"Who else, indeed?" sneered Pit.

"Lad's right." Fists clenched, Raven stalked up to an unconcerned Pit. "Afraid of a little risk, are you?"

Pit grinned. "And you? Afeared of a wee bit of dark and fog?"

Raven worked his jaw and spat in Pit's face. With a yell, Pit fell upon Raven, fists flying. To his credit, the thinner and more agile Raven gave out as good as he got, while Wart beseeched them to stop.

Unnoticed, Alain began working his bonds loose. He caught Ruaud's glance and nodded.

The act of Raven brandishing a seax brought the fight—and the Normans' efforts to free themselves—to a halt.

"If you want to stay here, stay," he growled at Pit. "We are moving on."

Raven mounted and kicked his horse into a trot. Ruaud's lead snapped taut, forcing him to grip it to keep from revealing his loosened bonds. The lead must have slipped in his hands, for he uttered a pained grunt. Alain, behind Wart, had enough warning to avoid suffering a similar fate. Muttering a creative array of curses against Raven, Wart, Alain, Ruaud, the other outlaws, the dark, and the fog, Pit guarded the procession's rear.

In the distance, beneath the waning moon, Alain made out the shadow of a conical hill that loomed larger as they approached. Instinct warned him their destination must be nigh.

After what seemed like an eternity, Raven drew rein at an oak and dismounted. While the other two secured the horses, Raven fished in the oak's bole, withdrew a hunting horn, and blew a horrific blast. He returned the horn to the tree, retrieved his saddle pack, and sat at the tree's base. Wart joined him. A sulking Pit chose a tussock within sight of the group, but not near his companions, and started gnawing on his travel rations.

The knights remained standing.

"Do as you please," Raven said as he tossed them each a hunk of bread and the wineskin, "but you're in for a wait."

They sat. While devouring the rations, they assessed each other's condition, which wasn't too bad under the circumstances.

Snores made Alain glance toward Pit. The outlaw had slid off the tussock to curl in the grass. Raven and Wart appeared alert, but Alain sensed this was the best chance he and Ruaud were going to get.

They eased off their bonds, shared a brief nod, and leapt up to rush Raven and Wart. Battle rage surged through Alain's veins, banishing pain and fatigue. The brigands' bellows roused their companion, and the fight became a blur of punches, kicks, trips, rolls, vulgar oaths, and blade thrusts.

In a lull, Alain found himself standing, panting, over Raven's body, the dead outlaw's seax gripped in his fist, dripping blood. A trembling Wart faced him, his back wedged against the oak tree.

Hefting the seax, he wondered whether anyone had made a vow for this lad's protection . . .

Ruaud's shout made Alain turn and see his friend wrestling across the ground, trying to keep Pit's seax at arm's length. Alain sprinted across the gap, judged the timing, and plunged Raven's war-knife downward.

Pit's startled yelp allowed Ruaud to strike the seax from Pit's grasp, throw the outlaw off him, and scramble to his feet. Alain raced to where the war-knife had landed and tossed it to his companion. Hand to neck, Pit staggered toward them, his eyes bulging with murderous intent.

He never made it. Eyes rolling, his head lolled, and he fell into an awkward heap. Ruaud, taking no chances, drove the seax through Pit's throat.

Of Wart there remained no sign.

Perchance the lad had run off to alert the others. Alain strode to Raven's corpse and began stripping it. At the moment of death, Raven had voided his bowels, and Alain shook the foul matter from the breeches as best he could.

"What are you doing?"

"Disguising myself." In spite of everything, he grinned. "I suggest you do it too. I expect we will be getting more trouble ere long."

Ruaud held up Pit's scraggly jerkin, shaking his head. "These will not buy us one scrap of protection once their companions realize we are not of the band."

"True." Alain donned Raven's breeches without difficulty but had to struggle to tug the jerkin over his broader chest. "I shall think of something."

"Hurry." Ruaud tossed a nod over his shoulder, where rhythmic splashing had begun to emanate from across the marsh.

Squinting let Alain discern nothing save a pale sphere of light bobbing toward them. He motioned Ruaud to help him drag Pit's and Raven's bodies into the tall fronds bordering the marsh. With any luck, scavengers soon would dispose of the evidence.

Alain instructed Ruaud to hide Waldron's gold while he checked both men's bodies. But his quarry eluded him.

Disappointed, he left the corpses and joined Ruaud in awaiting their visitor, a man poling a barge. They pulled their borrowed cloaks' hoods close about their faces.

"Wolf," said the bargeman in a heavy whisper.

Wolf? A name? Or a watchword? Alain looked at Ruaud, who twitched his shoulders in the barest of shrugs.

"Wolf!" the man repeated.

Alain made the only response that came to mind: he howled.

"Hey! Who the bloody 'ell are you? Who blew that—"

Ruaud and Alain plunged into the swamp and waded ankle-deep water toward the barge. The man raised his pole to wield it like a quarterstaff—credibly well, in fact, but no match for two knights. The cold water and sucking mud provided only minor obstacles. Ruaud snatched the outlaw's ankle and pulled him, screaming, off the barge, where Alain silenced his noise with Raven's seax.

They hauled themselves onto the barge and dragged up the body to dispose it with the others. Ruaud poled them toward the shore while Alain pondered their options.

"I say we ride back to Edgarburh with Waldron's gold and tell the old man his daughter is here," Ruaud suggested after the bargeman disappeared to join his lawless brethren. "Let him send his men out after her."

Fists on hips, Alain studied the island. "We don't know she is here. We need to verify it first."

"We, we, always with the we. Well, I say not *oui* but *non!*"

Alain whirled on him. "That is your choice, of course. But the next time I see William, I will inform him that one of his knights would prefer to turn his back on a fight, a friend . . . and on someone in need."

Ruaud laughed mirthlessly. "That was low, Alain."

"*Oui.*" Alain finished securing the barge, strode to where the horses were tethered, and untied their reins.

The sound of scraping steel drew Alain's attention, and he looked up to see Ruaud offering him one of the outlaw's scabbards, which he had removed from the saddlebow of the nearest horse. "Not the best of blades, but it will serve you better than a war-knife."

Alain couldn't agree more. He accepted the sheathed longsword, looped the baldric across his chest, and returned to the task of coaxing a skittish horse onto the barge.

"Why are you bothering to do that?" Ruaud asked.

Though not in a mood to explain to someone who didn't intend to help, Alain said, "The other outlaws will be expecting a certain number of men and mounts." He leveled his glare at Ruaud. "I shall devise a reason to explain why the man count decreased from four to one, never fear."

"Four to two, you mean." Ruaud strapped on Pit's sword belt, a snug fit but far better than Raven's would have been. The horse Ruaud led onto the barge went placidly enough, perhaps because one of its companions already had boarded.

"Thank you." Alain didn't bother to disguise his relief. "But I thought—"

"Don't thank me yet. God alone knows how many more outlaws we must face."

"Indeed." After they guided the third horse aboard, Alain gripped his friend's forearm warmly. "But our odds of success have just doubled."

"I knew the fool would spout some nonsense like that," Ruaud muttered, apparently to no one in particular.

Smiling grimly, Alain grabbed the pole to start pushing them across the swamp toward the island, praying with each thrust that he would find Kendra alive and unharmed.

Chapter 8

To ration their strength, they took turns at the barge pole, navigating by the hill. Although neither knight had suffered any wounds more serious than cuts and bruises, the exertion and pain, combined with the deprivation of sleep, food, and drink, exacted a steep toll. The food and drink problem they remedied with the outlaws' supplies, but progress through the swamp, chorused by howling that sounded louder as they neared the hill, remained slow.

Alain was thankful to have Kendra's image to spur him on. Between shoves, he studied Ruaud as the latter slumped against the bow, guzzling ale. Alain had sworn no vows for Ruaud's safety, but he felt responsible for their predicament none the less. Though his shoulder was aching, and the calluses on his palms had grown calluses of their own, he stayed an extra turn at the pole.

Just when he thought his arms were going to give out, he spotted the torchlit outline of a dock and huts along the shore.

"Here, let me bring us in." Ruaud levered to his feet and extended a hand. "You've been at it too long."

Alain surrendered the pole without protest and moved to the bow to study the landscape.

No one seemed to be patrolling the shore. Still, he would be a fool to assume the outlaws had not posted sentries. But where were they? In the huts?

They got their answer when Ruaud maneuvered the barge up to the dock. Two men appeared from behind a rock wall above the line of huts, spears at the ready.

"King!" challenged one.

Not again! Alain wondered which king this Saxon rabble would hold in such esteem as to incorporate into their watch-words. Surely not King William.

Then inspiration hit.

Clearing his throat and roughening his voice, he said in his best imitation of Wart's guttural Saxon accent, "Pit and Raven are making off with the gold!"

"What?" yelled the other sentry. "Where?"

Alain pointed across the swamp. "Take our horses. If you hurry, you can catch the fongers!"

The huts erupted with a dozen men, all armed and clamoring to pile onto the barge and hunt down their erstwhile companions. Someone ran up carrying an armload of extra barge poles, which he distributed among the others, and the expedition shoved off, their curses drifting back across the murky waters.

"Well done," whispered Ruaud.

"What in'ell was that all about?"

Ruaud and Alain turned to find another group of outlaws

bearing down on them with leveled spears.

"I told you—"

"Methinks you've told us a pack of lies," snapped the lead man. He caught Alain's hood with the spear's point and pushed it back. "Fongin' Normans!"

The knights exchanged a glance, drew their borrowed swords, and the melee began.

KENDRA HEARD the faint clash of steel on steel, rushed to a window, and threw open the shutters. But what the hill's slope didn't conceal, the darkness did.

She tried to keep from indulging in the hope that someone was attempting to rescue her, or who he might be.

The whine of a sword being drawn outside her chamber's door and the clatter of feet on the stairs told her the guard had left his post. But had he left the tower?

Only one way to find out.

She stepped to the door and gave the handle a tentative pull. Miraculously, it wasn't locked. She eased open the door a fraction and peered out: still no sign of the guard, thank heaven. She ducked back into the chamber and snatched the wineskin and the sack of oatcakes and dried beef the guard had brought earlier, and slung them over her shoulder. Praying for her luck to hold, she gathered her skirts and crept down the winding staircase, alert for sounds of the guard returning.

On the ground floor, her good luck ended at its door. The guard had moved the huge bolt to exit but must have locked the door via key from the outside. Gritting her teeth, she resisted the temptation to pound on the door's timbers; the last thing she needed was to draw the attention of her captors.

As she glanced around for another way out, her gaze fell upon the wooden-planked flooring. Her mother had spoken of the Tor's hill being riddled with caverns. What would be more natural than a tower with an escape route built into the hill?

'Twas worth a try. For the battle seemed to be dwindling, leaving no clue as to the victors. Regardless of who'd been fighting whom, someone would come for her soon.

She set the wine and food down, shoved aside the rugs, and tapped on the floor, feeling a rush of satisfaction when the hollow sound confirmed her guess. Upon moving a chest standing on bare wood, she discovered a rope handle attached to a square set of bound planks. She gave the handle a firm tug.

Fierce barks burst from the hole, along with an even fiercer stench.

Hand to mouth, she stumbled back.

When the noises subsided, she crawled to the hole for another look. Growling began, low and menacing. Acting on faith that nothing was going to leap out at her, she dropped a few beef strips into the abyss. The sounds of greedy gnawing replaced the growling.

Why would the outlaws keep a starving hound in an escape tunnel?

Before she could puzzle out an answer, she heard shouts and the renewed clash of arms. With a whispered apology, she closed the hound's prison, replaced the chest and rugs, snatched her remaining supplies, and bolted up the stairs. She fled into the opulent upper chamber, slammed the door, and braced it with her body, her chest heaving in time with her runaway heart.

Someone with a heavy, uneven tread thumped up the stairs. She whipped her head around, searching for anything that might serve as a better weapon than her dagger. But in this den of plush luxury, nothing presented itself. Nothing except . . .

The hearth—of course! She scurried over, grabbed the poker, and thrust it into the hottest embers for as long as she dared.

The footsteps thudded closer.

Fighting to control her breathing and her shaking hands, she took a position beside the door, cocked the glowing poker, and waited.

CLUTCHING HIS side, which was aching and bleeding freely where one of the outlaws had struck a lucky thrust, he dragged himself up the last few steps. By all accounts Kendra was being held in the uppermost chamber, but he needed the proof only his eyes could supply.

Even if she proved to be his final sight on earth.

He reached the landing and paused, gasping, to marshal strength. She might be guarded inside the room, though heaven alone knew how he'd battle a flea, never mind anything larger. In the heat of combat, he had killed the tower's guard before thinking to ask the man how many of his companions were stationed within.

Of Ruaud's fate he couldn't be certain. They had become separated soon after entering that Godforsaken maze, when foes kept leaping out at random intervals like sparks from a pithy fire. Alain thought he'd heard his friend's cheerful swearing after he had won free of the maze to reach the windswept summit, but whether or not the sound had been a trick of his battle-engorged senses, he had no idea.

After the initial clash, Alain had lost count of how many men he had maimed or killed. He shifted his hand to examine the flow of blood, unable to recall which outlaw had inflicted the wound. The number of men surviving to mount a second attack, he had no wish to contemplate.

As he stared at the door, pondering his next course of action, its edges blurred. Soon the loss of blood would render most options impossible.

He sucked in a breath, raised his sword, yanked on the handle, and stormed into the room.

Searing agony branded his torso.

As he gulped air, his knees buckled, and he fell. Darkness enveloped him. With the darkness came a single, devastating thought:

I have failed. Again.

RUAUD D'AUVAY tore through one of the huts near the dock, hunting for something to quell his hunger. As near as he could tell, all the brigands had either departed—thanks to Alain's foolhardy but brilliant ploy—or lay stiffening under the stars.

Poking into casks, boxes, and open shelves yielded him two loaves of crusty bread, a generous fistful of dried beef strips, a cheese wheel, and all the wine he could swill.

Not a bad start.

He slung a full wineskin over his shoulder, lopped off a hunk of cheese, and carried it along with the beef and a loaf outside. He selected the side of the hut that gave him a view of the marsh and maze's entrance, though he doubted any threats would come from the latter quarter. He and Alain had made short work of the ill-trained, ill-armed men.

As he chewed on the beef and washed it down with the surprisingly good wine, he reviewed the fight. Not counting the three who had escorted the Normans, the bargeman, and an unknown number who had abducted Lady Kendra, Ruaud and Alain had either killed or duped another three dozen outlaws. That made for a sizeable band by any reckoning, but Ruaud could not recall seeing anyone who had acted as the leader.

An unpleasant thought made him swallow his cheese hard. He eased it down his throat with several swallows of wine.

What if the outlaws' leader—in all likelihood their fiercest and most skilled warrior—was guarding Lady Kendra? How would Alain, weary from captivity, battle, crossing the marsh, and climbing the hill, fare against such a man?

The lad's passion for his bride ought to help, but everybody had its limits.

He changed positions, but the angle prevented him from seeing the summit and the tower that crowned it.

Resolve flared in his heart to make sure Alain and Lady Kendra were all right.

Ruaud collected himself for the ascent, but his left knee buckled as pain shot up his leg. He massaged the knee hard, willing the pain to abate, with no success. One of the fatherless sons had connected with a savage kick, toward the end of the skirmish, after Alain had broken away to go after the woman. He judged himself fit to fight on level ground, but the injury rendered climbing damned nigh impossible.

As if in a dream, he became aware of faint, angry shouts wafting across the marsh. The outlaws, no doubt, but why they were shouting Ruaud couldn't begin to guess. Brawling among themselves, perhaps?

Or had they found their dead companions?

He chewed on that thought a while, the implications souring more with each passing moment. If the corpses had been discovered, the men would return to confront him and Alain—probably were en route already. And they knew this lair far better than Ruaud did, in spite of any defense he could devise. Alain and Kendra, in the tower, would be safe enough for the present, unless they'd been captured.

In either case, Ruaud's injury had rendered him powerless to assist them.

A skiff tied to the dock presented another option: he could cross the marsh and seek help. According to Alain, this hill lay near Thane Ulfric's demesne.

By God, that arrogant Saxon should be dealing with this lawless band! Not King William's knights, who knew little about the land and less about its people.

Although Ruaud preferred the honesty of open combat, a fresh spate of muted shouts convinced him to hurry. Even if he neared the outlaws out on the marsh, the thick fog should shield him from notice.

He limped into the hut to refill his wineskin and replenish his food supplies, stuffing everything into a musty but serviceable sack. Upon striding to the dock as briskly as his knee allowed, he tossed the sack into the skiff's bow, stepped in, sat, and began rowing.

Bracing his feet against the skiff's sides didn't put too much strain on his injury, and he made good progress.

Progress to where remained the key question.

For, unlike when they had traveled toward the island, with its conical shape peering through the mist, Ruaud had nothing by which to navigate. He could be rowing in circles and never know it.

He mused about Alain's penchant for prayer, wishing that he, Ruaud, had cultivated similar habits. Surely God wouldn't bother heeding the supplications of someone who hadn't bothered with Him until well into his fourth decade of life.

And yet he couldn't let the logic deter him.

"Holy Father, I—" Biting his lip, he frowned. It seemed brash to petition God directly, when he didn't feel worthy to address the most minor of saints. But he had no idea which saint to call upon in this situation, so he let the skiff drift while he shut his eyes and hoped for the best.

"Father God, I know I haven't thought about You much over the years, but You must have seen how well my friend Alain honors You. I ask—no, I beg for Your help. Not for my sake, but for the sake of Your faithful servant Alain and the lady he loves. Please deliver them from their ordeal."

As he added a gruff "amen," a thought occurred that he hoped would ensure his petition's success. "And if it should please You, Lord, to deliver me from this infernal swamp, I promise to be more faithful in worship henceforth!"

"Dear God, no!"

Kendra dropped the poker as the familiar figure crumpled at her feet.

The poker and the body hit with loud thuds. He wasn't dead—his ragged breaths attested to that fact—although he would be soon if she didn't stop the bleeding from that nasty gash in his side.

Too bad her aim hadn't been lucky enough to cauterize the wound.

But since he was already unconscious, one more burn couldn't make any difference to him, and it could make all the difference in his survival.

She snatched up the poker and hurried over to the hearth. While the iron heated, she dragged him the rest of the way into the room, shut the door, blocked it with a heavy chest, and set about collecting pillows and coverlets to make him comfortable.

Once he was arranged to her satisfaction, she studied his attire. The jerkin, unevenly tanned and slashed in myriad places, appeared to be too tight to remove without risking further injury to him. She drew her dagger and sliced away enough of the leather to expose the wounds.

The scrapes and scratches had long since stopped bleeding, but blood welled from the deadliest gash. She found one of Dragon's clean undertunics, tore off several strips, and pressed the thick wad firmly into place. He groaned and writhed but didn't wake. After repeating the process with two more wads and tossing them aside, she was relieved to note that the flow had become a slow oozing. That, however, could change with any abrupt movement he might make. She applied another strip.

Stroking his limp hand, she glanced at the glowing poker while debating her plan. She despised the idea of having to hurt him again, but his condition left her with little choice.

When she couldn't put off the inevitable any longer, she stood, retrieved the poker by its wooden handle, and returned to his side. She removed the last bandage wad, pulled the ravaged flesh together as best she could and, grimacing, applied the heat.

His agonized moans wrenched her heart. To say nothing of the wretched sight and even more wretched stench of his charred flesh. Fortunately, he remain-ed unconscious. She laid the poker on the hearth, moistened a clean cloth with water from the basin, and swabbed his sweat-beaded face, unsure of what to do next.

To heal the pain, you must endure the thorn.

She gave her head an impatient shake, rocking back on her heels. That, again. Why now, of all times? This was Glastonbury, true, but the Tor could still be crawling with outlaws, and she stood a better chance of flying to the moon than obtaining the legendary plant.

Endure the thorn!

The thought's insistence gave her pause. As she studied the squire's form, her eyes lit on a small leather pouch strapped to his belt. Odd; it didn't bulge as a coin purse might. Her hand reached toward it as if controlled by someone else.

A flash of warmth heated her cheeks as she realized she would have to unbuckle his belt to free the pouch. Resolutely, she concentrated on the task at hand. She slipped the pouch off the belt and opened it to discover several tiny, muslin-wrapped packages.

As her fingers came into contact with one of them, the fabric's edges began to blacken.

Petals from the Glastonbury thorn!

She dropped the packet as if it were a live ember.

You must endure it.

He had begun to thrash about, uttering half-formed sentences punctuated with groans. She laid a hand on his forehead, and it felt far too cool.

The image of a dew-spattered red rose leapt to mind, given with no expectations and an implicit promise of forgiveness. Guilt stabbed her heart.

Endure the thorn.

She had no idea how the Glastonbury thorn could help, but goaded by memories of her mother's and brother's deaths, she yearned to ease Squire Alain's torment.

She grasped the packet. It began to smoke. She dropped it, her fingertips red and sore. Sucking them didn't relieve the pain.

Endure it!

As she reached for the packet again, fear froze her hand.

The thorn's Cristes-mæsse flowers were reputed to work miracles for the pure of heart. Yet how could she be "pure of heart" when she harbored venomous hatred for the man who had murdered her brother? How could she look her Norman bridegroom in the eye and proclaim her fidelity to him while she felt herself succumbing to this squire's forbidden allure? How could she reconcile the months of despising England's new king for what he had done to her people, her family, and her very existence?

"I can't!" Sobbing, she buried her face in her hands. "I just can't. The thorn won't work for me. I am not worthy."

Power does not come without sacrifice. But for Alain's sake, and yours, you must endure the thorn.

For Alain's sake.

Raising her head and drying her face on the sleeve of her gown, she gazed at the man—the Norman—who'd already sacrificed God alone knew how much for her sake. His chilled, waxy face convinced her that whether she was betrothed to another man or not, and whether Alain was kin to Del's murderer or not, she didn't want him to pay the ultimate price.

She had no right to permit him to make such a sacrifice.

The very least she could do for him was sacrifice a small piece of herself.

She drew a deep, shuddering breath, released her hatred as best she could, and pressed the packet between her palms.

Blinding agony seared her hands. She squeezed her eyes shut and clenched her jaw but refused to let go. Pain shot up her arms to her brain, torching every nerve in her body as if she had fallen into a vat of molten wax. In her mind's eye, she watched herself be consumed by leaping flames.

The stench of her burning flesh was no illusion. Her stomach roiled. Bile burned her throat.

Still she clung to the packet, not fully comprehending what bound her to this choice.

White flames engulfed her imagined self, and the pain remained intense, yet the flames did not char her. Even her hands, in her mind, appeared whole and hale, limned in the strange light.

The pain subsided to a bearable level. When it had become naught but a faint prickle, she opened her eyes and unclenched her hands.

She gasped, wide-eyed.

Snowy ash coated her palms. The skin—not red and blistered like the last time, and not black, as she'd feared—glowed a delicate shade of newborn pink. And the old scars were gone.

She checked her initial impulse to dust off her hands and instead worked up a mouthful of saliva and spat into them. Rubbing her hands together, she formed the spittle and ash into a paste and dabbed it onto the worst of Alain's wounds: the cauterized gash and the first burn she'd inflicted upon him.

Her second shock of the evening came when both wounds healed and the scars faded. Aghast yet curious, she probed the wounds' sites, feeling naught but firm, healthy flesh.

She sent a prayer of thanks heavenward.

"What—what did you do?"

She glanced down to see Alain touching his abdomen, his expression a mixture of confusion and horror. There would be no end of trouble if he thought she'd used devilry on him. So she opted for the simplest answer: "I applied a poultice and it healed you."

"I was bleeding, and . . ." He closed his eyes for a moment, as if struggling for comprehension. "And you burned me."

"For that I am sorry, good squire, but I had to cauterize the wound."

"But there is no wound any longer!"

"It was a very strong poultice." Offering a tentative smile, she laid a hand on his forearm. "And even stronger prayers."

Affection warmed Alain's smile. "Whatever you did, Lady Kendra, I thank you."

"'Tis I who must thank you for rescuing me."

"Don't thank me yet." Blinking, he uttered a short laugh. "Not until we are away from here."

He made as if to push himself up, convulsed with a moan, and fell back against the cushions.

"What's wrong?" she cried.

"Don't know. My side—" Eyes closed, he massaged the spot, his actions punctuated by gasps and grunts. "The flesh seems whole, but . . . still hurts. A lot."

"Here?" She pressed her palm against the spot. A tingling rush flowed down her arm and into her hand.

His face relaxed. "Ah, yes. Much better." He opened his eyes, the affection glowing brighter than before. "Your hand is very warm."

She jerked it up. "Too hot?"

"No, no." He caught her hand and guided it back to where it had lain. "It feels . . . good . . ." His eyelids drooped and his hand slipped as he surrendered to sleep.

She kept her hand in place for a few more moments before moving it to his brow. Its temperature felt much more natural, and she released a relieved sigh, willing him to enjoy a long, healing rest.

As she reached for the cloth to clean her hands, an idea hit. Quickly and gently, lest her ministrations wake him, she touched his other wounds. They too disappeared. Only his clothing bore evidence of the fight.

She bowed her head in profound gratitude, tempered by the profound regret that she hadn't discovered the Glastonbury thorn's secret in time to save her mother or brother.

After attending to her evening needs, she lay down close enough to Alain to be able to check on him during the night without overstepping propriety's bounds.

Sleep eluded her.

At last, she had obeyed her mother's final directive. Whether she would endure that hellish heat every time she attempted to use the herb, she couldn't begin to guess, but she was grateful beyond measure for this chance to heal her rescuer.

But at what cost?

She shifted onto her side to gaze at her charge, reveling in a forbidden surge of love. She kissed her fingertips and brushed his unshaven cheek. He uttered a pleased-sounding hum.

As she withdrew her hand, sadness enshrouded her heart at the thought of having to wed another man.

At what cost, indeed.

Chapter 9

ALAIN AWOKE WITH a start and sat up, reeling with disorientation.

A tower's walls surrounded him, though the profusion of cushions and tapestries refuted the notion that he'd been imprisoned. Darkness and the room's chill told him night blanketed the land. The figure sleeping an arm's length from him was no guard.

He couldn't recall reaching the tower, or whether Ruaud had accompanied him. Had Ruaud caught up with him later?

The figure shifted, uttering a soft groan. A feminine one.

His pulse quickened as he crept closer to her, scarcely daring to hope . . .

Kendra! And, as near as he could make out in the gloom, she appeared to be unharmed.

He released his gratitude with a heartfelt sigh.

Then he recalled the odd scene he'd dreamt.

He had been lying on a grassy field, mortally wounded, as storm clouds billowed and darkened overhead. Lightning flashed. Despite his struggles, his blood loss had left him too weak to seek cover. But when the storm broke, he saw not raindrops hurtling toward him but tiny white petals, numerous beyond counting. As they touched his skin, they burst into flame but did not burn him, leaving instead a tingling sensation and an ashen residue.

The memory of the fights slammed into his mind. He probed the place where one brigand's sword had bitten deep. Although some pain remained, the flesh felt as whole as if the thrust had missed him.

He withdrew his fingers and stared at them in wonderment. The tips were coated with a white powder unlike any simple or poultice he'd ever seen.

His heart shivered with the realization that he had lain near death, as the dream had implied. And Kendra—he now recalled from his few lucid moments of the night before—had saved him.

It had to have been a miracle; no good ever came of employing the devil's arts.

He inched closer to her and skimmed his fingertips over her cheek. It felt warm and soft. Bending down, he brushed her lips with his. An almost-smile tugged at her mouth, but she didn't wake.

Temptation goaded him to do more; honor commanded restraint.

He rolled away and stood, unsure how long honor would reign.

Duty chimed in with its own urgent request. What if the outlaws he'd tricked into leaving the island had discovered their companions' remains?

Stealthily, to avoid disturbing her, he peered out each of the chamber's windows but could see nothing beyond a vast shroud of mist, just beginning to pinken with dawn's glow, a few valiant trees thrusting through to dispel the illusion that the tower stood rooted in heaven.

But not seeing any outlaws didn't guarantee that he and Kendra were free from danger.

He girt on his war-knife and sword. The chest barricading the door scraped along the floor as he moved it, and he glanced at her. She remained asleep. He opened the door just wide enough for his body and eased it closed behind him.

A SHAFT of sunlight hit Kendra's eyelids, piercing her dream.

She didn't want to wake up.

Alain was kissing her, a deep and long and soul-satisfying kiss. She arched into his embrace, running her fingers through his thick golden hair and willing him to lift their passion to the next level. In this dream, Sir Robert de Bellencombre didn't exist. The outlaws didn't exist. Ulfric didn't exist. Nothing existed beyond her and Alain and their spiraling desires, and she clung to the dream in spite of her body's more mundane needs.

Her eyes still closed, she reached for him, though for what purpose she wasn't sure. The Alain of the waking world may have captured her heart, but he could never possess her virtue.

The abiding sense of happiness the dream had instilled within her shattered under the weight of her sigh.

He must have shifted in his sleep. She stretched farther but still couldn't reach him. At last, she opened her eyes.

Gone!

Sitting up, she fought to contain the welling panic. She hoped he had left to relieve himself, which sounded like a fine idea. This chamber boasted many sumptuous furnishings, but a privy pot didn't number among them.

She rose and removed the bandages swathing her legs, which, thankfully, no longer felt chafed, and pulled on her overdress. Combing her fingers through her unbound hair, she yearned for Rowena's help. Then the memory of that dreadful day returned, and she prayed that Rowena, Oswy and Cæwlin had escaped.

The tears wetting her cheeks heralded her doubts.

She blotted her face with the back of a hand, donned her veil and shoes, and strode from the room.

Halfway down the stairs, spooked by the tower's oppressive silence, complete save for her own tread and breathing, she paused.

Was he trying to escape her as she, regrettably, had done to him? Did he also fear what would happen if they succumbed to temptation and Sir Robert learned of their trespass?

Another thought gripped her. A trickle of sweat crawled down her spine.

What if Alain had fallen afoul of more outlaws? He couldn't have killed them all last night; he was just a squire, after all, and the lair had been swarming with more brigands than ants on spilt honey.

He might have had help in the form of his master, Sir Ruaud, but likely no more than that. If her father's fyrd had accompanied them, one of them would have found her. Even if Alain had been the first to reach her lofty prison, he never would have been permitted to sleep in the same chamber, despite the fact that he had been too badly wounded to act improperly.

She resumed her descent, all senses bristling with the possibility of danger.

When she reached the lower chamber, she heard a faint but hopeful-sounding whine through the floorboards and regretted not having brought any food. She murmured a promise to the hound, which seemed to satisfy it, for the whining stopped.

The room's dearth of windows left only the door through which to peer, and that didn't tell her much. A sea of pink-tinted mist swirled before her, smothering all clues as to what might lie beneath.

Prudence insisted she stay within the tower.

Concern for Alain propelled her outside.

An unmoving heap of stinking, leather-and-wool-wrapped flesh lying near the door made her gasp. It had already attracted a cloud of flies, in spite of the wind.

Please, not Alain!

Not Alain but the guard who had let her and Snake into the tower the previous day—had it been only a day? It seemed like an eternity.

So he had killed this man, but not without a price. The outlaw's sword, clutched in the stiff fist, bore a wide streak of dried blood. If Alain hadn't found her when he did . . .

Relief weakened her knees, and she sank down, heedless of the dewy grass and the corpse's stench that even the wind couldn't purge. She bowed her head, overcome with a rush of fatigue. A faint thought nagged her that she ought to finish the task she'd come outside to perform and return to the tower, but weariness prevented her from heeding it.

"Lady Kendra?"

What a pleasant dream, she mused, to hear her name spoken by that courtly voice.

"My lady, are you not well?"

Her eyes flew open, and she snapped her head up. Alain had dropped to one knee before her, concern etched across his face. He was breathing hard and fighting to control it, mayhap because he'd just climbed back to the summit.

Surreptitiously, she pinched the back of her hand. It hurt. She flashed a smile and offered him the hand she'd pinched. When he kissed it, and the sting gave way to a delicious tingling, she thought her heart would surely melt.

"I shall be fine, good squire," she managed to murmur, "if you will please give me a moment alone." She had no intention of admitting the rest of the truth to him.

"Of course, my lady."

He stood and helped her rise. Upon releasing her hand, he swept her a deep bow, straightened, and strode out of sight behind the tower.

She watched him go, cradling to her bosom the hand he had kissed, until the pressure in her vitals demanded her attention.

A short while later, she found him sitting on the ground with his back braced against the west side of the tower, arms wrapped around his knees, staring out across the thinning mist. More of the valley's trees were beginning to emerge, but they seemed insubstantial, dreamlike.

"'Tis like we're watching the creation of the world."

At the sound of her voice he began scrambling to his feet, but she bade him stay seated and joined him. The stone chilled her back, and she arched away from it. His nearness was having an intoxicating effect, and thought after inane thought tumbled through her mind, begging to be voiced. She selected the least inane and most important:

"How fare your wounds?"

He met her gaze, his own tinged with wonderment bordering on awe. "Except for some lingering aches, it's as if the fighting had never happened. How did you do that?"

"I—" As she pondered what to say, she could appreciate why her mother had kept her healing gift a secret. "Please forgive me, Squire Alain, but I used your Glastonbury thorn petals to make a poultice. Beyond that, I'm not sure I understand all of what happened either."

"Glastonbury thorn petals?"

"I found them in the pouch hanging from your belt." She knit her brow as an unwelcome thought occurred. "That was your pouch, wasn't it?"

He nodded. If her insinuation had offended him, he didn't show it. "I do have more than a passing knowledge of medicinal lore. But I have never known any herb to do this."

He unwrapped his arms and straightened his legs to pat his midsection where the wounds had been. Through the slashes in the jerkin she could see healthy flesh beneath. Only faint scarring remained.

So last night's event hadn't been a dream. Or a nightmare, she reminded herself with a mental shudder.

As if of its own accord, her hand reached toward him, but she paused before embarrassing either of them. "May I?"

"Of course, my lady."

He untied the jerkin's laces and peeled it off. The undertunic came next, revealing his broad, tanned, muscular chest, marred by several old scars.

Thank God Alain couldn't hear her galloping heart.

She concentrated on examining the sites of the burn and sword cut. His flesh felt cold, and the tingling sensation returned at once. Certain that she must be burning him again, she withdrew her hand and rocked back.

"What's wrong, my lady?"

"The heat in my hand—doesn't it hurt you?"

He reached out and pressed her hand between his. They felt even colder than his torso had. "No. This doesn't hurt." His smile seared her heart. "I do not believe you could ever hurt me." He pulled her closer.

His lips were so very tempting . . . but she had to resist them. She tugged her hand free. "You forget that I wield a fierce poker."

He laughed. "Ah, yes. The poker. Quite understandable, my lady, under the circumstances." His expression sobered. "Those men did not hurt you, did they?"

Other than making lewd threats, forcing me to chafe my legs raw, frightening me half to death on several occasions, and touching . . .

"Nay." The strong breeze was raising gooseflesh on his arms, and she handed him the tunic. "Although the one they called Dragon I should like to see roasted on a spit."

Alarm creased Alain's face. "What did he do to you?"

Just what I wish you would do to me, Alain, and so much more . . . she banished the wanton thought with a toss of her head. "He took certain—liberties—in the name of making sure his men had not harmed me."

He crumpled the tunic in both fists. His chest muscles flexed, and she ached to trace them with her fingertips. "I shall kill him. What was he called? Dragon?" His face brightened. "Perhaps Ruaud or I killed him last night. What does this Dragon look like?"

"He'd have been far better dressed than the rabble he leads." She tapped her chin to summon the unwelcome memories. "Not as tall as you, but just as well muscled. He had blond hair plaited into a thick braid, and his lower lip looked as if it had been sliced in twain long ago and had never healed right."

Alain gazed off into the misty distance as if reviewing his own memories. After a few moments, he shook his head and looked at her. "I do not recall any brigands of that description."

She touched his arm, drawing as close to him as she dared. "There should be plenty of time to track him down later." Reluctantly, she let go. "What of yourself? How did you find me so quickly?"

He shrugged the tunic over his shoulders. "Sir Ruaud surrendered us to the men who had come to demand ransom from your father. When we realized this was their lair, we freed ourselves, though I admit we were fortunate to find you here, since our captors had never mentioned where you were being held." He tugged the tunic into place and looked away. "The rest is not fit for my lady's ears."

She knew enough, anyway. "And Sir Ruaud? Is he—"

"I do not know."

And not for want of searching, she surmised, which would explain his shortness of breath when she first saw him. She laid a hand on his shoulder. Her fingers tingled again, but this time she did not let go. "I am sorry, Alain."

Though he kept gazing out over the marsh, his fingers closed over hers and tightened.

His friendship with the knight, his polished manners and speech, fighting skills, and scars—it made less sense than ever that he could be a squire. "Who are you, really?" she whispered.

His back stiffened, and he released her hand to give her a curious look. Finally, he smiled. "A complete fool."

She arched an eyebrow. "Hardly that, if you possessed the wit to locate me. I mean, you must be a knight. Don't bother to deny it. There can be no other reasonable explanation."

He regarded her for a long moment. "Yes. I am a knight."

"But why the disguise?" She recoiled as an unpleasant thought returned. "Sir Robert didn't send you to test my virtue, did he?"

"*Mon Dieu*, no! Never once did that cross his mind."

She felt her brow wrinkle. "How can you be so certain?"

"I have known Sir Robert my entire life." His smile turned enigmatic. "He would never resort to such a ploy."

"But he would send you and Sir Ruaud ahead to look me over, is that it?" Her ire rose on the wings of indignation. "To determine whether I am a worthy match for his lordship?" His smile inverted to dread. "Hah. I am right."

Denying him a chance to reply, she shot to her feet. Her instinct suggested escaping into the maze, but fear of becoming lost in the mist pushed her toward the tower's door. The bolt's heaviness prevented her from locking him out, so she concentrated on making best speed. Pounding footsteps warned her of Alain's pursuit.

He caught her wrist while she was still on the stairs, but she yanked it free and continued up. On the landing outside the upper chamber, she had to pause for air. He joined her before she could escape.

"Please, my lady," he said between breaths. "Let me explain."

"What's to explain? Sir Robert sent you to scout me out, and you agreed. You Normans are a despicable lot. Every last, stinking one of you! I thought I had met one who wasn't." She blinked hard to fight off the welling tears. "I was wrong."

She pulled open the door, fled inside, shut it with a heavy bang, and collapsed, the dam of her emotions bursting.

HER MUFFLED sobs lanced his heart. He worked the handle and gave the door a tentative push. It yielded. Unsure of his reception, he poked his head through and was grieved to see her huddled on the floor amid a scattering of cushions, sobbing as if she had lost her dearest love.

"My lady, I am so sorry." No response. "I never intended to cause you distress." Still no response. "Neither did Sir Robert."

"Sir Robert can go straight to—" The last word suffocated in a pillow, but he knew what she meant.

He winced. But she hadn't told *Alain* where to go, and it gave him a thread of hope. For there could be no mistaking the signals she'd been sending him scant minutes before.

Signals all too easily deflected by "Sir Robert."

Alain hated himself for the emotional mess his foolish deception had caused. Since she had reacted this badly to the story she'd concocted to fit her view of the facts—a story that struck too close to the mark for his comfort—he shuddered to imagine how she would react to the truth.

Perhaps she didn't have to find out.

Emboldened by his resolve, he shouldered into the room and closed the door.

"I truly am sorry, my lady."

She wiped her face on a pillow, sat up, and looked at him frankly. "Sorry—for Sir Robert?"

"No." He crossed the distance and, when she made no protest, sat beside her. "For myself."

"What is that supposed to mean?" she murmured, her eyes glistening like twin pools, cool and inviting.

Wanting nothing more than to lose himself in their depths, he stroked her dove-soft cheek. "It means that"—he drew a breath—"I love you."

She jerked her head aside as if he'd struck her. "How dare you say such a thing?" Her voice trembled, threatening to break. "I am promised to your friend." She squeezed her eyes shut but couldn't contain the escaping tears. "By royal decree, no less."

He caught one with his fingertip and smoothed it away. "We can change that."

"We?" She regarded him with pure scorn. "King William defeated my people and commanded Sir Robert to marry me. We are powerless to change either fact."

"*Au contraire, ma chere.*" In response to her puzzled look, he said, "William cares not who marries whom as long as your people and mine learn to live together in peace. When I explain the situation to him, he will grant his consent, I am certain." An odd expression on her face prompted him to add, half fearing her response, "That is, if you grant your consent first."

With a sigh she rose, walked to the nearest window, and threw open the shutters with such force that it seemed as if she were trying to open a prison door. "Would God it could be that simple, Alain." As he stood to follow her, she said, "I live under a vow that prevents me from marrying you—or any other Norman."

Surprise forced him back a pace. "What? Even Sir Robert?"

She gripped the window casing and leaned her head against her hand. "I shan't disobey the king. I cannot bear to imagine what he would do to my father or to the people living under our protection." Her chin quivered. "Marrying Sir Robert will cause me to break my vow, but I am willing to endure that for the sake of my people."

"What—" He swallowed hard, despising the question but craving the answer. "What sort of vow? Is it to someone you love but cannot marry?"

She uttered a short, mirthless laugh. "Aye." Her free hand crept up to the side of her neck, convulsed a few times in a motion resembling a halfhearted scratch, and fell away. She drew a shuddering breath. "A Norman ambushed my brother and dealt him a mortal wound. On his deathbed, I-I swore—" Her words dissolved into a flood of tears.

"And you swore never to marry a Norman because one of us killed him." He tried to leech the bitterness from his tone but wasn't sure how well he'd succeeded.

Nodding, she turned and sobbed against his chest. He circled his arms around her, sorry for her loss and wishing he could do more to comfort her.

"Alain, I am sorry," she rasped between breaths. "I wish it could be different for us." After her tears had run their course, she dried her face and regarded him earnestly. "But you understand that I cannot dishonor my brother's memory?"

All too well.

Between his mother and his brother, Alain had done enough dishonoring of loved ones' memories to fill a lifetime.

He curled his fingers beneath her chin. "I will speak to the king when he returns to England. He shall not force you to marry Sir Robert or any other Norman. As God is my witness, I promise you that."

Her eyes widened. "You would do that for me? But surely you don't stand that highly in King William's favor?"

"My lady might be surprised to learn how highly." He released her chin, suppressing the sigh born of the certainty that he could never touch her again. "I would count it a privilege and an honor to perform this service for you."

"I do know of a way that would ease your conversation with the king, though I doubt it would make either of us happy." She averted her gaze. "I could wed another man."

Astonishment prompted him to ask, "Who?"

"My cousin, Thane Ulfric." She looked at Alain, chafing her arms as if the mere mention of the man's name had given her a chill. "Second cousin, actually. You met him when you and Ruaud arrived at Edgarburh."

"I recall the meeting." And the emotions it had evoked, which he tried to submerge. "But even second cousins cannot marry without possessing the necessary dispensation."

"He arranged that when he tried to press suit with me a few years ago." Her laugh cut with a bitter edge. "I'm sure that forging a document to present evidence of our preexisting marriage would give him no trouble."

No doubt. "But, Kendra, I—" He ran a hand through his hair. How could he tell her he mistrusted her kinsman more than the devil himself? How could he admonish her for wanting to lie about her marital status while he perpetuated his own massive lie? "I just think that marrying Ulfric—or anyone else—is a bad idea."

HIS STRICKEN look shattered her resolve to remain stoic. "I may not have much choice about that," she said, stepping closer. "But would my lord knight grant me a boon that would enable me to fulfill an altogether different vow?" She slid her hands up his chest, reveling in the feel of his taut muscles beneath the tunic's thin linen.

"Name it, my lady," he said in a husky whisper.

"Please . . ." She stood on tiptoe to reach around his neck and pull his face to hers, drawing a deep breath. "Please kiss me."

He lost no time in honoring her request. Their mouths met, tentatively at first, then harder and more ravenously as their mutual hunger found freedom. Their tongues entwined, locked in a dance far more sublime than any pale dream. She felt the void left by her brother's death beginning, at last, to fill.

So this was why Del had been so insistent that she seek happiness. He knew it would help her heal, God rest his dear soul. She increased the pressure on Alain's lips, and he answered in kind.

Faint shouts forced them to step apart. Alain looked out the nearest window and hurried to each of the others in turn, muttering in French.

"Is it the outlaws? What do you see?"

"Nothing." He spat the word as if blaming it for the interruption. "The surviving outlaws must have returned. Does this tower have someplace to hide where they might not think to look?"

"I believe so."

She snatched the wineskin and food sack and grabbed as many cushions as she could carry. Alain, sword and seax secure at his waist, and similarly burdened at her request, followed her from the chamber.

Chapter 10

EVEN THROUGH THE tower's stout walls, the attackers' commotion sounded louder and more urgent. Kendra all but flew down the stairs; a wonder she didn't trip on her skirts. Alain wished he'd taken the lead but didn't have the faintest idea where she planned to hide.

When they reached the lower chamber, she dropped the pillows and provisions in a corner and began shoving aside a chest. He added his supplies to the pile, secured the door's bolt, and joined her to finish moving the chest. Their actions revealed a small door with a rope handle, which she bade him lift.

It came up after a yank; what he wasn't prepared for was the whine of a hound and the blast of fetid air. Kendra reached inside her food sack and pulled out several dried beef strips. Rather than dropping them straight down, she lowered herself to her belly and flung the offering into the chamber at an angle. The scrabbling of paws told him the dog had found the food.

"Are you sure this is wise? What if this is the animal reputed to be terrorizing the folk of this shire?"

She twisted her neck to regard him. "Would you rather face whoever is outside?"

He conceded her point. "How much of a drop is it?"

"I don't know. That's why I brought those." She spared a nod for the cushions. "Please throw them down there, along with yon pallet." She pointed toward the stained, straw-prickled woolen lump in the corner.

Despite his better judgment, he complied. The items vanished into the shaft's darkness and landed with soft plops.

"I wish we had a torch." He gazed about the chamber. Given time, he could have fashioned one out of the materials at hand, but a fresh spate of shouts, sounding closer than before, convinced him to abandon the notion. "Sit up, dangle your legs over the edge, and raise your arms. I will lower you down as far as I can."

She obeyed but gave him an inquisitive look. "You are coming with me, aren't you?"

"I must defend your escape."

"I nearly lost you once, and it could have killed me. I'd prefer not to go through that again." She folded her arms, her expression unyielding. "If you want me down there, you shall have to push me."

Someone tried the door. Moments later, a rhythmic banging began. Without any way to assess their attackers' numbers, Alain could not even begin to judge his odds of success or Kendra's odds of survival, should he be overcome.

The latter thought prompted him to sit beside her, grasping her hand tightly. As one they jumped into the stinking blackness.

SOMETHING WAS jabbing Kendra's ribs, and something else was panting onto her face.

Alain rolled aside with a grunt, and the poking quit. The hot breath gave way to a wet tongue. She put up a hand to fondle the dog's ears.

The pounding above continued, and she sat up, assessing her condition. Alain helped her stand.

"If you are all right, we must be away. As soon as they break into the tower"—he glanced toward the hole—"they will know where we've gone. Do you know anything about this cavern?"

Kendra shook her head, pressing the back of her hand to her nose to ward off the pervasive smell. She had considered these matters when she had formed her plan, but in spite of the drawbacks, it had seemed to be the best option. Now, with the enemy battering the door, she wasn't so sure.

She began kicking cushions into the shadows. Alain grabbed the pallet and helped to make short work of the task.

Holding hands, they stretched out their free hands as they crept down the corridor, ever mindful of outcroppings and puddles of liquid. After a score of steps, the path branched, with the stench of dog offal and urine much worse to the left. Her heart broke anew for the poor animal, forced to live in its own filth without adequate food, water, light, or exercise. Small wonder it howled so balefully each night.

When she tried to bypass the juncture, Alain stayed put.

"You believe we need to go down there?" The renewed stink obliged her to block her nose again. "I think the fresher air is coming from yon direction." She waved down the main corridor. "And fresh air may lead to a way out of here."

"I agree. But I—"

A crash sounded overhead that could mean only one thing.

Alain handed her their wineskin and food, scooped her off her feet, turned, and strode into the offending corridor. His boots squelched in the muck, and she grimaced.

"What—"

Furious barks and growls, mixed with the intruders' cries of alarm, drowned her protest. Alain bade her to feel for obstructions while he kept to his course, swerving, at her whispered advice, to avoid low-hanging formations. Within a handful of strides, the squelching yielded to the slap of leather on stone. He set her on her feet and nudged her forward.

The human and canine noises in the main corridor, echoing in frightening confusion off the walls of their bolt-hole, convinced her to remain silent. Then it occurred to her why he had chosen this route: no lady would have crossed that filth when the other path seemed to be the better option. She prayed that the outlaws, if they got past the hound, would reach the same conclusion.

Her hands contacted solid rock before her: a dead end. Alain groped around for a few moments and returned to take her hand and pull her beside him, into a narrow recess. She sidled closer and pressed to his body for warmth, she tried to tell herself. Her quickening pulse proclaimed the lie.

The cacophony seemed to draw nearer, and fear sharpened her senses.

One of the echoes sounded like her father's best scout. But what would bring Lofwin here? Had her father sent him to trail her? But that made no sense; how could Lofwin have known where to pick up her trail, unless—she scarcely dared to hope—unless someone in her escort had survived?

As she cocked her head to sort out the jumbled noises, she felt Alain turn and move as if he intended to return to the main corridor.

She laid a hand on his arm. "Nay," she whispered, "nay, please, you cannot—"

He disengaged her hand. "I thought I heard Ruaud."

"Are you certain?" His hesitation spoke volumes. "Alain, please don't go. It could be your imagination. Or a trap." She slipped her hand into his and squeezed. The walls felt as if they were closing in on her. Pressing a hand to her chest, she battled the urge to pant. "Please don't leave me."

Soon the dwindling voices became impossible to distinguish. She hoped he was having similar trouble.

"You are right," he said at length. "I probably imagined his voice." Disappointment leached through his whisper to wrench her heart.

"I'm sure Sir Ruaud is safe." She hoped she sounded more convincing than she felt.

This time he returned her squeeze.

RUAUD HAD to admit that when Alain didn't want to be found, he'd go to heroic lengths to ensure it. Employing a demon cloaked in fur and fangs, however, seemed a bit too much.

Grunting, he hauled himself out of the hole a bare step ahead of the snarling menace.

Lofwin and Garth grabbed him under each arm and helped him regain his footing.

"No good, this." Ruaud spat his disgust into the shaft and faced his allies. "Another way out?"

"Mayhap the others have found a cave entrance on the hillside." Lofwin's countenance looked doubtful as he addressed the other scout. "Wait outside in case they return this way."

"I search there first." Ruaud jerked a thumb toward the stairs. "Join you after."

Garth shoved aside the splintered remains of the door and stepped outside to take up his post. Waldron's chief scout clasped Ruaud's forearm and used the path Garth had cleared.

Ruaud stumped up the spiral staircase, cursing the fight that had caused Alain to spirit Lady Kendra into hiding.

Not that he could blame his friend's caution. That last batch of brigands—he hoped it would prove to be the last— had been the toughest to defeat. His knee was aching like fury now, though in the heat of combat it hadn't troubled him. Still, he'd been grateful to have Lofwin and his men guarding his back, whom he'd found soon after emerging from that Godforsaken swamp.

No, not Godforsaken, he amended, casting his gaze upward to offer a quick apology. Receiving aid in the guise of Waldron's retainers was nothing short of miraculous, even after Lofwin admitted to having begun trailing the Normans soon after their "surrender."

With one prayer answered, one remained.

THEY STOOD, neither moving nor speaking, for a long time after silence had descended. Alain brought all his scouting-honed senses to bear but couldn't detect anything amiss.

He *had* heard Ruaud. What he hadn't been able to ascertain was whether Ruaud had been acting under his own volition, trying to find them, or whether he'd been forced by his captors into the hole to flush out their prey.

But if the outlaws wanted them that badly, why didn't they just kill the dog and come after them? Or was that part of the ruse, to dupe Alain into thinking the exit was safe? Were the outlaws that clever?

Perhaps not this band, but death swiftly visited a knight who underestimated the enemy.

The fist farthest away from Kendra he ground into the rock.

There was no way on this side of hell that he was going to leave her alone unless he could make certain she would be safe.

A familiar, hopeful whine interrupted his musings.

"Our new friend may be telling us it's safe to come out," he said.

Kendra agreed but waited to move until he started forward. When he encountered the muck, he picked her up again to bear her across.

It felt so good, so right to cradle her in his arms.

But he had no right to keep her there against her wishes. There had to be a way to circumvent that accursed vow she'd made, but his wits felt as thick as what he was wading through.

Curbing a sigh, he took one last step to clear the offal and set her down in the main corridor. She dropped to her knees to hug the dog, who rewarded her with a faceful of licks. Alain offered his thanks with a pat to the dog's head but straightened quickly, hearing a faint creaking noise. He'd have dismissed it as the natural sound of the tower settling, but his senses tingled a warning.

They were not alone in this tower.

He grasped her elbow to encourage her to rise.

"Come. We must hurry and find another way out," he said, hoping to avoid alarming her by sounding as calm as possible. "They may return."

"I think you're right." Before rising, she gave the hound a final hug.

They inched into the dark unknown, feeling their way like the newly blind.

For reasons of its own, the dog had chosen to remain. Alain concentrated on trying not to crush Kendra's fingers as he struggled to banish the impression that perhaps their canine friend knew to avoid what lay ahead of them.

RUAUD REACHED the top landing and stared at the closed door, scratching the stubble on his chin. If Alain were guarding Kendra inside, he'd have rigged a trap.

He stepped up to the crack between the door and its frame. "Alain!" No response from within, not that he was expecting any. He tried a different tack. "*C'est moi, mon ami, seulement moi. Viens ici!*"

Still no sound. He tried the handle: unlocked. But when he would have opened the door, the threat of Alain and Kendra being held captive loomed as a distinct possibility.

Other, grimmer possibilities he refused to entertain.

He backed up, drew his sword, and readied it for attack. In one fluid movement, he kicked in the door and lunged into the chamber, sword leveled for business.

No trap, no bodies, nobody.

Discouragement warred with relief.

With the point of his sword, he poked a man-size heap of coverlets lying on the floor, revealing naught but pillows.

Something plain and white caught his eye amidst the opulence. He used his sword to pull it from beneath another coverlet: two generous lengths of bandage. From the lack of bloodstains, he surmised they had been used for some other purpose; binding sprains, perhaps.

He almost missed the other bandages that were so red they blended with the fancy furnishings. His gut twisted as he looked toward the door and saw the spatter trail, its biggest splotch near the threshold. Such severe blood loss didn't bode well for the injured person's chances of survival.

Fraying threads told him these bandages had been torn from something else, perhaps an underdress, unlike the other strips, which had been cut.

Lady Kendra, suffering a sprained ankle, had tried to stanch the flow of Alain's gash? If so, how in hell did she move him? Even in perfect health, with that petite frame of hers, he doubted she could have managed unassisted.

Forehead to fist, Ruaud slumped against the doorframe.

"Alain, where the devil are you?"

He sheathed his sword with a heavy heart and turned to leave the tower.

THE CORRIDOR widened into a large gallery lit by beams shining through holes formed by chinks in the rock. Heaps of gold, silver, and jewels glittered before them. Kendra gasped, half dreading to find the Round Table populated by a slumbering King Arthur and his knights and half disappointed when she didn't.

While she contented herself with standing to bask in the eye-popping sight, filling her lungs with sweet air, Alain examined several objects.

"It isn't enough for them to terrorize farmers and merchants." He held aloft a hefty gold crucifix. "They have looted churches too." Disgust oozed from his tone. "Bishop Odo will be livid."

"But this is Saxon gold. What is it to you, a Norman?"

He set the crucifix down, gave it a slight bow, and faced her, fists on hips. "The king is not deaf to the plight of your people. His regent in charge of southern England, Odo de Bayeux, dispatched Sir Ruaud and me to investigate the complaints and set matters aright." He relaxed his stance and pivoted, shaking his head. "It appears the complaints contain much substance indeed." Stooping, he picked up a large brooch wrought in a distinctive Norman floral design. "And not all of this plunder is Saxon."

"What will you do with this hoard once we get free?" *If we get free* . . . "Claim it for the king?"

An offended look darkened his features. "I will make every attempt to locate the rightful owners, of course."

She laughed in spite of their predicament. "Come, now. Do you believe you can show people this treasure and expect them to claim only what belongs to them? Are you Normans that blind to human nature?"

Irritation flashed across his face. "Regent Odo showed me some of the letters. The lists of stolen items were quite detailed. And there are other ways of testing honesty." He uttered a quick laugh, but she didn't understand the jest. Just as quickly, he sobered. "But of course we cannot do anything while we remain trapped in here."

Kendra couldn't agree more. While Alain searched for the means to climb toward the air holes in the hope of widening them enough to slip through, she searched closer to the ground for a more readily accessible outlet.

Their efforts met with no success before the light fled the chamber. She sank onto the lid of a chest, wishing she had brought the cushions.

At least the dog and its wretched living quarters had seemed to discourage pursuit; small comfort, that. The prospect of being above ground, even if as the outlaws' prisoner, was looking more attractive by the moment.

As the gloom deepened, Alain pulled several kneeling pads from the pile where he'd found the crucifix, along with an altar cloth embroidered with gold threads. He pressed the *Chi Rho* over his heart for a moment, head bowed, before unfurling the cloth over the kneeling pads, which he'd arranged into the shape of a pallet.

"I shall stand watch while you rest," he said.

"Mayhap later. But . . . thank you." His kindness forced tears to her eyes that she prayed he couldn't see, and it was all she could do to keep a quaver from invading her voice. "I—I'm not tired," she lied, squeezing her eyes shut.

"Here, then." She felt the wineskin brushing her arm and opened her eyes to find Alain bent low beside her with his offering. Taking the wineskin with a grateful smile, she shifted over to make room for him atop the chest. "You need to keep up your strength," he cautioned.

As the apple-sweet wine soothed her parched throat, she remembered the coarse but kindly Snake, who had told her the same thing.

That felt like half a lifetime ago.

A long blink checked her tears. She couldn't bear having to explain to Alain why she mourned someone he probably had killed.

He passed her an oatcake, but his hand lingered to clasp hers. "Why did you ask me to kiss you?"

"What? You didn't enjoy it?"

"Very much." His sigh warmed her neck. "I shall not make you break your vow, Kendra. I give you my solemn word as a knight of Normandy and a member of two kings' courts."

"Two kings?" She twisted, wishing she could see his face better. "William and—who else? Surely not Harold?" The implications of such a suspicious pairing of associations made her mind reel.

"I spent my early years in King Edward's court before joining William's cause."

"It still seems strange."

"My mother was a Saxon noblewoman and a member of Edward's London court, but my father was a Norman lord."

She chewed her oatcake as she chewed on his admission. Only half Norman, then . . . so very tempting, but half Norman was still Norman. And she couldn't recant her vow even though her heart pleaded otherwise.

After washing the cake down with another mouthful of wine, she asked, "What does your mother think of your newest allegiance?"

"She doesn't know." His shoulders shifted in a sigh. "Or perhaps she does somehow. She died many years ago," he whispered.

"Oh, Alain." She slipped her arm around his waist and leaned her cheek against his shoulder. "I am sorry. I meant no disrespect."

"I know." His fingers found her chin. "But you haven't answered my question."

"My vow to never marry a Norman was my idea. My brother—" Her voice caught, and she swallowed hard. "With his final breath, he made me promise to seek happiness. I hold that vow just as sacred as the other." It was her turn to sigh, overwhelmed by the anguish of memories. "For a moment, in your embrace, I—I was . . ." Her words collapsed within the trembling of her chin.

"Kendra, *mon amour*, nothing would please me more than to make you happy."

His lips met hers tenderly. She welcomed his touch, nestling her body closer to his. He kissed her harder, and his tongue thrust deeper. While one hand cupped her cheek, the other skimmed toward her breasts, persistently exploring, caressing, arousing . . .

With a supreme effort of will, she stopped him.

She sucked in a breath, suspecting he would not like what she had to say next.

"I cannot bed a man I cannot wed."

"Sir Robert won't—"

She stood and whirled to face him. "Won't what? Won't find out? Hah. Some friend you must be if you believe him to be that stupid." She felt her eyebrows lower as another idea occurred. "Or do you mean that he won't mind if you opened me up for him? Is that the mission he sent you to accomplish?

What do you two take me for, a tavern whore to go spreading my legs for any handsome face to look my way?"

"No, no." The whisper sounded no louder than a breeze whiffling through a meadow. "Good Lord, no."

The abjectness of his tone lanced her anger. Bending, she reached for his face but encountered the backs of his hands. She traced the strong fingers, knuckles, and tendons, awe welling within her. These hands had fought—and killed—for her to keep her safe. And pure.

With little effort, she pried them from his face. "You men aren't the only ones who cleave to honor," she said quietly but firmly. "But if you know of other ways to make me happy . . ."

He took her hand, turned it over, and kissed the palm, sending a tingle up her arm. "I do." He pushed up her sleeve, and his lips brushed the tender flesh from wrist to elbow. Waves of delight coursed through her.

"Show me." The huskiness of her voice betrayed her primal need. An exquisite throbbing assaulted her nethers, and an on-slaught of wet warmth battered her sense of honor. "Please."

HER QUIET plea woke a mindless, ravening hunger that took all his will to control. God in heaven, he wanted her so damned much! But not if she believed that "Sir Alain" would make a whore of her. He stood, grasping her hands.

"There is something I must—"

"Hush." She freed her hands and reached up to pull his face to hers. In the next breath she kissed him, hard, arching her body against his, delivering a silent invitation he couldn't refuse.

He loosened the laces of her bodice. As his fingers slipped beneath the neckline of her underdress and tugged it toward her shoulders, he reveled in the softness of her skin.

Forgive me, Father, for I am about to . . .

About to—what? Sin? How could it be a sin to bring enjoyment to another person? A person who had saved his life? A person who had revived feelings that he'd believed to be long dead? A person for whom he would sacrifice his final breath?

She finished unlacing her bodice and pulled it off. Her belt followed it. He kissed her throat, and she uttered a breathy gasp. Delighted and incited by the sound, he planted more kisses on her neck and the bare ridges of her shoulders. Her breath started coming in slow, soft pants. She wriggled her arms free of all their layers of fabric. The dress and underdress slipped to her waist, and she untied her cloth breastband.

He cradled the delicate flesh and tested her nipples first with his thumbs, then his lips and tongue. Her breathing quickened and she began to sway against him; she seemed as ready as he felt.

But he had to be certain.

He eased to his knees, leaving a trail of kisses down her abdomen and working her dress and underdress past her hips. The fabric slid the rest of the way off and mounded at her feet, leaving only the cloth that bound her loins. His lips continued toward their goal. Her fingers tangled in his hair and kneaded his scalp in time with her hips' shifting. He reached for the knot of her loincloth.

She tensed. Her hands gripped his like a vise.

Though he suspected the answer, he had to ask, "What's wrong?"

She shivered and shook her head. Sighing, she let him go and stooped to retrieve her breastband. "I can't. I'm sorry, but

I—I just can't." She wound the cloth around herself, tied it in place, and picked up the underdress.

"Because of Sir Robert." He shifted off his knees and sat, sighing. The rock floor's chill doused the heat she had ignited within him. "I must confess that I—"

"Not him. Dragon. When his men brought me to him, he insisted on making sure they hadn't harmed me. That insistence . . ."

"Took a form you didn't like." A wave of battle fury shuddered through his body. He clenched his fists to keep it under control.

"Not exactly. I mean, I did not like it at the time; I was his prisoner and terrified of what he would do next. But you—what you were doing just now made me realize . . . I did enjoy it a little." She poked her head and arms through the holes in the underdress and settled it about her with abrupt, angry tugs. "First Dragon, now you. Won't Sir Robert be pleased to have such a whore as me." Sighing harshly, she sat on the cavern's floor, hugged her knees, and bowed her head.

"Kendra, I am Sir Robert," he whispered.

The silence stretched so long that he began to believe she hadn't heard him. As he opened his mouth to repeat his confession, she tipped her head back and loosed a peal of laughter that echoed throughout the chamber.

"A tempting fantasy . . . but no. You are Sir Lancelot, and I am the faithless whore Guinevere. It shall end as badly for us as it did for them, I think." She pivoted toward him and laid her hand on his cheek. "But I do thank you for making me feel loved. Cherished. And happy, even if only for the briefest while."

Alain drew a deep breath and held it as he pondered how to respond. But protesting was pointless as long as he bore no proof of his identity to show her. Expelling his breath through pursed lips, he wrapped his arms around her. She leaned into his embrace. In moments her breathing softened and slowed, and her limbs felt leaden against him. He gently moved her onto the makeshift bed, hating that he had no right to join her there.

In two languages he cursed himself for the fool he was. As he rose and groped toward the cavern's entrance, he resolved to see Kendra safely home and prove his identity to her.

And to accept whatever consequences befell him as a result.

Chapter 11

GRUNTING AND SWEATING, the next morning, Alain heaved the chest into place atop the others and stepped back to survey his idea.

"Will it work?" Raw desperation darkened Kendra's tone.

Gazing at her tense face and disheveled hair and garments, he grieved to see the toll her ordeal had taken upon her angelic beauty. He swept an errant golden lock from her cheek, and she leaned into his touch. "I hope so."

He climbed to the top of the stack, which put him chest high with the hole he'd chosen to attack. With the seax he poked into the crevices around the hole and pried loose a few fist-size rocks. Not a bad start, but even if he managed to enlarge it downward, the much shorter Kendra would still need help to reach it.

Concentrate on overcoming one obstacle at a time, he reminded himself as he set to work.

They fell into a routine, with him dislodging rocks and her catching and stacking them, working as silently as possible to reduce the risk of being overheard.

Minutes blended into hours with the mind-numbing repetition. He looked down at the pile and felt a surge of satisfaction at how large it had grown. Testing the hole's width with his hands, he judged it a tight squeeze for him, though she ought to make it easily. He motioned for her to come up.

To his surprise, she held up a hand, retrieved the near-empty food sack, and scurried from the chamber. Shrugging, Alain set about digging out a few more chunks. She returned with the hound in tow, using the sack twisted into a lead. At the gallery's entrance, the dog braced its feet, whining.

"Come on, you silly beast," she coaxed. "Don't you see we mean to free you?"

She opened her hand to display the last strip of dried beef and waved it before the dog's nose. When it stretched to take the food, she stepped back a pace, murmuring words of encouragement. The dog whined again, but Kendra remained insistent.

When hunger overcame fear, the hound entered the chamber. Kendra kept backing up, and the dog kept pursuing, until she reached the stack of chests. The dog sat before her as she tore off a piece and offered it in the palm of her hand. With another piece, she encouraged the hound to stand with his paws braced on a chest in the stack.

Realizing her intent, Alain grasped the dog to haul it up, feeling a rush of panic as the chests shifted and his balance faltered. But the dog must have sensed its opportunity and found purchase for its paws, scrabbling to the top. Alain boosted the animal into the hole and watched it wriggle to freedom.

Frowning, he turned an ear toward the hole, trying to discern whether the dog was barking at intruders or expressing its joy in being released. He decided on the latter and signaled Kendra to ascend.

Her smile could have lit the cavern.

Upon tucking her skirts into her belt, she followed the hound's path. Alain thrust out his hand to help her up the rest of the way, which she accepted with obvious gratitude.

His hands settled on her waist in preparation for lifting her to the hole, and he paused. Once they left this cave, he would have to make good on his vow to free her from the king's command to marry Sir Robert de Bellencombre.

It was the last thing on earth he wanted to do, and yet after having failed to fulfill promises to those he loved, failing in this task simply was not an option.

He made the mistake of gazing too deeply into her alluring eyes, and a wave of longing crested and broke within his heart. Heedless of propriety, he sampled her sweet lips one last time, a kiss she returned with more passion than he deserved.

As she broke contact, unmistakable pain flashed across her face—pain he had caused her by being too bold, too male, and, ultimately, too Norman.

To say nothing of his being too deceptive and too downright stupid. Claws of self-loathing rent his soul.

"Alain? What have I done?"

He shook his head. "Nothing."

I have wronged you, dearest Kendra, by deceiving you and loving you and wanting you so much that I ache to even look at you. But he couldn't voice that confession, not here, not now; not ever.

After turning her to face the rock, he gripped her waist and lifted her into the world where they never could be anything beyond polite acquaintances.

If giving her up was the right choice to make, he mused wretchedly as he watched her crawl through the hole, then why did he feel as if he had committed an unpardonable sin?

KENDRA EMERGED and stood, arms outspread, yearning to proclaim her freedom to the four winds.

Mindful that she and Alain wouldn't be free until they quit this awful place and mindful that any noise could draw unwanted attention, she refrained.

Of the hound there remained no sign, though she wished it Godspeed and a belated, though no less heartfelt, thanks.

The sound of scraping made her bend down to see Alain attempting to widen the hole. His blade removed no more than a few pebbles.

"Will you be able to make it?"

"I hope so," came his grim reply.

With a grunt, he hoisted himself into the hole and began pushing himself through. But before his broad shoulders could win free, they stuck fast.

Horrified, she knelt and clawed at the rock, trying to dislodge stones from the outside, but her fingers were useless against the solid mass.

She dusted her hands with a handful of fine, dry dirt to improve her grip, grabbed Alain's arms at the wrists, braced one foot against the rock face, gritted her teeth, and tugged for all she was worth.

Wonder of wonders, his shoulder moved!

So did her foot. She lost her grip and began to fall, flailing her arms in a desperate bid to keep her balance.

A pair of sturdy arms encircled her from behind. She screamed.

"Well, you do seem to need rescuing after all, dear cousin," said a familiar voice as he pushed her upright.

"Nay, I do not." She cared far less about how Ulfric had learned of her plight than about freeing the man she loved. "But Alain does. Help me, please!"

"Just 'Alain,' Kendra? You seem to have become altogether too familiar with your visiting Norman squire."

His patronizing tone raised her ire. "What I choose to call him is irrelevant, Ulfric. What is relevant is that he needs assistance."

"Thank you most kindly, Lady Kendra, but no."

Grimacing, Alain forced himself through the hole, tearing his tunic and scraping his shoulders. She longed to learn whether her healing touch still worked, but with Ulfric in attendance, she didn't dare try. From behind Alain came a muffled crash, doubtless from his having kicked over the stack of chests.

Ulfric cocked an eyebrow. "What was that?"

Straightening, Alain brushed off his attire, ignoring the scrapes, his demeanor cool. "You would never believe what we have endured, Thane Ulfric."

"Try me, squire."

She stepped between them lest they both break their foolish necks by brawling on the slope. "Tales of our ordeal can wait until after Sir Alain"—she directed a warning look at Ulfric—"and I have recovered."

"Sir Alain, now, is it?" Ulfric's grin exuded arrogance. "Did the bandit chief knight you? You seem to be wearing his colors."

Alain glared at Ulfric. "I trust it is safe for the Lady Kendra to depart?"

"Quite safe. You and Sir Ruaud seem to have done a commendable job of obliterating this band of troublemakers."

"Sir Ruaud? You have seen him?" She could hear the hope in Alain's tone.

Ulfric stroked his chin, shaking his head. "I cannot say that I have."

Kendra shot her cousin an inquisitive glance. "Are you certain, Ulfric?"

He draped an arm about her shoulders. "Unless one of my men has found him among the corpses while we have been conversing, no. Sir Ruaud is not here."

She got the distinct impression that Ulfric was lying, but why would he mislead Alain about his friend? With nothing more solid than suspicion, however, she couldn't pursue the matter.

"Come, my dear," Ulfric continued, steering her down the path. "Thornhill shall be at your disposal while you recover."

"Sir Alain too?"

Ulfric tossed a glance back at Alain, who was following them, head bowed as if he was making a one-way trip to the gallows. "You too are well come."

It grieved Kendra to observe that the invitation did little to lift Alain's spirits.

ULFRIC'S ESTATE couldn't come close to Edgarburh in size, but in luxury Thornhill compensated for the lack of acreage. Vast tapestries hung from every wall, and Alain could scarcely take a step without bumping into an expensive chair, table, bench, or chest. Much of it reminded him of the bower where he'd found Kendra, and it awakened his suspicions.

No. His suspicions had awakened when Ulfric had so conveniently appeared to keep Kendra from tumbling down the hillside. Alain hadn't stopped berating himself for allowing her to endanger herself for his sake.

And yet her willingness to do so, with no apparent thought for her own peril, touched him more deeply than a thousand of her glorious kisses ever could.

He sighed at the realization that memories of her would have to sustain him for the rest of his life.

"Are you ill, Sir Alain?"

He would have laid even odds that Ulfric's solicitousness had been feigned for Kendra's benefit.

"I thank you for your concern, Thane Ulfric, but I shall live."

"Indeed." Ulfric's predatory grin made the hairs on Alain's arms prickle.

Their host clapped twice, and servants trooped in through doorways that led to side corridors or chambers. Ulfric entrusted Kendra into the care of several handmaidens, who spared shy glances and giggles for Alain before ushering their charge from the hall. He felt a wrenching in his chest, as though his heart had gone with her.

Ulfric assigned the remaining manservant to Alain, giving him instructions to implement Alain's every wish and to provide fresh clothing fit for Thornhill's "noble Norman guest." On Ulfric's lips, the phrase sounded like an epithet.

"Your generosity is most overwhelming, Thane Ulfric."

"I would be a poor host to do anything less," said the thane, "for a guest who will be leaving so soon."

Alain cocked his head. "Am I?"

"You should return to Edgarburh with news of Kendra's rescue. Her father must be quite worried."

"True enough. But she is in no condition to travel."

"That's why she shall stay here for as long as is needful."

Needful for whom? Alain fought to retain his civility.

Upon pondering the thane's suggestion, he decided it made sense. No doubt Waldron would be relieved to hear of his daughter's rescue, and from Edgarburh Alain could dispatch a report about the outlaws to Regent Odo. There would be sufficient time for Alain to confess his misdeeds to Kendra once she arrived; no need to rush that eventuality. "Then if I may have the loan of one of your horses?"

"For such a happy mission, of course." Again that predatory grin dominated the thane's face. "But first you must join us for our midday meal." When Alain opened his mouth to protest, Ulfric raised a hand. "I insist."

INSIDE THE large, well-appointed guest chamber, which was situated too close to Ulfric's quarters for Kendra's liking, the handmaids' inane chatter and giggling showed no signs of letting up, and it was threatening to drive her mad.

What hurt the worst were questions and speculations directed to her about Alain.

On all but the most basic questions, she demurred. It wouldn't be seemly to cast the impression of knowing too much about someone who by all rights should be a stranger.

And yet in the short time they had spent together, she had learned enough to realize . . . nay.

What she felt for the man who had conquered her heart was nothing short of selfish desire. Indulging any further wouldn't be fair to Del's memory, and it wouldn't be fair to Sir Robert. For, despite Alain's claims, she needed to steel herself for the possibility that he might not succeed in convincing the king to belay his command.

Most importantly, it wouldn't be fair to Alain.

By this time, the maidservants had finished bathing her, dressing her, applying cherry juice to her lips and crushed ochre powder to her cheeks, and combing the tangles from her damp hair. With a light veil settled over her head and secured with a slim gold circlet, she was beginning to feel human again.

If indeed *human* could describe a woman who had lost the volition to love any other man.

She rose from the stool and dismissed the women with her thanks. Alone at last, she closed the door and drifted back toward the bed. Wrapping an arm around the dark oak bedpost, she blinked hard to will away the welling tears.

The door opened with a creak, and she heard tottering footsteps cross the floor, but she didn't bother to acknowledge her visitor.

"Well come, my poppet!"

The familiar, aged voice made her turn. Ethel, Ulfric's old nurse and a favorite from Kendra's previous visits to Thornhill, was setting a tray upon a side table. Tendrils of steam curled from the mug, which doubtless held one of Ethel's herbal concoctions.

She couldn't reach the woman fast enough and favored her with a long embrace. As Ethel patted her back, Kendra was reminded of her mother, and her sobs erupted.

"My dearest poppet, you have had a bad turn these past few days, haven't you?"

Ethel gently but firmly disengaged Kendra and pulled a clean cloth from her sleeve. While Kendra used it to dry her eyes, Ethel inspected her with the intensity of an army commander.

"You don't know the half of it, Ethel."

Smiling enigmatically, Ethel grasped the mug and pressed it into Kendra's hands. "I do know that I see a lovely young woman in love."

Kendra snorted and took a long swallow. The warm, honeyed liquid soothed her from the inside out. "An impossible love. A love that's best forgotten." She took another swallow and stared into the mug. "If I can."

"Listen to old Ethel, poppet." She laid a cool, leathery hand on Kendra's arm. "Passion fades, but if you well and truly love this man, then no matter what happens, you never will stop loving him."

It confirmed what Kendra had suspected. "Then so much the worse for us both, Ethel, for we can never wed."

As if the tisane had loosened her tongue, she proceeded to explain why.

"Ah, poppet, love will find a way. It always does."

A lad entered with word that the midday meal was ready to be served, and that Thane Ulfric had requested the honor of Kendra's presence.

She followed the servants from the room, hoping with all her heart that Ethel was right.

EVEN MORE so than being in the midst of battle, astride his warhorse and bedecked with every knightly trapping under heaven, Alain felt like a target. He tugged at the stiff, high collar of the crimson velvet tunic the servant had brought, wishing he could yank the accursed thing off and knowing that to do so would declare to his host an insult Alain wasn't prepared to defend.

Forebodings redoubled when he considered this meal. His every instinct warned him away, and yet his failure to attend wasn't a viable option either.

At least this event should afford him one final opportunity to see Kendra.

A page, dressed in a linen tunic the same shade as Alain's but featuring a gray wolf snarling upon the chest, entered to announce the meal. The lad bowed, but his self-discipline yielded to several long moments of gaping at what was probably the first Norman knight he'd ever seen.

"We Normans do not eat children." Alain broke into a grin. "Well, perhaps only the naughtiest ones. But I shall tell you a secret," he whispered, drawing the lad closer. "Children do not taste very good."

That won a chuckle and a crooked grin. After another bow, the page scampered from the room.

The manservant, burdened with the remains of Alain's outlaw disguise and undergarments, gave Alain an approving nod and asked if he needed aught else. Alain declined, thanking him. The servant bowed as best he could and left.

What Alain needed was a means to marry Kendra without forcing her to foreswear her vow. And under the roof of his chief rival, he stood even farther from solving this conundrum.

With a final tug on the collar and offering a swift, silent prayer that he would survive whatever Ulfric might be devising, he strode from the chamber.

His host had spared no expense, Alain observed upon entering the hall. Fine linen sporting the gray wolf rearing on a crimson background adorned the high table. The lower tables were covered in coarser material bearing the same colors and lupine design. Ropes of ivy festooned every table and looped between the ornate brass wall sconces. Peering closer at one of the garlands, Alain noticed tiny purple flowers nestled among the leaves. Silver platters and gorgeous red blown-glass goblets adorned the high table, complemented by matching pewter and less finely wrought glassware throughout the rest of the hall.

Such preparations required several days to get everything scrubbed and ready. Alain searched his memory to determine whether this could be a holy feast day and failed. His suspicions ratcheted up another notch.

It made him seethe at how neatly Ulfric had maneuvered him into agreeing to depart before he could learn more.

A servant approached to conduct him to his assigned seat at the high table, a chair not much less ornate than the one belonging to the hall's master.

Out of deference to his absent host, Alain remained standing behind his chair, as did those assigned to the lower tables, whom he judged to be members of Ulfric's fyrd and their wives. Surrounded by the plethora of crimson banners, tunics, dresses, tabards, and table coverings, Alain felt less like a target than a member of the thane's household.

He preferred to be a target.

A pair of heralds stepped inside the hall's main doors. During the ensuing trumpet flourish, Alain gaped at the sheer ostentation as Thane Ulfric appeared, standing framed in the doorway, with Kendra hooked on to his left arm.

God, what a vision!

Her crimson gown—the exact hue of Ulfric's surcoat, though devoid of the wolf design—enhanced the high color of her cheeks. Tinged with a hint of pink, like the blushing dawn, her pale veil did its best to cover her golden locks, which had been brushed till they fairly glowed in the torchlight. Her eyes remained lowered as she and a beaming Ulfric strode toward the dais, but when she chanced to glance up, her gaze locked to Alain's.

She smiled briefly, sending a thrill through his soul.

Feeling Ulfric's glare boring into him, he restrained his response to the barest twitch of his lips.

"Before we begin the meal," Ulfric addressed the entire company, "I have a presentation to make."

At the thane's signal, the same page who'd visited Alain's chamber stepped forward bearing an object hidden in the valley of a plump pillow. The page marched to where Kendra was standing, in front of the table, and dropped to one knee, lifting the pillow.

Alain tightened his jaw. If Ulfric thought for one moment that he could propose marriage—

"Lady Kendra, I believe this is yours," Ulfric said.

He reached toward the pillow and withdrew a length of black cord. A slim silver box swung from the bottom of the loop. Ulfric held it aloft for all to see.

Kendra gasped, eyes wide.

"Wh-where did you find this?" She cupped her hand under the trinket, and Ulfric dropped it onto her palm.

"My men recovered it from one of the outlaws." Ulfric laid his hand upon her arm. "He shall not trouble you or anyone else ever again."

That had to be Wart, Alain thought regretfully, the only one of his captors who'd seemed to be an otherwise decent soul fallen in with the wrong company. Alain had searched the bodies of the other two for Kendra's locket after Wart had escaped.

She seemed not to have heard Ulfric, for she'd busied herself with opening the case.

An anguished wail pierced the ambient chatter.

"What have you done?" she cried to Ulfric. "Where is it?"

Ulfric gave her a helpless look. "What do you mean?"

But the only coherent words she could utter were, "'Tis gone! Lost! Forever lost!"

The open locket clattered to the flagstones. Tears spilling down her cheeks, she fled from the hall.

When Alain surged to follow her, a hand clamped around his arm and yanked him back. Alain spun free, glaring.

Ulfric raised both hands, palms outward. "I was merely trying to protect my cousin from suffering further distress."

Alain itched to point out that Ulfric was the one causing her distress but instead elected to exercise diplomacy. "She wishes to know what became of the contents of her locket, and she deserves to hear the truth from a witness."

Without waiting for Ulfric's response, he scooped up the locket and quit the hall as fast as propriety permitted.

Chapter 12

The pounding of her feet as she ran down the corridor intensified the pounding in her head. She found the right door, yanked it open, dashed through the antechamber, slammed the inner door, and collapsed facedown on the bed, sobbing.

"Poppet? What ails you, child?" Ethel's voice drifted through from the other room. Before Kendra could reply, she heard heavy footsteps enter the antechamber. "My lord, Lady Kendra cannot receive visitors," Ethel said sternly. "Please leave at once."

"Good woman, I apologize for the intrusion. But I believe Lady Kendra will want to hear the tidings I bring."

She rolled over and sat up, drying her face with the sleeve of her underdress. Mustering her courage, she crossed the room and opened the inner door. "Sir Alain may stay, Ethel."

"Aye, my lady." Ethel smiled and stepped out of Alain's path but did not leave the chamber.

Alain strode forward until he stood a pace from Kendra, proffering the locket. "Its contents are safe with your father, my lady." He knotted the cord's cut ends.

She bent her neck in an invitation for him to slip it on. His fingertips brushed her skin, leaving a fiery trail that snaked down to the pit in her stomach.

"Many thanks, good sir knight," she murmured, biting her lip to quell her rampaging emotions. "The relic this contained means a great deal to me."

When she looked up, she noticed the earnestness of his gaze. "I presume you plan to rest at Thornhill a while yet, Lady Kendra. Would you like me to retrieve it for you?"

His suggestion presented a tempting offer, but if fate was determined to condemn her to a lifetime without him, then the sentence may as well start sooner rather than later. "I thank you for your kind offer, Sir Alain, but I cannot in good conscience keep you from your other duties."

And, she thought glumly, it would just postpone the inevitable.

He cocked an eyebrow. "Other duties?"

"Finding Sir Ruaud and finishing the regent's mission."

"Ah." His smile, regretful yet affectionate, caused her heart to flutter. When he reached for her hand and raised it to his lips, she thought she might faint from the intensity of her longing. "My lady makes me forget all else while I stand in her glorious presence."

"My bri—my cousin had best not make you forget that you are leaving, Sir Alain."

Countenance darkening, Alain released her hand to turn toward Ulfric, who had shouldered past Ethel to stand in the center of the antechamber.

For a long moment, the two men faced off like a pair of bucks readying for the charge.

"Ulfric is right." Kendra glided between them. "If you leave now, Sir Alain, you will have ample daylight to begin your search for Sir Ruaud. Mayhap someone in Glastonbury has seen him. He is not an easy man to miss."

"And I have already ordered a horse to be saddled and provisioned for you," Ulfric said. "It would be a pity for you to miss the fine meal that was prepared today. If you are finished here, I shall escort you to the stables."

"Thane Ulfric, you have been more than kind." Alain bowed, but not before Kendra saw distrust flare in his eyes. Straightening, he faced her. "Fare you well, my lady." Although his face remained impassive, the muscles around his eyes tightened with unmistakable anguish.

"God's speed to you, Sir Alain, in all your travels," she murmured, thankful that her voice didn't betray her.

After Alain left the antechamber, trailed by Ulfric, she jammed a fist to her mouth to stifle the welling sob. The door swung to with a thump, and her sentence began.

The hand that came to rest upon her forearm startled her.

"Handsome, courtly . . . virile too, if I don't miss my guess," Ethel said. Kendra couldn't prevent the rush of heat to her cheeks, sparked by the vivid memory of Alain's caresses. Ethel's grin displayed pure mischief. "Child, you are three kinds of fool if you insist on banishing him from your life."

By "him," she presumed Ethel did not mean Ulfric.

"Aye." It came out more a sigh than a word as she collapsed upon a nearby chair. "But I am betrothed to another man. Until that fact changes, I know not what else to do."

Ethel stooped to grasp Kendra's hand, the one Alain had kissed. As Ethel's fingers touched Kendra's palm, the woman's eyebrows lowered. After a moment, the look of puzzlement grew into a knowing one.

"Have faith, poppet." She skimmed her wrinkled fingertips over Kendra's knuckles, taking care to avoid the skin that Alain's lips had touched. "Have faith in the power and magic"—Ethel winked—"of true love."

She gazed into the woman's bright black eyes, which sparkled with ageless wisdom. In that moment, she found her heart believing in Ethel's words, in spite of what her head insisted upon telling her.

PLODDING ALONG the road to Glastonbury—little more than a cart track winding through the wooded hills, rolling pastures, and fruitful grain fields—Alain felt like more of a target than ever. He drew curious stares from every company of pilgrims he passed. Not only was he still dressed in the bright crimson tunic, but Ulfric had gifted him with a fox-trimmed cloak and one of the best mounts in his stables.

That issue, however, did not absorb Alain's attention.

Kendra had rejected his implicit offer to see her. In so doing, she had rejected him.

And yet he couldn't have mistaken the love he'd seen glistening in her eyes during their final moments together.

She loved a lie, he reminded himself, a lie of his own devising. A lie he must set to rights before he could claim her hand and heart. A lie that scorched his soul.

Not only had he hurt her, but his ruse probably had resulted in the death of his closest friend. For if Ulfric had spoken the truth when he claimed not to have seen Ruaud, then chances were slim that he'd been seen alive by anyone else.

Yearning for a modicum of peace and forgiveness, Alain nudged the horse into a canter toward the abbey they had passed earlier that morning, en route to Thornhill.

If peace and forgiveness eluded him within those sanctified walls, at least he could ask to swap Ulfric's garb for something less conspicuous.

Halfway to his destination, along a deserted section of the track, a hurtling streak of midnight fur ambushed him. His horse shied, whinnying, as the hound he and Kendra had freed from its underground kennel sprang from the bushes, barking with obvious pleasure.

"Down, sir!" Alain admonished the hound, who obeyed with surprising alacrity. After bringing his horse under control, he dismounted, tied the reins to a branch, removed the saddlebags, and walked over to stroke the dog's head. "I am glad to see you too." The dog stretched his nose toward the saddle packs. "Ah, hungry, are we, lad?"

Alain opened one of the bags, first finding a bulging wineskin, which he pulled out and set beside him. He reached in again and withdrew a linen parcel containing a loaf of warm, fragrant bread. The dog sniffed it and backed off a pace, growling. Alain smelled the loaf. Its faintly musty odor reminded him of the lethal meadow saffron. He put the bread aside and repeated the process with a bundle of apples and several juicy slices of roast pork. The hound refused to consider the apples, but when he got to the pork, he sat, threw back his head, and howled plaintively.

A group of pilgrims, walking up from behind Alain, cast uneasy glances at the dog and hurried past, disappearing around a bend in the road.

His stomach rumbling, Alain wanted to howl too.

Sampling whatever Ulfric had put into the wineskin was out of the question.

"It appears we shall have to forage elsewhere." He threw the tainted food, as well as the wineskin and saddlebags, into the brush. The dog whined, sidling closer, and Alain scratched him behind the ears. Tongue lolling, the dog nuzzled Alain's hand. "I'm sorry I have nothing to give you, but I do thank you for saving my life."

The dog favored him with a lick that coaxed a smile to his lips as he wiped his cheek on his sleeve.

The animal's presence reminded him of Kendra, and he groped inside his pouch for the packet containing the lock of her hair that he'd found en route to rescuing her. His fingers drew out not one packet but two. Thinking he'd retrieved some herbs by mistake, he unwrapped the packets.

Both contained a lock of hair.

One was Kendra's as Alain fondly remembered it: glossy and golden. The other, much shorter lock, also blond, had a thin, brittle quality.

When the dog began nosing the packets, Alain folded them up and stowed them in his pouch, berating his slow wits.

The other swath of hair had to be the item missing from Kendra's locket, which Alain had watched the outlaws desecrate. He recalled that her father had slipped him a small packet before he and Ruaud had "surrendered;" this had to have been it, he reasoned.

He hoped the lock was from a family member rather than a beloved suitor.

No, not a suitor, unless he had misread the signals she had been arrowing his way.

Hair from her murdered brother, perhaps?

Whatever its origin, if Waldron had intended for Alain to use the token as a means of winning Kendra's favor, it was too late to avail himself of the opportunity. Kendra never wanted to see him again. She had made that all too clear.

He pounded the ground with his fist, making the dog jump to his feet. As Alain rose, so did his determination to carry out Waldron's implicit command to return Kendra's treasure to her.

But not while traipsing across the countryside, half starved and looking like an archery butt.

Before untying the horse, he checked each hoof for stones and loose shoe nails. Upon finding no problems there, he loosened the girth and removed the saddle and blanket, searching for burs, bits of straw, or anything else that might cause the horse distress. The mare stood patiently, mouthing grass and swatting flies with her tail. At one point, she swung her head around as far as the reins allowed, gazing at Alain as if to insist he was worrying for no good reason.

Only after he had finished examining the tack would he concede that perhaps the mare might be right.

Saddled, mounted, and moving onward once again, he was glad his canine ally had chosen to accompany him, though not always at his side. At intervals, the dog would veer off the path after a rabbit or bird, baying with joyous abandon, returning before Alain had traveled too far.

"What shall I name you?" he asked the hound between one of those forays, when he had dismounted to rest the horse. The dog's towering, majestic appearance inspired an idea. "What think you of *Seigneur Noir*?" Seated beside Alain, the hound cocked his head as if in confusion. Chuckling and fondling the dog's ears, he explained, "It means 'Black Lord.' You do deserve the title, though I admit it's a mouthful. *Noir* should suffice." He repeated the name several times, and the hound answered with an agreeable bark.

After getting under way, he caught sight of the abbey church's soaring walls within the hour, as the nones bells began to toll.

The lightness of spirit sparked by Noir's friendship yielded to the somber recollection of his purpose for choosing the church as his first destination.

Outside the town of Glastonbury, he passed the biggest encampment of pilgrims he'd ever seen. Had this been Normandy, he might have fallen in with these folk.

But the solace he sought did not exist in a crowd.

He arrived at the abbey's gates and explained his pilgrimage to the porter, who welcomed him and Noir and held the bridle while Alain dismounted. Conversationally, Alain remarked upon the pilgrims' camp, for he noticed far fewer visitors at the abbey.

"A pilgrims' encampment, sir knight?" The porter's squint gave him a befuddled look. "Ah, yes. They must be assembling for the feasts of Saint Peter, Saint Paul, and the First Roman Martyrs, though it seems a mite early for folks to be arriving already." Alain quirked an eyebrow upward. "The feast of the apostles Peter and Paul isn't for another six days, and First Martyrs' is the day after," the porter explained. He slapped his forehead and rolled his eyes. "Ah, what am I thinking? Tomorrow is John the Baptist's day, so the early ones probably have arrived for that. You will stay for High Mass tomorrow too, won't you, good sir?"

Although Alain suspected that the monk had tagged him as a wealthy benefactor, thanks to Ulfric's gift, he said, "Lord willing."

Upon Alain's request, the porter imparted directions to the stables. The path led past a tree the porter claimed had grown from a cutting of the original that had sprung from Joseph of Arimathea's staff. Leading the horse and hound, Alain passed the gnarled, haw-laden, and otherwise unremarkable tree without pausing to consider the legendary spiritual connection. He found the stables and entrusted both animals into the groom's care. Noir seemed content to curl in the straw for a nap.

Some part of Alain wished he could join the dog.

As a man in a daze, he followed the strains of soulful chanting toward the main church and slipped in through one of the small side doors.

By this time, the office of nones was almost over, but that didn't prevent him from kneeling and bowing his head. Guilt assaulted him from many angles: old matters, such as his failure to protect his brother, as well as the newer issues of deceiving Kendra and getting Ruaud killed.

He remained long after the chanting had been replaced by the rustling of the monks rising to leave.

"As I live and breathe—Alain!"

He jerked his head up.

A grinning Ruaud was standing before him, clad in a plain tunic and trews. Alain, grateful beyond measure, grasped Ruaud's forearm to haul himself to his feet.

Together they genuflected toward the altar and left by the same side door Alain had used. He resisted the urge to question Ruaud's behavior, but after they stepped outside, he could no longer contain his curiosity.

"What in heaven's name are you doing here, on a—what?" Alain took a moment to recall how many days he'd been held captive. "A Saturday afternoon? You, who would rather darken the doorway of a tavern than a church, even on Sunday mornings? Did those outlaws scare you into taking vows?"

Ruaud's paunch-shaking laugh was a joy to hear. "This attire was the only garb the abbey's wardrobe master could find to fit me, for the outlaw's gear got shredded during the fight." His expression sobered. "But I am fulfilling a promise. The good Lord does answer prayers."

"For me?" Alain couldn't disguise his surprise.

"And the Lady Kendra. Is she all right?"

"Yes." Alain snorted. "Somewhat. At present, she lodges with her cousin—and my chief rival."

"And how, pray, did you permit that to happen?"

Alain's stomach rumbled. "It's a long story, and I'm sorely in need of meat and drink first. Meat and drink that won't kill me."

Ruaud shot him an inquisitive glance as a small group of monks strolled by, but Alain gave a slight shake of his head.

"Come, then, my friend. The abbey boasts a fine and decently private guesthouse for visiting nobility." As Ruaud turned toward the building, he plucked at the shoulder of Alain's tunic. "I trust the story includes how you came by this finery?"

"Only if you tell me how you grew piety overnight."

"Done." Ruaud chuckled.

They reached the guesthouse door, which opened onto a spacious common room furnished with several tables and benches, three sideboards stacked with pewter plates and tankards, and a large hearth laid with a heap of glowing embers. A steaming cauldron hung from a rod wedged between the hearthstones, creating a heady apple-cinnamon aroma that was making Alain's stomach complain even more.

At this hour, the room stood empty, presumably because the other guests had not yet returned for the evening.

A monk wearing a stained apron over his habit approached Ruaud and Alain as they entered, greeting Ruaud by name and giving Alain a respectful nod. Ruaud introduced Alain and explained their needs in what Alain couldn't fail to notice was vastly improved English. Alain added his request for a plain tunic, offering the fine crimson one, as well as the fox-trimmed cloak, as payment for his bed and board.

The monk acknowledged Alain's generosity with profuse thanks, eyed him as if taking his measure, executed a bow, and left through a back door, returning a few moments later with a tunic similar to Ruaud's lying folded across his palms. Alain accepted the garment with thanks. The monk conducted him outside and up the staircase to Ruaud's chamber, while Ruaud stayed in the common room. Alain made quick work of stripping off Ulfric's gifts and passing them to the monk, who bowed again and departed to allow Alain to finish dressing.

As the undyed linen settled about his torso, he couldn't deny the feeling that he had shed a death mark.

"My God, but it is so good to see you!" Ruaud exclaimed upon Alain's return to the common room.

Alain smiled at Ruaud's seat selection, near the rear of the room, where they could enjoy an unimpeded view of the main door with their backs guarded by the wall.

Some habits did indeed die hard.

"I didn't take that long to change, did I?"

"You know what I mean."

"Indeed. And I cannot begin to tell you how glad I am to see you, Ruaud."

"So, what happened to you back on the Tor?"

"The what?"

"Glastonbury Tor. It's what the locals call that hill where the outlaws built their lair. Were you and Lady Kendra imprisoned in that tunnel? You must have heard us calling you, even over the infernal noise of that devil-dog."

"The dog acted to protect us. So that was you. I thought so, but Kendra feared a trap." Ruaud's statement prompted Alain to ask, "What do you mean, 'us'? Who was with you?"

The monk approached their table carrying a pair of trenchers piled with bread, cheese, roasted chicken, and stewed, spiced apples balanced across one arm, and a pitcher of ale and two flagons tucked under the other. Ruaud and Alain helped the man unburden himself, and he filled the flagons, leaving the pitcher on the table before departing to attend a large group of richly caparisoned Saxon guests that had just arrived.

Alain raised his flagon to celebrate finding Ruaud, and took a long pull.

"Thane Waldron sent a scouting party to track us."

Alain nodded. "That explains why I felt as if we were being watched—and not just by our captors. Where are Waldron's men now? And what became of the rest of the outlaws? How badly did you get hurt?"

Laughing, Ruaud held up both hands in mock surrender. "Toenails of God, Alain, even in French you talk too fast. You eat while I talk."

Alain was happy to comply, and he began demolishing the first good meal he'd eaten in half a week.

After swilling more ale, Ruaud said, "Waldron's men are dispersed throughout the town, seeking word of their lady. We parted with the promise of sharing any information we might uncover." He punched Alain's shoulder, almost jarring the chicken leg from Alain's grasp. "I had a strong hunch you would turn up here sooner or later."

Alain shared Ruaud's grin. "I have become too predictable. That's certain death for a scout. I shall have to work on changing that." After licking his fingers, he asked, "And the outlaw band?"

"All dead. The whores' sons gave me a few cuts and scratches—nothing worth talking about—though my right knee still aches where one of the sods kicked it."

"An elder-flower compress will ease your knee's pain."

Ruaud grunted. "That could be what the abbey's infirmarer uses. Save your supply, Alain. I am well cared for here." With both palms on the table, he leaned closer, frowning. "And what of you? I found bloody bandages inside the tower."

"Lady Kendra healed me," was the only explanation Alain felt prepared to divulge. It still awed him to contemplate the miracle she had wrought, and he understood it no more now than when it had occurred.

Ruaud downed his ale and poured more from the pitcher. "There's another story, I'll warrant."

Alain nodded, although he wondered whether he could ever relate it to Ruaud.

Instead, he asked, "If you were so certain of where we were, why did you and Waldron's men stop searching for us?"

Ruaud slammed down his flagon with an angry thump, slopping foam onto the tabletop. "We were ordered off the land by its owner."

"What? Who? The outlaws—"

"Had appropriated it for themselves, and their band was too large and too elusive for the thane to defeat, so he told me." Alain felt a disbelieving eyebrow lift. "Well, you crossed that marsh too, Alain. A fine natural defense, no?"

"Oh, come, now. If two determined knights could penetrate it and kill as many as we did, then a thane with as few as a score of men could have rooted them out long ago. Unless..." Alain furrowed his brow. "Unless the thane had no wish to defeat them. Did he give you his name?"

"Unnecessary. I had already met the man." Ruaud tore off a mouthful of chicken, took his time chewing it, and swallowed. "So have you."

"*What!*" Anger propelled Alain to his feet. Every head in the room swiveled toward him, and he sat again. With effort, he reined his voice to a whisper. "Now I know why he tried to kill me."

"No!"

With both hands, Alain signaled for Ruaud to keep his voice down. "Oh, yes."

Still whispering, Alain proceeded to relate his account, sans his intimate encounters with Kendra. Ruaud listened, enraptured throughout the tale, forgetting to eat and, more surprisingly, to drink. Alain eyed the other patrons as they consumed their meals and left the common room, but not before casting the two Normans appraising glances.

Yet another suspicion, centered upon Ulfric, presented itself to Alain, one that would explain why the thane was amassing a secret fortune.

"He knows that I know where the stolen gold is hidden, so I'm sure he means to kill me before I can trace the connection to him." Not to mention eliminating a rival for Kendra's affections, he thought acerbically.

"Doesn't that put Lady Kendra in danger too?"

"Only if she discovers her cousin's duplicity." He swigged his ale without really tasting it and stared into the empty flagon. "My guess is that he will take all measures to preserve her ignorance—at least until after he's married her and her father dies, leaving him free to inherit Edgarburh."

Alain refused to voice the concern that Kendra's life wouldn't be worth a wooden *sol* if that scenario came to pass. And with Waldron's male heir conveniently dead . . .

He smacked his palm onto the tabletop. "By God, I won't let him succeed!"

Ruaud looked doubtful. "What will you do, Squire Alain? Go charging back to his demesne and demand that he surrender her to you?"

"*Sir* Alain won't." In response to Ruaud's cocked eyebrow, Alain explained that Kendra had guessed about his knighthood, though she wouldn't accept his confession of his true identity.

The plan he envisioned would provide the opportunity to confirm his suspicions about Ulfric and, God willing, clear the way for Alain's marriage to Kendra—if she ever forgave him for his deception. If she chose not to forgive him, he would accept his penance and still do the right thing for her, her father, and their people.

He stood and gazed through the windows at the waning sunlight, feeling cold resolve course through his veins.

"Sir Alain won't demand that Thane Ulfric release Lady Kendra, but Sir Robert Alain de Bellencombre will."

Chapter 13

"WERE YOU BORN a lunatic, man, or has love addled your wits?" Ruaud latched on to his friend's arm and dragged him toward the bench. He had to push on Alain's shoulders to make him sit. "If you go there and make reckless accusations about the manor's lord, how long do you think you will survive?"

Alain shot him an annoyed glance. "I have no intention of bearding him alone." Ruaud began to mouth a protest, but Alain held up a hand. "Much as I appreciate your assistance, I understand I shall need more than one blade guarding my back."

"Merciful God," Ruaud muttered, casting a beseeching look heavenward, "my foolish friend has conceived yet another plan."

"Indeed."

"What is to be the idiotic disguise this time?"

"I truly am becoming too predictable." A smile tugged at the corners of Alain's mouth. "I shall explain later." He rose and extended his hand to Ruaud. "But first, if you please, tell me where I can find Waldron's men."

Ruaud gripped the proffered hand and stood, wondering yet again what it was about this man that enticed him to become involved in his wild schemes.

Perhaps he, Ruaud d'Auvay, was the one who'd been born mad.

ULFRIC, LORD of Thornhill and soon to become lord of Edgarburh and beyond, pulled a sweat-stained undertunic through his fingers. It wasn't enough to have that Norman—squire, knight, or whatever in hell he claimed to be—gone from his demesne.

Too much careful planning lay in the balance.

Clutching the garment, he rose, paced the length of his bedchamber to the unglazed window, and swept aside the leather covering. The sun, appearing reluctant to surrender to the night, cast long shadows with everything it touched.

Soon, Ulfric would cast a shadow across the length and breadth of England.

He held the cloth beneath his nose and inhaled its tangy Norman scent. Licking his lips, he pressed his empty hand to his chest and indulged in a feral grin. Tonight's unfinished business begged for completion.

The familiar tingling sensation flooded through him, and he dropped the cloth from a hand no longer able to grasp it.

After the transformation finished, he shouldered open the shutters and scrambled out the window. The need for stealth bridled his urge to howl until after he had wriggled through the concealed hole in the burh's wall that had been constructed for nights such as this.

Beyond the gaze of any who might mark his passage, he sorted through myriad tempting scents for the only one that interested him and broke into an easy, ground-gobbling lope.

He almost lost the trail near Glastonbury. Staying clear of the abbey grounds, he nosed about the main road, trying to make sense of what had happened. Here the scent grew fainter, as if the Norman had bathed before continuing on his way. And a second man-scent became mingled with the first. Had the Norman found his friend and exchanged clothes with him?

One target or two; in this guise, it mattered not.

Back in the desolation of the moor, he picked up a third scent worth noting: wood smoke. His prey had made camp for the night. Ulfric halted and sat on his haunches, swiveling his head and sniffing speculatively.

A low growl rumbled in his throat as he located the camp. Cautiously, yet brimming with eager anticipation, he approached his mark.

The Norman had no time to cry out before Ulfric leapt upon him, fangs bared and fur bristling. The unprotected neck proved no match for his jaws. His bloodlust, fueled by the stench of the man's fear, was not sated until long after the prey had ceased struggling.

THE KNIGHTS, accompanied by Waldron's scouts, doubled back past the Tor and its surrounding marshland to retrieve the thane's gold from its hiding place; a poor consolation, in Alain's mind, for having to leave Kendra behind.

A huge flock of crows rose up en masse nearby with a horrific cackling, making his mount whinny and shy. He crouched and sawed on the reins to keep from being thrown.

Baying, Noir vanished behind the thicket where the birds had emerged while Alain calmed his horse. The baying gave way to a series of expressive growls, as if Noir were worrying something, perhaps the carcass of a cow, which would explain the number of crows.

Alain dismounted and handed the reins to one of the fyrd members before rounding the bush to see what Noir had found.

The sight made him blanch.

The body of a man lay facedown in a long swath of dried blood, half concealed by the thicket. The man's fingernails and trail revealed that he'd crawled there to die. Oblivious to Alain's commands, Noir had clamped onto a leg and was dragging the corpse from the brush. Finally, he quit his grisly task and regarded his master.

Alain's shouts brought Ruaud and the others running.

"*Sacre Mère!*" Ruaud jabbed a finger toward the corpse. "Is that not—"

Alain nodded, swallowing hard. As he gripped Noir's scruff, Lofwin rolled the body over. The other men gasped their surprise, but Alain remained silent. The corpse's mangled throat confirmed his guess.

The unfortunate soul was wearing the tunic and cloak Ulfric had given Alain. No doubt the monks had sold the clothing to the man to raise funds for the abbey.

He squatted for a closer look. Massive paw prints dotted the soft earth surrounding the body and led westward with an increasingly longer stride. Alain traced one of the prints, a memory tugging at the fringes of his recollection. Nothing presented itself. With a mental shrug, he surmised that Ulfric must have a kennel of beasts like Noir, transformed into lethal monsters through deprivation and unconscionable cruelty.

Lofwin and his men retrieved spades from their packs and began to dig a grave. As Alain straightened to assist them, Ruaud drew him aside.

"That was supposed to have been you."

Alain nodded, grimacing. "I must stop this madman before he decides Kendra is expendable too."

"REPORT, ETHEL!" His kill had felt immensely satisfying, but the belated realization that he had found the wrong mark still infuriated him. With effort, he modulated his tone. "Is Lady Kendra ready to assist me?"

"She bears faint traces of ash on her palm. Lady Edwina's gift has awakened at last, my lord." The old woman Ulfric had known his entire life twisted her apron and shuffled backward one pace, two, three.

"About time." His eyes narrowed upon Ethel and her pathetic attempt to maneuver herself closer to the door. "But?"

Sighing, she held her ground. "I like Lady Kendra, my lord. I dislike seeing her placed in danger."

He tipped back his head and howled a laugh. When he regarded his servant, he hardened his stare. "What danger could there be in asking her to heal one hurting soul?"

"Healing a body carries risks aplenty. A broken soul elevates the risk tenfold." She lowered her gaze. "'Tis what weakened Lady Edwina for a fever to claim her life."

Ulfric knew well the event to which Ethel referred; he had been present when Edwina had attempted to heal his mother of the madness that had beset her following the death of his father. Edwina's failure had left both women naught but shells of their former selves. Both were dead within a month.

"Prepare my exalted convalescing guest for a meeting with Lady Kendra." When Ethel opened her mouth as if to ask a question, he lowered his eyebrows and pumped sternness into his gaze.

Gripping a fold of her apron, she looked chagrined. "He doesn't always have good days, my lord."

"I can wait."

As he waved a dismissal, and the woman obeyed with astonishing speed, he pondered her warning. After his careful steps to maneuver Kendra under his roof, he had no wish to lose her—or her lands. She was young and strong and feisty, Ulfric reasoned; Cousin Edwina had been demure and frail. Kendra would survive the onslaught that might result from wielding her gift on behalf of one special recipient.

She had to survive. His plans hinged upon it.

Chapter 14

TWO DAYS AFTER Alain's departure and almost a week since her abduction, Kendra had never felt so utterly miserable. She missed her rose garden at Edgarburh. She missed her evening ritual of selecting a blossom for Del's tomb and feeling closest to his memory during those precious few minutes. In spite of her recent differences with her father, she missed him terribly.

Worse, she ached with despair because Alain had ridden out of her life forever, and she had forced him to leave.

For solace she fled to Thornhill's bee garden.

Its lavender and hyssop hedge stood abloom with delicate purple and bluish flowers ready for harvesting. Inside the enclosure swayed tall hollyhock stalks just beginning to form bulbous buds alongside scarlet-blooming bee balm, bright yellow mullein on downy spikes, globular yellow tansy blossoms, and pink and blue star-shaped borage flowers. She sampled a few borage leaves for their refreshing taste of cucumber.

These tallest herbs stood among beds of ground-hugging thyme and hellebore, both of which had finished blooming for the year, the creamy blossoms of lemon balm, and the spidery leaves of meadow saffron, whose purple blossoms were not due to appear for several months yet. She wondered at the inclusion of this last plant, for it could make a lethal poison, although she supposed the beekeepers had planted meadow saffron just to extend the honey-making season.

The air thrummed with the buzzing of bees flitting from bloom to aromatic bloom.

An apple tree's branches arched over one corner of the garden, and in its shade the groundskeepers had planted a bench. As she neared it, she noticed the tiny greenish-yellow flowers of wormwood, an invaluable herb for protecting bee-keepers from suffering stings. The bees gave the wormwood a wide berth, making this bench an ideal spot from which to contemplate the garden's beauty—which included, on the far side, the ancient tree that had inspired this estate's name and whose Cristes-mæsse petals had ignited her healing gift.

What she wished to contemplate had naught to do with her present surroundings or her gift.

She picked another borage stalk, sat on the bench, popped a few more leaves in her mouth, and closed her eyes with a sigh.

Sending Alain away had been the worst mistake of her life.

But he had gone willingly enough.

Nay, she sadly corrected herself, recalling the anguish she'd seen writhing in his gaze at their parting.

She traced slow circles around the patch of skin on the back of her hand that he had kissed. Imagining that kiss aroused memories of his other kisses and caresses.

When she and Alain had stood in the depths of life-threatening danger, it hadn't seemed so bad. With him, her fear of the future's uncertainty had all but disappeared.

Not true. The uncertainty of their future together had loomed as a barrier between them even as they had fought to demolish it with their kisses. By far the largest block in the wall was her vow to never marry a Norman.

Bowing her head, she covered her face with her hands and wept. The prospect of recanting that vow, forsaking Del for Alain's sake, tore her heart asunder.

More than ever, she longed for her brother's counsel.

The wish's irony forced a rueful laugh from her throat: if Del were alive to advise her, she never would have had to make that accursed vow.

A shuffling tread upon the path invaded her thoughts. She rubbed her eyes and looked up to find Ethel standing before her.

"Please forgive me for disturbing you, my lady." Wringing her hands, Ethel sucked in a breath. "Thane Ulfric requires a service from you."

Surprise caused Kendra to overlook the odd formality of Ethel's tone. "What do you mean?"

The woman only bowed and gestured for Kendra to follow her. But rather than walking toward the manor house, Ethel set off in the opposite direction, toward what appeared to be a large cluster of storage sheds. As they walked closer, Kendra realized the sheds were in fact cottages.

What few folk Kendra saw abroad in this area of the estate seemed to be suffering a variety of ailments, everything from wracking coughs to missing limbs. Some women, wearing brown overdresses and wimples, mingled among the ill as the apparent caretakers, toting supplies, serving food and drink, assisting those having trouble walking, drying tears.

One man, who at first didn't seem to have anything wrong with him, dropped to the ground nearby, flailing his limbs and moaning. Two other men, wearing hooded robes of the same hue as the women's dresses, emerged from one of the cottages and ran to restrain the writhing man. Through the cottage's open door drifted more wails and groans.

Appalled, Kendra stopped and stared at Ethel. "What is this place?" she whispered.

"Those whose ailments have placed too great a burden on their families come here."

"To recover?"

"The lucky ones do." Ethel watched the men struggling with the man suffering from fits. When they calmed him enough to move him inside, she regarded Kendra. "Most come here to die."

Kendra felt her eyes widen. "And Ulfric cares for them?"

Ethel snorted. "My lord Ulfric keeps the cottages provisioned and in good repair. The Church"—she waved an arm toward a knot of nuns hauling bulging baskets of damp laundry toward ropes strung between the trees—"supplies the work and compassion."

A girl, aged no more than ten summers, wandered up to them. Her eyes were red-rimmed and bleary, and when she wasn't sniffling, her breaths came in high-pitched wheezes. She wiped her nose on her sleeve—not for the first time, to judge by the stains—and gazed hopefully up at Kendra.

She touched the girl's head. Heat rushed to her palm. The girl yelped and dashed away as fast as her illness permitted.

Mortified, Kendra watched her leave. "I'm so sorry," she whispered to the fleeing child. "I meant you no harm, little one."

"Na, na, of course you didn't, poppet," Ethel crooned, patting Kendra's arm.

"I—" She didn't want to confess her secret, but she needed to offer some explanation. "My hand felt so hot, I thought I was burning her." Tears stung as she considered the girl's response. "I must have burned her."

Ethel made no comment except, "Please follow me, my lady. Thane Ulfric wishes you to meet one of the residents."

She strode across the yard to another cottage, with a puzzled Kendra trailing after her.

A pair of monks blocked the door at their approach, arms crossed. The men's builds and demeanors reminded Kendra more of warriors than of God's servants. When Ethel explained that Ulfric had commanded Kendra's visit and produced a ring from her pouch they seemed to recognize, they nodded and allowed the women inside.

It took several moments for Kendra's eyes to adjust to the gloom. The windows were shuttered, with only a handful of candles to stave off the darkness, which Kendra found odd. Common wisdom stated that most ailing people benefited from fresh air and sunlight. She expressed her concern to one of the monks.

He shook his head. "Thane's orders, my lady."

She submerged her concern and absorbed the rest of the one-room cottage's details.

A large bed had been pushed against one wall; the hearth, its iron implements, and stacks of logs and kindling occupied the opposite one. Two straw-stuffed pallets lay spread near the hearth. In the center of the planked floor stood a square table and two chairs. Another pair of chairs graced the cottage's door, and a sideboard holding a basin, pitcher, trenchers, and flagons occupied the fourth wall. The scent of lavender permeated the air from flowers that had been strewn among the rushes.

From one of the chairs beside the table a figure rose slowly. He didn't seem capable of standing fully erect, and he supported himself by gripping the chair's tall back. After a monk stepped forward to assist him, he turned to face Kendra.

His plain garb hung loosely over his large frame, and he looked as if he might have been powerful in his prime. Wisps of tawny hair sticking out at odd angles combined with the crooked posture to bestow upon him a wizened appearance.

A black leather mask obscured one eye and half his face. The other eye looked pinched and haunted, as if he harbored inner torment beyond measure.

Kendra cocked a questioning glance at Ethel.

"One of Thane Ulfric's guests, my lady," Ethel said. "Can't speak much." With two fingers, she tapped the side of her head.

Something in the man's bearing, in spite of his infirmity, gave Kendra the impression that he had held an important office. She curtseyed deeply. This seemed to revive a memory, for he straightened and gave a slight bow. He swept a wave at the other chair as if he wanted her to sit beside him.

While she did, Ethel asked privacy from the monks, again citing Ulfric's request. By turns they eyed her, Kendra, and the injured man, finally exchanging a glance with each other. As if of one mind, they hefted the chairs from beside the door and carried them outside.

Their behavior strengthened Kendra's suspicion that they'd been charged to protect this man more so than to attend to his daily physical needs.

When Kendra returned her attention to him, his demeanor brightened. "Love . . . lee," he croaked. His lips formed the barest of smiles, and he seemed unaware of the tears slipping down the uncovered half of his cheek.

Without thinking, she began to brush away the tears.

She might as well have thrust her hand into a boiling cauldron.

Gasping, she pulled back. He leapt to his feet, flailing his arms and screeching an incoherent alarm. His chair clattered to the floor behind him, which seemed to agitate him further. Ethel hurried to his side, murmuring soothing words and trying to catch his hands.

Unsure what to do and feeling terrible for having upset him, Kendra rose and backed away.

The monks burst into the cottage, fists knotted and eyes flashing. "What happened, woman?" demanded the taller one.

Although the question was directed at Ethel, Kendra bristled. Being bodyguards gave them no right to bully an old woman. She drew the power of her rank about her like a cloak and, setting her jaw, stepped between Ethel and the monks.

"It was an accident, good brethren. The fault lies with me. I made a sudden movement that must have startled him."

"Aye," Ethel said. "You know how he gets, Brother Eric."

Kendra glanced over her shoulder at the injured man and was grateful to note that he had calmed. To both monks she said, "I assure you that it shan't happen again."

"See that it doesn't," grumbled Brother Eric. "My lady."

His companion, fists on hips, didn't appear to be as easily mollified. "Why are you here, Lady Kendra?"

"I—" Kendra stopped, stymied.

"She is a healer, Brother Oswald," Ethel insisted. "If you don't believe me, ask Thane Ulfric, though he shan't take kindly to having his orders questioned."

When the monk called Oswald offered no further objections, Ethel made a shooing motion. "Good brethren, Lady Kendra must have privacy for her work." She followed them to the door as if she didn't trust them to leave. "And, please, no more interruptions, no matter what you might hear."

Their eyes widened at that before narrowing in obvious suspicion. "Please," Ethel whispered as she stepped around them to fling open the door. "Trust us."

"Trust us? Trust me, you mean," Kendra said after the monks had trooped out and the door swung shut. "To do what?"

Ethel's gaze turned matter-of-fact. "Heal him, of course, my lady. That is well and truly why you are here."

"I—what?" Kendra regarded Ethel, who had busied herself with seating the injured man. "What are you talking about?"

Ethel chuckled. "Why, your dear mother's gift, of course. Nay, don't bother to deny it: look at your palms."

Kendra looked. And had trouble believing the evidence presented by her eyes.

Her left palm appeared normal. Her right one, where she had touched the child's head and the man's face, was coated with a fine white residue.

Wonderingly, she traced circles in it with the fingers of her opposite hand and held them up for Ethel to view. "What do you know of this?" She rubbed the powder between her fingers, and particles drifted into the candle's gleam.

"Not much, save that I saw it when your mother tried to heal someone." Ethel's gaze unfocused. "It's as if you—and your mother before you—have the power to draw forth a person's pain and scorch it." Shrugging, she looked at K-endra again. "More than that, I know not."

Kendra curled the afflicted hand into a fist so tightly the nails dug into her palm. Jaw clenched and eyes shut, she tilted her face toward the thatch and rafters.

If this gift is such a boon, then why couldn't it have manifested in time to save my mother's life, or Del's? Why did it have to manifest for the man I love but can never wed? Why must I use it for this stranger?

Why do I even possess this power at all?

In the midst of her mental railings, another thought intruded. She glared at Ethel. "Ulfric knows about this ability of mine. You! You told him, didn't you?" When the servant cast her gaze downward, Kendra forged on, "Now he wants me to heal everyone here, beginning with this man?" Perhaps so he could send them home and reclaim this land for some other purpose, she mused. A profitable purpose, probably, rather than a charitable one.

Considering the plights of the people she'd seen thus far, though, how could she refuse?

But, Lord, there are so many! Gift or no gift, how can I heal them all?

Ethel shook her head. "Not everyone unless you so choose, my lady. The only person Thane Ulfric would like you to help, if you can, is this man."

She motioned for Kendra to sit beside him, which she did without fully understanding the impulse to obey. Her fingers remained clenched around the ash coating her palm.

Ethel's cool, leathery hands gently but firmly pried her fist open and guided it to grasp another hand, one scarred and callused . . . from battle, Kendra realized.

The man's agony exploded within her brain. They uttered a long scream as if sharing one throat. She squeezed her eyes and his hand tighter, fighting to channel the pain away from them both.

Cheering peasants welcomed Alain and his escort to Edgarburh, although he suspected the people's warmth extended more toward the fyrd members.

Wherever they rode, however, one thing remained constant: the cheering ebbed to a confused murmur when the crowd realized their beloved Lady Kendra was not riding with them.

Alain knew how they felt. Without Kendra to brighten his days, he despaired of ever finding a reason to cheer again.

"Where is she?" Waldron demanded from the steps of Edgarburh's hall as the party dismounted. Noir bristled at the thane, but Alain silenced the dog with a reprimand.

"Lady Kendra lodges at Thornhill, my lord," Alain replied, "resting from her ordeal."

Her father looked none too pleased. He glanced at Ruaud before piercing Alain with his glare. "Your master still allows you to speak for him, squire?"

Alain stifled a sigh and went to one knee at Waldron's feet. So did Ruaud, to the surprised whisperings of Lofwin's men and other residents of the burh who had interrupted their tasks to watch the proceedings.

"Thane Waldron, I have sinned against you, your daughter, and God." Alain held up a hand to forestall the storm of rage collecting on the thane's face. "My lord, please accept my assurances that your daughter's virtue remains intact." *At least, as far as I know.* "My sin is one of deception, and I beg your forgiveness. I ask not as Squire Alain but as my true self." He drew a breath. "Sir Robert Alain de Bellencombre."

As the people's murmurings grew louder and more hostile, he bowed his head under the weight of shame and guilt.

Chapter 15

KENDRA FELT AS if her head were being roasted on a spit. With her eyes shut, and while grasping the injured man's hand, she visualized the flames being drenched by a cold torrent. As the imaginary rainstorm intensified, the fire died and the pain abated, praise God.

Beneath his pain lay a paralyzing blanket of numbness interwoven with strands of anguish, hopelessness, and despair. As she retained her grip upon the man's hand, the blanket threatened to suffocate her too. She lost touch with her senses, not knowing whether she imagined herself panting for breath or did so in truth.

Whoever this half-masked man was and whatever the source of his grief, its depth far outstripped Kendra's own. The realization both humbled and emboldened her. Without opening her eyes, she wrapped her other hand around his.

A frightening array of images branded her mind: horses rearing, screaming, and pounding foes into the ground; weapons shattering from the force of impact; men slipping, falling, and dying in the muddy gore; wounded warriors moaning for help. Soldiers looting the bodies of the fallen to raise new-found weapons against a relentless adversary. A shield wall buckling from within as greed asserted its dominion over the wall's members. The flight of a single arrow, its point bearing toward her with breathtaking speed, and the excruciating agony when it found its target.

Through it all ran an undercurrent of shock, disbelief, rage, betrayal, and, ultimately, dejected resignation.

Such a fathomless well of emotional pain she felt utterly powerless to combat.

Sir Robert Alain de Bellencombre, once known as Squire Alain, knelt in abject humility at Waldron's feet.

The Norman's admission robbed Waldron of his worry-fueled anger. Yet, while gazing down upon the knight guarded by the hellhound, he realized the revelation didn't take him by surprise. From the start he had sensed this man must be someone other than who he'd claimed to be.

And Alain—or Robert, or whatever he called himself—loved Kendra. Waldron knew this as surely as he knew the battle-forged contours of his sword hand. He had recognized the lad's anguished expression as one he'd seen on his own face whenever he encountered a reflective surface: the anguish of being separated from the better half of one's life, one's heart, one's very soul.

Although no one could ever replace Del, here knelt a man that Waldron would be pleased to call son.

He raised a hand, and his people fell silent. With a wary glance at the dog, he bent to address the knight, only one question straining for release: "Why?"

Sir Robert looked up, confusion darkening his features. "Why the deception, my lord?"

Waldron shook his head. "Why, in the name of everything holy, did you leave her?"

AN INSISTENT tugging on Kendra's hands broke her grip on the wounded man. Her head ached abominably. She massaged her temple, surprised by how gritty the skin felt. As if from a long distance away, she heard herself groan.

"My lady, will you be all right?" Kendra thought she recognized Ethel's voice, though lassitude had robbed her of the will to open her eyes. "Shall I summon the physician?"

"Nay." Her voice's huskiness startled her. She cleared her throat. "No need for that." And no need to share the knowledge of her special talent with anyone else. "I shall be fine."

It was far more than could be said for the man she had tried to heal. When she opened her eyes, she found him slumped over to one side and slack-jawed. Drool trickled from the corner of his mouth, which Ethel was daubing with her kerchief. Perspiration matted his hair. The exposed flesh of his face looked as waxy as a death mask.

Kendra touched her own head and realized that it too was damp. Again she felt that odd grittiness. She examined her fingertips and found more ash.

"I am so sorry, sir," she murmured, stroking his cheek, the portion not obscured by leather. "I wish I could do more to help you."

"And so you shall, my dearest Kendra, through more encounters of this nature."

She snapped her head up to find Ulfric standing on the threshold of the open door, hands resting on his hips, a smug grin seeping across his face.

Why had he left Kendra with someone he'd sooner spit upon than trust? An excellent question. He studied the dirt at his knee. "I should not have, Thane Waldron."

"Damned right," said her father.

An open hand thrust into Alain's field of view, a gnarled hand bearing more scars than the sum total of nicks on Alain's blade. He glanced up in time to see Waldron give a slight nod. He grasped the thane's forearm and hauled himself up, signaling Ruaud to stand too.

"My lord, we must talk." Alain pumped urgency into his tone. "Privately, if possible."

Waldron looked over his shoulder at the stream of people filing into and out of the hall. "Not in there." He turned and strode toward the living quarters, beckoning the Normans to follow him. Alain paused to ask Lofwin to secure the recovered gold. Waldron overheard and expressed profuse gratitude, which Alain accepted with a shrug; he considered the act as yet another facet of his duty.

With Noir trotting at Alain's heels, they crossed the yard and climbed the outer staircase in silence. Outside the door to Ruaud's chamber, Waldron halted. "Sir Ruaud, you are welcome to rest and refresh yourself while . . ." He rounded on Alain. "Sir Alain? Sir Robert? What in heaven's name should I call you, son?"

Son.

It had been far too long since Alain had heard that title directed at him, and it surprised him to realize how much he'd missed it. Since he was not his father's heir, he had no right to the patronymic *fitz*. Alain's sibling nemesis, Philippe FitzHugh, enjoyed that distinction and never wasted the chance to flaunt it in front of Alain. Hence he had chosen to affiliate himself with the village of his birth, Bellencombre. Alain had never thought of himself as being the "son of" any man until this moment.

The feeling wasn't at all unpleasant.

Waldron's raised eyebrow reminded him that the thane awaited an answer. Alain cleared his throat. "Formally, my lord, I am addressed as Sir Robert." Even after all the years spent with his English mother, he still used the Norman-French pronunciation favored by his father, "hro-*bear*." He continued, "My friends, like Ruaud and your daughter"—a tentative smile curved his lips—"call me Alain."

Waldron resumed his pace down the corridor. "Come, then, Alain."

The thane didn't see Alain's eyebrows hitch upward.

AFTER COMMANDING the monks to remain on duty outside, Ulfric slammed the door and stalked into the cottage.

Images of blood and battle whirled within Kendra's throbbing head, and she fought to steady her thoughts. "This man's condition is far worse than my poor skills can remedy."

Ulfric's grin broadened. "You underestimate yourself."

"What makes you believe I can cure him? That is, if I consent to try again." She touched her forehead and winced, though the pain did lessen a bit. "This is not easy for me."

"I am confident that you shall give your consent." He withdrew an object from the pouch at his waist and thrust it forward. From a heavy chain swung an ornate gold cross. "I know several men who would be most interested in this uncanny healing touch of yours." His grin took a sinister cast. "Highly ranking men itching for a spawn of Satan to burn."

She recoiled as if he'd struck her. "You wouldn't dare! My father—"

"Of course I won't, my dear, if you carry out my wishes." He stepped closer, leering. "All my wishes."

WALDRON LONGED to call the Norman knight *son*. Sir Robert—Alain—was bound to marry his daughter by royal decree. Welcoming Alain into the family in this manner felt so natural, so right . . . even though it sharpened the ache he felt whenever he thought of his own lost son.

Kendra mourned Del in her way, Waldron in his, and no less keenly, just not as openly.

And yet Alain's flash of anguish, when Waldron bestowed the title a few moments ago, made him wonder what might have transpired between the lad and his father. Waldron had no wish to cause this man any more pain.

He reached the door to his chambers, opened it, ordered the servants out, and beckoned Alain to follow him inside. The knight obeyed, escorted by that massive hound. The dog trotted about the chamber, sniffing here and there, before turning thrice upon a spot near the hearth and scattering rushes as he flopped onto the floor with a grunt.

According to Waldron's standing orders, the servants had left a well-stoked blaze in the hearth, a brimming pitcher of mulled wine, and one pewter goblet. As the last man prepared to leave, Waldron asked him to fetch an extra goblet and food. The servant bowed, eyeing the dog, and shut the door behind him.

Waldron filled the goblet and offered it to Alain. "I insist," he said when the lad put up a hand in polite refusal. "You will need this far more than I. You have much to explain."

The knight's mouth cracked into a half smile. "Indeed, my lord." He accepted the goblet with thanks and took a long swallow.

Waldron expelled an exaggerated sigh. "And you, lad, may dispense with the 'my lord' and 'thane' nonsense since you will soon become my son by marriage."

Alain's smile vanished. "Not if Kendra has any say."

"What? But the king's decree—"

"I have promised her that I shall seek to have it nullified. William may choose to grant her wish if I can convince him that the people of Edgarburh will cause him no further trouble. I do stand highly enough in the king's favor to offer her this hope."

With a twitch of his eyebrow, Waldron noted the lad's choice of words. "Her wish, not yours?"

"My lord—" He raised a fist to his mouth and cleared his throat. "Waldron. I have braved death to see Kendra delivered from that outlaw band. I would have braved the fires of hell itself for her—would rather do that, in fact, than be parted from her again."

"But you did part from her."

Alain stared into the goblet. "Not willingly." He drained the cup and set it down with a heavy thump. "She does not realize who I am."

The servant returned with the extra goblet and a platter of beef, bread, and cheese, which Waldron accepted and dismissed the man with thanks. The dog raised his head, pricking his ears, and Waldron tossed him a hunk of cold boiled beef. It expressed its gratitude with noisy chewing and soft growls of canine pleasure.

While Waldron filled both cups, Alain explained what had happened, including the hound's role, in gut-wrenching detail.

Good thing those outlaws were already dead, or Waldron would have galloped after them himself.

"And she told me why she cannot marry a Norman."

"That foolish girl!"

"Please don't think that, sir. She is determined to obey the king's command, believing that Sir Robert and I are different men." Alain thumbed the goblet's rim as if using it to shape his thoughts. "But if her brother's memory means this much to her, I shall not force her to dishonor it." He bowed his head for a moment before regarding Waldron. "I am very sorry for your loss—yours and Kendra's—and I regret that one of my countrymen was responsible."

Smitten by a wave of grief and not willing to trust his voice, Waldron patted Alain's shoulder, his gaze drifting, as it so often did, toward his newest chest.

Inspiration swept aside the grief. "I may know a way to circumvent that vow of hers."

He stood and motioned Alain to accompany him, and they crossed the chamber to stand before the chest. Waldron pulled the thong holding the key from beneath his tunic, unlocked the chest, and together they lifted the heavy lid.

As Waldron pawed aside several layers of wool, he said, "Here is the murderer's shield. If you recognize it and can help me bring the man to justice, it might persuade her to change her mind about you."

"It is a large army, sir, but I shall—" Alain paled, shook his head, and blinked hard. "No . . . it—it cannot be." He reached toward the shield, seemed to think better of it, and twisted to look at Waldron. "May I?"

Waldron nodded his assent, and Alain withdrew the kite-shaped shield from the chest. He peered at the device, a prowling saffron leopard, and reverently ran his fingertips over the wood's green paint, pausing at certain gouges as if he had expected to find them.

"You recognize it?" Waldron scarcely dared to hope that his months of frustration might be nearing an end.

Alan's nod was terse. "Did your son die at Hastings?"

"Nay. On his way home, several days after the battle, he was ambushed and suffered a mortal wound. Only by a miracle did he linger until Cristes mæsse."

"Then it's impossible that the man for whom this shield was crafted dealt that stroke." The lad tightened his jaw, but Waldron noticed a tremor in his chin.

"Why?" He refused to be denied an answer when he stood closer to one now than in the last nine months combined.

Alain's hand convulsed around the shield's iron rim as he stared at its face. "I watched him die by a Saxon's hand at Hastings. The Saxon took his shield. This shield. And I tried—God, how I tried! But I couldn't reach him in time. I was too far away, powerless to prevent his death." He inhaled a ragged breath. "I couldn't even prevent the looting of his body."

He hid his face with the arm holding the shield. The dog rose and padded over to nudge Alain's other hand, whining. Alain rested his hand on the dog's head.

Waldron gripped Alain's shoulder. "I know how much it hurts, son. I have lost far too many companions-at-arms over the years."

Alain stiffened and raised his head to regard the shield, grasping it with both white-knuckled hands. "But how many vows did you break to your dying mother when you failed to protect those men?" His glare, when he turned it upon Waldron, radiated raw fury.

"How many," he ground out between clenched teeth, "called you brother?"

ETHEL'S MINISTRATIONS seemed to have revived the injured man, and he straightened in his chair. His good eye conveyed grief, but something new glimmered there too: appreciation.

Pointing at the half-masked man, Kendra leveled her glare on Ulfric. "Tell me why his healing is so important, cousin."

"Ha . . . h-hold . . . ha, hold . . ." muttered the man, rapping his fist on the table.

Kendra said, "Is he someone of note? Is that why you're so anxious to see him hale and whole?"

Ulfric nodded, fingering his chin. "That would be one way of describing it."

"But who—" Someone grasped her hand. She turned to find the man lifting it to his lips. He completed the gesture with surprising grace.

"Ha. Old go . . . go in sin. Thankee, lay dee." He released her hand, squared his shoulders, and inclined his head in a regal gesture.

Old go in sin? Kendra shook her head, mystified. "What?"

"You have made excellent progress, Kendra," Ulfric declared. "He has chosen to reveal himself to you, which is far more than any physician has been able to achieve in the nine months he's suffered this condition." Ulfric waved the cross. "A few more healing sessions with you shall do him—and England—a world of good."

Chuckling, Ulfric strode away. As he opened the door and stepped outside, twirling the cross, it flashed ominously in the waning sunlight.

WALDRON RELEASED his grip on Alain's shoulder and stepped back. "I've lost no brothers in battle," he replied quietly. "Please forgive me, son—Sir Robert."

Son. Alain felt his rage drain. The ironic yearning to call this Saxon *father* hit the Norman with astonishing force.

Lord willing, he would refer to Waldron as father one day, after claiming Kendra as his bride.

But much had to transpire before that day's dawning, beginning with another unpleasant admission.

"Sir, you have done nothing wrong, save unwittingly revive a painful memory. I apologize for my outburst." He laid the shield inside the chest. "And I apologize for something I must tell you, for it concerns one of your kinsmen."

"Ulfric." Not a question but a statement.

Alain's eyebrows quirked upward. "You know?"

"What he's plotting?" Waldron grunted. "Sometimes I wish I did, but usually I'm thankful I don't. He's been sniffing after Kendra for years. He no doubt hopes to gain control of Edgarburh through her once I'm gone."

"Would that be such a bad thing?"

Waldron barked a laugh. "For you, most assuredly."

Alain couldn't help but smile. Noir nudged his hand, and he stroked the dog's ear. "Forget about me for a moment. If there had been no Sir Robert, no royal decree regarding Kendra's future, would it be detrimental to Edgarburh to have Ulfric governing it?"

"Lad, he has a hard enough time with the small estate he's got. Think of that outlaw band. They built their encampment under his nose, and he couldn't do a thing about it."

"Couldn't . . . or wouldn't?"

"What, exactly, are you implying?" Waldron's tone turned as flinty as his stare.

"I have no proof yet, my lord, but I suspect the outlaws were working for him."

"'Tis a most serious charge to lay upon my kinsman. I presume you have good reasons?"

"I do, sir." Alain held up a finger to discuss the first of many points he had omitted from his earlier recounting of what had happened at Glastonbury Tor. "The cavern I mentioned was stuffed to bursting with treasure."

"From the outlaws' raids, of course. So?"

"It appears to have been left untouched, even the mountains of coins, as if the outlaws had been ordered not to use it."

"How much are you talking about?"

Alain closed his eyes to summon the memories and had to squelch the sweet memory of Kendra's kisses and curves. "Enough, perhaps, to pay a sizeable army for a year."

"Sizeable?"

"An army large enough to put a Saxon back on the throne."

He omitted his speculations about where that army might be mustering; no need to alarm the thane about that just yet.

Waldron gaped as Alain continued, "Then there is the matter of Kendra's locket. Ulfric claimed he recovered it off the body of one of the outlaws, but who's to say the man didn't give it to him because he was in Ulfric's employ?"

"Pure speculation. You cannot build a case on that."

"No, I cannot. But if Ulfric is innocent of what I suspect, then why would he have tried so hard to kill me?"

"What!"

"Twice." Another memory intruded, and Alain felt his eyes stretch wider. "Perhaps even thrice. Ruaud and I were attacked at an inn on the way to Edgarburh." He recalled the odd packet of dried petals he'd found on the guide's body. That had to have been what Kendra had used to heal Alain's wounds: the Glastonbury thorn, she'd called it. Not to mention the large animal prints Alain had found afterward—the same prints, he realized, that had surrounded the man who'd been murdered on the moor. "I am certain the guide we'd hired in Sarum led us into an ambush. Somehow Ulfric must have found out about my other mission."

"Other mission? What other mission?"

"Regent Odo received several complaints from the outlaws' victims, and he charged me with setting the matter to rights."

"Hence your disguise," Waldron concluded. "And your avidness to trail the outlaws by surrendering to them."

"Kendra figured into both plans too." Alain drained his goblet and poured another cupful. "I wasn't keen on the marriage idea at first, so I embraced the disguise as a way to buy time before making my final decision."

"You would have disobeyed the king?" Waldron sounded aghast. "And rejected my daughter?"

Shame fixed Alain's gaze upon the goblet. "I had my reasons." Reasons that seemed petty compared with his burgeoning feelings toward her. "Please forgive me, sir. I intended no disrespect toward either of you." He looked up. "My decision to accompany the outlaws was motivated by my fervor to rescue your daughter."

Waldron rose, crossed to the window, and looked out over Edgarburh's bustling thoroughfare. "Now you believe she needs rescuing again and have returned to enlist my help."

Alain joined him at the window in time to see a heavily laden wagon lumber to a stop near the kitchens. The driver and his assistant jumped down and sauntered around to the back to begin unloading the crates and barrels, while several servants emerged from the kitchens to help them.

"I have no wish to worry you, sir, but I am concerned that Ulfric will not let Kendra go without a struggle."

"So am I, Alain." Waldron faced him, determination conquering the worry in his gaze. "Go. Take my men, provisions, weapons, horses—whatever you require."

"You will not come with me?"

Waldron sighed. "Although Ulfric and I claim kinship, my open support of King William has made me less than popular with him and his allies. Besides, this is your fight. All I ask is that you bring my Kendra safely home."

"I shall, sir." Alain felt his lips thin to a grim line as he prayed with all his heart for increased measures of strength, luck, skill—whatever it would take to fulfill this vow.

THE DOOR swung to. The candles flickered, casting the cottage back into gloom.

Ha, old? Ha-hold? Kendra squinted at the ailing man, mouthing the words he'd spoken. *Old go in sin? Go in sin? Go—*

Stifling a cry with the back of her hand, she rose from the chair and dropped to her knees at his feet, scarcely noticing that Ethel struggled to follow her example on age-stiffened joints. "Please forgive me for not recognizing you." Shame bowed her chin to her chest. "Your Majesty."

The man who, until the fourteenth day of October in the year of Our Lord one thousand sixty-six, had embodied the final hope of the Saxons' cause, rested his hand atop her head in silent absolution: King Harold Godwinson.

Chapter 16

"OUTRAGEOUS!"

The king crumpled the parchment and hurled it onto the hearth, where it hit the embers and ignited. Bishop Odo thanked God for inspiring him to order his scribe to craft a copy.

"Who do these Saxon miscreants think they are?" William braced his hand on the hearth stones, staring at the fire. "I show them mercy, and this is how they show their appreciation."

Habit forged by their years-long friendship—in spite of being half brothers—drove Odo across the slate floor of William's private reception chamber to clasp the shoulder that bore the burdens of two realms.

"The demonstration of mercy is always a sound policy in God's eyes, Will. I pray you do not regret your decision." Odo gave that broad shoulder a companionable squeeze before releasing his hold. "But some policies require more patience."

"Patience?" William snorted and turned his back on the fire, feet spread and arms crossed. "Hah. We are not at war, and yet I have taken up residence on this side of the Channel for mere days before being bombarded with ransom requests."

Odo cocked an eyebrow. "I would not consider one letter 'bombardment.' And this isn't a ransom demand. Thane Waldron reported that your knight and the knight's squire suggested the ploy, with the intent of rescuing Waldron's daughter." He stopped short of voicing his suspicion that William hadn't bothered to read anything other than the word *ransom*.

"Waldron." William stroked his beard. "Waldron . . . why does that name sound so familiar?"

"You decreed that Sir Robert Alain de Bellencombre become betrothed to Thane Waldron's daughter, Lady Kendra."

"Of course. But . . ." With his index finger, William rubbed the bridge of his nose, a familiar sign of deep concentration. "There's something else about that name . . ."

Glad he'd made inquiries prior to this audience, Odo said, "Thane Waldron Edgarson of Edgarburh attended your coronation to swear fealty to you and to present a rather unique petition."

William's expression lightened. "Ah, yes. He claimed his son was ambushed and mortally wounded by one of my knights." He tilted his head. "What was the investigation's result?"

Odo sighed as he strove to craft a tactful response. The bonds of friendship with powerful men could stretch only so far. "If you gave the command, Will, it was never recorded."

That wrenched a rueful laugh from William's throat. "In other words, I was too caught up in the coronation festivities to act upon the thane's request." Grinning, he raised both hands in mock surrender. "Guilty, Father Confessor. But if you dare breathe a word of this to another soul . . ." Seriousness eclipsed his countenance, and he rested his fists on his hips. "Might this matter be related to de Bellencombre's ransom?"

"I don't know." Odo battled the temptation to chide William for not fully reading the missive. "Waldron did not mention Sir Robert in his letter."

"What? Where is he, then? I'd have expected him to be the first to go charging after the men who'd abducted his bride."

"Perhaps." Odo scrunched his shoulders. "But I had ordered Sir Robert to investigate reports of outlaw activity and gruesome deaths in the region, and I have not heard from him since he left Winchester, almost a fortnight ago."

William's gaze turned thoughtful. "Sir Robert probably would have attended to that mission before wedding the woman. So he's either still pursuing the outlaws, or—God forbid—they have bested him. But if the latter is true, then why would they not have sent a ransom demand for him?"

"That's what I've been puzzling over," Odo admitted, "and why I chose to bring this matter to your attention."

"I don't blame you." William's quiet tone suggested he might have made similar choices, and it heartened Odo. "So, who is this other knight Thane Waldron mentioned?"

"Sir Ruaud d'Auvay."

William clenched his fists, staring at the ceiling. "God's bones in a gilt box!"

"Will . . ."

The king had the grace to look repentant for a moment. "D'Auvay is a fine frontline fighter; I knighted him myself years ago. But the man has never possessed a shred of subtlety or finesse, and both qualities would be necessary in rescuing the woman from these brigands against the level of odds I expect d'Auvay has had to face. De Bellencombre owns both traits in abundance, and is a shrewd soldier besides, but God alone knows where he is."

Odo closed his eyes to offer a silent prayer for the safety of Sir Ruaud, Sir Robert, and Lady Kendra. The sharp sound of footsteps interrupted his petition, and he opened his eyes. William had already crossed half the distance toward the chamber's only door. "Will? What do you intend to do?"

William paused at the wall where his battle sword hung in its hard leather sheath, supported by two oaken pegs carved in the shape of lions' claws. He removed the weapon from its perch as Odo strode closer to help William strap it in place.

Nodding his thanks, he said, "The very last thing I want to do is convey the impression that I don't believe my knights are capable of handling themselves in difficult situations. That would foster rebellion faster than I could blink.

"But there are too many mysteries at work here: Lady Kendra's abduction, Sir Ruaud's surrender, Sir Robert's disappearance, the death of Waldron's son." William enumerated the points on his fingertips. "All of those events are connected to Edgarburh."

After adjusting the sword to more comfortably ride his hip, William met Odo's gaze. "What I do will depend upon the answers Thane Waldron supplies me."

"A state visit?"

William laughed. "God, no. That would take weeks to arrange, for Matilda would insist on coming with me, and she'd insist on having her say regarding who and what to bring."

His expression sobered. "No, Odo, this venture shall include you and me and a company of my personal guardsmen. No wagons or pack animals; just what weapons and provisions we can carry upon ourselves and our horses."

"It might also be wise to arrange for a division to mobilize quickly, if necessary," Odo suggested.

William's eyebrows knotted into a thick golden line across his forehead. "You believe there may be more afoot?"

"I'm not certain what to believe, Will. All I can tell you is that my sources have reported some unusual movements in the Glastonbury district."

"Troops?"

Odo shook his head. "Pilgrim traffic has swelled, and many Saxon thanes and their entourages have been identified among the crowds."

"Saxon pilgrims at Glastonbury?" William sounded incredulous. "Won't Abbot Thurstin be surprised; I didn't think the Saxons were a particularly pious lot."

"My point exactly." The bishop gave a lopsided shrug. "But we could be wrong about them. Worshipping the same God does make us all brothers in the Lord's sight. As a precaution, I have the pilgrims' camp under surveillance, but I don't expect another report for several more days."

Fingering his sword's pommel, William strode to the man-size map of southern England—Odo's jurisdiction whenever William resided abroad—hanging on the opposite wall. The king traced the route from London to Glastonbury, tapping his finger first on Sarum and then on Edgarburh.

"I do not want to wait for confirmation. The lives of Sir Robert, Sir Ruaud, and perhaps many others," proclaimed the conqueror of England, "may depend upon how swiftly we can arrive." He inclined his head toward Odo. "I will, however, follow your advice and order a regiment to muster at Sarum. God willing, we won't need them, but it is prudent to be prepared."

Odo could not have agreed more heartily.

Chapter 17

ALAIN'S MAIL CHIMED as he rose from his knees following the conclusion of Wednesday's dawn prayer service. In London's West Minster, such a sound would have jolted off the stones and echoed embarrassingly throughout the nave. Not so inside Edgarburh's humble timber chapel, where the only stone took the form of the altar and two granite sarcophagi decorated with carved marble panels.

With a voiceless apology to its occupant, he used the closer tomb to lever himself to his feet. It felt good to be arrayed in war's trappings once again, but the leather and steel ensemble did impose limitations.

"That's my son. Sir Delwin Waldronson." Sadness muted Waldron's voice as he stopped beside the sarcophagus, hands clasped behind his back. "We call—called him Del."

Alain studied the effigy, carved as a comely knight dressed in full Saxon battle gear, a longsword at his left hip and a seax strapped to his right, his expression stern and hands folded in prayer. A pair of dried roses lay entwined across the granite knight's chest on a nest of petals: a white and a red.

His spine tingled in recognition. Wonderingly, he reached out to touch the blooms. The petals felt brittle, but his fingertips released a cloud of fragrance. He withdrew his hand to keep from damaging the flowers.

"Kendra laid those there before she—she—" Waldron sucked in a breath, studying the tomb. "It was—is her custom, every day the rosebushes bloom, to select the best one for Del. Only one rose, without fail. Yet for some reason, on the morning of her abduction, she placed two here. And two the day before, now naught but loose petals . . ." He glanced at Alain, dashing tears from his eyes. "I haven't had the heart to remove them."

Alain felt his lips twitch into the semblance of a smile. "The red one looks like the rose I gave her that morning."

Waldron nodded as if it came as no surprise. "Del planted the roses for her after their mother, my beloved wife, died several years ago." He sighed, gazing at the other sarcophagus. Its lovely female effigy led Alain to presume it housed the remains of Kendra's mother. "I think Edwina and Del would have liked you, despite your fighting on the other side at Hastings."

"You didn't approve of your son's choice to join Harold's cause, did you?" Alain asked.

"Approve? I was proud of him, aye. But how can any parent approve of a child's decision to risk life and limb, no matter how worthy the cause?" His expression turned frank. "I will not lie to you, Alain. I would have rejoiced to see Harold defeat your duke and send him fleeing tuck-tailed for Normandy. But Harold failed, and so here we stand with a Norman overlord rather than a Saxon one, and life muddles on. Del must have accepted that fact and was prepared to live with it; he was a realist at heart. I believe he was murdered for his realism."

That rang true enough in Alain's ears, based on the suspicions he harbored. "Lord willing, I shall return with answers."

"Just returning with your bride will make me happy." Waldron thrust out his hand, and he and Alain gripped forearms. "God speed you and guard you well, son."

The fatherly benediction bolstered Alain's spirits more than he ever would have imagined possible.

With a sharp nod to Kendra's family, dead as well as living, he strode from the chapel to join Ruaud and those of Waldron's fyrd who had not been ordered to guard the burh, tugging on his leather riding gloves as he went.

Alain's warhorse, Chou, saw him coming and tossed her head, pricking her ears and nickering a greeting. Ruaud, already mounted astride Azure at the head of the unit, added his admonishment for Alain to hurry. Dawn had yielded to a glorious summer morning; with favorable weather, the hundred-member company could cut half a day off the two-day journey to Thornhill.

A stable hand steadied Chou as Alain climbed the mounting block and hoisted himself into the saddle. After he settled in, the lad handed up Alain's shield, emblazoned with the de Bellencombre rose. Alain drew his sword and held it aloft, glinting bright and deadly in the morning rays.

"For God, Lady Kendra, and Edgarburh!"

With a thunderous whoop, echoed by the surrounding crowd, the men took up Alain's shout as they set spurs to their horses' flanks and cantered away from the rising sun.

While streaming past the stables, they were joined by a noisy black streak that scattered chickens and children in its wake. Alain allowed himself a smile as Noir adopted an easy lope beside Chou, who sidled a bit but calmed when she realized the hound wasn't a threat. Alain welcomed Noir's presence.

He could use all the help he could find.

WHAT HAD begun in Sarum as a dreamy summer morning had by nones transformed into a dreary, drizzly nightmare. Odo pulled his sable-trimmed cloak's hood closer to shut out the damp. Much more of this, and his mail would rust solid.

He slid a glance toward his half brother, who rode tall in the saddle, sans hood, defying the weather. That William bothered wearing a cloak gave mute testimony to the fact that defiance sometimes had to be tempered with wisdom.

In due course, William's messenger returned with the welcome news that Edgarburh stood ready to receive its king. When they topped the final rise separating them from their destination and Edgarburh lay before them, Odo wanted to whoop for sheer joy.

Instead, he nudged his black mare to keep pace with William's sorrel stallion as the king ordered their company to canter the remaining distance.

Edgarburh's residents greeted William and his troop with respectful if wary bows, the hoods of their drab cloaks making the people kneeling in the mud appear like giant mushrooms.

One mushroom rivaled the eye of a peacock feather.

"Thane Waldron, well met," said William as amicably as possible, given the sodden conditions. "If memory serves, I believe you met my regent and half brother, Bishop Odo de Bayeux, the last time you visited court."

The man in the peacock-blue cloak lifted his head. The rain had plastered his white hair to his forehead in haphazard strips. His eyes shone clear and unafraid. "Your Majesty and his regent honor humble Edgarburh with your august presence. To what, pray, may we ascribe this good fortune?"

William's stallion pawed the muck and shook his head, spraying droplets everywhere, doubtless as eager to retreat from this miserable weather as everyone else was. The water muffled the tack's jingling.

"Two of my best knights are missing," said the king. "I want to know why."

"Then might I suggest that Your Majesty and his men join us for hot mutton and mead in the feast hall?" The thane swept a cloaked arm in the general direction of the timber building behind him. "I believe my tale shall be easier to stomach in that manner."

Chortling, William swung down from the saddle and ordered his men to do likewise, admonishing them to see to the comfort of the horses before accepting the thane's hospitality. He entrusted his stallion into the care of one of his men as Waldron rose and directed his guards to assist the soldiers.

Odo and William's three ranking bodyguards handed their reins to other soldiers, and the five Normans followed their Saxon host into his small but warm and aromatic hall, where a feast awaited them. While William and his retainers fell gustily upon the mountains of mutton and bread, Waldron regaled him with what he knew of the events surrounding Sir Robert and Sir Ruaud.

"In fact, Your Majesty just missed seeing them," concluded the thane. "They departed at dawn this morning to return to Thornhill for my daughter."

"Thornhill?" asked Odo.

"In the Glastonbury district, Your Grace."

That the thane had mistaken Odo's question for ignorance, the bishop let pass without comment.

William, who had claimed what had to be the thane's dais chair, straightened to regard Waldron. "Are you aware that an upsurge of pilgrim activity has been sighted in that area? Numbers that might suggest an army?"

Waldron appeared genuinely surprised. "Alain—that is, Sir Robert expressed concern that he might face armed resistance, but he said nothing of the proportions you indicate, my lord." Color drained from his face. "Do you think he and Ruaud and my men may have ridden into a trap?"

"I know not what to think, Thane Waldron," William snapped, "other than perhaps my policies toward the Saxon people have been too lenient."

Odo whispered into William's ear, "Your Majesty will do well to recall that this Saxon is not your enemy."

"No?" William all but roared, startling a nearby maidservant into sloshing her mead pitcher. As she squeaked an apology, curtseyed, and withdrew, another servant rushed to mop up the spill. Oblivious, the king continued, "How do I know Thane Waldron didn't plan to send my knights into harm's way to be destroyed by the traitors with whom he is in league?"

To his credit, Waldron returned William's glare with steady calmness. "Thane Ulfric of Thornhill is my late wife's kinsman; that fact is pointless for me to deny. But I have no knowledge of his plans beyond his longtime desire to marry my daughter." His bushy white eyebrows lowered. "Ulfric knows well my loyalty to Your Majesty. Why, therefore, would he confide in me?"

The tension crackling between king and thane prickled the hairs on Odo's arms.

"Perhaps that loyalty," William ground out, "stretches only as far as you believe you can seek justice from me for the Norman knight who murdered your son."

Waldron's eyes widened, his face flushed, and he glanced away for a moment. "That might have held true at Cristes mæsse when I presented my petition to Your Majesty," he admitted. "But no longer. Sir Robert has reason to believe that someone else, not a Norman, is responsible."

"Who?" asked Odo.

"Good my lords, I would rather not say until I have proof, which I have every confidence Sir Robert shall obtain. He did confirm that the Norman shield my men found at the ambush site had been looted from someone who perished at Hastings."

Confronted with the king's impassive stare, Waldron went to one knee at William's feet. "I seek nothing from Your Majesty now other than your trust. Not even that much, just your willingness to believe that I have not betrayed your excellent knights."

Odo sharpened his senses as he scrutinized the thane. "My lord," he said to William, "I discern no guile in this man. I believe his tale is worthy of Your Majesty's consideration. I also believe it would be in the best interests of the realm to move the regiment from Sarum to the Salisbury Plain, perhaps invoking combat drills to avoid alarming the local residents until we receive more information."

"And what would be in the best interests of the Crown?" The years of their kinship had taught Odo to recognize the almost-smile flirting with William's lips as eagerness for action.

"That, of course, depends on whether the Crown wishes to discover in person what has happened to the Crown's knights. In that event, the Crown would be wise to wait for reinforcements."

"Order them here, to Edgarburh, rather than the Salisbury Plain?" William pinched his chin between thumb and forefinger. "What says a Saxon thane to the prospect of quartering a Norman regiment upon his doorstep?"

Waldron, still kneeling, jutted his chin. "Your Majesty, although I am weary unto death of battles and wars, I would quarter the devil in my own bed if I thought that could help forge peace between our peoples."

The king tipped back his head and uttered a throaty laugh. "Well said, Thane Waldron. Well said. If even half of your peers possessed a fifth of your humor, ruling your lot would be tenfold easier." William swiveled his head toward Odo. "Pen the order to bring the troops to Edgarburh with best possible speed."

As Odo moved to obey, he saw the king signal Waldron to rise, which the latter did without hesitation. William grinned at the thane. "It appears you shall be required to host me and my retinue a while yet," he said.

Waldron, his hand resting over his heart, bowed double. "Your Majesty, nothing would please me more." Not one trace of sarcasm corrupted his tone.

Odo strode toward the corner where the company's saddlebags had been stowed, chuckling to himself. That canny Saxon could give many a young Norman courtier lessons in diplomacy.

Chapter 18

SWIRLING THE WINE at the bottom of her crimson glass goblet, Kendra languished on her tall-backed chair in Thornhill's feast hall, wistfully listening to the rain pummel the roof timbers. The sound reminded her of her beloved Edgarburh, but it also reminded her how foolish it would be to attempt traveling under such unpredictable conditions.

If Ulfric would let her leave.

Thus far she'd been unable to complete King Harold's healing, and although this didn't seem to anger Ulfric yet, she suspected that could change without warning.

Just as, without warning, more thanes arrived each day to take counsel with Ulfric.

Four days ago, following Sunday's High Mass, the burh had experienced the largest influx yet. Some thanes Kendra recognized; most she didn't. Some looked handsome enough to flirt with if she'd been of such a mind; most ogled her whether she appreciated their attentions or not.

Hence, Ulfric had made a point of parading her upon his arm before the assembled crowd at mealtimes, during mass, and for every other excuse he could devise. Even though no plans had yet been made—and she was not about to press Ulfric on the issue—he made it clear to everyone that she was his intended bride.

Inwardly, she cringed at each mention of the word.

The man whose bride she wanted to become was probably entrenched at his favorite tavern with a wench in his lap and a flagon of ale in his hand.

Nay, that was unfair. Alain wasn't the wenching type.

With the heel of her hand she rubbed the spot over the source of her ache, closing her eyes and tipping her chair back against one of the hall's vertical timbers.

"My dear, are you ill?"

She didn't need to open her eyes to know who'd addressed her. "Merely fatigued, Ulfric." *And heartsick.* She righted her chair and regarded him, not bothering to disguise her weariness. "I thank you for your concern."

He patted her hand. "Perhaps you should retire to your quarters and rest in preparation for this evening's"—his smile turned avaricious—"event."

She suppressed a groan. These "events," as Ulfric publicly called her secret healing sessions with King Harold (and she refused to regard the man in any other manner, regardless of the current political landscape), were taking a toll on her. Each time she finished, the king appeared to rally, but Ulfric would enter the cottage and order her outside. And the next day His Majesty would seem to have lost whatever ground he'd gained.

Kendra would have given her eye teeth to know what Ulfric did inside the cottage after she left, but the king's monk-body-guards rendered any effort to eavesdrop impossible.

Casting her cousin a grateful smile for the reprieve, however small, she rose, stepped down from the dais, and began threading her way past the lower tables toward the door.

A messenger entered and rushed toward the head table, knocking a platter of roast pork from a manservant's hands and almost colliding with a woman pouring ale. The messenger scarcely noticed Kendra as he hurtled past her, except to nod an apology for jostling her arm. Believing his message was none of her concern, she continued out the door.

The rain had ebbed to a drizzle. She still felt obliged to pull up her cloak's hood, but the lighter rainfall permitted her a change of plans.

Rather than the manor house, she headed toward her favorite retreat at Thornhill: the bee garden. Gratefully, she discovered the bench had been kept dry by the apple tree's canopy. Congratulating herself for having escaped the feast hall's cloying atmosphere, she inhaled the garden's earthy fragrances.

The problem of Alain she felt powerless to remedy. Unless he returned to her—and she wished for that moment with her entire being—she would never see him again, for it would be unseemly for her to seek him out if she ever left Thornhill.

If.

She shook her head to dispel the disturbing notion.

Her mind wandered to other questions that had been nagging her for several days. Why was Ulfric being visited by a constant parade of thanes? Why, despite her best efforts, was King Harold's condition showing no improvement? And why did Ulfric insist upon the king's recovery?

Perhaps it was the association between the fruit-weighted boughs overhead and the wine she'd imbibed with her midday meal, wine bearing the familiar taste of apples. Perhaps the king's healing sessions had drained her far more than she'd realized, and her mind was losing touch with reality. Or perhaps the garden's herbs wrought a special brand of healing magic.

Whatever the reason, ludicrous ideas began to form . . .

She recalled where she'd tasted that unique wine before: as the outlaws' captive. They could have stolen it, true. But the cavern had contained only gold, silver, jewels, and objects crafted from those materials, nothing as mundane as wine casks. Nor had she seen such stores inside the tower.

While the outlaws could have kept plundered wine elsewhere, she couldn't shake the impression that Ulfric was connected to them. In retrospect, it seemed too convenient that he'd been standing on the hillside as she and Alain had finished digging out of the cavern, as if he'd known where they were going to emerge.

And why didn't the dog bark a warning when he'd defended them so vehemently before? The animal had to have seen Ulfric. Could her cousin have been familiar to him and thus not perceived as a threat?

What if Ulfric knew about the fortune in the cavern, how it had been acquired, and he had plans for its use?

Kendra chewed her lip and frowned, certain the visiting thanes factored into those plans, but their contingents seemed far too small. Unless most of the men were being quartered elsewhere.

One by one the pieces fell into place, and she did not like the picture they formed.

She rose, gathered her skirts in her fists, and pelted from the garden, heedless of the many puddles. She had to turn her cousin from the mad course he'd chosen. Her chances for success would be slim at best, but she had to try.

If she didn't, the consequences unleashed by his perilous plan would consume her and everyone she held dear.

ULFRIC CRUSHED the parchment in his fist. With his other hand gripping his chair's carved armrest, he leaned forward, feeling a fierce scowl drag at his mouth.

"Tell Dragon he shall ready his followers to commence another 'pilgrimage' as best he can in this accursed weather. He is to await my signal to depart," he told the messenger.

The man saluted, turned smartly, and strode away, snatching a mutton joint from one of the far tables before quitting the feast hall.

Ulfric narrowed his eyes upon the retreating figure. Under other circumstances, he'd have taught the whelp a lesson for displaying such insolence. But time had allied itself with William the Bastard.

He stood, and so did the other thanes. With a word to the men-at-arms to continue their repast, Ulfric motioned their leaders to join him behind the dais. Menservants hurried to bring forth enough benches for Ulfric's distinguished guests.

"What has happened, Ulfric? Why have you ordered another"—Oesc's grin showed more gaps than teeth—"pilgrimage? And to where?"

Ulfric kept his tone low and even. "His Majesty's orders," he lied. "It seems the Norman usurper has gotten wind of a stench he doesn't like. He is mustering troops at Sarum."

Wihtred muttered a curse. "We're not ready, are we? How can we be? We cannot hope to move until this rain lifts. Besides"—the old thane cast a nervous glance toward the servants' entrance—"His Majesty isn't ready, I'll wager."

"We shall have to be ready, His Majesty included." That last bit he uttered for his listeners' benefit; the only man privy to the full extent of Ulfric's plans and powers was commanding the "pilgrim" camp outside Glastonbury.

His pronouncement was greeted with assorted mutterings but no real dissent. Yet.

Time to lay the matter to rest.

Ulfric stood and regarded each of the thanes in turn. "Does anyone here wish to return home and become enslaved under a Norman yoke? If so, then do it now." As he had suspected, no one was willing to admit to cowardice. "Good. Leave His Majesty to me. When the weather breaks, he shall march with us."

More than a few thanes wrinkled their brows in obvious skepticism, but Ulfric ignored them and continued, "I need each of you to return to the encampment and help Dragon prepare our men for the 'pilgrimage' to meet the Bastard of Normandy on the Salisbury Plain."

HALFWAY TO her intended destination, Kendra saw Ulfric striding toward her.

"Ah, cousin, well met." Ulfric's smile seemed tense. He slipped his hand beneath her elbow and began escorting her toward the king's cottage. "I—that is, my honored guest has need of your services much sooner than anticipated."

Kendra stopped. When Ulfric tried to tug her along, she refused to budge. "That is why I came looking for you, Ulfric." Planting her hands on her hips, she pumped disapproval into her glare. "This isn't right."

"What? Healing a man who's badly wounded in body and spirit?"

"You shouldn't use him to foster a dead political cause."

Ulfric's laugh sounded genuine. "You think I'm trying to get him well enough to put him back on the throne?"

"Aren't you?" When he refused to respond, she asked, "How else do you explain your noble visitors—visitors with a well-known dislike of King William?"

"As have you, my dear." He clutched her arm and bent so low that his lips brushed her ear. "You are involved too deeply to start growing a conscience."

She looked at him, aghast. "Involved—in what, exactly?"

"Why, returning England to Saxon rule, of course."

She noted his choice of words but felt it safer to remain silent. He appeared to mistake her silence for acceptance and started pushed her onward.

"Remember, Kendra, I will make a lot of trouble for you with the Church if you refuse to comply."

That, she could well believe. Better to feign obedience while formulating an escape plan. She allowed Ulfric to resume their course with no further resistance.

"My lord Ulfric," said Brother Oswald with a stiff nod as they drew near. "Lady Kendra, your appearance is most fortunate. I was about to send for you."

All concern for Ulfric and his schemes fled. "Why?" She pulled free of her cousin's grasp. "What has happened?"

The monk cast a worried glance toward the cottage's door. "He has had a seizure, my lady. One moment he was sitting in his chair, talking—or trying to. The next moment, he was writhing on the floor, clawing his chest and gasping for breath. Ethel and Brother Eric are tending him." Palpable relief washed over his face. "But I am glad you've come."

She burst through the door, shed her sodden cloak, and hastened across the room. The monks had heaved the king onto his bed, but sloppily, as if even in his emaciated condition his frame was too large for them to handle. His pallor and labored breathing alarmed her. Brother Eric twisted around to glare at the intruder, but the moment her identity registered he surrendered his seat.

"Was he eating anything?"

"Nay, my lady," said Ethel, swabbing the king's face with a damp cloth. The gesture seemed to lessen the tension crouching there, though his eyes didn't open.

Kendra pried apart his jaws and forced her fingers down his throat until he gagged, just to be sure. Satisfied that the airway was clear, she sat and grasped his limp hand. The familiar heat flared, and neither of them flinched.

The mental picture that formed was one of infinite, empty blackness.

Not knowing what else to do, she willed her healing energy into the void, hoping to contain and conquer it. But weariness weighted her mind, and the blackness intensified around her.

"Your Majesty, please," she whispered, feeling her voice quiver. "Please don't leave us. We need you."

"England needs you," said Ulfric, hovering over Kendra's shoulder.

England? England is done with me.

The strength of the voice in Kendra's mind caused her to open her eyes and study the man sprawling on the bed. His color had improved, and he seemed to be breathing easier, but her sense of his imminent danger remained.

She closed her eyes and plunged into the blackness, where a faint pinpoint of light glimmered. She concentrated on coaxing that light to brighten and spread.

My cousin doesn't seem to think England is done with you.

Your cousin has his own plans, and I factor into them only to a limited degree.

'Tis not true.

Oh, yes. What do you think we talk about after you leave?

I don't know, Your Majesty. Battle strategies?

An odd, buoyant sensation shivered through her, as though King Harold had laughed.

Mundane matters, Lady Kendra. My childhood, my family, my training, my friends. Ways I had gotten into trouble, and the punishments that had been meted out. My favorite food, favorite drink, favorite horse, favorite hound. Likes and dislikes. My greatest joys and worst fears. Strengths. Weaknesses. Things about me that no one else would know. Things no one else would even care to know unless he was planning to take my place.

What? Sheer determination kept her gripping his hand. *Ulfric looks nothing at all like Your Majesty. How can he believe he could take your place? Perhaps he knows someone who does resemble you.*

If that were so, then why doesn't that man talk to me? As Kendra's mind spluttered about for an answer, the king continued, *You and your mother are not the only ones in your family with strange abilities.*

How do you know about my mother, my lord? What abilities do you believe Ulfric possesses?

Your mother, dear lady, I learned about from your conversation with Ethel a few days ago. My body may no longer obey my will, but I hear and comprehend everything. A long pause ensued, as if the king were contemplating a weighty matter of state. *Thane Ulfric I am less certain about, for I have not seen him use his power upon himself. But when he and I are alone together, he grasps my hand, and it feels as if a portion of me is flowing into him, somehow—the exact opposite of what your healing power does for me.*

No wonder the king had appeared to suffer a reversal after each of Ulfric's visits. She felt her mind reel from the implications. *But how—draining your life force? How can that be possible?* Anger ignited. *Never mind how he accomplishes it; how dare he even contemplate such a despicable act?*

How, indeed. I have no answers for those questions, Lady Kendra.

I will stop him, my lord. I must stop him if you are to recover. He shall harm you no longer.

Your cousin's ambitions run dangerously high. How can you hope to combat that?

I don't know, but I shall try. Please sleep now, Your Majesty—feign it, if you must—and leave Ulfric to me.

As she sensed his consciousness relax, she pondered his startling revelations. With her pouring her energy into him, only to have Ulfric suck it out, small wonder she kept feeling like a piece of damp, wrung linen. Nevertheless, before severing contact she willed as much energy as she could spare to bolster him.

For she feared that if King Harold died, Ulfric would cease to find her useful, especially if he suspected her of understanding his scheme.

Her pulse racing, she released his hand and opened her eyes. Ulfric reached for him, but she tangled her hand in Ulfric's and stood. "I believe I've pulled him back from the brink, cousin, but he needs to sleep." She tugged Ulfric away from the bed and disengaged her hand.

"But—"

Brother Eric courteously but firmly grasped Ulfric's arm and escorted him toward the cottage's door. "Remember, my lord. Brother Oswald and I serve him, first and foremost. Not you."

Ulfric glared at the monk, but he wrenched his arm free, snatched his cloak from a peg by the door, flung it about his shoulders, and stormed out of the cottage without comment.

After the door had swung to, she noticed that Ethel had resumed her bedside vigil. Kendra stepped to within whispering distance of Brother Eric.

"If you value your lord's life, don't let *her* lord back in here ever again."

Eric's wide-eyed expression demanded her to elaborate, but she pointed a glance toward Ethel. "Trust me," she mouthed.

Nodding, he ushered her outside. Ulfric, thank heaven, was nowhere in sight, though Kendra couldn't help but associate the roiling rain clouds with the political storm he was fostering. After pulling up her cloak's hood to fend off the downpour, she dashed for the manor and the tenuous safety of her chambers, wondering how long she could remain safe while protecting King Harold's life.

Chapter 19

HAT HAD BEGUN late Wednesday afternoon as a drizzle had by Thursday morning transformed into a deluge of biblical proportions that persisted, to varying degrees, through Friday. Rations, clothing, bedrolls, skin: nothing escaped the wetness. Even when Lofwin led the rest of the troop to make camp in an old Roman temple, the structure's ruined roof offered little respite.

As the waters rose, so did tempers. Horses snapped at each other and their riders. Men snapped at each other and their mounts. Noir snapped at everyone.

Two things kept the group from each other's throats: food, sodden as it was, and their mutual desire to see Kendra safe.

Alain suspected he wasn't the only one chafing at the fact that the rain and mud had almost doubled their journey's time. He'd hoped to confront Ulfric yesterday. Now, Friday morning found them with a long day's ride before reaching Thornhill.

After the men had broken fast and buried the meal's remains, he ordered them to don their pilgrims' robes. If Ulfric could use the trick to hide troops, then, by God, so would Alain. Riding would present a challenge, but traveling all day in the mucky spray thrown up by the horses' hooves would soil the robes and lend more credibility to the disguises.

Having another layer of cloth to cut the wind was welcome too.

At sext, when the sun deigned to show itself at its zenith and the company paused for the midday meal, Alain selected Garth and Lofwin to ride ahead and scout Glastonbury and Thornhill.

"Sir Alain, let me go with Lofwin instead." Grizzled Cædwlin, his injured shoulder still bandaged, gazed at Alain steadily, fierce determination masking whatever pain he must be feeling. "I may not be much good in a fight, but I can help keep you out of one until the right time."

Alain had to smile, as much for Cædwlin's pluckiness as for the fact that he'd called him "Sir Alain," a habit that had been adopted by most of the fyrd as a sign of acceptance.

While Chou tossed her head and splashed a hoof in a puddle, her rider pondered Cædwlin's request. The pilgrim garb would help shield their identities, especially given Lofwin's gift for exercising stealth. Besides, Alain could well imagine Cædwlin's yearning to expunge his guilt for having allowed Kendra to be abducted by contributing to her return.

He nodded at Cædwlin and Lofwin in turn. "God speed and protect you both. Report back as soon as you can."

Their report, when they returned after nones, he didn't like in the least. The pilgrims' encampment, which had lain south of Glastonbury, now sprawled east of it, between Alain's troop and Thornhill. A washed-out bridge along the road leading south from town had necessitated the camp's move, but the river's course bent around to flow beside the east-west road for a while, and it had flooded that road as well.

"You think they were moving out when the bridge washed away?" Ruaud asked. "Where do you suppose they were headed?"

"Planning to move, yes. But as to where . . ." Alain stroked Chou's neck, trying to recall the deerhide map he'd seen in Regent Odo's workroom. "I wager they want a good road that heads east to Sarum, where they can pick up the road that will take them to London and William's doorstep."

"If he's in residence," Ruaud reminded him.

"Perhaps he has returned and they know it. Or they might be planning to make trouble for Regent Odo, hoping to lure William back across the Channel." Alain made a fist and pounded his thigh; never before had duty yanked him so hard in different directions. "We must stop them."

Ruaud rolled his eyes; it was Lofwin who voiced the objection. "With all due respect, Sir Alain, what chance do you believe a hundred will stand against more than a thousand?"

"Using armed force?" Alain pinched thumb and forefinger together to indicate his answer and regarded Lofwin levelly. "Besides, your lady—and mine—comes first."

That won a grunt of approval from Cæwlin, who, busy massaging his shoulder, had been content to let Lofwin deliver their scouting report. "We could skirt the camp." He squinted up at the soggy skies, swiped rain from his face, and shrugged. "'Twould take the rest of the day, mayhap past nightfall, but it could be done. Any patrols they might have out won't be ranging far in this weather."

"Did you find a ford?" Ruaud asked.

"The river has flooded the road for quite some way, Sir Ruaud," Lofwin replied, "but doesn't cross it. An army would have a lot of trouble, what with wagons and such, but a troop our size could pick our way around the flooded areas."

Alain heard the hesitation in Lofwin's suggestion. Staring toward the as yet unseen army and river that blocked his path, he pondered his options. "Either way, we lose too much time. We will be unable to assist Kendra until the morrow." Lofwin and Cæwlin nodded resignedly. Alain continued, "Therefore, we shall gather as much information as we can—"

"And hope we survive to report it to the king, eh?" Ruaud gave Alain an incredulous look. "You, who live by stealth and subterfuge, shall ride straight into the enemy's encampment? Is that what you propose?"

Alain grinned. "My mother had a cardinal rule for mingling within the various circles at King Edward's court:

"Always act like you belong."

"*Ah, oui, mes amis,*" Ruaud said to their gaping Saxon companions, chuckling. "Alain, he always does this. He loves to makes life—what is your word? Interesting."

EOSA THORGUDSON hunkered on the cot in his rawhide tent, tracing patterns in the muck with his dagger's point while waiting for the end of the deluge or the end of the world, whichever came first.

At the rate this damned rain was falling, with no letup in sight, he felt the end of the world to be the safer wager.

The hides kept the rain off his head, and his men had done a credible job of trenching around the tents, but water blew in every time someone poked his head through the flap.

He should be thankful for this weather, he reminded himself, for it kept all but the most intrepid folks indoors and away from the temptation of asking too many questions about the "pilgrims."

Oh, his men had frequented the abbey church, and no mistake. With the help of his scribe, Eosa had developed a rotation so that a contingent attended all services during daylight hours: prime, at dawn, followed at three-hour intervals by tierce, sext, nones, and vespers. Men of a more religious bent—and he had several, along with a huge number of lazy sods seeking to escape camp chores—could attend as many services as they wished.

A farthing apiece seemed a reasonable fee to assure the monks' silence. Thinking about what his "brethren" were doing under the nose of the fat Norman abbot gave him a smile.

But the delay was straining the men's tempers and the "pilgrims'" credibility.

The plan had called for a mustering period of three days. Now, here they sat with more than a week gone, halted by shite-laden water, of all things! And no sensible choice but to wait for the Brue to recede. It was as if the finger of God Himself had pinned them to this place.

The finger of God, in the form of two formidable Norman knights, had squashed most of the members of Eosa's earlier assignment like so many ants.

His thick braid whispered across his leather-armored back as he shook off an involuntary chill.

That fonging rabble had served their purpose, and Eosa considered himself well rid of them. He still wasn't sure why he'd consented to allow their sole survivor to join his group, but Snake had proven adept with a sword and had not caused any trouble so far. Nor would the bastard, if he wanted to see more sunrises.

"My lord Dragon?"

Eosa looked toward the tent flap to regard the hooded face of Bertred, his scribe, whose camp name was Nib. Rain had molded the woolen fabric to his skull and made him stink like a wet sheep. Nib looked as miserable as Eosa felt, and he waved him into the tent.

"Report," ordered the man known inside the camp and beyond as Dragon.

"Sir, another troop has arrived."

"What?" Eosa felt his eyebrows lower. "How?"

"'Tis a cavalry unit, sir. They must have found a small ford downriver."

Damn. He would have liked to have learned of a ford that could be traversed by wagons.

Another thought occurred, and he gave Nib a sharp stare. "They could have missed us. Why the bloody hell were they so late?"

"Their commander, Lofwin Octhason, claims the weather delayed them."

That, Eosa could believe, but . . . "Lofwin? I know a man by that name. Where does this unit hail from?"

"Edgarburh, my lord."

"Indeed." It took all of his self-control not to gape at the scribe. What in hell could have persuaded Thane Waldron, a Norman shite-eater, to change his diet?

Or had he?

"Send Lofwin Octhason to me at once."

ALAIN STOOD, cloaked and hooded, between two of Lofwin's subordinates inside the camp commander's tent while Lofwin stepped forward to converse with the man everyone called Dragon.

Here, no one bothered with the pretense of being a pilgrim. Two armed men flanked Dragon's camp table, which consisted of planks balanced atop two pairs of tripods. Maps and parchment lay scattered across the work surface, illuminated by several oil lamps, though Alain stood too far away to discern any useful information. Two men guarded either side of the tent's flap, with hundreds more a shout away.

The tendrils of smoke from the lamps did little to dispel the tent hides' mustiness.

Dragon stood behind the table, clad in an unpilgrimlike leather jerkin and breeches, a seax strapped to his right thigh and a longsword riding his left hip. A hauberk hung from a rod suspended between two short posts nearby. An unpainted, iron-rimmed oval shield stood beside one post, and a pointed iron helmet surmounted the other.

Arms folded, Dragon scowled like his namesake, his cleft lip making the expression appear even more sinister.

A vague recollection stirred within Alain's mind.

"Prove to me that Thane Waldron has changed his opinion of the Bastard of Normandy," Dragon demanded of Lofwin.

"Our presence, in support of this cause, should be proof enough, Eosa," Lofwin replied.

Dragon bounded from behind the table to within inches of Lofwin's face. "That name has no meaning here. If you or any of your men"—he glared at Alain and the others—"utter it again, you shall need a map and a torch to find your ballocks. Understood?"

The tattoo of raindrops on the tent's roof intensified as if to underscore the threat.

Lofwin nodded calmly. As Dragon's stance relaxed and he backed up a pace, Alain chastised himself for failing to anticipate that Ulfric could have appointed a commander who might recognize Waldron's men.

"Why should I believe that you are here to help our cause," Dragon continued, "not acting as William's spies?"

To Alain's surprise, Lofwin laughed. "How long have you known me, *Dragon*? Do you believe I would have marched my men into the heart of your lair if I'd been ordered to spy upon it?" He crossed his arms, smirking.

Dragon grunted. "Perhaps you've been spying on us already, and you've shown yourself only to cover your tracks."

"My friend, if I had tracks to cover, you would never find them. Even with a map and a torch." Lofwin's expression turned somber. "As to why Waldron has sent us, I'll wager you know about the commanded marriage between Lady Kendra and one of William's knights?"

Dragon's lips twitched. Alain could have sworn the man was trying not to leer at the mention of Kendra's name.

A fact clicked into place. He hadn't met the man, but Kendra had . . . and Dragon had damaged her ability to enjoy the pleasures Alain had offered her.

He fought the impulse to run this *tas de merde* through. Lord willing, the opportunity would arise later.

"I know Waldron didn't attend William's coronation to protest the marriage decree," Dragon replied to Lofwin's question.

"Nay," Lofwin allowed, "but he's had half a year to watch her become more miserable because of it."

That much was true. Recalling her reaction when he'd tried to present the de Bellencombre brooch, Alain swallowed a sigh.

Dragon appeared about to speak, but Lofwin cut him off with his upraised right fist. Dragon's guards tightened their grips on their weapons, and Alain wished he had not surrendered his sword to the guards outside the tent.

"I would give this arm to see Lady Kendra happy. So would every member of Thane Waldron's fyrd." Lofwin lowered his hand, and the guards relaxed visibly, if not completely. "We hope our participation here can prevent her from being forced to marry the wrong man."

Alain almost smiled.

The camp's commander scrutinized them for several long moments apiece, fingering his sword's pommel. Alain's pulse kicked up a notch when it seemed as if Dragon were paying particular attention to him.

When assent came, he wasn't certain he'd heard aright.

"You are most fortunate, Lofwin Octhason," Dragon added. "If there was any way for me to keep watch over you and your troop myself, I would." His snarl grew more pronounced. "Make camp where you can, but if you or your men so much as piss where you shouldn't, it will be the last transgression you ever make."

As Alain exited the tent behind Lofwin and the other fyrd members, he scowled. *Dragon* would not make any more transgressions after Alain finished carving him into raven bait.

ALAIN WOKE, stiff and sore from having spent a fitful night in his dreams on the Hastings battlefield. He sat up, massaging his left shoulder, the one that had been injured in battle and now ached with the weather's every turn.

Fervently, he hoped that saving Kendra would help him to atone for his failures—if he could devise a way to get the fyrd away from this encampment without raising suspicions.

He rose, already clad in tunic and breeches, and donned his boots. Stepping over Ruaud and his eight other tentmates, he made his careful way toward the flap and peered out. A glance at the graying skies confirmed his guess that dawn was nigh. Fog had rolled in off the swollen river, bathing everything in mist.

Alain was surprised to notice that this section of the encampment was already bustling with activity. Men emerged from other tents, clad in pilgrims' robes, and departed in the same direction.

He left his tent in time to stop one. Roughening his voice to mask his accent, he asked, "Where's everyone going?"

The man gave him a curious look. "You don't know?" Before Alain could respond, he said, "Ah, you must be one of the new ones. Didn't Dragon put your unit on the rotation?"

"For what?"

"For going to mass at the abbey is what, though you're allowed to go even if it's not your unit's turn."

Alain felt his mouth stretch into the widest grin he'd made in days. "Many thanks . . . Brother."

Chuckling, the man moved off to join another group.

Alain ducked inside and rousted everyone else.

"Cæwlin, wake the rest of the fyrd. Have them arm themselves, don their pilgrims' robes, and meet outside this tent."

The fyrd veteran nodded, dressed, and departed to fulfill Alain's command.

"You have a plan to get us out of camp, Sir Alain?" Lofwin asked.

"I hope so. We shall join this morning's procession to the abbey but peel off, a few at a time, outside the camp and circle back to the picket lines for our horses. Lofwin, I want you in the first rank to break away. If the picket sentries challenge you, tell them that Dragon has ordered our unit to ride to Thornhill."

"Brilliant, Alain. That will put him on our trail faster than you can blink," Ruaud protested.

"Not if Dragon thinks we have tried to throw him off the scent," Lofwin said. "But our departure will be noticed."

"Sooner or later," Alain agreed. He shrugged into his robe and cinched it about his waist. "We leave our remounts and everything that isn't armor, weapons, or tack." By this time, his tentmates had finished dressing. Alain spread his hands like a priest preparing to deliver a benediction. "Brethren, let us pray that our skill, luck, and the fog will see us to our destination before Dragon realizes aught is amiss."

"You LET them leave camp?" Eosa, seated behind his field table, couldn't believe what he'd heard. "All of the fongers?"

The sentry ducked his head and scrunched one shoulder in a shrug. "Don't rightly know, sir. Hard to tell, what with everyone hooded and leaving at nigh unto the same time."

"Find out, and report back to me. Wait," he said as the sentry saluted and began to leave. The man halted. Eosa rose from behind the table, snatched his cloak from the post, and pinned it in place as he strode past the sentry. "Show me their camp."

The heavy fog caused both of them to pull up their hoods.

Eosa's thoughts churned as he squelched with the sentry through the camp. If Waldron's men had come to spy on them, why in hell would they leave after just one night? Eosa had ensured that nothing incriminating had been present during his meeting with Lofwin. Their mission could be one of confirmation—but why would Waldron have sent a hundred men? Why not just two or three to observe from a distance and depart?

And how the fonging, bloody hell had Waldron learned of the pilgrim ploy?

Not from Ulfric; Eosa would have staked his share of the mercenaries' payment on that fact.

Unless . . . his thoughts wandered back to a much more pleasurable task he'd enjoyed recently, though it had been cut short. Ulfric would have killed him if he'd dared to take any further liberties with Lady Kendra than he had done. And the temptation had been so strong, with the bitch brazenly baring her legs to show where they had been chafed. In fact, if Ulfric's summons hadn't come when it had, Eosa might have swived her anyway, in spite of the strict orders to the contrary.

A startling realization halted him. If not for Ulfric's summons, he, Eosa Thorgudson, might be feeding the ravens along with the rest of the outlaws.

"Sir?" The sentry looked at him, puzzled. "We're not there yet."

Feeling stupid for the lapse, Eosa motioned the man forward and matched his stride. When they reached the area near the encampment's eastern edge where Waldron's men had pitched their tents, he was not surprised to find them all empty.

Oh, the bedrolls, shovels, flagons, wineskins, rations, and cooking utensils lay strewn about, but not one scrap of saddle leather or so much as a dagger had been left behind. It looked as if the men might return, but Eosa knew better. He also had a strong suspicion he'd find a hundred horses missing from the picket lines and dispatched the sentry to confirm his guess.

After the man departed, Eosa berated himself for not discerning Lofwin's true intent soon enough to have prevented it.

Ulfric was going to be livid.

Resisting the urge to clutch his throat, he strode away as fast as dignity allowed. Before reaching his headquarters tent, the sentry caught up with him and blurted out the news that Waldron's men had retrieved their mounts.

"Any idea where they went, man?"

"Thornhill, sir, on your orders, or so they claimed." The sentry shrugged. "In this bloody fog, the picket guards couldn't rightly tell which way they went."

Naturally. But was Thornhill a ruse, or their intended destination?

Having worked out a plan, he stopped at an adjacent tent to speak with his second-in-command. He shouldered between the sentries, yanked aside the flap, and thrust his head through.

"Dirk, I need two hundred of your best men, armed and mounted." Eosa would have preferred a much larger force but couldn't afford to give Waldron's men the advantage of time.

"When?" The warrior everyone called Dirk—in reality Ursa, the oldest son of Thane Oesc—was sitting on his cot, paring his fingernails with the garnet-inlaid weapon that had inspired his camp name.

"Now."

Dirk stood and sheathed the blade. "The mission?"

Eosa couldn't suppress his smile in response to Dirk's undisguised eagerness. After so many days of waiting out this Godforsaken weather, he wasn't immune to the lure of proposed action either. But his smile soon soured.

"Thornhill." Whether a ruse or not, it was the logical place to start, for either way, Ulfric would have to be apprised of this development. "Our king—and perhaps our entire endeavor—stands in grave danger."

KENDRA, USING Ulfric's arm as a crutch and wishing she didn't have to, was sitting down to the morning meal on the dais inside Thornhill's feast hall when the far doors burst open and banged against the walls. Thanes and men-at-arms alike swiveled their heads toward the intruders.

Swords drawn and blood spattered across their clothing, dozens of panting, sweating, grim-faced men poured through the doorway.

Ulfric and the others leapt to their feet, groping for weapons that they hadn't brought for breaking fast.

"Guards!" Ulfric shouted, whipping his head about.

The only men to answer his summons emerged from the servants' doors behind the dais.

As the thanes' men gripped their meat knives and adopted guarded poses, the intruders spread throughout the hall while their leader, trailed by two of his men and a black hound, stalked toward the dais.

Kendra, who had jumped up to stand behind her chair, clinging to its tall back, all but fainted from relief.

The skirmish—with Ulfric's watchmen, she guessed—hadn't winded Alain as much as it had the others, for he was the first to regain control of his breathing. But his color ran high and what she could see of his hair beneath the hood was matted by sweat. Blood smudged his right cheek, though it did not appear to be his.

If Alain's scowl could kill, Ulfric would have died where he stood.

She glanced at her cousin, who was . . . smirking?

"So. The squire pretending to be a knight has returned to reclaim his ladylove."

"No squire stands before you, Thane Ulfric, or ever has." Alain shoved the hood back to reveal his mail coif. He stripped off his robe, let it fall to his feet, and stepped free of the woolen puddle. A sleeveless, calf-length, dark saffron surcoat flowed over his mail, embroidered across the chest with a white rose surrounded by a tangle of greenery.

Kendra, I am Sir Robert.

Her jaw dropped open and her eyes stretched wide. Her heart's joyful dance turned to dread. She slapped a hand over her mouth as her entire world teetered on the brink of flipping upside down.

There remained one chance to salvage reality. "You—" After clearing her dust-dry throat, she lowered her hand. "Sir Robert sent you, Alain? Is that why you wear his colors?"

His gaze reflected an odd pairing of love and regret.

"I am profoundly sorry, Kendra. I tried to tell you the truth in the cave." Squaring his shoulders, he tore his gaze from hers to regard Ulfric. "Upon the command and authority of William, Duke of Normandy and King of England, I, Sir Robert Alain de Bellencombre, have come to claim Lady Kendra of Edgarburh as my bride."

"Nay . . . nay, it—it cannot be . . ." Her heart shuddered from the force of her erupting anger. "Nay!" She glared at the man she thought she loved. "I shall never marry you, *Sir Robert*, un-unless—" A sob welled as she recalled the last time she'd uttered the phrase that popped to mind. "Unless it snows in July!"

Tears streaming, she spun and fled out the servants' door as fast as her weakened condition would permit.

Chapter 20

ER DECLARATION SADDENED but didn't surprise him as he watched the love of his life race through the back door, dodging past a pair of startled menservants.

No royal decree could ever bring her back.

Ulfric's harsh laugh claimed his attention.

"It seems my dear cousin has some difficulty with your pronouncement, Sir Robert."

"What transpires between Lady Kendra and me is no concern of yours."

"Ah, but it is my concern."

The thane's smile turned predatory as he raised his fists to shoulder height. He closed his eyes and crossed his arms, laying his palms flat against his chest as if he were preparing for burial. When he opened his eyes, their color had changed from blue to sea green . . . exactly like Alain's.

The changes didn't end there. Ulfric's face seemed to blur. His hair muted into a darker shade of blond.

Alain gaped. Behind him, he heard Ruaud's swift intake of breath. The resemblance was far from perfect—with a too-high forehead and eyes too widely set—and Alain had no clue how Ulfric had managed such a feat, but he found himself confronted with a face he knew better than the back of his sword hand.

Still grinning at Alain, Ulfric uncrossed his arms and thrust an open hand toward one of his guards. The man filled it with the hilt of his own sword.

"I remember where I have seen you before, Sir Robert." The more words Ulfric spoke, the more his voice modulated into a light but unmistakable Norman French accent. "At Hastings, you stood rooted by fear, while I"—he swept his free hand toward the face that looked uncannily like Étienne's—"died."

"You lie!" Frustration and rage propelled Alain forward. His sword hit Ulfric's with a deafening clang. Ulfric parried the stroke and dodged around the dais, dealing out as good as Alain gave him. "There were too many men in the way. I couldn't get to you—him in time!"

Alain whirled away to disengage and sharpen his focus. If he allowed Ulfric's ploy to distract him, he'd never live long enough to even contemplate how he might earn Kendra's forgiveness.

He clung to that hope. It was the only thing that kept his sword arm moving.

Grimly, he reapplied himself to his work, but he had found a worthy opponent in Kendra's kinsman.

Shouts and the clash of arms erupted throughout the hall. Alain glanced up as another group of men burst in to engage

Waldron's fyrd. The already wounded Cæwlin and a dozen others fell in the initial onslaught, victims of a barrage of spears.

Alain faced Ulfric in time to watch the thane make another transformation . . . into the likeness of Noir. He almost dropped his sword. Noir began to growl.

Ulfric the hound wriggled out of the pile of discarded clothing, bounded to the servants' door, leaned on it with his front paws, and pushed through.

The real Noir, teeth bared and fur bristling, sped to the door and stopped, looking imperiously over his shoulder at Alain as if ordering him to come along.

Alain regarded the melee before him, recognizing Dragon and other men he'd seen in the encampment. Dragon's presence, and the familiar ease by which he seemed to move through Ulfric's hall, confirmed what Alain had believed all along. Ulfric must have engineered this plan, aided by other thanes, to build a mercenary army with the intent of deposing King William, financing it through the outlaws' raids of Norman and uncooperative Saxon estates, merchants, and churches.

Though outnumbered by three to one, Ruaud and the others seemed to be acquitting themselves well against Ulfric's men. Bodies sprawled everywhere, only some belonging to Waldron's fyrd. But their surviving opponents fought with desperate determination, and Alain knew the fyrd from Edgarburh could not hold them off forever.

Never in his life had he felt more torn.

He hefted his sword and advanced upon the fray.

"Go, Alain," urged Ruaud between breaths after dispatching another foe. Alain grieved to see his friend bleeding from several cuts on his arms where mail had yielded to steel's bite. "We help you fight for your lady, but only you can save her."

Five men, led by Dragon, rushed them. After Alain killed one of Dragon's men, he found himself facing the point of the leader's sword. The man's lip twisted, deepening that perpetual snarl. The memory of Kendra's distress flooded Alain. "This one is mine," he growled to Ruaud, who was busy either killing or maiming the other three assailants.

"Why such vehemence, Norman?" Dragon asked as they traded preliminary blows to test each other's strengths and weaknesses. "I have done nothing to you." The scarred lip tightened into a distorted grin. "Yet."

"You molested my bride."

Alain's thrust grazed Dragon's rib cage, slicing the leather jerkin and drawing blood. If the man hadn't dodged, the blow would have struck home. Alain recoiled to await another opportunity.

"Ah, Lady Kendra. What a delightful morsel of female flesh." Dragon initiated a rapid series of blows, trying to wear Alain down. Alain countered, but one lucky chop landed on his left arm, cutting through the mail to nick his flesh. "Sampling her was one of the greatest pleasures of my life."

If Dragon had thought to enrage Alain into fighting carelessly, the warrior had miscalculated. Alain saw his chance and, in a great sweeping arc, struck away Dragon's sword. Dragon's hand went with it. He crumpled, clutching the spurting stump and howling.

Others weren't so eager to attack Alain after that.

Pointing at Dragon, Alain said to Ruaud, "That's their leader; keep him alive for questioning."

"I know," Ruaud insisted. "Lady Kendra needs you more than we do." He lunged toward someone who had just felled Garth and was attempting to take Lofwin unawares. Ruaud plunged his sword into the enemy's side. The Saxon went down with an agonized scream. Lofwin gave a brief nod of thanks before engaging the next threat. Ruaud grinned at Alain. "You plan to leave her alone with Ulfric, then?"

That was all it took.

Alain sheathed his sword and sprinted for the door. Noir raced out with him. In the thick fog, the hound loped ahead, nose to ground and baying. Alain increased his pace, loath to lose sight of Noir. The shadowy outline of low buildings co-alesced out of the mist. The clamor of pursuit, probably made by some of Ulfric's men-at-arms, sounded fragmented and dis-organized. But he could not afford to stop and deal with what might lay behind him.

While he had no clue where Noir was headed or the buildings' purpose, or what threats lurked nearby, he held unflagging faith that Noir would lead him to Kendra and the madman-dog-demon standing between them.

KENDRA'S LEGS felt leaden, and she thought her lungs would burst. Without thinking, for her impulse was to put as much distance between her and Alain as possible, her steps had taken her toward King Harold's cottage. As she entered the in-valids' village, she stopped, doubled over with hands to knees, to catch her breath.

"Lady Kendra, most excellently well met." Brother Os-wald's voice crackled with relief. Kendra rose, still winded, to regard him. Worry deepened the creases of his face and not, she suspected, because of her own frail health. "He is dying and wishes to see you."

Brother Oswald's first announcement came as no shock. King Harold had been dying, by agonizing inches, for almost a year. Kendra had just prolonged the inevitable, and everyone privy to his condition knew it.

However, that the king wished to see her, a lowly thane's daughter, she had trouble believing.

Without waiting for her reply, the monk strode toward the cottage. Kendra strove to keep up as best she could. She felt as if she were wading hip deep in muck.

She wondered if she might be dying too.

It had happened to her mother, who probably had endured far less strain than Ulfric had forced upon Kendra.

But the thought of dying didn't frighten her as much as it once might have. By passing from the earthly realm into the eternal one, she could escape the many men who would try to use her to achieve their own ends.

Alain included.

The more she pondered the idea, the more earnestly she anticipated being reunited with those who loved her for who she was, not for what she could do for them.

She reached the cottage door, which Brother Oswald was holding open, drumming his fingers on the frame. Smiling apologetically, she stepped past him into the gloom.

The aromas of mint and lavender scented the air, emanating from an iron pan discharging smoke beside the hearth. She glanced toward the bed where the king lay, wheezing, attended by Ethel and Brother Eric. If Ethel had thought the scents would aid the king's breathing, the pan needed to be placed closer to him to do any good. Kendra snatched a small cloth from the table, wound it around the pan's handle before grabbing it, and walked it over.

Brother Eric looked up and, as he had done so often before, surrendered his seat to Kendra and left the cottage, probably to resume his post outside the door. She set the smoking pan on the floor near the headboard and seated herself.

But when she took the king's limp, cool hand into her own, she felt not even the most tenuous of connections. She glanced toward Ethel and shook her head. "His body still lives, but I—it is beyond my power to reach him."

She couldn't bear to voice the fear that if she could not reach the king's mind, she had no hope of coaxing him back to the realm of the living.

Ethel rose and walked around to Kendra's side of the bed, holding a small pouch. She disengaged Kendra's right hand from the king's, shook a few petals into Kendra's palm, spat, and pressed the mixture into a paste. With that hand Kendra grasped the king's and closed her eyes.

Ah, Lady Kendra, you have come.

Of course, Your Majesty. How could I fail to obey your summons?

No. No more 'Your Majesty' nonsense for me. There is but one Majesty where I am going, and He tolerates no pretenders.

She felt her lips bend into a slight smile. *If it pleases Your— if it pleases you, sir, I shall accompany you.*

A wave of the king's surprise rippled through her. *Why? Your entire life lies before you. A good life, I should think.*

This? Healing you, and others? This is no life. It is killing me. She never would have spoken the words aloud. But inside the raw reality of their mingled thoughts, she never could have held them back.

I know, dear lady. You may try to mask it, shrug it off as nothing, but I know. I am grateful for what you have done for me, but I must release you from this duty.

My lord, I— She squeezed his hand. Into her hesitation seeped memories of Alain and the tender moments they had shared. But the shock of his lies crashed upon her like breakers against the cliffs. If he had thought nothing of deceiving her by posing as someone else, what other deceptions would she suffer at his hands?

How else could he shatter her heart?

Did he even care about what he'd done?

I can feel your anguish. Someone you love very much has done this to you.

Aye, my lord, she admitted, unable to say less and unwilling to say more.

Kendra, dying is not—

Agony gripped her like a vise. She willed past the pain to try to locate it. Her heart or King Harold's was starting to falter. Considering this weird linkage they shared, probably both.

Dying might not be the best option for her in his opinion, but it would give her the release she craved.

If she could ever make it past this excruciating pain.

Chapter 21

ULFRIC ENJOYED CANINE form more than any human shape for the nonhuman benefits it afforded him. Tracking, for instance. While the dense fog might have confounded a man, to his canine senses Kendra's trail appeared as clearly as if it had been painted on the ground and torchlit. And on four nimble legs, he traversed the distance much faster than he could have ever managed on two.

Surprise was another benefit. Without breaking stride, he gathered his legs underneath his lean, muscular body and leapt atop Brother Eric before the monk could cry out. He sank strong jaws into vulnerable flesh, executed a quick jerk of his canine head, and it was done.

He butted his head against the dying man's and extracted the last of the monk's life force. The effort yielded only a small spark, not enough for a complete transformation.

No matter. The weak-minded always saw what they most desired to see.

Thankful for the fog and drizzle that had penned the timid indoors, Ulfric willed his body back into a human form that bore a passing resemblance to the dead monk. He stripped off the robe, sucked as much blood as he could from its neckline, and donned the garment. He dragged the naked corpse into the narrow, windowless passage between the cottages, snugged the robe's hood around his face and, hoping for gloom to complete his disguise, calmly entered the cottage.

NOIR DID not disappoint Alain. The fog parted to reveal a cluster of cottages, and the hound raced up to one of them unerringly.

But rather than approaching the door, he darted, barking, between two buildings.

Alain bolted after the dog, praying for Kendra's safety.

What he saw made him pull up short.

Noir was nosing about the naked body of a man, lying face-down, his head twisted at a sickening angle. A puddle of blood had collected beneath his neck. Alain did not have to roll over the victim to know how he'd met his end.

Battle rage flooding his veins, Alain drew his sword and stalked toward the cottage's door.

Ulfric had much to atone for.

"Brother Eric," Ethel said as she scurried over to the disguised Ulfric. "The king—Lady Kendra—" Wringing her hands, she looked up at him hopefully. "Please, you must help them."

Resisting the urge to slap some sense into the old woman, Ulfric hurried over to the bed, where Harold sprawled on his back, his limbs and body twitching violently. Kendra, who must have been seated beside him, to judge by the chair's placement, lay slumped across his chest, her body convulsing to the same rhythm as Harold's.

Brother Oswald was attempting to separate them, but each time he took hold of Kendra's shoulders, she shuddered out of his grasp.

Ulfric stepped closer and disentangled Kendra's fingers from Harold's. In midtwitch she uttered a loud moan and jerked back into Ulfric's arms, head drooping to one side.

Kendra represented the least of Ulfric's concerns. He lowered her to the floor beside the bed and moved closer to the king, laying a hand on Harold's unshaven, clammy cheek. As always, he reveled in the surge of power as the last of Harold's energy flowed into him.

"What are you doing, Brother Eric?" Suspicion clouded Oswald's tone.

Ulfric removed his hand from Harold's lifeless face and pressed it flat against his own chest for a few moments, over his heart. Feeling the transformation become complete, he turned, threw back his hood, and smiled at the astounded monk in a way Ulfric knew was uniquely Harold's.

He shouldered past Ethel, who lost her balance and fell to the floor, hitting her head with a dull thud. As Ulfric approached Oswald, the monk tried to raise his staff in defense. Empowered by the strength of the hound and dead men, Ulfric wrested the staff from the monk's grip and snapped it in two as if it were a child's toy. Oswald's neck followed.

Glancing over his shoulder, he felt a stab of pity for Kendra. It wouldn't do for his bride—his queen—to wake up lying on the floor. He shoved the dead king aside, scooped her up, and laid her on the bed. Her face, though creased with sadness, looked exquisite, and Ulfric bent down to take that which she had yet to willingly give him: a kiss full on her moist, pliant lips.

God, it was great to be king.

"Get away from her, you animal!"

Ulfric laughed. Casually, he straightened and faced his foe. The Norman nuisance calling himself Sir Robert stood in the open doorway, sword leveled. Tendrils of fog twined around the Norman's mail-clad legs like a feline spirit. Blood streaked his sword, and his rent surcoat sported far more red than any other color, though how much blood had come from the knight, Ulfric couldn't tell without the benefit of his canine senses.

Outside the cottage, the hound Ulfric had used to guard the Glastonbury Tor treasure hoard was savaging one of Ulfric's men.

So be it; Ulfric's enhanced state rendered the need for reinforcements unnecessary. Besides, he wanted nothing more than to split the Norman from crotch to throat.

"Is that the best insult you can muster?" Crossing his arms, he grinned as his voice modulated to match Harold's. "Or do you believe God will send you to hell if you curse me any worse?"

Sir Robert bared his teeth in what looked like more grimace than grin, advanced into the room, and slammed the door. "I could never presume to top the curses God has already heaped upon you for your sorcerous abominations." He lifted his sword into a stance of wary readiness. "I prefer to let this blade talk for me, Ulfric."

"Wolf-king isn't here, you puling Norman infant." Ulfric drew himself up to his full height, exulting in Harold's stolen majesty. "The true Saxon king of England is."

ALAIN SPAT on the floor. "All I see is a pathetic Saxon pretending to be another pathetic Saxon pretender."

Ulfric's head snapped up, and his eyes—Harold Godwinson's glittering gray eyes—narrowed to slits. "You're improving. That insult deserves death. I thank you for affording me the first opportunity to exercise my royal authority." Ulfric-Harold dipped his head in a parody of respect. "I shall even grant you leave to defend yourself, if you permit me to become armed."

Wisdom decreed that Alain should run Ulfric through; honor forbade it. He jerked a nod.

Ulfric's grin broadened. He dropped to all fours, rummaged beneath the bed for a few moments, and stood, cradling a long, slim, linen-swathed object as if it were a babe. Reverently, he loosened the top folds to reveal a ruby-encrusted hilt. The blade, as the wrappings slid free, gleamed no less magnificently.

It was a foot longer than Alain's weapon, two fingers wider, and double-edged.

His heart kicked into a canter.

Ulfric swung the blade to the vertical as easily as if he were twirling a twig. "A sword worthy of a king, wouldn't you agree, Norman?"

"Most assuredly." Alain tightened his grip and shifted his weight into a more solid stance. "Too bad you, Thane Ulfric, are not worthy of it."

Roaring, Ulfric charged. The first jolt of the massive sword against Alain's blade sent him reeling backward. More staggering blows followed, and it was all Alain could do to prevent them from connecting with his flesh. For if Eosa's sword had been able to cut mail, Harold's weapon surely could slice steel and bone like butter.

To defeat this demon, he needed a better plan.

They lurched about the cottage as if playing a children's game of touch-and-run, with Alain toppling the table, chairs, crockery, foodstuffs, and anything else he could find to keep Ulfric off balance, and Ulfric chopping at whatever Alain hurtled in his path.

Whenever Ulfric managed to get close enough to land a blow, Alain's arms felt as if they were going to wrench out of their sockets. Weakened by the old wound, his left shoulder ached fiercely, and his right wasn't in much better condition.

Then he spied his chance.

He feigned a stumble and hit the sideboard. The candlestick rocked. Pretending to grab it, Alain deliberately missed, knocking it onto the floor. Molten wax spattered the dry rushes. The flame snuffed out, releasing a pungent odor.

Laughing, Ulfric closed in. "I just recalled something that may interest you. Today is the Feast of First Martyrs. How very appropriate." He raised Harold's sword high overhead.

Such a blow would cleave Alain from crown to breastbone. Grimacing through the pain—real and anticipated—as he lifted his sword and braced for the block, he prayed for a miracle.

"You, Norman, can count yourself privileged to become the first martyr for your soon-to-be deposed king."

The blow fell.

Amid a shower of sparks, Alain deflected it.

With a soft *whoosh*, the rushes burst into flame. The hem of Ulfric's robe ignited, and the fire raced upward.

Shrieking, Ulfric dropped Harold's sword to beat out the flames. Alain righted his stance, cocked his sword arm, and drove his blade into Ulfric's unprotected side, burying it to the hilt and giving it a savage twist before yanking it free.

Ulfric's eyes rolled back and his features blurred. The demon in Harold's likeness fled, leaving behind the Ulfric Alain recognized. The thane fell, smothering some of the flames but not enough to halt the inevitable. Alain glanced around the room. Through the cottage's lone window he saw monks and nuns scurrying over, their faces contorted with alarm. Harold's body, Alain was more than willing to consign to the oblivion it deserved, but he needed to get Kendra out soon.

However, he needed answers first.

He knelt, grabbed a fistful of bloodstained wool around Ulfric's neck, and shook him. Ulfric woke with a sharp cough. The thane's malevolent glare made everything click into place.

"You killed my brother in battle. And you used his shield and face as a disguise to ambush Kendra's brother. You led the attack upon Ruaud and me at the inn and escaped as a hound, but not before tearing out our guide's throat so he couldn't betray you to us. You even tried to kill me twice more—first by meadow-saffron poison, then as a hound."

Between the smoke, fatigue, pain, blood loss, and the dizzying implications, Alain's head was starting to reel. He ducked lower to suck in the clearer air and forged on, "The outlaws, Kendra's abduction to extort money from a man you knew would never support your cause, the plunder hidden beneath Glastonbury Tor, the army—all of it was part of your grand design, wasn't it?"

"Why should I tell you a damned thing?"

"Because you will be damned if you die unshriven."

"I am damned already." Frowning, Ulfric turned his head away, though whether to watch his blood soaking the rushes or the advancing fire, Alain couldn't tell.

Tensely, Alain watched both.

A spate of coughing near the bed caught Alain's attention. He released Ulfric and faced the sound, hoping Kendra had awakened, which would make rescuing her easier.

No such luck. The bruised head of an old woman popped up from beside the bed, looking fearful and confused.

"Hurry and get out," Alain warned her.

"But Thane Ulfric, Lady Kendra—"

"I will see to them. Go, woman!"

She didn't need another command. Through the open cottage door, as she scurried to safety, he saw the other people forming a bucket brigade and heard sizzles as water met fire. But once the thatch caught, the entire cottage, along with everyone trapped inside, would be doomed.

Alain crouched low over Ulfric's face. "You know I am right, Thane Ulfric. Confess! You haven't much time."

"No Norman swinhund will act as my father-confessor."

"This Norman swinhund is all you have. Would you rather take your chances with the Lord God Almighty?"

Ulfric closed his eyes with a sigh. Alain thought he'd lost him and his confession. But when he rose to get Kendra, a hand wrapped around his ankle and yanked. He lost his balance and fell with a startled yelp. His sword jarred from his grasp. While groping for it among the rushes, he almost missed Ulfric's frayed whisper:

"You are right, Sir Robert. About everything. May God forgive me." He gripped Alain's forearm with surprising strength. "But never forget, Norman, that I made my choices for the good of England—Saxon England."

"And for yourself."

Ulfric smiled wanly. "That aspect lies between me and God."

True enough.

Kneeling and holding up the hilt of his sword to form a cross, he hastily murmured the Latin words he'd heard far too often on the battlefield, words of pardon and assurance of divine forgiveness. Ulfric's eyes glazed before Alain could finish.

As the first thatch bundles ignited, spewing sparks onto the bed, he sheathed his sword and hurried to Kendra's side. He had to brush embers from her gown before gathering her into his arms. Her head lolled, but he had no time to discern whether she was alive or dead.

The doorway was already wreathed in flames. He lowered his head, led with his right shoulder, and charged through.

Sweet air filled his starved lungs, triggering a coughing fit so intense that he nearly dropped her. A monk and several nuns broke rank from the bucket line to help him, along with the servant he'd chased from the inferno and a few folk whom he guessed to be residents of the other cottages.

He refused to let anyone take Kendra.

Noir ambled over, sniffed her hair, and licked her neck. When that elicited no response, he sat, whining.

Alain could well imagine how the hound felt.

As the servant felt Kendra's neck for a pulse, she asked about Ulfric, forcing him to relive their fight as he decided how much to tell her. Something in the tone of her question suggested that the thane had meant a lot to her.

"Thane Ulfric died of his wounds, good woman, not in the fire." Noting the tremor in her chin, he added, "But he died shriven." King William and England might fare better without being troubled by this rebel, but she didn't need to hear that. "I am sorry for your loss."

After releasing a heavy sigh and swiping her eyes, she gave Alain an appraising stare. "Thank you, my lord."

"And . . . Kendra?"

"Your lady lives."

He couldn't think of any other words that could have brought him more relief, and he sent his gratitude heavenward. "Will she wake soon?"

The woman shrugged. "She will rest easier in her chambers at the manor house."

He executed a staggering turn in that direction, but the persistent fog—which, mercifully, had helped to keep the blaze from spreading to the other cottages—and the billowing smoke blocked his view, hindering his decision.

"I agree, good woman." The croaking of his voice startled him. He drew a breath and cleared his throat. "But first I must know whether it's in the hands of Thane Waldron's men or Ulfric's."

The monk who'd left the bucket line to assist Alain gave him an understanding nod, hitched up his robes, and sprinted off. The aged servant woman followed him at her own doddering pace. Supported by the remaining onlookers, Alain sank to the ground, still cradling his precious burden.

He drew a thumb across her soot-smudged cheek. No matter how he tried to justify his original actions, her plight was his fault, even the abduction, for his forwardness as a love-smitten "squire" had driven her outside Edgarburh's protective walls.

And even if other circumstances had led to her capture, she might never have chosen to stay with Ulfric if Alain had not deceived her.

His heart constricted, and tears welled. Grief and guilt branded his soul.

As Ruaud directed the efforts to secure the prisoners, tend the wounded, remove the corpses, and restore order to the hall, he itched to know what had befallen Alain. He wrenched his gaze from the servants' door where he'd last seen his friend and tried to concentrate on the task of binding the wrists of a man with a serpentine scar running the length of his face. Although no more than an hour had passed since Alain's departure, it had seemed like eons.

"Go, Sir Ruaud." Lofwin's voice wafted to him as if in a dream. It took Ruaud a few moments to register why Lofwin was attempting to remove the rope from Ruaud's grasp. "Go and see to Lady Kendra and Sir Alain while we finish here."

Ruaud released the rope, communicated his thanks with a nod, and started for the rear door.

He didn't get far.

The door banged open and Alain staggered in. His surcoat was charred and sooty, and his hair looked—and smelled—singed. Fatigue and pain had gouged deep lines across his face. The unmoving bundle he carried, also soot-blackened in several places, seemed more the size of a child than a woman. Ruaud could have sworn that the vapors swirling about them were smoke, as if they'd escaped through the gates of hell.

That hellhound of Alain's flanked its master, its eyes glowering as if to challenge all comers.

A hush blanketed the hall as everyone paused to watch Alain's halting progress.

As Alain neared, Ruaud felt loath to break the silence, but he had to know: "Lady Kendra, is she—"

"She lives," Alain rasped.

The prisoner in Lofwin's charge reached his bound hands toward Alain's lady, seemed to think better of it, and lowered his hands. His bowed head couldn't hide the tears that slid free, or the trembling of his chin.

Ruaud cocked an eyebrow, vowing to find out later how this man, who appeared to be more ruffian than soldier, knew her and what she meant to him.

First and foremost, however, Alain needed help. But the fool refused it.

"At least let me accompany you, in case you stumble."

"As you wish." Alain's voice sounded hollow; his gaze remained fixed on the doors leading to the outside staircase and, presumably, Lady Kendra's quarters.

"What of Ulfric?" Ruaud whispered, hoping to keep Alain's mind engaged to stave off the shock that had already taken hold.

"Dead."

"What of his plan? Were you right?"

"Oh, yes."

"Details, if you please."

A spark of the old Alain ignited in his eyes as he gave Ruaud a puzzled look. "Now?"

"Of course, now."

Ruaud wouldn't have cared if Alain had chosen to recite the entire Book of Genesis, as long as he kept talking.

Alain answered Ruaud's question in French.

Ruaud marveled at the picture that emerged, from Ulfric killing Lady Kendra's brother as the first step toward increasing his power base, to hiring mercenaries to rob Normans and Saxons who supported William, to building an army—now a leaderless and potentially even more dangerous one.

By this time, they had left the hall and turned to mount the stairs. Alain interrupted his monologue to concentrate on this new obstacle. As his dog raced past him, he overbalanced and would have pitched backward had Ruaud not been standing ready to catch him.

"Allow me, Alain." Ruaud stretched out his arms. "Please. Unless you wish to endanger her as well as yourself?"

Alain surrendered his lady into Ruaud's care and began hauling himself up the stairs, his mail chinking heavily on each tread. Ruaud wished he'd thought to have Alain strip it off in the hall. Ruaud's mail dragged on him too, but his battle hadn't included a journey to hell and back.

A crone met them at the top of the stairs, holding open the door and beckoning them inside. She gave the hound a disdainful look, which went ignored as it trotted through the door and halfway down the corridor, where it paused and turned back with a questioning whine. After Ruaud entered with Kendra, followed closely if unsteadily by Alain, the servant closed the door and bade everyone to follow her. The dog fell into step beside Alain, working its head under his dangling hand as if to support him.

The woman led them to an open doorway and through the anteroom into a spacious chamber sporting more luxurious pillows, furs, tapestries, and furnishings than Ruaud could count. A fire was crackling in the hearth, with several logs stacked nearby. Pungent lavender scented the air from the dried flowers strewn among the rushes underfoot.

While Alain braced against the doorframe, Ruaud crossed the room and laid Lady Kendra on the bed. Her servant bustled about, fluffing pillows and arranging the covers to her satisfaction as Ruaud withdrew to join Alain.

"Many thanks." Although Ruaud knew Alain was addressing him, Alain's gaze remained fixed on the bed's occupant.

"What happened to Ulfric? I presume you killed him—how?"

Alain shook his head. "Later."

That Ruaud could understand. He'd witnessed enough this day to require a lifetime to come to terms with it all; he couldn't begin to imagine what his friend must have experienced.

As the servant approached them, Ruaud asked for spare clothing and a place to store their armor.

She gave them both measuring glances. "Fitting you, my lord," she said to Ruaud, "may take some doing, but mayhap his lordship has something that shall suffice." She nodded at Alain. "For both of you."

The servant ushered them out of Lady Kendra's chamber and bade them wait in the anteroom. Alain stood, staring at the closed door to his lady's chamber as if he had left his soul in there. His dog circled thrice in one corner and flopped down with a loud grunt but kept watchful eyes upon Alain.

As Ruaud began stripping off Alain's armor, he whistled softly at the sundry breaches he found in the mail links.

He had just gotten to the laces of Alain's quilted undertunic when the servant returned, bearing a pile of folded robes surmounted by two pairs of doeskin shoes. She laid her burden on a chair to help Ruaud finish removing Alain's sweat-stained padding. Together they pushed him this way and that, and he didn't seem to care.

She handed a burgundy velvet robe to Ruaud because she was too short to get it over Alain's shoulders. Through the entire procedure Alain stood unmoving, as if he were asleep.

Ruaud cinched the robe closed with a matching velvet cord, and the servant took Alain's hand to pull him toward Lady Kendra's bedchamber.

That seemed to break the spell.

"What are you doing, woman?" Alain planted his feet and refused to take another step. "This is not seemly."

"Horse dung. My lord." Hands on hips, the woman gave Alain a frank appraisal. "You may have rescued Lady Kendra's body from the flames, but her mind has chosen to remain. If you love her as much as I suspect, then you may be the only one who can coax her back from the brink."

Chapter 22

ALAIN LOOKED DOWN, running his hands over the plush velvet and seeing it for the first time. Ruaud, still clad in his blood-spattered hauberk and surcoat, looked as spent as Alain felt. "I should help you."

"*Merde, Alain.*" Ruaud blew a rude noise with his lips, tapping his temple. "That is what you possess for brains. Any servant can assist me. If this good woman is right"—he nodded politely in her direction—"you must help Lady Kendra."

Alain wished he could share Ruaud's optimism.

Ruaud clapped Alain's right shoulder and gave it a brief squeeze. Calling Noir to heel, Ruaud turned, grabbed the remaining robe and shoes, and clumped out of the anteroom. Noir looked to Alain as if for confirmation, and Alain gave an encouraging nod. The dog rose and followed Ruaud.

The woman, who, when Alain prompted her, called herself Ethel, tugged Alain into the inner bedchamber and closed the door behind them.

Kendra lay as Ruaud had left her, on her back with her head turned onto her left cheek, her right arm cocked overhead as if warding off a blow. Even in sleep, her face looked taut with apprehension and sorrow. Alain's guilt resurfaced.

"Go on, my lord." Ethel made a shooing motion with both hands, directing him toward the bed.

He strode to Kendra's side, stooped, and felt her face and neck. Her skin was cool, and her pulse beat weakly. "I have dressed wounds and set bones and treated fevers, but this?" He made a helpless shrug, dropping his voice to a whisper. "She has no injuries or fever. This is beyond my skill."

The servant thrust one hand into the pouch hanging from her belt. With the other, she grasped Alain's right hand, flipped it over, and opened her fist to reveal myriad tiny dried white petals. The petals fluttering onto his palm reminded him of snowflakes.

And snowflakes reminded him, with an unpleasant jolt, of Kendra's reaction when confronted with the proof of his identity.

Small wonder she refused to awaken.

"What is this flower?" he asked, although he had a fair guess.

"The Cristes-mæsse blooms of the Glastonbury thorn, my lord." She ground her knuckles into his palm, crushing the petals. Then she reached up to brush her index finger across his cheek, collecting tears that he didn't realize had slipped free. She used her fingertip to stir the mixture and closed his hand into a fist when she had finished. "Use this to reach her—quick, my lord, before it's too late."

His hand felt unnaturally warm. He stared at it as if it were an alien thing. "How? I know nothing of this herb."

She uttered a low chuckle and reached for Kendra's left hand, lifting it closer to Alain's and directing him to sit in the chair beside the bed. He complied and opened his fist to find that a thick, white paste had formed from the petals and tears.

Ethel held Kendra's limp hand a finger's width from the mixture in Alain's. "Follow your heart, lad." She pressed Kendra's hand to his.

Light and heat flared. Alain raised an arm to shield his eyes, squeezing them shut. He opened them and blinked several times, turning a slow circle, but the bedchamber had disappeared. All he could see was a dense, disorienting, featureless mist.

He thought he must be outside again, but this fog felt much warmer and drier. He took a few hesitant steps—toward what, he had no clue—but no shadows of buildings or trees or animals or people emerged.

Then he heard it: the distance-muffled but unmistakable sound of a woman weeping.

Kendra.

His heart twisted.

Guided by the sound, he broke into a run. The burst of energy, so soon after his battle with Ulfric, suggested that he must be experiencing a dream. A glance at his mail and surcoat, bearing the white de Bellencombre rose, with no trace of blood or soot, confirmed his guess.

But whose dream was it?

If it was his own, how could he help Kendra? And if this was her dream, how could he be participating in it?

Believing the answer to be somehow tied to the workings of the Glastonbury thorn, he dashed toward the cries.

The mist ended. The sobbing did not.

A large old hawthorn tree appeared, very much like the one he'd seen at Glastonbury Abbey, though this one had a granite sarcophagus standing beneath its arching branches. The sides of the sarcophagus were overlaid with marble carved in grand battle scenes. Where the effigy would have lain, decorating the lid, a flat slab remained. Kendra sat atop the tomb, her face buried in her hands and her shoulders shuddering. The hawthorn, past its blooming prime, showered her with hundreds of tiny white petals. They dotted her veil and gown like snowflakes, in stark contrast to the black fabric of mourning enshrouding her.

Alain approached her, but she heeded him not.

Across her lap lay two roses, a white and a red.

"White for Del's soul," she whispered, "and red for the blood he coughed forth with his final breath."

Alain said, "White for the rose on the brooch Sir Robert wanted to give you, and red for Alain's gift."

She did not bother to look up. "White for my love for Squire Alain."

Strangely, he felt lighter, and he looked at his chest and arms. The mail had been replaced by the plain leather jerkin and breeches he'd favored while posing as a squire.

"Red," Kendra continued, "for how I despise Sir Robert!"

The weight of his mail returned, matching the guilt that weighted his soul. His knees sagged before he could push himself upright.

Her vehemence stunned him. In the same breath he realized he shouldn't be surprised; his deception had wounded her, perhaps irrevocably.

Unwilling to accept the latter possibility, he knelt at her feet and grasped her hands. She refused to acknowledge his presence, but that did not deter him from offering, "Red for my sorrow for having deceived and hurt and angered you; white for my repentance."

He longed to pledge his love and plead with her not to give up on life—or on him—but his tongue felt wooden, as if it belonged to someone else.

Sighing, he released her hands and glanced down to discover that his pouch dangled from his belt. He reached in to pull out a packet and pressed it into her palm, knowing its contents without having to open it.

Her fingers made a fist around the packet, and she flung it down, glaring at him.

Her unspoken answer broke his heart.

Alain rose, bowed stiffly, and wandered back into the mist.

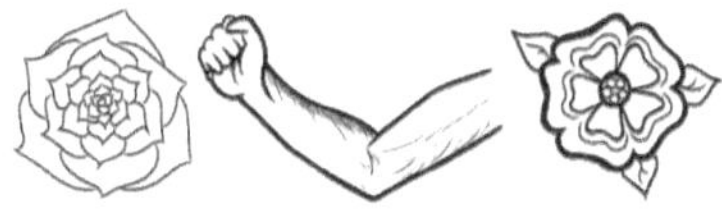

KENDRA TORE her gaze from the rejected gift to see Del standing before her, in full armor, posed with hands pressed together against his chest in the same manner as his granite effigy. Uttering a joyful squeal, she jumped down from the sarcophagus lid to embrace him.

The roses slid from her lap and fell beside the packet.

Alain halted at the sound of Kendra's outcry and turned to find her hugging another knight. Curious—and reasonably certain of this other man's identity—he moved closer to them but kept a respectful distance. In spite of the fog, he overheard their conversation easily.

Del's eyes opened and his stance relaxed, but he would not return her embrace. "Why have you failed to fulfill your promise?"

She drew back, puzzled and hurt. "I have honored your memory by refusing to marry a countryman of your murderer."

"That is not what I asked of you."

"I—I know. But I cannot"—fighting tears, she thrust out her chin—"I cannot and shall not marry a lie!"

Alain winced but could not fault her for feeling that way.

"But you would go to your grave defending another lie in the name of honor?" her brother asked.

She gave Del a hard stare. "What do you mean?"

"Are you so certain that a Norman ambushed me?"

"Of course! That's what..." A stunned expression cascaded over her face. "What Ulfric told me." Hands on hips, she regarded Del. "You have not come to escort me to heaven, have you?"

Sadness overshadowed his features. "I shall, if that is your choice."

"Why are you so sad, Del? Father Æthelward says there is no sorrow in heaven, only joy."

He cracked the lopsided grin she loved so well, though it was tinged with ruefulness. "True. But this place is not heaven. I sorrow for you because I have been shown what earthly happiness you will be denied if you accompany me now. And the misery your death will inflict on others."

"On our father? Or on"—bitterness invaded her tone—"Sir Robert?" She made his name sound like a curse.

Del raised a hand. "I am forbidden to say more."

"Can you at least tell me who caused your death?"

"Ask him." Del pointed toward Alain. "He knows."

Her gaze met Alain's. The look he gave her seemed laden with remorse. "I—" Longing and anger grappled to control her heart. "Nay. I would rather die with king and kin than marry someone who has already betrayed me once. What's to stop him from betraying me again? How can I ever trust him?"

"Do you indeed seek the answers to those questions?" Del asked.

Do I?

Kendra closed her eyes. Into the blackness rushed memory after memory of Alain's kindness, generosity, tenderness. Courage. Strength. Valor.

Self-sacrifice. Not once but many times.

Alain didn't deserve her rejection without an opportunity to explain his ruse. But neither could she entrust her future to him—king's decree or not—without obtaining crucial assurances.

Do I want to give Alain this chance?

She gave Del a firm nod.

"Then, dearest Kendra, you must let me go."

"I—" She knew he was right, but, "Even if I wanted to, I don't know how!" Tears blurred her vision. Alain, standing a few paces beyond Del, seemed to waver and fade.

Her admission anguished the soul of the man who would have been proud, in life, to have called this Norman knight brother. "You have two choices."

Del stooped to pick up the packet Alain had tried to give her and unfolded the fabric to reveal his precious strands of hair. He placed the packet into her cupped hands, and she cradled it against her heart.

"I have seen how you have treasured this token. And I do feel honored, Kendra, but . . ." Del wrapped his hands around hers and gently pried them away from her chest, encountering some resistance, which grieved him. "What you do with it will signal your choice"—with his head, Del motioned a clear invitation for Alain to join them—"to both of us."

Surprised yet more than willing, Alain surged across the gap to stand beside Kendra's brother. The Saxon knight assumed the pose of his effigy.

"Del, wait! Please don't leave me!"

Del opened his eyes. "I am permitted to remain until you have chosen. But you must understand the nature of your decision. Remember the promise I asked of you."

Seek happiness; of course, she could never forget that. But happiness seemed impossibly elusive. She stepped close to Del and gripped his forearm. "What have you seen? Will I be happy with"—she dropped her voice to the barest whisper—"him?"

"I cannot tell you any more than your heart already knows." Del closed his eyes again.

Standing mute before her, Alain felt utterly vulnerable until he espied the roses lying near her feet. He dropped to his knees, grasped them, and entwined their stems. He yearned to take her into his arms, beg her forgiveness, and kiss away her hurt and anger, but all he seemed permitted to do within the confines of this weird dream was raise the roses toward her.

"Red for Kendra . . . and white for Alain?" he managed to whisper, hopefully.

A memory flashed in her mind's eye. The last two roses she had picked to decorate Del's tomb had been a white and a red. The next day, she had picked the white blossom and Alain had given her the red. Both times, unable to choose between the blooms, she had entwined their stems and left them on the lid of Del's sarcophagus.

Her heart had made its choice.

She pulled the silver case from beneath her dress, sprang the catch, and returned Del's hair to the compartment.

As Alain watched in tortured silence, she approached Del and slipped the locket's thong around her brother's neck. Del relaxed his stance to embrace her. They clung to each other for what seemed like ages. Kendra's eyes watered, and her chin quivered.

"I shall always love you, Del." Unable to say more, she buried her face against his chest, tears bathing the locket.

"I know." Del kissed the top of her head. "And that is just the smallest token of my eternal love for you, dearest Kendra." He released her, his expression earnest. "But I do not have an eternity to spend here, and neither do you."

She dabbed her eyes with her gown's sleeve. "I will see you again, won't I?"

"Of course." He favored her with one final, lopsided grin. "*À Dieu, ma soeur chere.*" His grin broadened as he caught Alain's astonished gaze. The look exchanged by the Saxon and Norman warriors thrummed with mutual understanding and respect.

Still grasping the roses that she wouldn't take from him, Alain watched intense light flare around her brother. The silver case glistened against Del's chest as he disappeared.

Kendra too began to fade.

Alain lunged for her hand but caught only vapors.

Chapter 23

"SIR ROBERT?"

Alain fought through the thinning mist, trying to place the voice. Female, but not Kendra's: this one crackled like oak leaves in winter. At least it didn't sound as if the speaker was using his name as a curse.

"Wake up, Sir Robert, I implore you!"

Wake up? How could he? Kendra was still lost to him.

"My lord, the king has summoned you."

King William? *Here?*

That had to be part of the dream.

Alain willed his eyes open. Kendra's servant—he couldn't recall her name—loomed over him as he sat on the floor beside the bed, one hand stretched up, clutching Kendra's. The fingers of his other hand were wrapped around the thorny stems of a pair of roses so dry, the petals rattled as he moved.

As in the dream, one blossom was white and the other red. How he had acquired them, God alone knew.

His joints were aching like fury, though nothing compared with the pounding in his head. He disengaged his hand and pressed it to his temple, groaning. The pain abated.

He studied his palm, recalling the paste that the servant—Ethel, that's what she'd called herself—had made. All that remained was a coating of white ash.

He unknotted his legs and attempted to stand. Dizziness obliged him to cling to one of the bedposts for support, still holding the roses. He waved them as Ethel offered him a steaming posset. "What do you know of these flowers, good woman?" He displayed his other hand, palm outward. "Or this?"

Ethel took the flowers in exchange for the mug. As Alain swigged a deep draught of the herbal concoction—chamomile, valerian, mint, honey, and God alone knew how many other ingredients he was too groggy to identify—he watched the servant study the roses.

"Many believe that the Glastonbury thorn harbors miraculous healing powers when used by someone pure of heart," she began, "though how it works no one knows."

Pure of heart. Alain snorted. That phrase couldn't apply to him, the worst deceiver to fall into this world since Satan.

After he drained the mug, Ethel took it and returned the flowers to him. "As for the roses, my lord, all I know is that when I woke, I saw them in your hand. I didn't think you were holding them before, but"—she shrugged and gave him a gap-toothed grin—"I may not have noticed them."

Alain knew he hadn't brought the roses with him.

"But come, my lord. King William knows you were fighting yesterday, but he cannot be kept waiting forever."

Alain swallowed hard. "The king—here, now? I didn't dream it?"

"Most certainly not, my lord."

Ethel bustled into the anteroom and returned with an armload of fresh clothing. She deposited her bundle on the table, guided him behind an ornate oaken screen, and began handing him garments. He felt his cheeks heat to imagine Kendra asleep in the bed just beyond. He knew he shouldn't be intruding like this, but since he didn't have quarters in this manor yet, and since anyone could burst into the anteroom without notice, the screened area would have to suffice.

When the servant gave him the tunic, dyed bright crimson and trimmed in fox fur much like Ulfric's original gift, Alain surveyed it with resigned distaste before pulling it over his head and tugging it into place. Appearing before His Majesty in either a dressing gown or a charred, torn, bloody surcoat did not constitute valid options.

He emerged from behind the screen, and Ethel helped him gird the tunic with his sword belt. The sword itself she'd left in the anteroom, where Ruaud had removed it, along with Alain's mail and ruined surcoat, last night.

Before following Ethel from the bedchamber, he stole a final glance at Kendra's sweet face, gratified to observe that she seemed to have found a measure peace at last.

Whether she would ever deign to share that peace with him remained to be seen.

Honor constrained him to placing a chaste kiss on her forehead, though love urged him to express himself more fully. Such liberties, however, would have to wait until they'd been earned.

His lips brushed her soft, warm skin, but she did not wake.

He laid the roses beside her and slipped from the room.

KENDRA AND Alain had worked out all their difficulties, and he sealed his promise with a kiss that, while chastely planted on her forehead, conveyed the breadth of his vow and the vast depth of his love.

She knew she must be dreaming.

Although . . . she didn't seem to be as angry as she'd been the day before. She recalled having spoken with him; how that was possible when she'd been unconscious, she had no idea.

The prospect of having everything set to rights between them, however, was not an unattractive one.

The squeal of the door's hinges intruded on her reverie, and she opened her eyes to watch a familiar figure exit the bedchamber.

In trying to call his name, all she could manage was a throaty rasp. The door shut with a soft but no less final-sounding thump. Tears stung her eyes and nose.

In a rush, the events of the past day thundered into her mind: Alain's arrival and shocking revelation, her flight to King Harold's cottage, and her failure to either heal him or accompany him in death.

The latter puzzled her, because she'd stood upon eternity's threshold, close enough to recognize her brother and mother. She tried to recall her experience—the light, the love, the joy—but earthly words could never suffice.

Nor could she describe the fathomless sense of loss she'd felt when the eternal radiance faded, ending her chance to accompany king and kin.

That was when she'd dreamed of seeing Alain—Del again too, she recalled. Del had spoken at length about choices and promises while Alain, oddly, had remained silent.

Habit compelled her to reach toward her neck.

The locket was gone.

She sat up and groped around the pillows and covers, thinking that it might have slipped off while she slept.

All she found was a trail of dried white and red petals strewn across the bed, leading to a pair of roses. She pressed a hand to her mouth to stifle a gasp.

Stretching forward, she touched the stems and pricked her finger on a thorn. The bright bead of blood testified to the flowers' reality, but how could they possibly be what her heart claimed they were?

She sucked her finger, her mind awhirl with snatches of memories; whether real or dreamed, she couldn't discern. Recollection of Ulfric's voice convinced her that he'd been inside the cottage with her, though she couldn't remember what he'd been doing. But she also recalled hearing the clash of metal against metal and smelling the greasy smoke's acrid stench.

Smoke inhalation would explain why her throat felt on fire. Absently, she pressed her left hand to her neck.

The pain stopped.

That got her attention.

She withdrew her hand to study her palm and recognized the Glastonbury thorn ash.

Where in heaven's name had that come from? Was it the residue from her final attempt to heal the king? Had Ethel put more of the herb in her hand, hoping that Kendra could heal herself?

Or—the name came unbidden to her mind—had Alain done this?

He must have carried her here, she reasoned, but why hadn't he waited for her to wake?

I wouldn't marry you unless it snowed in July!

Her cheeks burning, she rolled over and buried her head in the pillow, unable to stem the flood of tears.

Even the creak of the door opening couldn't penetrate her grief.

"Poppet?" Ethel's concerned hand patted her shoulder. "Weep not, child. Things cannot be as bad as all that."

"Worse. I cannot die. And I"—she swallowed a sob—"I cannot live." Not without Alain, and her accursed tongue had ruined whatever chance they might have had.

"Of course you shall live, my lady. Many people are depending on it."

Kendra pushed herself over and wiped her eyes. "Would one of them happen to be a certain Norman?" she whispered.

"Several, in fact."

"What? Besides Sir Ruaud, what other Normans would be here?"

"His Majesty, the regent, and their guards. The army itself is camped below the hill."

She felt her jaw drop. "King William, with an army? Is Thornhill under siege?"

"Nay, my lady." Wringing her hands, Ethel glanced over her shoulder. "But the queen didn't accompany His Majesty, only soldiers did."

A queasy pit formed in Kendra's stomach. "Ulfric cannot be pleased with this development."

Ethel looked down. "My lord Ulfric lies beyond caring about such matters." She covered her face with her apron.

"You mean he's—" Kendra's breath caught, and she let it out slowly. "Oh, Ethel, I am so sorry." Although she'd never cared for him in a romantic sense, and she had despised how he'd tried to use King Harold as well as herself for his own ends, Ulfric was, after all, kin. And this woman had known him the longest of anyone alive.

Ethel dried her face with the apron and gave Kendra a frank look. "I'm sorry too, but his lordship did bring his end upon himself with his choices."

"How—what happened?"

"I don't rightly know, my lady. He—well, that is, after he—" She shuddered and averted her gaze, but Kendra prompted her to continue. Ethel sighed. "You'll think me daft for certain, but he made his face into His Majesty's likeness."

Kendra knew Ethel wasn't referring to King William, and the report of what Ulfric had done came as no surprise. "The transformation killed him?"

"Nay." The servant chewed her lip. "Leastwise, I don't think so, but my lord—that is, I fell and hit my head. When I woke up, the cottage was afire, and Thane Ulfric was lying in a puddle of blood with Sir Robert bending over him, whispering. Sir Robert was fair baptized in blood too."

Kendra's head began reeling, and she pressed a hand to her temple. "And Sir Robert—did he save me from the flames?"

"Aye, my lady. Carried you all that long way to the manor. Any fool with eyes could see he was half dead on his feet, but he wouldn't let anyone help him till he got to the stairs. He'd have fallen too; you both would have if it hadn't been for his friend, Sir—Sir—"

"Sir Ruaud," Kendra supplied when it became obvious that Ethel didn't know.

Ethel tried the name once or twice, pronouncing it more like "rood." She shrugged. "Anyway, Sir Robert's friend bore you up the stairs, with himself scarcely a step behind."

"Sir Robert kept vigil beside me all night?"

"Vigil, aye, 'twould be one word for it."

Kendra felt her eyebrows tighten. "What do you mean?"

"I intend no offense, of course, my lady, but"—Ethel's chest heaved as she sucked in a noisy breath—"but you looked like death itself, all pale and still. I feared for you, so I gave him this." She opened the pouch attached to her belt and extracted a pinch of tiny white petals.

"He healed me?" *Did he yank me away from my reunion with Mother and Del too?*

Ethel replaced the petals and spread her hands in a gesture of ignorance. "Mayhap he helped you heal yourself. He sounded unsure that it would work, though he seemed plenty eager to try."

Kendra wished she could recall more details of that odd dream, but she could conjure nothing past what she'd already remembered: the fog, Alain standing before her dressed in full, spotless battle gear, and Del, looking by turns like his effigy and as she had remembered him in life.

And the roses.

She studied them. "How did these get here, Ethel?"

"Sir Robert, my lady."

"But how did he come by them?"

Ethel shrugged.

That these were the roses from Del's tomb, Kendra no longer had any doubt. But what had become of the locket?

WALDRON EDGARSON heard more than felt his joints creak as he labored to his feet inside Edgarburh's chapel. Until Kendra's disappearance, he hadn't spent half as much time on his knees in his entire life.

Since the departure of the fyrd, led by Alain, his prayer time had more than doubled.

The other worshippers filed from the chapel. With most of the fyrd away, the building did not take long to empty. Father Æthelward gave Waldron an inquiring glance, but the thane expressed his preference for being alone. Giving an understanding nod, the priest went about the business of tidying the chapel.

Waldron made obeisance to the crucifix and limped to the bank of candles representing Kendra, Alain, Ruaud, Lofwin, and the rest of the fyrd.

So many flames, each one bravely holding back the gloom.

Swiping at eyes that had become too moist, he wondered how many would remain lit after everyone else's return.

The association prompted him to turn toward Del's tomb and the tall, thick tapers that illuminated it and Edwina's in perpetuity. A shaft of sunlight piercing the chapel's high, round window was dimming the candles' effect, bathing Del's sarcophagus in an ethereal glow.

Something else glowed there too. He cautiously approached.

Astonishment halted him.

Del's effigy claimed its usual position atop the lid, but Kendra's roses had disappeared. In their place on Del's chest lay her silver case, its black velvet cord tied in a second spot, where it must have been cut by the outlaws, and stretched taut.

Had Alain recovered the piece, brought it to Edgarburh, and left it behind? Waldron couldn't recall him having mentioned it; surely the lad would have returned it to Kendra rather than leaving it here.

Unless Alain thought he might not live to present it to her? Waldron's gut gave an uneasy twist.

He picked up the locket and hefted it. Not sure what he'd been expecting, he acknowledged that it felt real enough.

Strangest of all, he discovered after springing open the case, Del's hair lay nestled inside. He had given it to Alain while the locket was still lost.

Wagging his head, he snapped the lid closed and returned it to the effigy.

He had prayed more times than he could count for some sign that Kendra, Alain, and the others would be all right. If this was indeed the requested sign, then God had to be the undisputed master of the impossible.

REMEMBER THE *promise I asked of you.*

Kendra jerked up her head, feeling her eyes moisten. "Del?"

"My lady?" Ethel's look radiated concern. "No one else is here."

Kendra shook her head.

Seeking answers shall free you to seek happiness.

The fog enshrouding her mind dissipated to reveal the whole dream and its attendant grief and joy. And she knew where she'd find the locket.

She laid the flowers down and swung her legs over the side of the bed.

Ethel rushed to her. "Nay, my lady! You must rest."

"Please bring me a gown, Ethel."

Kendra stood on legs more wobbly than a newborn foal's. Dizziness threatened, but between the bed post and Ethel's support, she managed to stay upright.

"Are you certain about this, my lady?"

"Absolutely." Kendra gazed toward the bedchamber's door. "I have answers to seek."

If Alain believed he had no further reason to stay at Thornhill, she might not have enough time to finish her quest.

Twitching her shoulder in a slight shrug, Ethel pulled a forest-green overdress from the chest and helped Kendra into it. As the servant was smoothing the linen, a ferocious pounding rattled the bedchamber door.

"Open in the name of King William!"

Kendra's stomach clenched. "Go see what he wants, Ethel," she whispered.

Ethel tried to keep the door open just a crack, but the soldier would have none of it. He yanked it wide and shouldered past Ethel. She stumbled back with a whimper as more soldiers trooped in, swords drawn.

"Lady Kendra of Edgarburh, you stand accused of high treason against the Crown—"

"Nay!" she cried.

"—for aiding and abetting Ulfric of Thornhill," continued the soldier, "and the other Saxon thanes allied with him in his rebelion."

"'Tis not true," she protested as one man gripped her shoulders while a second bound her wrists with rawhide cords. A third prodded her with the point of his sword. She planted her feet and glared at the contingent. "Even my lawless kidnappers treated me better than this. I demand to see the king!"

"So you shall, Lady Kendra." The soldier who had recited the charges grinned. "His Majesty prefers to pass sentence against traitors himself."

As the soldiers marched her from the chamber, a single thought looped in her mind:

Alain shall denounce me as a traitor too.

She was unprepared for how much devastation it wrought within her soul.

Chapter 24

ALAIN APPROACHED THE line of King William's guards stationed in a tight perimeter around Thornhill's hall. He suspected that more of the king's men were watching the gates and manning the wooden palisade's towers.

Prisoners who'd survived yesterday's action fit to work today had been pressed into service to erect a gallows in front of the hall. He grimaced at the irony.

Had the battle occurred only yesterday?

He felt as if he'd aged a hundred years overnight.

Feigning cheerfulness, he returned the guards' greetings. Many of these men, each one chosen by the king, Alain had fought beside at Hastings and during William's earlier campaigns.

Perhaps he might find a place among them if he and Kendra couldn't—

He clamped off that line of thought. No battle was ever won on pessimism.

But questions still battered his brain.

What had become of the rebel Saxon army? How William had discovered it, Alain could guess: a conquering monarch who failed to monitor his new realm would soon become a deposed one, as evidenced by the events of the past several days. But how had the king arrived so quickly?

The summons prevented him from lingering with his friends to learn these answers, although his mounting apprehension made the idea sorely tempting. Alain expected William to demand a full report, but his gut warned him that something else might have prompted this commanded appearance before the Crown.

On a more personal level, Alain longed to learn how Lofwin and Waldron's other men had fared. Ruaud had seemed well enough last night—he'd demonstrated little difficulty in carrying Kendra up the stairs—but the summons had left no time to search the infirmary for the fyrd members.

And Kendra—how was she feeling? How fast would she recover from her harrowing experiences? What did she remember of them?

Would she ever forgive him?

For now she could add the death of her kinsman to her list of grievances against him.

"Alain, wait!"

He spun about to see Ruaud striding toward him from the manor house. His friend's mouth was set in a grim expression that didn't ease when he reached Alain and took his tunic sleeve to draw him away from the guards.

"What is it?" Alain asked. "Quickly, if you please, for the king has summoned me."

"I know." Ruaud's expression became grimmer. "And I know why: Lady Kendra has been accused of treason."

"*What!*" Several guards looked at them curiously. "Why?"

"One of the prisoners implicated her in Ulfric's scheme," Ruaud said quietly but no less urgently.

Alain grunted. "I can guess who that was."

Seething, he tried to jerk away, but Ruaud held him fast. "Have a care, Alain. If the king is in a foul humor, he may decide you're a traitor too, who only wants to protect his ladylove."

"I am no traitor. The king ought to know that well."

Too bad he had no time to search the cottage's charred ruins for a certain object that might appease his liege.

He stalked up the stairs and on into the hall, hearing Ruaud's heavy tread behind him. More soldiers, bristling with weapons, crowded the hall, where William had ensconced himself on the dais at the far end. His Majesty had traveled lightly, Alain reasoned. The royal banner, twin gold lions prowling across a crimson field, had been nailed to the wall timbers behind William's seat, but the chair was not ornate enough to be his field throne.

Having no wagons or pack animals to hinder progress explained how William's unit had made such excellent time.

Alain studied the other Norman warriors as he strode among them. To a man, they bore evidence of recent action: a blood-splotched hauberk here, a bandaged arm there. Though the king's surcoat looked pristine, his mail, to Alain's surprise, bore a smattering of dark red flecks.

Neither King William nor Regent Odo, also arrayed for battle and sitting beside the king, looked pleased as Alain approached them. He dropped to one knee, lowering his head. From the corner of his eye, he saw Ruaud strike the same pose.

"Rise, Sir Robert, Sir Ruaud," intoned the king. "And report."

They obeyed. Alain bowed to the king before regarding Regent Odo. "Please accept my apologies for not reporting to you sooner, Your Grace. I have been quite thoroughly occupied."

He began with Kendra's kidnapping and proceeded to her rescue, the discovery of the outlaws' plunder, Ulfric's attempts to kill him and why, infiltrating the rebel camp, the ensuing battle, his duel with Ulfric, and its lethal result.

Of his original disguise, and of his rescuing Kendra from the burning cottage and the overnight events, he said nothing.

"Most impressive, Sir Robert," Regent Odo said. The king gazed at Alain intently. "Sir Ruaud, do you avow that Sir Robert has spoken the truth?"

"Your Grace, I witnessed everything he spoke of, save the plunder and Sir Robert's final fight with Thane Ulfric. I have no reason to doubt his word about the rest of his report."

Alain shot Ruaud a grateful glance.

William cleared his throat. "Where was Lady Kendra yesterday while you fought the other traitors, Sir Robert?"

He couldn't fail to notice the king's choice of words. "Lady Kendra fled from the hall before the fighting began. I engaged Thane Ulfric, but he escaped. I suspected that he had followed her. I broke free of the battle and tracked him to a cottage on the far side of the hill. Lady Kendra and Thane Ulfric were both inside, Your Majesty, though Lady Kendra was unconscious when I arrived."

"There were others inside the cottage too, were there not?" asked Regent Odo.

"Yes, my lord. I saw an old female servant, also unconscious, and one—no, two male corpses. Three, counting the man who had been murdered outside. Two men I didn't recognize." Alain drew a deep breath, unsure of the reaction he would get. "The other corpse was Harold Godwinson."

The soldiers began to whisper among themselves.

King and regent exchanged a glance. "Have you proof of your claim?" William demanded.

Alain shrugged. "He was wearing a mask that covered one eye and half his face, presumably to hide the arrow wound many of us saw him take at Hastings. That mask—along with the rest of his body—may have been destroyed in the fire, but I expect that his sword did not burn."

The regent dispatched a unit to secure the site of the immolated cottage and to search it once the rubble cooled.

Odo returned his attention to Alain. "But you have no idea what Lady Kendra was doing prior to your arrival at the cottage?"

"No, Your Grace." Alain didn't like the direction this line of questioning had taken. "As I said, she was already unconscious—near death, in fact, when I found her."

The king nodded at Regent Odo, who in turn called for the accused to be brought in.

To Alain's surprise, not one but two prisoners were marched in by a cluster of guards. One prisoner he loved with his entire being; the other he should have gutted when he'd had the chance.

The guards forced both prisoners onto their knees.

"You!" Kendra hurled the word at Dragon, who leered back at her. With her cheeks blazing scarlet, she dropped her gaze.

"You know this man, Lady Kendra?" asked the regent.

"Aye, my lord. He was the leader of the outlaw band that abducted me." She appeared to be on the verge of saying more but remained silent.

"And he was in command of the Saxon rebel encampment," Alain added.

"Do either of you know his name?"

Curious as to what Kendra knew, Alain waited for her to speak.

"Dragon, my lord," she told the regent, "though I daresay that's not his Christian name."

"That is the same name I heard in the camp, Your Grace," Alain confirmed, "in addition to his given name of Eosa. Many items in the hoard match the lists you showed me and prove that his outlaw band plundered Saxons and Normans alike."

Regent Odo faced the Saxon who called himself Dragon. "Sir Eosa Thorgudson, for the crime of banditry, you are hereby stripped of title and lands. For the crime of treason against the Crown, you shall hang." Odo paused to give his scribe time to record the sentence. "Unless, perchance, you would care to repeat your earlier statement for all assembled here."

Hope lessened Eosa's permanent scowl. "It is true, Your Majesty, that Thane Ulfric raised an army against you. As his second-in-command, I was privy to all his plans." He waved his bandaged stump at Kendra, grinning slyly. "Including the role this woman agreed to play."

Her head snapped up. "Your Majesty, I agreed only to heal someone, nothing more."

"Silence, woman. No one gave you leave to speak," said the regent. "And what was that role, Thorgudson?"

"To prolong Harold Godwinson's life so that Thane Ulfric could take his place."

"Is this true, Lady Kendra?" inquired Regent Odo.

"My lord, I—" She bowed her head. "I didn't know at first. After Ulfric's motives became clear, I resisted his orders." When she lifted her face, her eyes glittered with resolve. "If attempting to heal a severely hurting soul is wrong, Your Majesty, then I am guilty."

"All the more so when you use sorcery to accomplish it," Eosa added.

With a gasp, Kendra blanched.

The regent jumped to his feet, fists knotted and eyebrows lowered, and the king canted forward in his chair. When Odo opened his mouth, William raised a hand. "Witchcraft is a grave charge to level in front of any man of the cloth, especially a highly ranked one," said the king, referring to Regent Odo, who still served the Church as an ordained bishop. "Explain, Thorgudson."

The Saxon appeared unruffled. "Harold Godwinson should have died months ago from wounds he received at Hastings. Lady Kendra's efforts extended his life beyond anyone's expectations."

"But you do not know how she did it?" pressed Odo.

Eosa shook his head.

"I don't even know!" she wailed. "It—it just happens." One of the guards poked the iron-capped butt of his spear between her shoulder blades. She flinched and dropped her gaze, but not before Alain saw the welling tears.

He had had quite enough. Willing himself to resist clenching his fists, he took a pace forward.

"Your Majesty, Your Grace, if I may speak frankly?" Both men nodded. Alain inhaled, offering a silent prayer for wisdom. "With all due respect, my lords, I am astounded and dismayed that you seem so quick to believe a convicted traitor, and I appeal to your sound judgment. Eosa Thorgudson possesses no proof of his accusation and therefore cannot present a valid case. Lady Kendra healed me too, and she delivered me from the brink of death without resorting to witchcraft. She used an herb local to this shire, the Glastonbury thorn. I do not know how it is expected to behave when used by most physicians, but I have learned that it can effect great miracles when wielded by the pure of heart."

Into the expectant silence, Alain forged ahead. "Lady Kendra possesses the purest heart of anyone I know. I believe she has been granted a special healing gift from God."

He tried to give her an encouraging smile, but she wouldn't look at anyone.

"This knight has been smitten by her charms," Eosa declared. "That renders his testimony unreliable."

"Hah. As if the word of a criminal is any more reliable." After giving Eosa an annoyed glare, which the miscreant dared to parry, Alain gazed beseechingly at the king. "Your Majesty, Lady Kendra is no witch but is a faithful daughter of the Church. At worst, she assisted those whose purposes ran contrary to the Crown. But I am confident that she was motivated by compassion for the injured man, not for what she thought he might accomplish for England, either in his own person or through the devices of others. In my company, Lady Kendra has always demonstrated the strictest obedience to Your Majesty's wishes."

"That may all be true," said the king, "but Thorgudson has raised a valid point. One would expect nothing less than for you to argue eloquently in defense of your bride."

Alain sucked in a breath, held it, and released it slowly, expelling with it the host of sharp retorts that sprang to mind. "I argue on her behalf because I believe she stands wrongly accused before Your Majesty. If not for the fact that her life is in jeopardy, I would be begging from Your Majesty an entirely different boon."

He heard Kendra's soft gasp but couldn't bring himself to look at her.

"What boon is this, Sir Robert?" William asked.

Sinking to his knees, Alain bowed his head. "I must confess to Your Majesty and all assembled here that I have not comported myself as a servant of the Crown ought. I willfully deceived Lady Kendra, Thane Waldron, and everyone else I met in the conduct of this mission by presenting myself as someone I was not."

"Your Majesty, Sir Robert is being too harsh with himself." Ruaud stepped closer to lay a hand upon Alain's shoulder. Alain disagreed but did not voice it. Ruaud squeezed the shoulder before withdrawing his hand. "He chose the guise of a squire upon my suggestion as a means of learning more about the outlaws and their activities than he might otherwise have accomplished as a knight."

"I appreciate your support, my friend." Alain diverted his attention from Ruaud to William and Odo. "But Sir Ruaud relates only what he and I have discussed. He does not know my private motives." This time Kendra did look at him, and he hoped she could sense his unspoken apology. "I needed some way to ascertain that Lady Kendra would not be like Ma—my previous fiancée, who was interested only in prestige and deserted me for a wealthier prospect."

"You were betrothed before?" she asked, risking another jab from the guard.

He sighed. "Her name was Marie."

"Did you love her?" she whispered.

"I thought I did, Kendra, until I met you." He set his jaw to mask his breaking heart as he regarded the king. "If Your Majesty requires blood for Lady Kendra's transgressions against the Crown, then please allow me to suffer her punishment. All I ask, if I may, is the assurance that she need never marry anyone—Norman or otherwise—against her will." Closing his eyes, he let his head sink until his chin rested upon his chest.

"Alain, you—you would do this for me?"

"It is done," he said, "if the king agrees."

Moments felt like years as silence invaded the hall.

"The king shall do nothing of the kind," William boomed. "Get up, both of you." He made an impatient gesture with his hands, and Kendra and Alain scrambled to their feet. William ordered a guard to cut Kendra's bonds and said to Ruaud, "You deserve a special commendation for enduring Sir Robert all the time so that I do not have to."

Ruaud laughingly rolled his eyes. "A weighty cross I must bear, Your Majesty."

The king leveled his gaze upon Alain. "All jesting aside, Sir Robert, I do appreciate your honesty, your willingness to sacrifice yourself for the sake of another, and the valuable service you have rendered unto the Crown. And," said the king, lowering his voice, "I'm not certain I wouldn't have made similar choices myself." Louder, he continued, "Let it be known to all that the Crown has granted Lady Kendra of Edgarburh a full pardon for any wrongdoing in Thane Ulfric's rebellion."

As the scribe recorded the pronouncement, Kendra and Alain each loosed a relieved sigh.

Eosa spluttered a protest, and William glared at him. "It is obvious that you have been obeying your dead master's wishes by attempting to condemn someone who was only marginally involved in his scheme." He nodded at Eosa's guards. "Remove this filth from my sight, but do not execute him yet. I shall want to watch him—and the rest of the rebels—swing."

At spearpoint, the guards hustled a slump-shouldered Eosa out of the hall.

Regent Odo's face creased with consternation. "Your Majesty, I recommend offering clemency to as many as are willing to swear fealty to the Crown." Alain's proximity allowed him to hear the regent's quiet but earnest remarks. "Otherwise, I fear you may run a threefold risk: leaving this shire devoid of leadership, without enough laborers to support the people's needs, and creating an entire generation who will grow up to resent Your Majesty for leaving them fatherless."

The king stroked his beard. "The leadership aspect can be remedied forthwith. Sir Robert Alain de Bellencombre, the Crown grants deed to Thornhill to you and your heirs in perpetuity, in exchange for service as sheriff for the Glastonbury district."

The scribe made more annotations on his parchment.

Alain had heard of this new office of the Crown, "sheriff," a position of William's invention to assist his dozen chief tenants in ruling England. A sheriff was commissioned to administer justice, collect taxes, and lead the local militia during times such as this—though, Lord willing, Ulfric's rebellion would be the last this shire would ever see.

Even without leading men into battle, the office of sheriff promised to be a heavy and no doubt unpopular responsibility.

"Instead of Edgarburh?" Alain asked.

"In addition to that estate," snapped the king. "I have not rescinded my earlier decree."

I noticed. Alain swept the king a deep bow. "Your Majesty's generosity is overwhelming. I am pleased to serve the Crown in this new capacity." He girt himself for the gamut of possible reactions to what he planned to say: "But the matter of freeing Lady Kendra from the obligation to marry me has become a point of honor."

"Because of the Norman who slew her brother?" asked William.

Simultaneously, Kendra said to Alain, "You don't want to marry me?" Hurt throbbed in her voice.

"I never said that. I only wish to give you a choice." Alain turned toward the king. "No Norman killed Sir Delwin Waldronson, Your Majesty. Thane Ulfric did, behind the shield of my brother, Sir Étienne de Bellencombre, whom he slew at Hastings, plundering his body to obtain a disguise to confound Saxon and Norman alike."

"What? Nay! It cannot be . . ." Eyes wide, she clapped a hand over her mouth.

"Ulfric confessed everything to me before he died," Alain told her. "I think he was hoping to expand his power base through marriage to you until the king's decree wrecked that aspect of his plan." He said to William, "As penance for my heinous deception, and with Your Majesty's permission, I still would like to honor her vow to never marry a Norman—"

"Alain, wait. I vowed to never marry someone of the same race as the man who murdered Del. He was slain by—by his own kinsman." She shook her head as if struggling to believe it.

"I am but half Norman," he reminded her glumly. "My mother was a Saxon."

Kendra curtseyed to the king. "Your Majesty is most wise for selecting a knight of dual heritage to help unite our races. I shall be delighted to comply with Your Majesty's decree to marry Sir Robert Alain de Bellencombre, if"—she rose and faced Alain with crossed arms, sternness dominating her features—"if you swear never to deal deceitfully with me again."

"Then first I must confess my other private motive for deceiving you." Alain swallowed hard, trying to dislodge the lump closing his throat. "I swore to my dying mother that I would protect my brother. At Hastings, that vow was shattered, and I—" Gritting his teeth against the rising tide of guilt, he forced himself to finish. "I doubted that I could ever protect anyone, least of all a bride who would depend on me as her protector."

"But you did protect me. From the outlaws, from Ulfric—"

"My brashness drove you from Edgarburh that day. If you hadn't been abroad, lightly escorted, none of this would have happened."

"You don't know that, Alain. If Ulfric was bent on getting to my father through me"—she glanced at the king—"because of my father's unswerving loyalty to Your Majesty, then he would have found some other way to accomplish it." When she returned her gaze to Alain, it was flooded with compassion. "Your brother's death wasn't your fault either."

How I long to believe you! He closed his eyes.

"Oh, Alain." He felt her fingertips press his cheek.

Heat branded his face, and intense light turned the insides of his eyelids bronze. When he opened his eyes—or thought he had—he found himself standing in the same dense fog that had accompanied the earlier dream of Kendra and Del.

The figure standing before him was no Saxon.

Shame forced Alain to avert his gaze.

"Greetings, my brother! Mama and Papa send their love." The hands gripping his shoulders felt real enough. Alain tried to wrest free but couldn't. "Mama understands, as do I."

This time he did pull away, and he folded his arms. "Then explain it to me, Étienne, for I do not understand." Feeling his eyebrows lower, he stared at the eternally youthful face. "Explain, if you please, why it had to be you and not me to die at Hastings. And why I couldn't prevent it from happening."

"Did you honestly believe that you could shield me forever? Come, Alain. I was a man grown when I chose to enter Duke William's service. Fully grown—and fully prepared to accept any consequences that befell as a result."

Alain clenched his fists. "I do not accept them!"

"You must if you are ever to truly live."

"How can I accept an outcome I should have been able to prevent?" he asked with asperity.

"I forgive you, Alain, and so does Mama. Most importantly, so does God. Now you must forgive yourself." Étienne's countenance clouded. "Otherwise, it is as if you are rejecting our forgiveness, considering it of no value."

Lord God, no, never that!

One problem remained, however.

"How do I begin?" Alain whispered.

"Lay my memory to rest." Étienne gripped Alain's forearm in farewell. "Learn to focus not on yourself but on others." He grinned. "Beginning with your beautiful bride."

That was the most sensible thing Alain had heard anyone utter, living or dead.

Determined to demonstrate his trust in Étienne's advice, Alain broke contact first. At once his mental burden began to lift. He knew his guilt would take time to conquer, but he felt encouraged by the start.

"Thank you," he said.

"For what?" Not Étienne's voice but Kendra's.

Blinking, he shook his head and glanced around. Thornhill's hall had returned, sans fog and sans Étienne—though that didn't disturb him as much as he'd expected. Everyone was looking at him curiously, but from the candles' heights it seemed that no time had passed.

He gripped her hands, stroking the dovelike skin with his thumbs and gazing into her slate-hued eyes. "I thank you for your understanding and patience. I have regretted my deception since the first hour I met you, as Ruaud can attest."

"I forgive you, Alain, with all my heart."

He resisted the urge to kiss her and instead squeezed her hands before releasing them.

"What is this, Sir Robert?" asked the king querulously. "Do you love this woman or not?"

"I do, Your Majesty. More than I can ever say."

"Then"—William's brief grin at Odo hinted defiance—"hang propriety and show her, you imbecile."

That was one royal command Alain wasted no time obeying. His sole regret, as he clasped her body to his and their mouths met in sweet reunion, to the cheers erupting throughout the hall, was that he could not keep kissing her until all the stars fell from the sky.

Chapter 25

RM IN ARM with Alain, her lips atingle from the imprint of his, Kendra couldn't have felt more ecstatic.

She beheld the gallows and the ragged line of prisoners snaking around it, entrapped by three concentric ranks of Norman guards, and choked back a gasp.

Several of the prisoners were Edgarburh men.

Apparently drawn by the sound of the king's party emerging from the feast hall, they seemed to notice Kendra, and hope flickered through the despair clouding their faces.

Alain must have seen them too. He excused himself from her company and lengthened his stride to catch the king, who was mounting the viewing platform, accompanied by his bodyguards. Kendra grabbed her skirts and broke into a most unladylike trot. Ruaud passed her to join Alain at the base of the platform.

"I need a word with His Majesty," Alain told the guards. "Some of these men are innocent."

The king heard Alain over the guards' refusal. He ordered the executioner to wait and signaled Alain to ascend the platform. Ruaud and Kendra followed him too closely to be denied passage.

Regent Odo stepped forward. "His Majesty has decided to offer the rest of the rebels the opportunity to swear fealty to the Crown. But these men"—he swept a mail-clad arm toward the prisoners—"were members of the upper echelon, and their executions are to commence forthwith."

Morbid curiosity turned Kendra's attention toward the scaffold. Six ropes hung looped, knotted, and waving in a perversely inviting manner. A large wagon, hitched behind a pair of shaggy brown draft horses, waited to bear away the corpses. No doubt the soldiers stationed closest to the scaffold had been tasked to remove one group and prepare the ropes for the next.

She chafed her arms to ward off the chill that defied the warm July morning.

Alain's jaw tightened. "May I ask whose testimony has condemned them, my lord?"

"Eosa Thorgudson identified them as members of Ulfric's army. Some tried to deny it, of course," said the regent.

"He was right, after a fashion," Alain conceded. "Your Majesty, Your Grace, the fault is mine for not rendering a complete report. Please accept my humblest apologies."

He bowed low and held the pose until the king bade him to rise and continue.

"When I reported that Ruaud and I had infiltrated the camp, I neglected to state that a hundred of Thane Waldron's men were accompanying us. We pretended to enlist because the army lay encamped between us and Thornhill. Skirting the camp undetected in the rain would have taken far too long. In fact, my plan could not have succeeded without the help of Lofwin Octhason and his companions-at-arms."

A hundred of the fyrd? Kendra squinted through the forenoon glare toward the bedraggled men. She didn't recognize threescore in the entire group. None of their injuries seemed too severe; perhaps some were yet recuperating in the infirmary.

Her heart ached to imagine that even one of her father's warriors had died helping Alain rescue her.

"If it pleases Your Majesty," Alain was saying, "and on behalf of my betrothed and her father, I respectfully request that the Crown consider releasing the surviving members of Thane Waldron's fyrd in recognition of their valiant service during these last several days, culminating in yesterday's battle."

"Now that I think about it, I do recall Thane Waldron having mentioned that he had given you some of his men to rescue Lady Kendra. They fought beside Normans against their own kinsmen?" The king sounded incredulous.

Kendra realized that in his place she probably would have been hard pressed to believe it too.

Alain ducked his head in a half bow, half shrug. "In all honesty, Your Majesty, I am quite sure their beloved lady's plight stood foremost in their minds. But—"

"But what Sir Robert is too modest to say, Your Majesty," Ruaud broke in, "is that Waldron's men looked to him for leadership." Kendra wanted to hug the man. "The Edgarburh unit was the sole reason Sir Robert was able to quit the fray to seek and rescue Lady Kendra."

King William strode over to grip the rail, gazing across the square. It didn't surprise Kendra that the only men to return his gaze were Norman soldiers; most of the prisoners kept their heads lowered, with but a few stealing a glance toward the platform.

"Who shall identify the Edgarburh men?" asked the king.

"Please allow me, Your Majesty."

Kendra dropped into a curtsey, not daring to look up even when she heard the chink of mail nearby. Gentle fingers lifted her chin, and she found herself staring into the king's compelling green eyes.

"Lady Kendra, your father's men shall still be required to swear fealty to the Crown," he said, not unkindly.

"The oath that binds my father to Your Majesty binds everyone at Edgarburh." She blinked, not certain where those words had come from; they sounded more like something Del would have said. His memory made her smile, bolstering her resolve. "The fyrd should have no objection to swearing this oath to you in person, my lord."

"Well spoken, Lady Kendra." The king offered his hand to help her rise and bade Alain and Regent Odo to escort her among the prisoners.

Reunions were, by necessity, brief but heartfelt as she greeted each fyrd member by name and pulled him from the line. Some kissed her hand. Many saluted her with unabashed tears.

As she had predicted, every member of Edgarburh's fyrd rushed to swear allegiance to King William.

One man, however, gave her pause.

He was standing next to Dragon—Eosa, she reminded herself, who leered at her until one of the guards cuffed him. Dragon's accomplice had hidden his face from her, but not before she saw the scar that slithered across his exposed cheek.

She rejoiced to see him alive.

"Is this everyone, then?" asked the regent.

"Yes," Alain said.

"Nay," she told Regent Odo and her husband-to-be.

Alain shot her a puzzled glance. She smiled at him, took the last prisoner by the hand, and pulled him away from his condemned companions.

Her betrothed regarded the man for a long, intense moment before giving Kendra a look of pure astonishment. "You wish to pardon one of the brigands?"

She gave Snake's hand a squeeze and released it. "If he is willing to swear fealty to King William and renounce his former lifestyle, aye."

"An outlaw?" Regent Odo's eyes narrowed. "What is this man to you, Lady Kendra?"

She thrust her chin to ward off the insinuations in his tone. "My lord, Snake was one of my captors. But he offered me kindness on several occasions, guarding my dignity, privacy, and comfort when the others refused to do so. I believe he has a decent heart and deserves another chance."

Snake's face became a study in remorse, surprise, and hope. "My lady is most merciful, but"—the hope died—"I cannot accept."

"Why not?" Kendra couldn't bridle her surprise or dismay.

"I have no place," he replied. "I know no other life save a lawless one."

A bruised and bandaged Lofwin, having just sworn his oath to the king, approached them. "The fyrd's numbers are sorely diminished. He fights well and could make a new life with us, if Thane Waldron and"—he nodded toward his liege—"Your Majesty agree."

"Sir Robert?" called King William from the viewing platform, over the heads of those still queued to swear allegiance.

"For Edgarburh's future lord, you have remained remarkably silent."

Alain inclined his head. "Silent, Your Majesty, but pondering." He faced Snake. "You abducted Lady Kendra?"

Snake's eyes flinched, making his scar seem alive. "One of them what was sent to fetch her, I was, my lord." He squared his shoulders. "But I did treat her ladyship with all the respect owed a fine lady, I swear by Saint Dunstan's bones!"

"Saint Dunstan?" Alain asked the regent.

Amusement creased the craggy face. "A well-connected Saxon who lived in this shire a hundred years ago. By all reports, he was a Godly man who served both as Glastonbury's abbot and as a close adviser to many Saxon kings." Regent Odo turned his eyes skyward for a moment. "Would God that I may serve King William even half as well."

"If I swear by Saint Dunstan, will you let me go free too?" Dragon sneered.

"You shall be swearing to the entire company of saints in person soon," remarked the regent. "If they'll deign to have you, which I doubt." He ordered a guard to escort Eosa up the gallows steps.

Kendra gave the regent a grateful smile; she wasn't sure how much more of Dragon's presence she could have tolerated. Regent Odo responded with a polite nod.

"My lady, I am so sorry for taking you captive. I was only following"—Snake jerked his head toward the first man of the lot to be fitted for a noose—"Dragon's orders." He knotted his hands in an imploring gesture. "I swear to serve you better than ever I served him."

She glanced at her husband-to-be, who seemed undecided. "Alain?"

At length he asked Snake his name.

Snake hesitated, as if he couldn't recall it at first. "Liam Fletcher, my lord."

"You make arrows?" Alain asked.

Snake—Liam looked chagrinned. "'Tis been right many a year, my lord." He scratched his bewhiskered chin. "I may recollect a mite or two of the craft."

Alain clapped him on the shoulder. "Well, Liam Fletcher, you have already sworn fealty to my lady. Now you need only swear to the king, and we shall have you back into an honest trade before the next market day. Enlisting you in the fyrd as well as having you supply arrows for it ought to keep you clear of the gallows."

Liam's expression exuded gratitude as he bobbed an awkward but respectful bow. "My lord, 'twill be my pleasure."

Kendra too felt immense pleasure for having helped to deliver a lost soul—this time without benefit of the Glastonbury thorn's magic.

She commanded Liam to stay with Lofwin, turned her back on the gallows, where the executions were getting underway, and addressed the king once more: "May I search the infirmary too, Your Majesty?"

"You may," he replied. "The Crown had already decided to leave those men's fates in the hands of God."

This, Kendra presumed, meant minimal care, but perhaps she could reach some in time. She curtseyed her thanks. Alain helped her rise, and with the king's leave they departed for the infirmary.

Chapter 26

ALAIN HAD SENT a courier to Edgarburh with the news that Kendra, Ruaud, and most of the fyrd were on their way back. But Waldron had regretted not accompanying his men, and he yearned to see them all as fast as his best horse could carry him.

He and his ten-man escort intercepted the much larger party half a day west of Edgarburh. Only because Waldron had been forewarned did he know that Kendra wasn't the sole beneficiary of the soldiers' protection; not even so much as a kerchief bearing the royal colors betrayed King William's presence. The foremost ranks of the king's bodyguards drew their swords against what must have looked like a dervish churning across the rolling plains.

Somehow, even from her position in the formation's center, Kendra must have guessed what was happening. Over the din, Waldron heard a high-pitched shout of "Father!" and she and her horse emerged from the pack. A tall, helmed knight carrying a rose-emblazoned shield shadowed her.

As the distance narrowed, it pained Waldron to notice evidence of Kendra's trials in her disheveled hair and clothing, but her beaming smile eclipsed whatever discomfort she must be feeling.

Relief coursed through him. He couldn't spur his horse to hers fast enough. She all but launched herself from her mount into his arms, crying and laughing all at once. He hugged her so tightly, he feared she might not be able to breathe, and he loosened his grip. She didn't complain but nestled against him, sighing contentedly. If she'd wanted to remain thus forever, Waldron wouldn't have minded in the least.

He did know of someone, however, who would mind. Over Kendra's head, he gazed at the man fated to take his place in her heart.

Nay, that wasn't true. Blood forged a bond that might bend but could never break.

Alain removed his helmet, and Kendra stepped out of Waldron's embrace to take Alain's gloved hand. The couple shared a brief but tender glance that told him everything he needed to know about their future. He hoped his bow to the courageous Norman knight conveyed the vast depth of his gratitude that mere words could never express.

King William, flanked by the regent and a handful of their soldiers, swaggered toward them. Waldron dropped to one knee at his sovereign's feet, prompting his escort to do the same.

"England is once again most well come to humble Edgarburh." Waldron meant it even more sincerely than ever.

"England appreciates Edgarburh's gracious hospitality." The king cracked a grin. "But England wonders when Edgarburh was planning to extend an invitation to the wedding."

Waldron opened his mouth, shut it, opened it, and shut it again, feeling as foolish as a bloody carp. Astonishment constricted his throat. He needed a drink. Since nothing strong enough was available, he sucked in a breath and forced himself to think straight. "Of course, if it pleases the Crown to attend this event, we would be honored and delighted beyond measure by Your Majesty's august presence—as well as that of Queen Matilda, Regent Odo, and your retinue."

"Indeed." King William nodded, first at Waldron, then at Kendra and Alain, who were standing so close together that Waldron doubted even the sharpest sword could ever part them. "It pleases the Crown very much."

To say that Edgarburh celebrated Kendra's return would be like saying folk celebrated the birth of Jesu at Cristes mæsse, though these festivities were tempered by mourning Cæwlin and the other fyrd members who had perished at Thornhill. But whether one grieved or rejoiced, each state provided an excellent excuse to remain in a drunken stupor for days.

The bride, of course, couldn't afford such a luxury.

If Edgarburh with King William and his troops in residence had been, according to Kendra's father, busier than a month of market days, adding Queen Matilda and her entourage to the mix created a maelstrom of activity.

Moving trancelike from task to task, Kendra felt as if she were trapped within the storm's eye. Never mind that she'd accomplished most of her wedding's details prior to her abduction; the queen would have none of it. Once Her Majesty had learned of the "poor, motherless dear" slated to marry one of the king's favorite knights, she insisted on rearranging everything to her own exacting standards. Kendra's gown, the fragrant profusion of lavender garlands festooning the chapel and feast hall provided by the wagonload from the queen's Norman farms, the guests' attire, the sumptuous nuptial feast, even the finely woven and embroidered linens swathing the bridal bed didn't escape the queen's notice.

Fortunately, Kendra thought with a private smile as Her Majesty's personal dressmaker tugged the gorgeous silver-brocaded blue damask fabric this way and that, the queen had brought an army of workers.

Feeding them for the fortnight leading up to the ceremony might have posed a problem if the king hadn't granted Alain a generous portion of the gold recovered from Ulfric's stolen hoard. Alain, in turn, gifted much of it to Waldron as Kendra's brydgild, since his status as his late father's second son had left him with no estates from which to draw funds.

Two details Kendra remained firm on, however.

Although she had intended to wear the veil she'd made for this occasion, at the last moment she decided to honor her parents' union by wearing her mother's wedding veil instead. Even if its grayish blue color had not complemented her gown's darker hue so well, she'd have worn it regardless.

Queen Matilda, a knowing sparkle lighting her eyes, expressed profuse approval.

Kendra also insisted on carrying a bouquet fashioned of roses plucked from the bushes Del had given her following their mother's death. All the other changes the queen had effected should have taught Kendra a lesson; the royal florist used Del's roses to create a breathtaking cascade of red and white blooms at least as large—if perhaps not quite as heavy—as Alain's shield.

Surviving the madness of preparations and bouts of nervousness, thus she came to be seated sideways across the saddle of Alain's charcoal warhorse, whose ebony mane and tail had been braided and woven with snowy rosebuds. Chou's bridle and harness featured new silver fittings that shone in the morning sun.

As arranged months ago, four of Kendra's unmarried cousins—daughters of Waldron's younger brother and sisters—accompanied her, similarly dressed and mounted, escorted by Ruaud and three of Alain's other knightly friends. Noir wouldn't let himself be left out either. The giggling bridal party's play-acting began at Edgarburh's main gate, as a modified nod to the ancient custom of the groom sending his best men to steal his chosen bride from her home.

Having suffered a real abduction, Kendra would have preferred to bypass this tradition, but Edgarburh's residents seemed to enjoy chasing them through the burh to the chapel's steps. Noir and his newfound canine friends scampered among them to add profuse encouragement. After the hardships Kendra's people had endured for the better part of a year following the Hastings disaster, she wouldn't have denied them this bit of sport for all the gold in the world.

Her father, waiting at the base of the steps, which had been strewn with dried petals saved from the roses with which Kendra had decorated Del's tomb, looked ten years younger as he puffed his chest and extended his arms to help her dismount.

She lingered in his embrace, her mind bursting with a thousand different things she wanted to tell him. But all she could trust herself to say was, "Thank you, Father."

Even those words had to compete with her welling tears.

"My beautiful little girl," he murmured, hugging her close. "I have always loved you, even though I may not have always shown it." He released her with obvious reluctance. After she relinquished her bouquet to her nearest attendant, Waldron placed her right hand into Alain's left. "Well come to our family, son."

Alain, breathtakingly handsome in his gleaming chain mail and new surcoat, laid his right hand over his heart and bowed to Waldron. "The honor and the pleasure is all mine." He drew a deep breath and held it for a moment. "Father."

As they gripped forearms, both men were blinking rapidly.

After Waldron withdrew to his assigned place, Alain noticed Kendra's struggle for composure and caught her tears with a fingertip. "Are you all right, *ma chere*?"

"I—I'm happy . . . my dearest love," she managed to say.

They shared a smile and faced their future.

On the chapel's steps, before the king and queen, the royal attendants, the bridal party, Kendra's extended family, and as many of Edgarburh's people as could pack into the yard, Regent Odo, acting in his capacity as bishop, intoned the sacred Latin words uniting Alain and Kendra until death.

At the bishop's signal, Ruaud produced a silver ring from the pouch at his belt and passed it to Alain, who held it aloft for a moment before snapping it along its scores. The crowd raised a hearty cheer. Next, Ruaud pulled out two lengths of blue silken cord and gave them to Alain, who tied one to each half of the ring and knotted the cords to form loops. This should have occurred at the betrothal ceremony, but their betrothal period had been anything but normal.

Before Alain slipped the cord around her neck, he showed her what he had chosen to have engraved upon her half ring.

"*Mon coeur tu as?*" she asked haltingly, certain she'd butchered the pronunciation.

He repeated the phrase in his lilting accent. "You have my heart," he whispered as the ring settled into place against her chest, where Del's locket once had resided. "Always."

She smiled, needing no reminder of what she had known from the first moment of their first meeting but treasuring the sentiment none the less.

"*Amot vincit om,*" she quoted to him in practiced Latin without looking at the phrase she'd selected to adorn his half.

"Indeed," Regent Odo agreed, glancing at King William. "Love does conquer all."

Alain bent so she could slip the cord over his head. The half ring gleamed proudly against his surcoat as if it had always belonged there.

The prickling sensation of something fluttering onto her head startled her. His grin turned mischievous, and she followed the line of his gaze skyward as the "storm" intensified.

Several fyrd members, perched on the chapel's timber roof, were shaking canvas sacks of dried flower petals—rose, crocus, chamomile, hawthorn, apple blossom; apparently, every white flower they could find—onto the assembly below. Once they'd been discovered, they erupted with peals of laughter as the "flakes" drifted down to coat king and commoner alike.

"You did it," she whispered in awe to her husband as everyone else enjoyed the jest.

He radiated innocence. "What?"

"You . . ." Love surged through her with palpable force. "Alain, you made it snow in July."

He squeezed her hand. "But of course, *ma chere.*" His expression sobered. "I could not enter into this marriage leaving its most important condition unfulfilled."

Taking advantage of Kendra's stunned silence, the bishop bade Sir Robert Alain de Bellencombre to kiss his bride.

Alain lifted her veil to provide her first clear sight of her husband, crowned with a chaplet of plaited lavender and white roses similar in design to the one that secured her veil. Loose petals scattered across his shoulders and head. The smile he gave her, that only she and God could see, hinted of the pleasures they would share later this night.

Her heart raced wantonly in anticipation.

The warm touch of his lips on hers so engorged her senses that she scarcely heard the crowd's thunderous approval. She felt as if the entire world had been made anew, with herself and Alain the first couple to populate it. This teetered on the edge of blasphemy, to be sure, but she could imagine no other way to describe the soul-satisfying intensity of her euphoria.

Later, if anyone had asked her to relate the homily Father Æthelward delivered at mass following the wedding ceremony, she wouldn't have had the slightest idea what to tell them.

What occurred on their way out of the chapel after the mass's conclusion, however, she would never forget.

Gripping Alain's arm, she stopped in front of the sarcophagi housing her mother and brother. Doubtless sensing her need for privacy, the king and queen paused a respectful distance away, preventing anyone else from disturbing her.

She let go of Alain and slipped between the tombs, first turning to her mother's effigy and caressing the cool, prayer-folded granite hands. Although she still didn't understand the full measure of the talent her mother had bequeathed her, she silently thanked her for the gift of healing even though it had manifested too late to save either her mother or Del.

Not too late, daughter. The voice whispered through her mind like a summer morning's breeze. *Precisely in God's good time. Wield it well, with His blessings and mine.*

For one astounding moment, the stone felt fleshlike. In the next moment, it cooled and hardened, making her certain she must have imagined the sensation.

With the back of her hand she pressed her moist eyes, though why she bothered, she had no idea, for the tears welled in earnest as she faced Del's tomb.

Around his effigy's neck, and extending to the sideways *V* formed by his chest and hands, lay the locket she had worn night and day for half a year. Its black cord, knotted in two places because Snake had cut it on the fateful day that now seemed another lifetime ago, was stretched taut. Although she suspected it would prove unnecessary, she sprang the catch to look inside.

It was Alain who voiced the question that leapt to Kendra's mind: "How did those get there?" He pointed at the brittle blond strands of Del's hair that once again lay in their rightful place. "Your father gave them to me, to return to you, but I thought . . ." As he trailed off, staring, she shot him an inquisitive look. He shook his head with a smile. "I thought I had lost them at Thornhill."

Kendra could guess what he might be thinking about, but now was neither the time nor the place to inquire about a certain dream that had felt altogether too real.

She kissed her fingers and pressed them against the effigy's cheek. It too grew fleshy for a miraculous moment before behaving like granite ought.

"I shall take good care of her, Delwin Waldronson," Alain murmured, gazing at the statue.

Kendra noted his emphasis on the word "shall," as if he were answering a question posed by Del himself. She resolved to ask Alain about it later.

You take care of him too, Kendra. In this new office for the Crown, Alain will need all the love and support you can give him.

Del, that is one promise I am delighted to make to you.

She didn't think anything else could have surprised her until the effigy—briefly but unmistakably—displayed her brother's distinctive lopsided grin.

Blinking as they emerged from the candlelit chapel into the bright July sun, Kendra and Alain were obliged to duck and run for the feast hall as the people laughingly pelted them with fistfuls of barley. The bridal party was hard-pressed to keep up, the more so when they stopped to arm themselves with grain.

Kendra's brilliant idea to pull apart her bouquet bought them a respite as people scrambled for the roses she dropped in her wake. But she couldn't appease the crowd fast enough, so she heaved the entire concoction at them, grabbed her skirts, and lengthened her stride.

Although the barley-pelting ceased when the newly wedded couple crossed the hall's threshold, by unspoken agreement they continued to run, hand in hand, until they reached the dais. They turned, panting and grinning at each other like moon-mad fools, until the growing noise at the far end of the hall signaled the arrival of everyone else.

The king and queen led the procession at a stately pace, followed by the bridal party, Regent Odo, Waldron and the other members of Kendra's family, Waldron's fyrd, and the king's men-at-arms. The remaining crowd eschewed dignity to jostle for seats. Noir beelined for the dais, where he proceeded to make a nuisance of himself until Alain called him to heel.

Alain, beaming at his gorgeous bride, knew he had the best seat in the hall on this, the very day he once had dreaded above all others.

Seated on Alain's right, Ruaud, bless his wicked heart, started the chant, "Kiss! Kiss! Kiss!" Soon the word was echoing throughout the hall, accompanied by clapping and the drumming of dagger hilts on the tabletops. As Kendra and Alain complied, the drumming grew louder and more intense.

Fortunately, the guests had more important business to attend to as the honeyed mead started flowing and royal-liveried servants set the feast before them.

Upholding tradition, however, someone at the high table would revive the chant time and again, most often waiting until either the bride or groom had a full mouth. The king and queen seemed pleased to contribute to the hilarity, and Alain's kisses got sloppier after every empty goblet.

Before the hall started spinning too badly, he leaned toward Ruaud and asked for Kendra's gift. He must have spoken more loudly than he imagined, for Kendra made a similar request of the demoiselle sitting beside her.

"You first," Kendra and Alain said simultaneously, once they had their gifts in hand, and laughed.

At her insistence, he presented his gift: the rose-enameled brooch that had belonged to his mother, the same brooch he had tried to give Kendra while posing as Squire Alain. Her swift, soft intake of breath prompted him to apologize for reviving unpleasant memories.

"Don't, Alain. Please." She fumbled with the catch for a moment before securing it to her gown, over her heart. "This is perfect. Thank you."

He had wondered what she might give him. After untying what felt to his mead-fuddled fingers like a hundred ribbons, though in truth it was only four, he had his answer:

"Your locket?" He turned the shiny silver case over and over in his hands, looking for its catch.

"Its twin." She took it from him, deftly opened it, and displayed its contents. A lustrous lock of her hair lay nestled inside. She snapped it closed and slipped the cord over his neck, where it clicked against his half ring. "So you will always remember me when you're off on your knightly pursuits."

"Hah, as if I could ever forget you, Kendra of Edgarburh!"

That earned another kiss-kiss-kiss chant from Ruaud. When they finished, Ruaud clapped his hands and whispered something to the servant who'd answered his summons. The queen's woman rushed off and returned a few minutes later bearing a perfect apple sitting atop a polished silver tray, which she presented with a curtsey to the bride and groom.

"Ah!" squealed Queen Matilda. "Now we shall find out how many children the happy couple may expect." She gave Waldron an exaggerated wink. "Your grandchildren."

Alain's new *beau-père* blushed to the roots of his white hair and took a long pull of mead.

"What is this for?" Kendra asked as Alain positioned his dagger's blade over the fruit.

"Norman wedding custom," he said as steadily as he could. "Our apples are tart but very fruitful." He grinned at his bride. "Just as our people are. As many seeds as show inside an apple when the bride and groom cut it open, that's how many children they may expect to be blessed with."

"The number in the right hand is the number of sons," added the queen, projecting her voice for the benefit of the mostly Saxon crowd, "and in the left is daughters."

With Kendra's hand to steady him, Alain severed the apple in twain. She snatched the halves, giggling. "Then we had better get started soon, my husband." She held the fruit aloft, announcing to the assembly with the vigor of a seasoned battle commander, "Three sons and a daughter!"

This time they defeated the crowd in its game, their lips meeting before the first syllable of "Kiss! Kiss! Kiss!" could be uttered.

Their final public kiss occurred, by Saxon custom, over a tower of honey-and-oat cakes almost as tall as Kendra. Alain felt certain he could lean over to reach her, God—and mead—willing, but the formidable stack seemed to frustrate his bride, who had trouble seeing past the cakes.

So he did what any other considerate bridegroom would have done, or so he thought: he drew his sword, cautioned her to stand clear, and slashed the stack.

After an awkward moment of stunned silence, thunderous whoops of laughter erupted.

"I'll wager I wasn't supposed to do that." Feeling his cheeks heat, he wiped the crumbs from his sword with the hem of his surcoat and sheathed it.

"Nay, my love." Grinning, she stepped through the sticky mess to fling herself into his arms. "But I believe that you—we have just birthed a new tradition."

The resounding chant of "Kiss! Kiss! Kiss!" faded into oblivion as Alain lost himself in the unfathomable depths of Kendra's love.

Epilogue

KENDRA ORDERED ROWENA to hurry with weaving the last ribbons into her braids. The messenger had reported that Sir Robert—even three years later, hearing Alain's formal name and rank made her smile—and his company were due to arrive soon. The manor's lady wished for everything to be in perfect readiness for the lord's return.

She donned her veil and pinned the de Bellencombre rose brooch in its rightful place next to her half ring. Her fingers lingered upon the white and green enamel's graceful contours to revive the cherished memories it evoked.

It had been a dreary six months without Alain.

But how much worse must it have been for him, being called away from hearth and home by the king to help quell yet another Saxon uprising, this time in the northeast, near York.

She sighed, easing her gravid bulk from the chair to stand, and tottered with Rowena's assistance to gaze out the tall, stone-framed window. From the castle's vantage on the ridge crest, halfway between Edgarburh and Glastonbury, she felt as if the entire world lapped at her feet.

Although her love for Alain, coupled with his just governing of the shire, had inspired the folk of Edgarburh and Glastonbury to abandon their resentments, she wished the rest of her people would choose to live in peace under their Norman masters. Then mayhap King William wouldn't feel compelled to be so brutal to them—and mayhap she could have her husband for more than a few months at a stretch.

"Is that such a selfish wish?" she murmured.

"My lady?" Rowena asked.

Kendra smiled ruefully. Her unborn baby nudged her, and she patted her swelling belly. "'Tis nothing, Rowena." Nothing but the fondest wish expressed by every warrior's mother.

As if on cue, she heard her firstborn warrior, two-year-old Étienne, shrieking and clattering about the adjacent room, old Ethel raising her voice over his din, admonishing him to slow down.

The woman might as well try taming a whirlwind.

A cloud of dust approaching from the north held Kendra spellbound as she watched it grow larger, her heart dancing in anticipation.

Alain would receive several surprises this day.

She hadn't quite grown accustomed to the time it took to traverse this immense, manmade cavern called a castle, and advanced pregnancy slowed her steps that much further. By the time she stopped at the wine cellar to fetch a goblet full of their finest vintage for the ceremonial welcome and hurried into the main yard with Étienne and their servants in tow, Alain and his men had already cantered under the portcullis and dismounted.

The man she had once known as "Snake" noticed her and raised his right hand in salute before ordering the other men to feed and stable their mounts. Liam Fletcher had proven to be an invaluable liaison to Alain's Saxon troops, and in public settings Kendra had rarely seen her husband apart from his second-in-command, who fletched fine arrows as necessity demanded.

Liam took Chou's reins as well as his own mount's and, with a respectful nod at Kendra, led the soldiers and their horses toward the stables.

The love of her days and lover of her nights circled about the courtyard, his helmet tucked under one arm, taking in his newly completed home for the first time. Pleased wonderment worked its way into the road grime streaking his face—along with a darker, crustier streak that had to be dried blood.

The castle's defensive walls had been completed, but the towers and great hall were naught but foundations when Alain left. The household was living in timber buildings that had since been converted to storehouses.

Noir, whom Alain had taken to war, padded around the yard, barking after the occasional chicken, cat, or pigeon and poking his snout into every crevice and cranny.

"I have much to show you, dear husband."

He whirled at the sound of her voice, a grin leavening his weariness. After entrusting his helmet to the waiting squire and striding toward her, he halted as her condition appeared to register. "Kendra! All those letters, and you never told me."

"You never asked." She smiled sweetly, pressing her fingers over the cut on his cheek. As the wound faded, so did her smile. "What injuries are there among the men?"

"Of the survivors, nothing too bad this time, praise God." He opened his arms. "The men can wait a while yet."

Sidling as close to him as her belly allowed, she reveled in the simple pleasure of his embrace. She slid her hands over his chest to trace the dual lumps under his surcoat: the small arc representing his half ring and the larger rectangle defining the case containing her hair.

With his palm he caressed her rounded flesh, his eyebrows quirking upward when he felt the baby kick. "Little Delwin?"

"Or Edwina."

During her first pregnancy, they had agreed to name their children in honor of their departed loved ones. Margaret and Hugh, Alain's parents, also would be future candidates for names if the de Bellencombre brood ever grew that large.

Lord willing, it would be years yet before they would be forced to consider naming a son "Waldron" or "Ruaud." Both men enjoyed robust health, although Ruaud had not visited since returning across the Channel to his Norman wife, sons, and estate soon after Étienne's birth.

Alain peered around Kendra to find his son clinging to the back of her overdress. Although he squatted to the boy's level, Étienne whimpered and shrank back, rounding his eyes and sticking a thumb in his mouth.

"My armor must frighten him," Alain said with a sigh.

Kendra's heart broke for her husband. "*Étienne, cher, tu sais ton papa,*" she scolded lightly. And again, in English, "You know your father." She grasped the boy's chubby fingers and gently but firmly pulled him forward. "Come and bid Papa well come to our new home."

"Your French has improved markedly, Kendra." Pride reverberated in Alain's tone as he scooped up his wriggling son and held him close. After a few moments, he set Étienne down, though Kendra was relieved to see their son clutching his father's mailed leg, poking his fingers into the chinks.

"I've lots of time to talk to the stones now that I don't have to oversee their placement," she said, only half in jest. "They don't help me if I get it wrong, but they don't laugh either."

Alain's face turned comical with disbelief. "When have I ever laughed at any of your efforts, *ma chere*?"

"Not recently, that much is certain." As he spluttered a protest, she motioned to the servant carrying the goblet and ordered the man to present it to his lord. "This should help you find your tongue."

He downed the wine in three gulps, thrust the goblet back at the servant, wrapped his arms around Kendra, and kissed her soundly, revealing exactly where his tongue could be found. She melted into his embrace, feeling very much the giddy bride again and adoring every moment.

"Now that," he declared as he released his breathless wife, "is a proper welcome for the castle's lord."

"If you liked that"—her grin radiated pure mischief—"then you shall love trying our new bedchamber."

He reflected her grin with his own. "Even a cave would feel like a home with you to share it with me."

She laughed. "You haven't seen the bedchamber yet."

After charging Rowena with Étienne's care, Kendra dismissed the servants to their regular duties, rested her right arm atop Alain's left, and with Noir bounding beside them, began showing her beloved Norman husband the fruits of their fondest dreams.

Le Fin

Jubilate Deo
kih, 12 June MMXIV

Author's Notes

NOW IN JULY began in 1999 as a collaboration with my longtime writer-friend Patricia Duffy Novak, who had intended to write Alain's viewpoint while I wrote Kendra's. But life events prevented her from continuing the project, and she gave me her blessing to finish it.

I shall always be grateful to Patricia for her suggestions regarding the story line, and for her contributions in its research. Being a professor at Auburn University gives her access to that library's resources, which in our case yielded such gems as a map of medieval Winchester, England. The paragraph describing Alain's route from St. Mary's Church to the tavern was adapted straight off that map.

The basic story line of the romance was Patricia's idea: a Norman knight being ordered by King William to marry a Saxon noblewoman. Historically, William did employ this policy to stabilize England . . . with varying degrees of success. And he did, as described in the text, invent the office of sheriff. Bishop Odo de Bayeux really was William's half brother, regent, and confidante—and there exists evidence to suggest that he commissioned the Bayeux Tapestry, but probably several years after the events described in *Snow in July*, which is why I never mention this famous scrap of cloth in my text.

The Glastonbury thorn tree is a Middle Eastern strain of hawthorn, which lends credence to the legend that it sprouted from the staff of Joseph of Arimathea, a merchant who imported tin from Britain in Jesus' day. Whether the young Jesus accompanied him on any of these buying trips is a matter of British national pride which I chose not to speculate upon in this story. Hawthorn is known to have medicinal value for treating ailments of the heart and circulatory system, and the Glastonbury strain is famed for producing blooms at Christmas, so I was pleased to imbue the plant with a miraculous dimension to its healing properties.

Longtime fans of my work know that I love playing with legends, and in that regard *Snow in July* is no different. In addition to mentioning the local tradition that associates King Arthur with Glastonbury—though his alleged grave would not be discovered at the abbey for another century beyond the lifetimes of Kendra and Alain—I adapted the legend that the wounded King Harold Godwinson survived the Battle of Hastings and lived out his remaining days as a monk.

The primary liberties I took were in regard to Glastonbury Tor and its surrounds. The Tor's association with being an island dates to the millennia-old memory of the River Severn creating annual floodplains that inundated areas bordering the Bristol Channel as far inland as Glastonbury. This geologic event had ceased, for the most part, by the dawn of the Middle Ages, though the Glastonbury district still existed as swampland in the 11th century. The present-day tower is all that remains of the 14th-century Church of St. Michael, built upon the site half a century after its wooden predecessor was destroyed by an earthquake. I presume that the older church was built upon the foundation of a much earlier structure, since the site has yielded evidence of habitation dating back to Neolithic times. The maze ruins constitute just one of the hypotheses about the Tor's terraced slopes.

All other details are fictional, including the treasure cavern, although I made every effort to integrate them with historic facts as seamlessly as possible. As for some of the more exotic language choices, such as *Cristes mæsse* and *ma demoiselle*, I have either adapted or invented them to lend an ancient flavor to my story without going through the exercise of inventing a new language, as I have done with The Dragon's Dove Chronicles (*Dawnflight*, et al.)!

Thank you for your interest in my work, and I hope you enjoyed my first foray into the realm of paranormal historical romance.

People

Entry format:

Full Name (Pronunciation). Brief description, which may include rank, occupation, country, shield description in non-heraldic terms, nickname(s), name's origin, and meaning. Place-names and other affiliations are given in the person's native language.

Viewpoint characters are listed first, with their glyph(s), followed by everyone else mentioned in the text, fictional or otherwise. Approximate pronunciation guidelines are supplied for the less obvious names. Phonetics for pronouncing Saxon names follow the guidance given on the WikiBooks page "Old English/Fōresprǣc" (https://en.wikibooks.org/wiki/Old_English/F%C5%8Drespr%C7%A3c). When in doubt, pronounce the name however it makes sense to you. Or purchase the audiobook edition!

Alain
(chapter heading)

Alain
(scene heading)

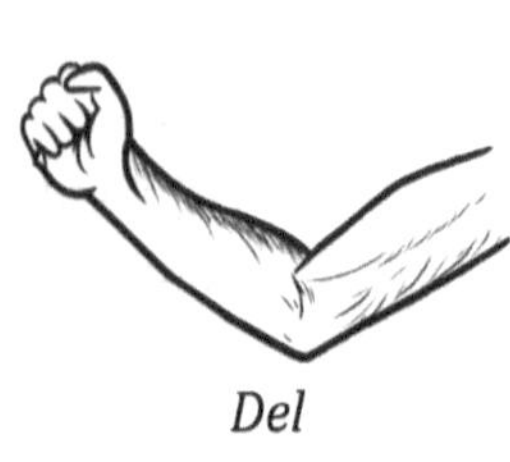

Del

Robert (hro-BEAR, with a silent *t* unless followed by a word beginning with a vowel) **Alain de Bellencombre.** Second son of Hugh FitzWalter and Margaret, younger half brother of Philippe FitzHugh, older brother of Étienne de Bellencombre. Knight of Normandy in the service of William the Conqueror. Shield: white rose nestled in tangle of greenery, on saffron yellow. Nickname: Alain.

Alain (ah-LEN). Name preferred by Sir Robert Alain de Bellencombre for informal address by family and friends. He chooses the name Alain Bellefleur for his squire persona. Sarcastically called Sir Robert the Pious and Squire Bellefleur by Ruaud, and Saint Pretty Boy by their captors.

Delwin (DEL-ween) Waldronson. Son of Waldron Edgarson and Edwina, older brother of Kendra. Saxon knight of England in the service of Harold Godwinson. His name means "friend of he who lives in the valley." Shield: bent dark blue arm with fist on gray. Nickname: Del.

Eosa

Eosa (ayOH-sah) Thorgudson. Son of Thorgud. Saxon knight of England in the service of Harold Godwinson; Ulfric's second-in-command. His name means "war horse." Nickname: Dragon.

Kendra

Kendra Waldronsdotter. Daughter of Waldron and Edwina, younger sister of Delwin. Saxon heiress of the estate of Edgarburh. Her name is the female form of Kendrick, meaning "keen power."

Chapter-heading glyph (pictured, left) appears in chapters 5, 7, 12, 14, 15, 18, and the Epilogue, and the blossom by itself appears as a scene heading throughout the text.

Odo

Odo de Bayeux. Younger half brother (via his mother Herleva) of William the Conqueror. Served as a soldier, Bishop of Bayeux, and regent of southern England in King William's absence; depicted on the Bayeux Tapestry (created in England circa the 1070s) as riding a black horse. His name means "wealthy," and he certainly was.

Ruaud

Ruaud (hroo-OHD) d'Auvay (doh-VAY). Knight of Normandy in William's service, and Alain's best friend. Married, with sons, and estates deeded him by William in England as well as Normandy. Name meaning unknown; selected from list of knights accompanying Duke William during the Norman invasion of England.

Chapter-heading glyph (pictured, left) appears in chapter 13, and the bear's head appears as a scene heading.

Ulfric

Ulfric (OOLF-reej). Thane of Thornhill. Kendra's second cousin and onetime suitor. Saxon knight of England in the service of King Harold. His name means "wolf-king." Shield: rearing gray wolf on crimson.

Chapter-heading glyph (pictured, left) appears in chapter 21, and the wolf's head appears as a scene heading.

Waldron

Waldron Edgarson. Saxon nobleman; thane of Edgarburh. Oldest son of Edgar, for whom the estate of Edgarburh is named; widower of Edwina; father of Delwin and Kendra. His name means "powerful one." Shield: upward-bent dark blue chevron on gray.

Non-viewpoint characters and others mentioned in the text:

Æthelward (AH-thel-ward). Saxon priest at Edgarburh; his name means "noble guardian."

Alexander. Pope Alexander II (born Anselmo de Baggio), who in 1066 granted papal favor to Duke William's envoy for proceeding with preparations for the Norman conquest of England. This written edict, accompanied by a papal ring and the Standard of St. Peter, became instrumental in the submission of the English clergy to William's rule.

Arthur of the Britons, King Arthur. Enemy of the Saxon people whose reputation had already gained five centuries of embellishment by the time of the Norman conquest of England; therefore, his legend was terrifying to Kendra. Rumored to have been buried near Glastonbury or under Glastonbury Tor, though the abbey's monks would not milk this claim via the discovery of "Arthur's grave" for another 125 years.

Bassa. Saxon physician at Edgarburh; his name is the Old English form of the Old French *basse* ("short").

Bertred (BAIR-traid). Saxon warrior in Ulfric's army; Eosa's scribe. His name means "bright counsel." Nickname: Nib.

Cæwlin (KOW-leen). Saxon soldier serving in Edgarburh's fyrd; Waldron's longtime friend. His name means "cave lake."

Cynewulf (KEEneh-woolf). Saxon thane; his name translates to "king wolf."

Dirk. Camp name of Ursa Oescson, a Saxon knight in Ulfric's army; Eosa's second-in-command. His birth name of Ursa is derived from the Latin *ursum* ("the bear").

Dunstan, Saint. Tenth-century abbot of Glastonbury; later appointed Bishop of Winchester and Archbishop of Canterbury; and adviser to Saxon kings Edmund, Eadred, Edgar, Edward (II) the Martyr, and to a limited extent Æthelred the Unready. The legend of how Dunstan defeated the Devil by shoeing his hoof is the origin of the practice of nailing a horseshoe with the ends pointed upward above a door for good luck. Canonized in 1029; feast day May 19. Considered one of the patron saints of England, alongside Edward the Confessor, until the 14th century, when St. George was given the job by King Edward III.

Ecgfrith (AIDJ-freeth). Saxon man hired by Alain and Ruaud in Sarum to guide them to Edgarburh; his name means "the edge of peace."

Edgert (AID-gairt). Saxon thane, but not one of the thanes in Ulfric's alliance. His name is a variant of Eadgard, meaning "keeper of his oath."

Edith of Wessex. Widow of Edward the Confessor, sister of Harold Godwinson, and the fourth wealthiest individual in England at the time. She did reside in Winchester until her death on December 18th, 1075.

Edward the Confessor. Brother-in-law of Harold Godwinson; King of England from 8 June 1042 until his death on 5 January 1066. Called "the Confessor" for having lived a reportedly saintly life but having died of natural causes, he was canonized a century after his death. His sarcophagus may be viewed in Westminster Abbey.

Edwina. Late Saxon noblewoman; wife of Waldron; mother of Delwin and Kendra; cousin of Ulfric. Her name is the female form of Edwin, meaning "rich friend."

Eric. A Saxon monk serving as bodyguard to the convalescing King Harold; his name means "always mighty."

Ethel. Saxon servant at Thornhill; Ulfric's former nursemaid; her name means "noble."

Étienne (ay-tee-EHN; "crown") de Bellencombre.

1. Youngest son of Hugh FitzWalter and Margaret, younger brother of Alain, younger half brother of Philippe FitzHugh. Knight of Normandy in the service of William. Shield: prowling dark saffron leopard on green.

2. Oldest son of Alain and Kendra.

Garth. Saxon soldier and scout in Edgarburh's fyrd; his name means "enclosure."

Guinevere. King Arthur's queen, who selected Lancelot as her champion—and the rumors of their alleged illicit relationship began to fly from that point on. Whether a Saxon noblewoman of Kendra's era would have known that version of the story is a matter of debate . . . but this is why poetic license was invented.

Harold Godwinson. Son of Godwin, who was one of the most influential Saxons in early 11th-century England, and brother-in-law of Edward the Confessor, alleged to have been Edward's deathbed choice as successor. An early scene in the Bayeux Tapestry depicts Harold as having met with William to swear fealty to him prior to Edward's death, which is an unsubstantiated but fascinating snippet of Norman propaganda.

Hedda. A Saxon maidservant at Edgarburh; her name is the diminutive form of the Old High German name Haduwig, meaning "contending battle."

Hugh FitzWalter. Late Norman nobleman bearing the title Comte; husband of Margaret, his second wife; father of Philippe, Alain, and Étienne.

Jesu (YAY-soo). A medieval variant of Jesus.

Joseph of Arimathea. Jewish merchant of Jesus' day reputed to have traded with sources in Britain that exported tin throughout the Roman world. The supposition that the young Jesus had accompanied Joseph of Arimathea on at least one of these buying trips remains a source of English national pride to this day.

Lancelot. Although some scholars argue that this famous knight and infamous lover was inserted into the Arthurian Legends by French troubadour Chrétien de Troyes a century after the events depicted in *Snow in July*, I believe he is based on a much earlier personage, King Auguselus of Scotland, mentioned in Geoffrey of Monmouth's quasi-factual *History of the Kings of Britain* as being one of Arthur's staunchest supporters.

Lofwin (LOHF-ween) Octhason (OAK-thah-son). Saxon soldier and chief scout of Edgarburh's fyrd; son of Octha. His name means "little friend."

Margaret. Late Saxon noblewoman, second wife of Hugh FitzWalter (at which time she was conferred the title Comtesse), mother of Alain and Étienne; her name means "pearl."

Marie. French noblewoman betrothed to Alain until she decided that his half brother Philippe—titled and standing in possession of their father's estates—was the better catch.

Matilda of Flanders. Wife of William the Conqueror. Historically, Matilda was not crowned queen consort of England until 1068, and she probably stayed in Normandy until then, governing the duchy in William's stead, and later as regent for their oldest son, Robert Curthose. In preparation for the invasion of England, Matilda outfitted a ship, the Mora, out of her own funds and gave it to William. Over the course of their marriage she bore William at least nine children (including two kings, William I of England, and Henry I of England), the first seven of whom were already born by the time of the invasion, though I elected not to mention any of them in this text.

Oesc (ohASK). Saxon thane who actively supports Ulfric; his name means "divine."

Oswald (OHS-wald). A Saxon monk serving as bodyguard to the convalescing King Harold; his name means "divine power."

Oswy (OHS-wee). Saxon soldier and one of the younger members of Edgarburh's fyrd; his name is a diminutive form of Oswin ("friend of God").

Philippe FitzHugh. Oldest son of Hugh FitzWalter; half brother (by their father) of Alain and Étienne. Sole heir to their father's estates and title in Normandy.

Pit. Scottish outlaw and one of Alain's captors; the name is a corruption of the ethnic term "Pict" and was chosen to reflect his Highland heritage.

Rat. Saxon outlaw and one of Kendra's captors.

Raven. Saxon outlaw and one of Alain's captors.

Robert the Magnificent. Robert I or Robert II, depending on the source. Late Duke of Normandy, father of William the Conqueror.

Rowena (roh-WAY-nah). Saxon maidservant at Edgarburh; her name is the English form of the Celtic name Rhonwen, meaning "white skirt."

Snake. Saxon outlaw and one of Kendra's captors; born Liam Fletcher.

Thorgil (THOR-gheel). Saxon soldier and captain of the guard at Edgarburh; his name means "Thor's pledge" or "Thor's gold."

Thorgud. Saxon thane; father of Eosa. A supporter of Ulfric; his name means "Thor is good."

Thurstin. Eleventh-century Norman abbot of Glastonbury. There is some dispute as to whether he was appointed to this post soon after the Norman Conquest or as much as a decade later; regardless, I needed a Norman abbot for the purposes of this story, and his predecessors were all Saxons.

Wart. Saxon outlaw and the youngest of Alain's captors.

Wihtred (WEEHTraid). Saxon thane who actively supports Ulfric. His name means "white counsel."

William. Son of Robert the Magnificent and Robert's merchant-class mistress, Herleva. Succeeded his father as duke of Normandy, and defeated Harold Godwinson for the crown of England. Depicted on the Bayeux Tapestry mounted on two different horses: a black and tan, and a red (sorrel), of which I selected the latter for use in *Snow in July*. Nicknames: William the Conqueror, William the Bastard. Also known in various historical sources as Williame (Old Norman), Willelm (Bayeux Tapestry), and Guillaume le Bâtard (French).

William FitzOsbern. William the Conqueror's other close friend and adviser, appointed coregent in charge of ruling northern England whenever the king was out of the country.

Glossary

THIS APPENDIX INCLUDES place-names and foreign terms. Pronunciation guidelines are supplied for the less obvious terms, especially those of French or Old English (Saxon) origin. In the case of a term having multiple translations or variations used in the text, the most commonly referenced term is listed first. Word and phrase origins and English translations are given wherever possible.

Language choices throughout the text include a deliberate "aging" of certain present-day terms in French as well as in English. The "aged" English terms (such as *well come* for "welcome") may be inferred from the context. The "aged" French terms may also be inferred from the context, but I have included them here, along with all the other French words and phrases, for the reader's benefit.

À Dieu (ah DEW; "aged" French). Phrase of farewell meaning "to God;" in other words, "until we meet again before God." Based upon present-day French *adieu* ("goodbye").

À gauche (ah GHOSH; French). Phrase meaning "to the left," the opposite of *à droit* ("to the right").

Amot vincit om (Latin). "Love conquers all."

Anjou. A medieval province in western France, approximately 100 miles due south of the Normandy border corresponding to the present-day district of Maine-et-Loire, governed by a count during the era of the Norman Conquest; its principle city was Angers (Angieus in the early 12th century; current urban population 200,000).

Au contraire (oh con-TRARE; French). Phrase meaning "to the contrary."

Azure. Ruaud's warhorse. Name origin: Old French *azure* (heraldic term for the color blue).

Battle of Hastings, the. Fought on 14 October 1066, about seven miles from the town of Hastings, between the forces of Harold Godwinson and Duke William of Normandy, this battle is arguably the watershed event of all English history because it led to the permanent end of Saxon rule.

Beau-père (boh pair; French). Colloquial term meaning "father-in-law;" literally, it means "handsome father." Origin: compound of *beau* ("handsome" or "boyfriend") and *père* ("father").

Bee balm. A plant with scarlet flowers favored by beekeepers for honey production.

Bellencombre. A village in the northern region of Normandy which existed in the 11th century and is home to approximately 650 people today; birthplace of Alain and Étienne. The name translates as "pretty entanglement."

Blessed Mother, Blessed Virgin, Holy Mother (French *Sacre Mère*), Mother of God. Terms of respect conferred upon the Virgin Mary.

Borage. A star-shaped flowering plant favored by bee-keepers for honey production. The leaves are edible and taste like cucumber.

Brydgild (BREED-geeld; Saxon). Literally, "bride-gold," the term referring to the ancient custom of the groom paying an agreed-upon sum to the father of the bride for the privilege of marrying his daughter, since the bride's family would thenceforth be deprived of her services. Origin: Old English compound of *bryd* ("bride") and *gild* ("gold").

Burh (Saxon). The term applied to the fortified town of a nobleman, linguistically comparable to Old English *byrig*, German *burg*, English *borough*, and Scottish Gaelic *broch*. The *h* of *burh* is sounded at the back of the throat as in *broch*.

C'est (SAY; French). "It is."

Chamomile. A medicinal herb.

Chere (SHARE; French). The feminine form of the word for "dear." The masculine form is *cher*.

Chi Rho. One of the earliest ecclesiastical symbols for Christ, an overlay of the Greek capital letters *chi* (X) and *rho* (P), so chosen for being the first two letters of Χριστός (Latinized as *Christos*, "Christ").

Chou (SHOO). Alain's warhorse, a charcoal gray mare. Name origin: French *chou* ("cabbage"). If this seems an odd name for a horse, I chose it because I learned in my high school French class (lo these many, *many* moons ago) that "chou" was used in France as a term of endearment by dating couples. I have no idea whether French people are still calling each other "my little cabbage" today!

Comfrey. A medicinal herb.

Compline. The last of eight Christian canonical hours of the day, occurring at approximately two hours past sundown. Origin: Latin *complere* ("to fill up").

Comte (French). Landed title equivalent to that of Count. A region governed by a *comte* is the origin of the present-day Anglo-American civic term "county."

Comtesse (French). Landed title equivalent to that of Countess.

Creech Hill. Site of an Iron Age hill fort near the present-day town of Bruton (Somerset, England), and the location of the ruins of the Roman temple used as a travelers' way-station in *Snow in July*.

Cristes mæsse (KREE-stehs mah-seh; Saxon). Old English term meaning "Christ's mass;" i.e., Christmas. Hyphenated as *Cristes-mæsse* when used as an adjective.

Edgarburh. Fictional Saxon-controlled fortified manor, market town, croplands, and pastures located west-southwest of London in the vicinity of the present-day town of Shrewton in Wiltshire, England approximately five miles north of the A36-A303 intersection and 20 miles east of Glastonbury. Governed by Thane Waldron Edgarson. Historically, Shrewton (Old English *scīr-rēfa tūn*, "sheriff's settlement") evolved from the medieval village of Addeston ("add stone")—the name of which is tempting to believe might have been inspired by Alain's Norman-influenced building activities after he and Kendra inherited Edgarburh. Although I refer to Edgarburh as a burh in the text, and it fits the description since the manor is a walled compound, it does not represent any of the thirty-three burhs of medieval England that were established by Alfred the Great and used as important commercial centers, royal currency mints, tax collection, and so forth. The closest royal burh to Edgarburh would have been Wilton, near Salisbury, about eight miles to the south.

Elder. A medicinal plant whose leaves and berries were harvested for various uses.

En Anglais (on AHN-glay; French). Phrase meaning "in English."

Et (AY; French). The conjunction "and."

Farthing. Shortened form of "fourthing;" i.e., one-fourth of a penny, so named because the state of the medieval English economy was such that people needed smaller coins than a penny to make change for goods purchased.

Feast of Saint John the Baptist, the. Liturgical feast celebrated June 24 in honor of the birth of Saint John the Baptist, kinsman of Jesus, who "leaped for joy" in his mother's womb when the pregnant Mary visited her (Luke 1:44).

Feast of Saints Peter and Paul, the. Liturgical feast in honor of the martyrdom in Rome of the apostles Peter and Paul, which is observed June 29, of ancient origin and of major importance on the present-day Roman Catholic calendar.

Feast of the First Roman Martyrs, the. Liturgical feast in honor of the first Christians to be martyred in the city of Rome during Nero's persecution in A.D. 64, observed June 30.

Feverwort. A medicinal herb so named for its effect in reducing fevers.

Fitz (Norman French). The patronymic title meaning "son of," used only by the firstborn male heir. Origin: Latin *filius* ("son"). Linguistically related to the *–vich* patronymic suffix used in Russian male names and words like *Tsarevich* ("Tsar's son").

Fong, fongin(g), fonger(s). Slang terms referring to the act of fornication or its participants; i.e., the medieval "f-word."

Fyrd (FEERD; Saxon). A company of men-at-arms under control of the local thane. The fyrd described for defending Edgarburh in *Snow in July* represents the core soldiers that would remain in service during times of relative peace. When the thane was commanded by the king to supply troops for military action, the thane's villagers and peasants would be conscripted into temporary service to make up the difference in the number required by the king.

Glastonbury, Somerset, England.

1.   The market town; current population 9,000.

2.   The region encompassing the town, abbey, and Glastonbury Tor and its surrounding marshlands.

Glastonbury Abbey. Christian monastic site dating from at least the 7th century A.D., though legend claims its founder to be the 1st-century merchant Joseph of Arimathea.

Glastonbury thorn, the. Tree reputed to have grown when Joseph of Arimathea struck his staff into the ground to indicate his chosen site for the establishment of the first Christian church in Britain. This legend is borne out in the fact that this species is a Middle Eastern hawthorn that grows naturally nowhere else in Europe, and it displays "miraculous" (but infertile) blooms annually on Christmas Day, which no other hawthorn species exhibits. Hawthorn is known to have a beneficial effect on the heart and circulatory system, but its supernatural healing abilities described in *Snow in July* are entirely of my invention.

Glastonbury Tor; also, the Tor. Name of the conical hill surrounded by swampland near Glastonbury's town and abbey. Origin: Scottish Gaelic *tor* ("conical hill").

Hastings. Coastal town in East Sussex (historically, Sussex) on the southern coast of England, 53 miles southeast of London; current population 89,000.

Hauberk. Sleeved shirt of chain mail reaching to midthigh.

Hellebore. A flowering, ground-hugging plant favored by beekeepers for honey production.

High Street. Part of the geography of medieval Winchester, according to a map in the collection of the library on the main campus of Auburn University, Alabama.

Hilde (HEEL-deh). Kendra's mare.

Hollyhock. A tall, flowering plant favored by beekeepers for honey production.

Hyssop. A plant with bluish flowers favored by beekeepers for honey production.

Ici (ee-SEE; French). Word meaning "here," sometimes used with the command *viens ici* (literally, "come you here," informal form; formal form is *vienez ici*).

Ilchester. A village in southeastern Somerset, England dating to the Roman occupation and known as Lindinis during that era. In the *Domesday Book* of the late 11th century it was called Sock Dennis; current population 2,000.

Je m'appelle (jheh mah-PELL; French). Phrase used colloquially to say, "my name is." Literally, it means "I call myself."

Jerkin. Leather battle tunic that could be made of varying styles, features, and quality, depending upon the customer's wealth.

Jerusalem. Ancient Middle Eastern city controlled by the Arabic Fatmid Caliphate at the time of the Norman conquest of England, 30 years before the start of the First Crusade.

Lady's mantle. A medicinal herb favored for treatment of female health issues.

Lavender. A medicinal and aromatic strewing herb.

Lemon balm. A flowering plant favored by beekeepers for honey production.

Linden. A medicinal herb.

London. King William's base of operations, and the most important city in England dating to before the era of the Roman occupation.

London's West Minster. Westminster Cathedral.

Lungwort. A medicinal herb favored for treatment of upper respiratory health issues.

Ma chere (mah SHARE; French). Phrase meaning "my dear" as spoken to a woman. If addressing a man, it becomes *mon cher*.

Ma demoiselle ("aged" French). Phrase meaning "my lady," based upon present-day French *mademoiselle* ("miss;" i.e., a polite form of address for a girl or unmarried woman).

Mais (MAY; French). The conjunction "but."

Mark.

1. Slang term for a coin of large denomination, usually gold.

2. Slang term for "target."

Matins. First of eight Christian canonical hours of the day. Properly occurring at midnight, the prayer service is sometimes combined with lauds, which is held at dawn. Origin: Latin *matutinus* ("of the morning").

Meadow saffron. An herb that attracts bees for honey production but also can be distilled into a lethal poison.

Merde (MAIRD; French). Slang term for excrement.

Minster, the. Colloquial term for a cathedral church. Derived from Old English *mynster*, which probably evolved from Church Latin *monasterium* ("monastery"), implying that the term originally applied to any church connected to a monastic settlement.

Mint. An herb used for aromatic, culinary, and medicinal purposes.

Moi (MWAH; French). "Me."

Mon ami (pl. mes amis; French). "My (male) friend(s)." When pronouncing *amis*, the *s* is silent unless it occurs before a word beginning with a vowel.

Mon amour (French). Term of endearment meaning "my love;" suitable for addressing persons of either gender.

Mon coeur tu as (mohn cur too ah; French). "You have my heart" (familiar form; formal form is *mon coeur vous avez*).

Mon Dieu (French). Phrase meaning "my God," often used as an exclamation of surprise or shock.

Mon seigneur (mohn sin-YOUR; "aged" French). Phrase meaning "my lord," based upon present-day French *monseigneur* ("mister").

Mullein. A plant whose downy yellow flowers form on spikes, favored by beekeepers for honey production.

Noir (NWAR; "black," French). A huge black hound probably descended from the original *Pugnaces Britanniae* ("combative ones of Britain") breed of war-dog exported from Britain throughout the Roman Empire and often used to fight bears, lions, and other large animals in gladiatorial arenas.

Non (French). "No." The last *n* is silent.

Nones. Sixth Christian canonical hour and ninth hour of daylight, around 3 p.m. Origin: Latin *nonus* ("ninth").

Norman. Of or pertaining to the inhabitants of Normandy, who were predominantly Scandinavian (Viking) in origin, not French (Celto-Goth).

Normandy. Duchy centered around the city of Rouen that came under the control of Scandinavian king Rollo in the 10th century.

Otherworld, the. Domain of elves and fairies in Welsh mythology.

Oui (WE; French). "Yes."

Pardonnez-moi (par-DOH-nay mwah; French). "Pardon me" (formal form of address; informal form is *pardon-moi*).

Persephone. Greek goddess of spring and mythical analogy to Kendra's experience with Ulfric.

Prime. Third Christian canonical hour and first full hour of daylight, around 6 a.m. Origin: Latin *primus* ("first" or "chief").

River Brue. A sea-bound river originating in the White Sheet Downs that flows south of Glastonbury. It was a major source of flooding in the area, along with its companion watercourse, the River Axe, disrupting travel on a regular basis. This situation was improved over time, starting with the construction of a channel in the 12th century.

Rose hips. The bottom portion of the rose blossom, which is rich in vitamin C and therefore useful in treating upper-respiratory ailments.

Saffron. An herb that yields a yellow dye.

Salisbury Plain. A 300-square-mile chalk plateau in southern central England (Wiltshire and Hampshire counties), largely uninhabited to this day and most famous for being the site of Stonehenge.

Sarum. A hill fort in Wiltshire, southern England dating to three millennia before the Roman occupation, now in ruins and referred to as Old Sarum ever since the early 13th century, when the settlement was relocated due to the burgeoning population; and the old castle, cathedral, and other buildings were razed for materials. Also known historically as Sorviodunum (Latin, in Roman documents), Caer Gradawc (P-Celtic, in *History of the Kings of Britain*), Searobyrig (Anglo-Saxon documents), and Sarisburia (Norman-French, in the *Domesday Book*).

Saxon(s). Of or pertaining to the inhabitants of southern England who emigrated to the island from the Saxony region of Germany in the mid-5th century A.D.; name possibly derived from their weapon of choice, the *seax*.

Seax (SAHox; Saxon). Saxon war-knife, usually measuring 15-18 inches from point to end of hilt.

Seulement (SOO-leh-mone; French). "Only."

Sext. Fifth Christian canonical and sixth hour of daylight, around 12 p.m. Origin: Latin *sextus* ("sixth").

Shite (Saxon). Slang term for excrement.

Sign of the Rose, the. Fictional tavern located near the tannery district of medieval Winchester.

Soeur (SUR; French). A word meaning "sister," which Delwin uses in the phrase *ma soeur chere* ("my dear sister").

Sol (French). Old French word for a small bronze coin of low denomination; origin of the more recent slang term, *sou*.

Somerset. Region of southern England where Glastonbury is located.

St. Mary's Church. A poor backstreet church in Winchester that did exist on Tanner Street in the 11th century, according to a map in the collection of the library on the main campus of Auburn University.

Surcoat. A garment worn over armor and embroidered with the knight's shield design. Historically, it wouldn't begin to see this type of use consistently for another hundred years, when the rules of heraldry began being formalized.

Swinhund (SWEEN-hoond; Saxon). An epithet literally meaning "pig-dog," a compound of Old English *swin* ("pig") and *hund* ("hound").

Swive (SWEEV; Saxon). A colloquial term for the act of copulation, from Old English *swifan* ("to move" or "to sweep").

Tabard. A short, sturdy coat worn by peasants and foot soldiers; in the case of the latter, it is emblazoned with the lord's coat-of-arms.

Tanner Street. Part of the geography of medieval Winchester, according to a map in the collection of the library on the main campus of Auburn University, Alabama.

Tansy. A plant whose flowers form as yellow globes, favored by beekeepers for honey production.

Tas de merde (tah deh maird; French). Alain's Saxon companions-at-arms would say "shite pile."

Thane (Saxon). An ancient English landed title roughly equivalent to that of baron, but status was ranked by how much acreage was governed. "Thane" is the Shakespearean-era spelling of the older form *thegn*, which I elected to use for ease of pronunciation. Origin: Anglo-Saxon *þegn* or *ðegn* (both mean "retainer"). Under the Norman system of governance, the wealthiest thanes eventually became designated as barons, and the less wealthy thanes were integrated into the knightly class.

Thornhill. Fictional manor, pastures, and croplands adjoining Church lands near the town of Glastonbury and Glastonbury Tor, governed by Thane Ulfric. Corresponds to present-day Wearyall Hill, where Joseph of Arimathea was reported to have planted the staff that subsequently became the Christmas-blooming Glastonbury thorn tree.

Throne of England, the; also, the Crown. Terms applied to either the office of kingship or to the king himself.

Thyme. A flowering, ground-hugging plant favored by beekeepers for honey production that also has culinary uses for flavoring meats and salads.

Tierce. Fourth Christian canonical hour and third hour of daylight, around 9 a.m. Origin: Latin *tertius* ("third").

Trews. Loose-fitting trousers made of leather, wool, or linen.

Tu sais ton papa (too say tone paPA; French). The informal phrase meaning "you know your father." In formal speech, the phrase is *vous savez votre père.*

Un cadeau (uhn cah-DOH; French). Phrase meaning "a gift."

Valerian. A medicinal herb used in the treatment of pain.

Vespers. Seventh Christian canonical hour, occurring at sunset. Origin: Latin *vespera* ("evening").

Vite (VEET; French). Word meaning "hasten" or "hurry," and often used as an interjection.

Wessex. Ancient kingdom designation derived from the phrase "West Saxons" (as opposed to Essex and Sussex, realms of the East and South Saxons, respectively), which became a county when England was unified under a single king.

Willow bark. A medicinal herb used in the treatment of headaches and other types of pain.

Winchester, Hampshire, England. One of the original 33 royal burhs designated by Alfred the Great, capital of England until just after the Norman Conquest, when King William transferred that function to London, and headquarters of Regent Odo whenever William was residing somewhere other than England.

Wormwood. A flowering herb favored by groundskeepers for its ability to repel bees.

York, North Yorkshire, England. Headquarters of Regent William FitzOsbern whenever King William was residing somewhere other than England.

Acknowledgements

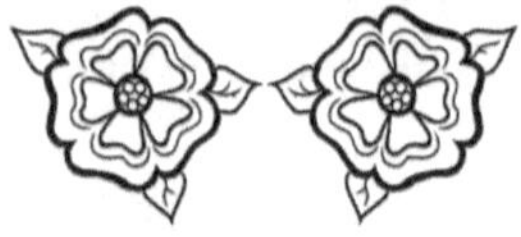

THOUGH A ROMANTIC concept, in this day and age of social networking there is no such thing as the "lonely writer's garret." As much as I would like to wall myself into a garret at times—providing it came equipped with a good enough Internet connection to conduct research, keep tabs on my family, and place orders—I am grateful to writer-friends such as K.R. Thompson, who has been instrumental in pulling me out of my shell to get my books into the hands of local readers; and Robin Allen, a "pre-Facebook" friend who always stands ready and willing to critique a cover concept or a synopsis.

In one of life's little ironies, Robin also happened to be one of the contest judges for a prepublication version of the first three chapters of *Snow in July*, unbeknownst to either of us. Imagine our surprise when I sent her the first cover concept for her feedback, and she realized the title sounded very familiar! Even funnier was her underlying thought as she had critiqued the contest entry itself: "I have to tell Kim about this one. It seems to be right up her alley."

Indeed!

No list of acknowledgements would be complete without grateful nods to my fantastic editor, Deb Taber, and equally fantastic cover designer, Natasha Brown. I hope to keep them on my team for a long time to come.

kdh, Wytheville, VA
June 1, 2014

About the Artist

JESSICA HEADLEE STUDIED art at Marion Senior High School of Marion, VA, during which time she won Silver Key designation in the national Scholastic Art & Writing Awards for her white-charcoal drawing titled "Reality." Jessica graduated as valedictorian in 2014, she earned 11 varsity letters in three sports (indoor track, outdoor track, and softball), and she achieved All-State status in indoor track.

In 2017 she graduated magna cum laude from Coastal Carolina University with a Bachelor of Science degree in marine science. She had begun to pursue a career in coral reef ecology and conservation when she contracted cancer and passed away in 2021. Jessica's remains are interred in reef artifacts off the coasts of Maryland and South Carolina. Her hobbies included fiction writing, video gaming, and nature photography. She was an avid conservationist, especially regarding our oceans, and you honor her memory by removing even just a handful of trash from every beach you visit.

Other art by Jessica Headlee appears in Kim's novel *Liberty*. Of the art she created for *Snow in July,* her bear glyphs appear in Kim's novel *Raging Sea*, and her Tudor rose was adapted into two illustrations by Jennifer Doneske for *King Arthur's Sister in Washington's Court* by Mark Twain as channeled by Kim Iverson Headlee.

About the Author

Photo Copyright by Chris Headlee

KIM HEADLEE LIVES on a farm in the mountains of southwestern Virginia with her family, cats, fish, goats, Great Pyrenees goat guards, someone else's cattle, half a million honey bees, and assorted wildlife. People and creatures come and go, but the cave and the 250-year-old house ruins—the latter having been occupied as recently as the midtwentieth century—seem to be sticking around for a while yet. Kim has been an award-winning novelist since 1999 and a student of Arthurian literature for more than half a century.

Other published works by Kim Iverson Headlee:

Raging Sea, The Dragon's Dove Chronicles, book 3, Pendragon Cove Press, 2019.

The Challenge comic book, illustrated by DC and Marvel Comics artist Tim Shinn, Pendragon Cove Press, 2019.

Twins, the novella genesis of The Dragon's Dove Chronicles book 6, Pendragon Cove Press, 2017.

The Business of Writing*: Practical Insights for Independent, Hybrid, and Traditionally Published Authors*, Pendragon Cove Press, 2016; updated annually.

Kings, a sword-and-sorcery crossover novella by Kim Iverson Headlee and Patricia Duffy Novak, Pendragon Cove Press, 2016.

The Challenge, a Dragon's Dove Chronicles novella, Pendragon Cove Press, 2015.

King Arthur's Sister in Washington's Court by Mark Twain as channeled by Kim Iverson Headlee, illustrated by Jennifer Doneske and Tom Doneske, Lucky Bat Books, 2015.

Liberty, second edition, Pendragon Cove Press, 2015.

Morning's Journey, The Dragon's Dove Chronicles, book 2, Pendragon Cove Press, 2014.

The Color of Vengeance, a novella excerpted from Morning's Journey, Pendragon Cove Press, 2013.

Dawnflight by Kim Iverson Headlee, The Dragon's Dove Chronicles, book 1, second edition, Pendragon Cove Press, 2014.

Liberty by Kimberly Iverson, HQN Books, Harlequin, 2006.

Dawnflight by Kim Headlee, first edition, paperback, Sonnet Books, Simon & Schuster, 1999.

Forthcoming:

King Arthur's Sister: The Once and Future Queen, the sequel to *King Arthur's Sister in Washington's Court*, Pendragon Cove Press.

Prophecy, the sequel to *Liberty*, Pendragon Cove Press.

Zenith Glory, The Dragon's Dove Chronicles, book 4, Pendragon Cove Press.